The Gospel of Jesse

By

S.H. McCord

Unless otherwise noted, all scriptural quotations are taken from the King James Version of the Bible. (Public Domain.)

ISBN-13: 978-1507740279

ISBN-10: 1507740271

Library of Congress Control Number: 2015901466

CreateSpace Independent Publishing Platform, North Charleston, SC

for Allison

Acknowledgements

Thank you to the following people for making this a better story than I could have written alone:

Mom, Dad, Joan and Jeni for reading a pretty raw first manuscript and for all your suggestions for its improvement.

Olivia and Anna Claire for your love and patience as Daddy snatches what time he can to write.

But mostly Allison, without whom nothing would be possible.
I sure do love you.

Prologue

Cunningham was the last town before the final drop-off to the Chagrin River. There was nothing beyond for another forty miles and no bridges or roads to get there. Bordered on one side by steep bluffs and on the other by the swirling water of a temperamental river, it was as if Cunningham settled in the heel print of God, fated and perfectly suited for a government craving hydroelectric power.

A single highway ran up the bluff, through Hawkinsville, and out to the rest of the world. Anywhere you could go was literally uphill from Cunningham, so we commonly referred to every place else as *Uphill.* It didn't matter if you were from the town next door or Paris; if you weren't from Cunningham, you were from Uphill. It's funny how a word for outsiders can bind a community together tighter than bailing wire. It kept us separate…maybe even better.

Cunningham was beautiful, and as a child looking from the inside out, it was a wonderful place to grow up. Except for the farm families, we lived in clapboard houses, modest but well kept, on tree-lined avenues just outside of town. Small stone retaining walls held our front yards back, making way for shaded sidewalks that were well traveled after dinner in the spring and early summer. Old Glory hung from porch posts every day, and on weekends strangers drove in from Uphill to patronize our vegetable stands, picnic by the Chagrin, or eat at our diner and swear it served the best peach pie in the whole world.

The town square centered on two ancient oaks that stood well apart at their trunks but reached for each other higher up, clinging together until it was hard to tell one from the other. We called them the Bride and Groom. The trees shaded a grassy plaza, supposedly for special events, but mostly used for touch football and a farmers market for our weekend guests. The ladies of Cunningham took special pride in this part of town, trimming everything in tulips, impatiens, and daisies. A manicured azalea hedge bordered the interior. At Easter, the bushes ran blood-red with blossoms, but with warmer days, the petals dropped to the sidewalk like crimson confetti, leaving a thick green wall around the garden spot of town.

I can almost see the storefronts of Cunningham. There was Murdock's General Store, where you could buy anything from fertilizer to a frying pan; Katie's Diner run by a man named Mac, an Uphill favorite for its peach and strawberry pies; and Wallace's Hardware & Lumber Supply. There was City Hall and the Sheriff's Department, a pharmacy with an ice-cream counter, our doctor's office, and the single-pump Gas & Grocery run by our mechanic and his sickly wife. There were a couple of other stores I've forgotten now, but the biggest business of all, occupying one full side of the square all by itself, was the God's Glory Church of Cunningham, pastored by Dr. Reverend Dodge.

God's Glory stood tall among the other buildings, looming large like an ivory fortress with a big brass bell calling its congregants to hear the Word of God. The church, with its great steeple, resting poetically among the quaint village shops, live oaks, and azaleas, was famous for drawing the giving masses out of Hawkinsville every holiday season. Reverend Dodge would offer a well-rehearsed sermon, and our semi-annual brothers and sisters would leave having given or pledged enough to last the whole year. Even so, Cunningham residents never neglected their tithe or directed their charity anywhere but God's Glory, which always seemed hungry for the Lord to reveal how the money was to be used. Of course the reverend's house never lacked for paint or new curtains.

God's Glory Memorial Park, which is a fancy way of saying *cemetery*, sat adjacent to the church and was as neatly kept as the town square itself. The white granite headstones, marble plaques, and concrete angels added to the beauty and allure of the church, making it seem peaceful and worthy of trust. During the holiday season, Reverend Dodge saw to it every monument was donned in flowers, meticulously arranged to accent the somber beauty of the cemetery. The Holiday Committee members were masters at introducing enough hodgepodge to the floral arrangements to maximize the effect without making it look decorated or the overall scene contrived. That would be in poor taste. A lot of planning goes into spontaneity. The pristine tombstones and carefully arranged flowers softened the hearts of visitors as they stopped to point and stare. Everyone wanted to believe there might really be a better place, and perhaps God's Glory and Reverend Dodge held the key.

Beyond God's Glory was River Road, the back way into town, and one of Dad's favorite long-cuts. The road ran along the railroad tracks and would take you as far as you wanted to go into the farmlands on either side of Cunningham. The train rails kept company with River Road for a while but then continued on, running along the wooded riverbank to wherever they began or ended. The line was rarely used, but the tracks were well maintained by the railroad company as part of a government pork deal landed by a congressman somewhere else in the state. There were no more roads, farms, or businesses after that. The tracks were the last thing Cunningham claimed before the final drop to the Chagrin River, Tracker Island, and the edge of nowhere.

Tracker Island was a narrow strip of land formed by a brief split in the river. It was mostly swamp at the southern end, not buildable and prone to flooding. There were no roads from town, just an old cattle bridge long past using that had been repaired over and over again with timber and scraps of lumber by the squatters living there. We used to laugh and say it looked like a bunch of drunk beavers built the stupid thing. Town kids weren't allowed on the bridge, but Cunningham didn't hold much more for teenagers than time to kill, so it was another place to go until the sheriff ran us off or we were old enough to leave for real.

The squatters living on the island were called *Trackers*, a term of derision, because they lived on the other side of the railroad tracks. They were dirty, shabby mixed-breeds who never came to church, kept their children from school, and pillaged our dump. Trackers were rare in town, and even so, we never spoke to them. They kept their eyes low and mumbled their business to whoever was behind the counter at the general store or the Gas & Grocery. Only the sheriff and his deputies had any regular dealings with the squatters, mostly to keep them in their place and out of Cunningham on weekends and special occasions.

When the floods came every year, the townsfolk watched as the Trackers abandoned their island home with arms full of all they could carry. They piled broken dishes, old handbags, tools, clothing, anything useful, on the railroad tracks and waited as the river carried the rest of their pitiful lives away. They sat with their belongings like statues in the rain, long enough for the sky to clear and the Chagrin to recede before moving back to reassemble life however they could. I remember as a child seeing the Trackers sitting in the drizzle with all of their earthly possessions piled around them. I stared through the window at the families as we drove past on our way to church, wondering why Cunningham offered no shelter, until I finally realized, it was because the Trackers deserved all that was happening to them.

1
Able Lake

There always seems to be so much time, but the truth is, a lifetime is no better than a day; you wake in the morning at sixteen and by lunch you're forty-two. Later, when the sun lowers in the sky, you struggle to recall things you should know, things that make you who you are. It's the horrible fear of forgetting that takes me on the pilgrimage home—or as close as I can get to home—every year, ending here in Hawkinsville at this cabin on the shore of Able Lake. I guess I'm hoping against hope the familiar yellow days, when the pollen hangs in the woods like a gold-green ghost, will somehow preserve what I feel slipping away. Twisted dogwoods twinkling among sturdier trees remind me it's spring…it is always spring when I'm here.

Beyond the azaleas down by the dock, I can hear water lapping the bank, gently rippling from a distant swimmer or a boat that passed by some time ago. I've been coming here for decades, alone, always alone, to sit and stare across the lake and lament what happened. Although there are plenty who do, I never fish or swim, or even touch the water. I'm not sure if it is sacred or cursed, but either way I'm afraid of the effect it may have on me. I've been comfortable having my sins neither washed nor punished, but I have this terrible feeling my indecision won't be allowed much longer. Wisteria perfumes the breeze, soothing my mind and coaxing me to remember. This place knows me, and it knows the story I've told only to myself.

These days I have waves of perfect clarity, but there are times when I'm sure my beloved Maggie is still here, having slipped gently out of bed to make the morning coffee, and the men and women hovering about are simply strangers claiming to be my children. I guess they are as loving as they can be with a forgetful, argumentative old man. The pills do help my memory, though, and kept me from getting lost on the way here. I hope the two bottles I have will be enough to help me remember everything that happened before the dam was built and Able Lake swallowed the little town of Cunningham. My children will be coming for me soon, probably by morning, so, as Maggie used to say, I need to "make hay while the sun's shining" and get done with as much of my confession as I can.

I struggle knowing where to start. I could go on and on about Dad working at the factory, Mom's fried chicken, or how fast I used to drive my truck on River Road. Maggie used to say I could talk five whole minutes on a single breath. She thought she was funny. But there isn't much time, and being long-winded won't add to anything I have to tell, so I'll take Maggie's habitual advice and "hurry it along." After all, when they find me and pull me away from this place, there'll be no more hope of remembering.

Sometimes the past seems like a story I read a long time ago, and other times it feels like a weight I've never been able to shed. I dread the past, for it cannot be changed and it's often more terrifying than we recall. I'm worried I'll find I'm not the man I remember being or I think I have become. I'm sure I've forgotten too much already and I may no longer have my facts straight, but I've been told facts are like boulders to be negotiated on the way to the truth, so I'll take another memory pill and pray there's forgiveness waiting for me somewhere.

It seems now, things started to unravel before Jesse ever arrived in Cunningham…probably about the time John saved Natalie Wallace from drowning in the Chagrin.

***

Natalie was the daughter of Mr. Wallace, the man who owned the lumber supply store in town. Something was wrong with her; I can't remember exactly what—maybe she was Downs or autistic—but the condition was definite in her appearance, so just by looking at her, you knew she was a special child. She couldn't stand her dresses to be soiled and had a horrible phobia of loose strings hanging from her clothes. It was as if a dangling thread running across her bare skin might slice her open like a razor. When Natalie was little, she would throw screaming fits, crying, "It hurts, it hurts, Daddy," until Mr. Wallace realized he needed to cut all the tags from her dresses and inspect the hems of anything she would wear. A touch of fatherly care dispelled the only true demon she had. Natalie lisped when she spoke. I'm not sure if the odd mixture of her speech impediment and Southern accent was cute or pitiful, but in Cunningham we were used to it.

A widower, Mr. Wallace dearly loved his daughter, and by the way she dressed for town and church, no one would ever guess she had no mother at home to pick out her clothes or tie bows in her hair. Mr. Wallace and Natalie lived on a farm lying fallow out along the infamous bend in River Road.

The bend was a tight curve, dangerous and blind, that Natalie would dumbly cross in the warm months, drawn to the blackberries growing along the railroad tracks on the other side. Mr. Wallace spanked Natalie to keep her off the road during blackberry season, but the call of the black fruit was stronger than his belt, so Natalie often came home with purple stains on her fingers and mouth, promising she'd only been picking flowers. Mr. Wallace did everything he knew to destroy the thorny bushes, but no matter how much he cut and burned, the blackberries miraculously survived, growing fuller and more alluring every year. He finally gave up and posted big yellow road signs warning drivers on the approach to his property. They simply read, "Watch Out for Natalie."

The whole town knew to be careful driving out River Road, and throughout the spring and summer months, Reverend Dodge's benediction always concluded with "remember to watch out for Natalie." That could have been our town motto. Cunningham sort of measured itself by the kindness shown to her.

2
Tracker Bridge

The Chagrin was still angry with the recent spring rain. The water was swift and deep, rushing along to the seething rapids sweeping down around the low, stony beach of Tracker Island. It was still early enough for the morning to be chilly, and a light fog hung low over the river like a wispy companion. Everything was damp, and Cunningham's crops were just beginning to peek up from the soil as the farmers all prayed against another frost. The fruits and vegetables that drew weekend crowds from Uphill wouldn't be ready for another few months, and with an early Easter past, there wasn't much for two sixteen-year-olds to do. I found myself on Tracker Bridge with Kirby Braddock, intending to kill the morning spitting into the water and talking about nothing much.

Kirby was a genuinely nice guy, heavyset and as goofy as they come. His only true failing was he could be talked into almost any inane thing me and the rest of my buddies could think up. One time we got him to collect a grocery sack full of dog poop and smuggle it to school. I remember him opening the bag on the bus and dropping his nose inside for a deep long sniff, as if the sack contained homemade cookies. He tried not to gag as he grinned over at me. "Hey, PJ," he snorted, "see what Mom made me for lunch? Chocolate dogs and chili. Sure smells good. Want some?" Then he curled over in his seat, laughing as the rest of us tried not to throw up.

When we got to school, Kirby spread his chocolate dogs and chili all over the floor in the boys room. The bell rang at the change of class, and the usual flood of students spilled into the restroom, but no one knew to expect a minefield of turds until it was too late. Most just stepped in Kirby's surprise, but when the pushing and shoving to get out started, some of the unfortunate ones fell to the ground, thoroughly ruining the rest of their day. When the principal asked Kirby about the incident, he said he was sorry, but it was an honest accident. He said his mom made collards the night before, and they hit him so fast that he couldn't make it to a stall in time. Kirby said he was actually afraid his colon would rupture, so the whole thing was more of a medical issue than anything else. He promised he was on his way to get the janitor, but class let out before he could alert anyone about the mess. Kirby got suspended for two days. Maggie tells me that's not a funny story, but it still makes me laugh.

Anyway, Kirby and I were out on the bridge, where we shouldn't have been, killing time early in the day. The cool morning and the sound of the Chagrin sloshing below stirred in my body, calling forth the primal urge to urinate. I unzipped my pants, ready to impress Kirby with a grand yellow arc, when he tapped me on the shoulder.

"Hey, PJ," he sang. "You might want to hold your wee-wee while your girlfriend is here."

"What?" I huffed as I turned to see Natalie standing on the bank among the scrub brush and trees. She must have seen us walk down and followed along. She knew we weren't allowed on the bridge, but in her mind, she wasn't breaking any rules as long she stayed off the structure itself and remained on the riverbank. The truth is, where she stood on the leafy slope, damp with the morning mist and a twelve-foot drop to the water below, was far more precarious than being on the bridge. She was wearing a white dress that made her glow like a patch of daisies in the under trees.

"Hey, Natalie," Kirby called while grinning at me. He knew she liked me and thought it was big fun to see me squirm with her innocent attention. She was never ashamed of the way she felt.

"Hey, Kirby Braddock. Hey, PJ. What you boys doin' out here on that ol' busted bridge?"

I didn't bother to answer. I stepped closer where I knew she could hear me plainly over the sound of the river. "Natalie, you need to get outta here. You know you shouldn't be in these woods wearing that pretty white dress. What's your daddy gonna say when you get home with dirt and hitchhikers all over it?"

"You think my dress is pretty, PJ?" She swayed shyly, looking at the ground. She took a single step forward, and the swift Chagrin churned a little louder. "This is a town dress me and Daddy got in Hawkinsville. It's not a play dress for being in the woods or eating blackberries, but it's not as fancy as a church dress either. That's why it's a town dress, for being in town. I'm glad you think it's pretty."

"That's great, Natalie, but you need to go home. A slippery bank in the dirty woods is no place for a girl in such nice clothes."

"You know you're not supposed to be on that busted ol' bridge. Daddy says it could fall down any second, and whoever is on it when that happens will be swept all the way to the ocean. You need to get off there right now, and you, too, Kirby Braddock, before the both of you wind up in the middle of the great big ocean somewhere far out to sea."

Her last comment made Kirby turn away and snort as he tried to contain his laughter at her colorful but idiotic warning.

"What's so funny, Kirby Braddock?" Natalie scolded as she took a step closer. I felt a sudden rush of electricity tingle up my back as I watched her slip on some wet leaves and regain her balance by grabbing on to a scrub tree. She was oblivious, but Kirby and I both sighed with relief. The Chagrin was not friendly here, and concern for where Natalie was standing began to pool in my stomach. Still, Kirby and I did not leave the bridge.

"Now, Natalie, see there? You almost fell and messed up your clothes. You're too close to the bank, and if you're not careful, you're gonna end up in that river somewhere in the middle of the ocean. If you won't go home, why don't you at least come over here with us? It'll be okay. We'll help you." I tried to coax her to safety, but the suggestion of joining us on Tracker Bridge was more than she could take.

"No, no, no, PJ. You need to come off that bridge before something bad happens!" She let go of the tree she steadied herself with. "Daddy says that bridge is gonna fall. He says it's dangerous. He says not to ever catch me on it. Please, PJ, come off the bridge!"

It was as if the river raised its voice to mute her plea. The roar of the water filled my ears, and all I could do was watch as Natalie took another slow step forward, slipped, fell softly to her back, and slid gently over the edge. The Chagrin swallowed her as smoothly as a morning pill, without so much as a ripple or a splash. Before Kirby and I knew what happened, the river pulled her in deep, sucking Natalie away as if she had never been there at all.

The air left my body as I stood dumbly looking down into the river.

"Oh, my God, oh, my God!" I could hear Kirby panicking somewhere in a dream. I finally took a breath. "PJ, where is she? Do you see her? She went down like a rock! Where is she? Do you see her?" Kirby was at my side, but Natalie was nowhere to be seen, only a remorseless river churning below.

"I'm goin' in!" Kirby kicked off his shoes. "I got to get her! I got to get her now!"

I was shaking. I couldn't believe how much I was shaking! There was a reason we weren't allowed to be here! The water was dangerous and deep, full of eddies and undertows even the strongest swimmers could never manage. *Why was I out here? Why hadn't I just taken Natalie home?*

Only a few seconds had passed, but Kirby already stripped himself out of his jeans and was headed over the side. I almost let him, but I threw my arm up to stop him instead. I was afraid. "She'll come up. We'll get her when she comes up. We gotta see where she is first. She'll come up, and then we'll get her." I was trembling, and I wasn't sure if I was right about not jumping in, but it seemed like the careful thing to do. That probably makes me a coward.

"Where is she? Where is she? Do you see her?" Kirby rattled as we scanned the water for any sign of Natalie. The seconds crawled like hours but time was running dry and real help was too far away.

"Okay, let's go." I kicked out of my shoes and tore off my pants as fast as I could. We moved to the edge of Tracker Bridge and stared into the seething river below. It was eager to have us as well.

"Let's go together, PJ. Are you ready?"

I nodded, and then, right as we were about to jump, I caught something out of the corner of my eye. "Wait! Look! What's that?" I pointed downriver to a dark man running along the opposite bank. He broke from the woods in a full sprint, faster than anything I'd ever seen before. He made short distance between the thicket and the river and went crashing into the water like a giant bull about forty yards from where we stood.

"What's that?" Kirby gasped.

"I don't know."

We watched in silence as the big man half waded and half swam into the currents. The river was strong and high around his chest when he was finally beaten by the rushing water and the Chagrin took him under.

"We have to go," I heard Kirby say, but my eyes were still downstream where the man had been swallowed. "Trackers can't swim—everybody knows that. We gotta go!"

With my toes curled over the side, I took a deep breath and closed my eyes as the roar of the river wrapped around me. I had to jump now or cower on the bridge forever. There was no more time to wait on courage. I could feel Kirby ready to jump.

I don't know if I would have gone or not, but something massive rising from the water interrupted my moment of indecision. The river spat hard as the Chagrin choked and gagged, trying to hold down what it swallowed. It couldn't. The big man wrestled to regain his footing, and when he stood up from the water, he had Natalie in his arms. She was limp, and her white dress dripped from her body. As I stood in my underwear, weak kneed and dumb, watching the stranger take Natalie back from the river, I thanked God honestly for the first time in my life.

I don't know why we didn't cross over to get Natalie, but we waited instead, watching the man tend to her as she lay on the stony beach of Tracker Island. She seemed to be in better hands. I saw her begin to stir and felt another wave of relief. Natalie was conscious now and more upset over the condition of her dress than having nearly been washed out to sea, but the big man was gentle and his touch was kind. He soothed her.

From atop the bridge, we could see Natalie smile and nod. Words passed between them as naturally as a niece with her uncle. She calmed, and when she was collected enough, the big man whisked her into his arms and carried Natalie up the river's edge toward us. Kirby and I stood in awe. We could see bruises beginning to purple on Natalie's arms and face where the river had beaten her against its rocks, but other than that, she seemed okay. Natalie was unfazed by the whole ordeal, and with her arms around her savior's neck, she laughed and chirped as they made their way upriver. Kirby and I gaped at the pair of them until the big man stood at his end of the bridge with Natalie still in his arms.

"Hey, PJ. Hey, Kirby Braddock. Look who carried me all the way up from far out to sea."

He was a powerful mixed-breed with tattered clothes soaking wet from the river. It would be difficult to guess his years—some people age more gracefully than others—but he was handsome by all rights, and he glistened as the water dripped from his body. The big man started to put Natalie down, but she squirmed to stay in his arms.

"My daddy don't allow me to be on that ol' busted bridge, John. He'll tan my hide if he finds out I been on it."

She clung to his neck, and her eyes locked into his as she explained her daddy's rules. John nodded, and with Natalie in his arms, he stepped onto the bridge. He looked at us and paused. Kirby and I instinctively moved to the side so John and Natalie could pass straight across.

As John strode by with Natalie, I got the sensation I'd been brushed by something strong…special…like a timber wolf or a twelve-point buck. He eased Natalie to the ground so her foot never touched the "busted ol' bridge," keeping her innocent and without offense. She reached up and hugged him, whispered something into his ear, and then kissed him on the face. He wasn't comfortable with her affection.

When Natalie let him go, John crossed silently back. I thought the big man was going to leave without a single word, disappearing to his island without us hearing his voice at all. He was three or four strides on his way when he turned back. His voice was low, not threatening, and easy to catch over the sound of the river.

"Boys."

"Yes, sir," we answered together.

"Your folks don't allow you on this here bridge, do they?"

"No, sir," we answered again.

"Then," John said flatly, "don't be on it. You hear?"

"Yes, sir, we hear."

John started to walk away but was struck by another thought first. "Boys, Miss Natalie's father's gonna be pretty upset 'cause of what happened today and on account of her dress gettin' all ruined. Trouble's coming 'cause of it—ain't nothing to be done about that. But it would go a bit easier on everybody's mind if you two put your trousers on before you take this girl home."

"Yes, sir." I didn't know what else to say. "Thank you, sir."

"Yes, thank you, sir," Kirby echoed.

John gave us one last look and nearly seemed to smile before he turned and disappeared into the thicket.

"I see London, I see France," Natalie sang when she noticed Kirby and I were standing in our underwear. She chortled up, "I see PJ's underpants." She snickered and giggled and sat down on the bank and laughed some more while Kirby and I got dressed.

Not much of the day had gone by, but I was exhausted by all that had happened. There was nothing to say yet, so I took Natalie by the hand and Kirby followed us up out of the woods without a word. We'd figure out what we were going to tell Mr. Wallace when we got back to my truck.

3
The Lie

I'd left my pickup off the road behind some trees so it couldn't be seen unless you were really looking for it. Just like hanging out at the bridge, it was against the rules to park in the woods back here. As soon as Natalie saw my truck, she let into me about how many laws I'd broken and how, if I didn't "straighten up and fly right," no good was going to find me and then where would I be?

Kirby ordinarily enjoyed Natalie giving me what for, but today we were both pretty rattled, so I didn't pay much attention to Natalie, and the scolding she gave me didn't draw the slightest grin from Kirby. Other things were preying on our minds.

"What do you want to say happened?" I muttered as we came up on the truck.

"I don't know. I guess I'll say whatever you want to say."

"We're not supposed to be down here, Kirby, and something bad, really bad, almost happened 'cause we were."

"I know." Kirby looked down and kicked halfheartedly at the ground. "If it hadn't been for that Tracker, it would've ended up worse than bad."

Our conversation fell silent as we considered the options, hoping Natalie would go along with whatever we decided. She was tired and no longer interested in what we were saying, so she popped the door to the truck and climbed in to wait for her ride home. She looked sleepy as she scooted to the middle of the seat in her soggy white dress.

"Maybe we shouldn't mention the Tracker." I was more thinking out loud than offering a suggestion.

"You might be right. You know we're partly to blame for that Tracker having his hands on Natalie." Kirby looked me straight in the face, and I could see he was scared. "She was across the bridge, on the island. That's bad. That's real bad." He took a deep breath. "Maybe we should say we were driving by and saw Natalie come down here by herself. We can say she fell in and we pulled her out."

Kirby was an honest guy, so he wasn't looking for us to be heroes when we weren't, but like me, he had a terrible sense we were in trouble and the Tracker, John, might be in the worst trouble of all. Not that we cared as much about him as we worried about what might happen to us. Some people aren't as precious afterward as they are in the moment.

"No one's gonna buy that. We have to say we were on the bridge and Natalie followed us down, just like it happened. We'll say we tried to get her to go home, but she wouldn't listen. We'll say she fell in, but she held on to the bank, and we were able to climb down and pull her out. There's gonna be hell to pay, but I think that should be the story, and we won't say one word about the Tracker or what he did. Who'd believe it anyway?"

Kirby looked at me and nodded. "Okay, I'm with you, but how are you gonna get Natalie to go along? You know how she is. She's only gonna say what's true."

"I know." I sighed and glanced at Natalie. "Maybe I can…scare her into it."

Mr. Wallace's store was only five minutes away, but I drove around a good half-hour trying to convince Natalie not to tell anyone about John or being on Tracker Island. But Natalie was Natalie and, understanding only the value of blackberry lies, wouldn't agree to say something *wasn't*, when it *was*. So I made up bigger lies about all of us going to jail and never seeing our daddies again if we told about the Tracker. When Natalie started to tear up, I relented and said how great it was for the three of us to have our own secret and how it made us real friends. She smiled through wet eyes at the thought, but even so, she shook her head, indicating she would still tell about John.

I ran my hand over my head as frustration started to turn me mean. I dug for something terrible to say. I told her she was dumb and no one would believe her story anyway about a stupid Tracker if Kirby and I said otherwise. She started to sob and threw her hands up to cover her face as a bump in the road jostled the truck. She wanted to go home, but she hadn't yet agreed on the day's events, so I kept at it. I felt sick and cruel as I went on telling her everyone was going to think she was crazy and she and her daddy would have to leave Cunningham and go someplace bad, but if she listened to me, they might be able to stay. She kept her hands pressed hard against her snotty wet face, continuing to shake her head no to our lie. Kirby stared out his window in silence the whole time I tortured Natalie. He didn't intercede for her, but I felt his disappointment settling in the cab as we both learned how despicable I could truly be. Natalie loved me, but her feelings were not as important as my resolve.

"Okay, okay," Natalie blurted. "I won't tell! Stop being so mean, PJ! Please stop being so mean."

She broke into harder sobs and turned away, leaning over to comfort herself under Kirby's arm. He stroked her shoulder, quieting her and telling her everything would be all right.

The guilt of breaking Natalie stirred in my stomach like sour milk. I lowered the window, hoping the outside air would keep me from throwing up. Kirby reached over, turned on some music, and we drove around a little longer until it was hard to tell Natalie had been crying at all. She was back to her regular self, sitting up in the middle of the truck, telling Kirby and me something about her dad's store. She seemed to forget about everything, and I was pretty sure she would let me and Kirby tell our lie without correction. Her face and arms were bruised and scraped, but there was nothing to be done about that here. It was time to take her home. I wheeled into the square, passed the church, and rolled into a parking space directly in front of Wallace's Hardware & Lumber Supply. We opened the doors, stepped out, and escorted Natalie in without saying a word.

Inside was darker than the bright morning we'd come from, so my eyes needed a moment to adjust. There were no customers, just the sheriff sipping coffee and making light conversation as Mr. Wallace swept behind the counter. As soon as I saw the sheriff in Wallace's store, my heart dropped through my stomach, and it took all I had not to turn around and run out the door.

Sheriff Johnson was a tall, big-bellied man with a bulldog's face and a deep, bellowing laugh that could shake pictures right off the wall. He'd been the sheriff in Cunningham as long as any of us could remember, and even though he wasn't fit enough to run to the corner, we all knew he was not a man to be trifled with. His good nature was shallow and evaporated the instant he felt the law in Cunningham wasn't being properly respected or attended to. In Cunningham, laws of tradition were as important as any other on the books, which left a great deal of what was and wasn't legal open to the sheriff's interpretation. Of course, when it came to law enforcement, our visitors from Uphill always received generous leeway, but that had more to do with the policies of Reverend Dodge than the benevolence of Sheriff Johnson.

The morning sun silhouetted us against the front door, providing another moment or two before the two men at the counter could see there was something wrong.

"Hey, sweetie, hey, boys," Mr. Wallace called over as the sheriff blew on his coffee.

I swallowed hard, not quite ready to respond, and Kirby stared at his feet.

"Daddy, Daddy." Natalie broke from where we were standing, ran to her father, and buried her head in his aproned chest. "I promise, I promise to God, Daddy, I wasn't pickin' no blackberries, and I didn't set foot on that ol' busted bridge." All of the emotions she'd managed to contain flooded right out of her at the sight of her dad, and her heavy sobs made it impossible to understand what she was saying.

Mr. Wallace tried to push Natalie back to see her face, but she held on tight, so he did too. The sound of her weeping in her father's arms filled me with such shame; I couldn't do anything but stare down at my shoes alongside Kirby.

"Shhh, I've got you," Mr. Wallace said. "Are you hurt, sweetheart?"

Natalie, with her face still pressed to her father's chest, shook her head no as her muffled tears began to subside and she started to reclaim herself.

"PJ, Kirby." We looked up to see the sheriff summoning us over with a single finger, but my feet were glued to the floor, so I couldn't move.

"Sweetheart, what happened? Where did you get these?" Mr. Wallace pried himself away from his daughter enough to finally notice her bruises. The sheriff noticed them too.

"Boys!" boomed Sheriff Johnson hard enough to make me jump, "come here now!"

Fury over Natalie's condition was welling inside the big man, and even though he was doing his best to keep it contained, I was afraid to get too close. Still, I was even more terrified of not doing as I was told. Kirby and I moved slowly toward the sheriff, not as two heroes who pulled Natalie from the Chagrin, but as two liars looking to protect themselves from their hand in an accident that nearly took her life. I began to doubt whether the story we concocted would hold.

The big man never looked away as Kirby and I skulked over to where he was waiting beside the counter. His nose twitched, and his lips curled into an involuntary snarl. He wasn't blaming us for anything yet, but he aimed to have the truth about Natalie, and we'd better pray he believed whatever we had to say. We stopped an arm's length from the sheriff, but he wasn't satisfied, so he stepped up to cut the distance between us tight enough to smell BO through his aftershave. Hot coffee breath wafted across my face as he brought his nose down to mine. His radio crackled with a call from one of his deputies, but he reached down and snapped it off. Nothing was more important than this.

"Tell me what happened to that little girl," Sheriff Johnson growled, "and tell me now."

The sheriff was better at getting the truth than I was at lying, so I wasn't sure I had the courage to go through with what Kirby and I agreed to say. But there are times when the truth is so terrifying that getting caught in a lie can't make things much worse, so you hope in the lie and bury the truth where even you might not be able to find it again. Besides, I'd fully committed to telling my tale the moment I started torturing Natalie in the truck.

"Well, sir," I stammered, "me and Kirby..." My eyes went to my shoes, and I struggled for words, making me look even more guilty than I was. "Well, we were out on Tracker Bridge, and…uh, well…" I strained to remember what I was supposed to say as Kirby stayed silent and Natalie watched me from her father's arms. I could feel her staring from across the room as I stood nose to nose with the monstrous sheriff, trying to spin my lie, but not finding the words.

"He carried me over the bridge, Daddy," Natalie piped up, catching the sheriff's ear. The big-bellied man turned away from me to listen to her, and Kirby looked up from the floor for the first time.

"I told him I wasn't allowed on that busted ol' bridge, Daddy, so he carried me across."

"You were on the other side of the river?" Mr. Wallace's voice cracked as he leaned in to question his daughter. Sheriff Johnson twisted as he adjusted his belt and thumbed the top of his holster.

"I sure was…but not really, because he carried me the whole way."

"Sweetie," Mr. Wallace was shaking now, "this person who carried you across the bridge, did he give you these?" He touched her on the cheek and then on the arm.

Natalie looked down, noticing her bruises for the first time and wincing at the sight of them. "Maybe," she whimpered, "when we were in the water."

The sheriff writhed and gritted his teeth as Mr. Wallace continued to glean only pieces of what really happened. Maybe Natalie was doing her best to keep Kirby and me out of trouble because of what I said in the truck, or maybe it was the trauma of the morning, but she was telling everything backwards and out of order, making things sound far worse than they were. I can't blame Natalie, though, because if Kirby and I had come forward immediately, what was about to happen might never have.

"Sweetie," Mr. Wallace was saying, "who were you in the water with?"

"It was me." Kirby stepped up to the counter to take the blame. "I was down at the bridge, and I—"

"It was not you! Kirby Braddock, you liar! It was not you at all, or you either, PJ! Neither one of you saved me from being carried away far out to sea," Natalie snapped and then buried her head back into her father's chest.

"Mr. Wallace," I finally spoke up, "she's got it all wrong."

"PJ, you had your chance. Now, not one more word out of you, you hear?" Sheriff Johnson snarled before turning his attention back to Natalie.

"Natalie." Her father pulled her away so he could see her face. "Who carried you over the bridge? You need to tell me, honey."

"Well," Natalie sniffled, "it wasn't Kirby or PJ like they want to say.…It was…John."

"The Tracker?" Sheriff Johnson asked.

Natalie looked up and with an exhausted smile nodded yes.

The sheriff took a deep, red-faced breath as anger seethed through his big body. "I know him," he growled to Mr. Wallace.

"Get Natalie to the doctor right now, and don't you worry about that Tracker. He'll be under my jail before half an hour's gone." He reached down, snapped on his radio, and pressed the speaker to his face. "Carl, Eddy," he summoned his deputies as he paced toward the door, "meet me at the bridge right now."

"Ten-four, copy that, Sheriff. See you in seven," the radio crackled in response.

The sheriff, single-minded and boiling for justice, seemed to forget all about Kirby and me as he brushed by on his way out of the store. But he paused and turned back, eclipsing the doorway. He was large and dark with the late morning sun at his back. His face was hidden in the shadow. "You two boys," his voice was low and threatening, "get yourselves home right now. We're not done by a long shot, and the last thing you want is for me to have to come looking for you. You got me?"

Kirby and I nodded, and the sheriff disappeared down the sidewalk.

I felt heavy as Mr. Wallace started getting Natalie ready to see the doctor. Kirby and I shuffled quietly out of the store and climbed into my truck. Mr. Wallace locked the door behind us.

I tried to tell myself I hadn't done anything wrong, this had just been an accident followed by a terrible misunderstanding, but guilt wasn't letting me go that easily. I hadn't been the person I wanted to be all day long, and even though I may have been technically innocent, technicalities are just another way of skirting the truth. It didn't help. I felt ashamed, and since feelings are often more powerful than facts, I couldn't talk myself into being okay with what happened.

Kirby and I rode home in silence until I touched the brakes and we came to a stop in front of his house. I'd never seen Kirby like this before. He just sat staring out the windshield. I put the truck in Park and waited for him to get out.

"We should have gone in after her," he muttered.

"I know," was all I knew to say, and I put my forehead down on the steering wheel.

"We shouldn't have lied."

"I know," I sighed without looking up.

We sat for a few minutes more before Kirby opened the door and I watched him cross the yard and disappear into his house. Ordinarily I would have driven around a while or headed down to River Road to clear my head, but the sheriff told me to go home, and I was too afraid not to. I didn't say anything to my parents about Natalie or John that night. I just pushed dinner around my plate until my mom asked if I was feeling well. She put her cheek on my forehead and sent me to my room to lie in the bed and stare at the ceiling as the final breath of day began to fade away.

4
The Next Morning

I was sure I hadn't slept as the day ran through my mind, but twenty-seven minutes after two was the last I saw of the clock until I heard Mom shuffling breakfast pans in the kitchen. I lay quiet and tired, watching the morning sun stream across my room, illuminating small particles of dust that would have otherwise gone unnoticed. I could hear coffee percolating and bacon hissing as the smell of both wafted up the stairs. Mom would be calling me down to eat soon. The sound of the oven opening and a sheet of biscuits sliding over the rack, followed by the clinking of plates and silverware being set around the table, made yesterday seem far away and today more hopeful. I took a deep breath, rolled to my side, and continued to drift in the sound of my mom in her Sunday morning ritual.

Tap, tap. A light knock at the front door broke the rhythm of the breakfast sonata, and I heard my mother move out of the kitchen to receive the unexpected caller. All of the worry and fear I'd taken to bed immediately woke inside me. Sunday morning visits were rare and only when a neighbor needed to borrow a cup of sugar or a few eggs, but this time I was sure something else wanted in. I was certain the sheriff had come to talk about Natalie and John. My heart was pounding, and the lump in my throat was big enough to choke on. I pulled myself up and crept to the bedroom door to eavesdrop on my mother and the visitor. I could hear her talking with a man, but I couldn't tell who it was until my father greeted him as well and the volume of the conversation grew. I listened as my mom offered some coffee to Mr. Wallace and heard him politely refuse.

"So, you need to talk to PJ," I heard Dad say. "Well, he should be up by now. Let me holler at him."

"Thank you," Mr. Wallace answered.

Dad walked to the foot of the stairs. He had given up waking me gently long ago.

"PJ! PJ! Get those feet on the floor and put some clothes on! Mr. Wallace is down here to see you!"

"Yes, sir!" I called back, but I was already half-dressed, hoping to get downstairs before Mr. Wallace told my parents more than I could explain.

My dad and Mr. Wallace were standing just inside the front door when I came down. Mom was in the kitchen checking on the biscuits. I nodded good morning to Mr. Wallace, and he nodded back.

"PJ, Mr. Wallace wants to know if you would help him with something this morning before church."

I could tell by his voice that Dad thought this was an unusual request, but he was always about service to others and thought it was terribly important to teach me the same. My father seemed to think the more inconvenient the help, the more pleasing it was in the eyes of God. I'm not sure he was wrong. Anyway, when I agreed to go with Mr. Wallace, my parents were so delighted at my opportunity to serve, especially on a Sunday, they didn't ask any questions, assuming Mr. Wallace needed me at church.

"See you in service," Dad called from the stoop as I followed Mr. Wallace down the walk.

"See you there," I hollered and slid into the pickup to find Natalie waiting.

Mr. Wallace turned the key, and his truck rumbled to life as his daughter caught me in syrupy stare. She looked a lot better than I expected. I smiled as embarrassment turned in my stomach.

Mr. Wallace waved to Dad, and we rounded the corner at the end of the street.

Mr. Wallace wasted no more time. "PJ," he started without looking over, "tell me what happened yesterday. Every bit of it, and don't leave a single thing out."

He wheeled the truck around another corner to take the long way into town, and Natalie reached over to put her hand on my knee. I closed my eyes, took a deep breath, and told Mr. Wallace all about Natalie falling into the river and how Kirby wanted to jump in but I made him wait. I told him how fast the water was and how far away Natalie had been swept when the Tracker jumped in to pull her out.

"I thought I was never coming back," Natalie interrupted. "That ol' Chagrin held me on the bottom and wasn't gonna let go for nothing. Then, when I was near far out to sea, I felt the strongest hands ever, like steel, take ahold of me and pluck me right on out. I didn't know if I was here or there, but I was pretty sure I was in the arms of God. I must've been. Then I woke up, and John carried me across the bridge so I wouldn't be a disobedient daughter." She leaned over to whisper in my ear, "Daddy don't allow me on that busted ol' bridge." She turned to her father with a giggle. "And then, Daddy, PJ and Kirby Braddock were in their underpants!"

She brought her hand to her face and snorted up a little laugh at the thought, but her father never cracked a smile. "PJ," he said flatly, "keep going."

So I told him how scared Kirby and I were about a Tracker carrying Natalie around the island and what everybody in town might think. After all, it was our fault Natalie was at the bridge, and we never even tried to save her. I didn't tell him about being mean to Natalie after that, but I did say Kirby and I tried to get her to lie about what happened. She was safe, and we thought we were doing what was best for her.

Mr. Wallace listened as he drove, and about the time I finished telling what happened, he pulled up to the sheriff's office and cut the engine. He looked over at me and gave a disappointed sigh. "Let's go," he said. He turned to Natalie. "Honey, you wait in the truck, okay?" Natalie nodded she would, and Mr. Wallace and I got out.

A bell chimed as we walked through the door. I wasn't clear what more Mr. Wallace wanted from me, and I sure didn't like being in the sheriff's office. I tried not to let it show.

We stepped past an empty counter with "Loraine" on the nameplate to find Cunningham's two deputies sitting at their desks, one reading the newspaper with his feet propped up and the other scribbling on some paperwork.

"Good morning, Mr. Wallace," the deputy with the propped feet greeted as he folded the paper to his lap. "How are you this morning?"

"I'm fine, Eddy. Where's the sheriff?"

Eddy grinned. "Well now, Mr. Wallace, the sheriff would be in the back there along with the prisoner and, uh, well, his veterinarian." Eddy, still smiling, slid his feet to the floor and leaned forward to look for Mr. Wallace's reaction to what he said.

"What did you say, Eddy? Did you say he's back there with the vet?"

"That's what I said, Mr. Wallace. That is surely what I said." Eddy leaned back in his chair with an oily grin.

"Why in the world would the sheriff have the vet back there?"

"I don't know," Eddy smirked. "Maybe the prisoner needs to be wormed." Eddy snickered like a weasel at his own joke, reached over, and jabbed at the other deputy. "Ain't that right, Carl? The sheriff wants to be sure that big Tracker has all his shots."

"Why don't you shut up, Eddy. You ain't a bit funny, you know that?" Carl shot back. The grin dropped from Eddy's face. "To answer your question," Carl went on, "looks like the prisoner fell last night and hit his head pretty bad on the bunk."

"Not only that," Eddy interrupted, "he smashed three fingers in those big iron doors when we shut him in the cell. I told him to be careful and watch his hands, but he didn't listen too well, did he, Carl?"

Carl ignored Eddy and continued with Mr. Wallace. "The prisoner had a pretty tough night, so when I got in this morning, I went to fetch the doctor, but I couldn't get him to come, being Sunday and all, so I got the veterinarian instead."

"It seems fittin'," Eddy interjected.

"The sheriff just came in, and he's back there with both of 'em now," Carl finished.

Mr. Wallace stepped past Eddy to the edge of Carl's desk. "Carl, your prisoner, did he say anything about yesterday?"

"He ain't made a single peep since he been here. He ain't asked to pee, he ain't asked for a drink o' water, he ain't even said his own name. He just sits there, quiet as a mouse, and we can't get him to talk for nothin', not for nothin' at all," Eddy answered the question meant for Carl.

"Will you shut up, Eddy?" Carl barked.

Mr. Wallace seemed to pay no attention to what Eddy said, but it clearly affected him as he moved closer, put his palms down on Carl's desk, and leaned in. "The prisoner you have back in that cell of yours being patched up by an animal doctor, his name is John. And according to PJ here," Carl glanced past Mr. Wallace, noticing me for the first time, "he saved Natalie's life yesterday. She fell in the river, and that man back there pulled her out when he could've gone about his own business…which would have made this a very different kind of day for me. Now," Mr. Wallace's voice went low and hard, "I talked to Reverend Dodge about all of this last night, and he said if PJ could corroborate Natalie's story, he didn't see any reason the sheriff should hold on to John. You know as well as I do, Carl, Reverend Dodge likes to keep these things all in the family and out of the Uphill news. I'm not sure I'll be able to do that unless you get the sheriff out here right now."

Mr. Wallace's tone surprised Carl, but he nodded he understood and waved Eddy in to get the sheriff. When Sheriff Johnson emerged from the back, he was furious. Eddy obviously filled him in on what was said, and he was incensed by the interference with his police work. The sheriff wasn't interested in having any public conversations with private citizens about his prisoner. He stomped across the floor, pausing only to order Mr. Wallace to follow him into his office, and then he slammed the door hard enough to rattle the outside windows. The deputies and I stared silently through the glass of the sheriff's office as the big man raged at Mr. Wallace. Their voices were muffled but heated until the sheriff finally sat down behind his desk and Mr. Wallace picked up the phone to dial a number. He spoke into the receiver briefly and handed the phone to Sheriff Johnson.

"That would be Dodge," Eddy muttered.

The sheriff scowled as he leaned forward on his desk with the phone to his ear. He boiled as he listened. "No, Reverend, we won't!" the big man exploded, standing straight up and slamming his fist on the desk hard enough to bounce a cup of pencils off the side. He paused as the other half of the conversation came over the phone. "I *am* the law in this town!" he boomed in response and then stopped to listen again. That was the last time the sheriff spoke loud enough for us to hear, but we watched as he rubbed his forehead between his two fingers and sat down. He nodded a couple of times before hanging up. He leaned back deep in his chair, glaring at the ceiling, but when Mr. Wallace turned to leave, the sheriff followed him out to where the deputies and I had watched the whole episode.

"Alright, Carl," Sheriff Johnson growled, "apparently we have an eyewitness," he glared at me for a moment and then continued with his deputy, "who says that Tracker back there is innocent of all charges and this is nothing more than a misunderstanding. We got no need to hold him anymore. So as soon as the doctor finishes up and these civilians clear the premises, I want you to haul his butt on down to the bridge and see he takes himself across."

"I'll carry him down, Sheriff," Eddy volunteered.

"If I wanted you to carry him," Sheriff Johnson snarled, "I would've told you to carry him. What I want, Deputy, is for you to stay away from that Tracker. You've done enough already."

"Yes, sir," Eddy grinned. "You're the boss."

Mr. Wallace put his hand on my back, indicating it was time to leave. We walked out and piled into his truck without me being asked a single question. Natalie already told Mr. Wallace the truth, and all he needed me to do was stand there. I guess sometimes that's all it takes to make things right. Still, I felt bad about what happened, so I threw some extra money in the offertory at church that morning to ease my conscience and grease the palms of heavenly justice. Mr. Wallace closed down his store for three full days after that, and the next thing I remember, it was summertime.

5
Summertime

Mr. Wallace replanted that spring for the first time since Mrs. Wallace passed, so by summertime, Natalie was in the square with the rest of the farmers selling produce to weekend visitors from Hawkinsville. Everybody's stands were full of beans, snap peas, okra, tomatoes, cucumbers, peppers, scuppernongs and almost anything else you can imagine for the crowds to pick over, squeeze, smell, and finally purchase. I can still see the farmers and their old wives sitting in front of their vegetables under big straw hats, fanning themselves and smiling wide as customers and admirers milled through the best of Cunningham. It's a pleasant memory and smells of heat and purple hull peas.

Our visitors seemed to believe they got the best deal on whatever they bought, but to tell the truth, there were no real bargains to be had. Cunningham was family, so no matter what stand the folks from Uphill visited, they found the prices were all the same—except for the year Mr. Wallace started growing again. Natalie charged twice as much for her tomatoes as any other seller on the square.

It wasn't for pride or money Natalie set the price so high, but the tomatoes grown on the Wallace farm that summer were so clearly superior in every way a tomato can be, the other farmers broke tradition and demanded Mr. Wallace set a higher price. Even so disadvantaged, the early lines formed at Natalie's stand,

and she was sold out, packed up, and off the square by midmorning almost every weekend. I remember she used to tell the folks from Hawkinsville that those were God's tomatoes until Reverend Dodge stopped her with some biblical quote about blasphemy or taking the Lord's name in vain, so she called them Track tomatoes instead. When customers asked her what Track tomatoes were, she would lean in close and whisper, "The roundest, reddest, tastiest in the whole big world. I 'spect these are the kind of tomatoes God would make if it weren't blasphemous for Him to do it."

The unusual success of the Wallace farm was the talk of the town that summer. Everyone wondered how Mr. Wallace had the time, between Natalie and his lumber supply business, to whip a farm that lay fallow for so many years into such great shape in one short spring. It's a good thing Mr. Wallace didn't allow Natalie to sell God's beans or God's peas or any of His other staples also growing on the farm, because in towns like Cunningham, wonder turns to suspicion in the bat of an eye.

As the days heated, we spent a lot of time on the river south of town where the water gurgled happily around big rocks and never dipped below chest deep. Just across the tracks with gentle banks of fine brown sand, this was the spot Cunningham and warm Uphill guests came to picnic and enjoy the cool water of the Chagrin. The church bought tables, benches, and grills as a token of hospitality to our visitors, and volunteers from the congregation collected the litter left at the end of any given day, making it ready for the next. The water was broad with low, welcoming banks on the Cunningham side, swirling around comfortable boulders and flattening out to a marsh of thick reeds and cattails near the horizon.

The marsh was beautiful from a distance, but up close it was nothing more than slow, murky water full of leeches and cottonmouths. We were careful never to wade or swim too close to the other side.

This spot in the river was called Sandy Shores, and even though the town couldn't officially claim this place as its own, we did anyway because it was beautiful and people loved it.

Sandy Shores with its warm beach, soft sand, and friendly shallow waters was the only safe place to swim in the whole Chagrin, making it a popular draw for weekend pilgrims and Cunningham residents alike. Kirby and I killed a lot of lazy days watching out-of-town girls sun themselves or cool off in the river under the careful eye of their boyfriends or fathers.

Then like clockwork, the vampires from the Hawkinsville Medical Center descended on our town to take advantage of the quarterly blood drive put on by the God's Glory Church of Cunningham. Reverend Dodge set aside one day every three months for all residents of age to donate blood. He used to tell us if Christ could shed His blood for us, we could certainly spare a few drops for Him. After all this time, that still sounds right to me. Some churches take pride in their nativity and others take pride in their Easter egg hunt, but at God's Glory the Give Blood to God blood drive was one of our biggest events, and it happened four times a year, once every season.

It was a huge production with a flock of cookie-cutter nurses in white from the Hawkinsville Medical Center setting up shop in the fellowship hall of God's Glory. The church was decorated in big red crosses with ambulances and fire trucks parked out front. Strangers from Uphill thanked everyone and offered peanut butter cookies and juice to all who donated. No one dared miss it. I've always been squeamish about needles and groups of women all dressed alike, but even so, I gave every season, if only to earn the little badge letting everyone know I fulfilled my duty to God and Reverend Dodge.

I'm sorry I can't remember more about that summer. I must have been fond of some unimportant girl or pulled some thoughtless prank the way aimless teenage boys do. There does seem to be a memory of earning a speeding ticket or two out on River Road, but it's hazy and stands beyond my recollection. It's frustrating! I just hope I've recounted what's necessary and important to know before I continue. I need to make sense. I overheard the doctor explain to someone my memory is broken, but that's not true at all. It is not broken, it is simply running out.

Dusk is crawling through the trees now, bringing to life a forest full of lightning bugs and crickets in its wake. I've always loved fireflies, and I could sit on this porch right up 'til bedtime counting their green and yellow beacons, partly because they're beautiful and partly because they're one of the few things I'm still sure about. The darkness is bringing in the mosquitoes too. They're not as appreciative as the nurses from Hawkinsville, and since they didn't bring any juice or cookies, I'd better move inside. Besides, whatever Maggie is making smells wonderful, and I do love keeping her company while she cooks. Some guys like golf, but to me, kitchen talks with Maggie as she fusses about are the very best part of retirement. No, no, that's not right, that's not right at all. Oh, I feel myself starting to fade. I'm not sure, did I miss my last pill? I must have. I'd better go ahead and take two so I can squeeze all I can out of my memory about what happens next. After all, what happens next is why I'm here.

6
Jesse

It was the last Sunday before Christmas and winter hadn't quite settled in to full swing, but with the town hung in red bows and lights, the nip in the air was enough to cast the spell of the holiday. We filed into church for the final instructions and reminders about how we were to behave, where we were to sit, and what we were to say to the influx of semiannual visitors who would be coming to make their offerings Christmas Eve. After all, we owed it to God to maximize the Christmas experience of all our unchurched Uphill brethren. The pianist was playing something somber inside the sanctuary as I halfheartedly shook hands with the usher, accepted his program, and followed Mom and Dad to our usual pew. The big oak cross hanging over the altar watched as we settled in.

Annual wreaths of evergreen trimmed with gold ribbon hung on every window, and the smell of pine from the Chrismon tree wafted thick through the air. The murmur of two hundred conversations droned through the room until the music finally tapered to an end and Reverend Dodge took the pulpit. The congregation fell silent.

"Good morning," he offered in his usual resonate tone.

"Good morning," we dutifully responded.

The reverend nodded, stepped around the pulpit, and held his arms up like he was offering us all a big hug. "Isn't the sanctuary beautiful today?"

"Yes," we all answered with a man somewhere up front adding a belated "Amen!"

"Amen is right, brother," Reverend Dodge agreed. "We owe a special thanks to Sandy Strozier and the ladies of the Holiday Committee for making our church so very beautiful during this time of great joy and celebration."

The congregation applauded, and taking our cue from the "Amen" gentleman up front, we rose to our feet and applauded some more.

I've always disliked how standing ovations in church are equally afforded to decorating the windows and the divinely remarkable. Sometimes we should sit, sometimes we should stand, and sometimes we should stomp our feet. But we never stomp our feet in church, and we'll stand for the slightest of anything. What's to distinguish the mundane from the marvelous if all we ever grant is our highest praise? Maggie never agreed with me.

The reverend raised his hand, signaling it was time to move along, and we took our seats once again.

"Before we begin the servicc, I have a few announcements. Remember, next week is Christmas, and we're expecting as large a crowd as ever to visit from Uphill. This will be the only church a lot of these people will get the entire year. As usual, we'll be setting up folding chairs in the narthex and around the walls for our regular members so our visitors can have the pews. Please do not sit in the pews."

The congregation nodded compliantly. No one from Cunningham would dare be caught in a pew on Christmas Eve or Easter Sunday.

"Don't forget," Reverend Dodge continued, "the first Saturday after the New Year is our quarterly Give Blood to God blood drive, so don't overdo your holiday. There's no sense in contributing an overdose of cholesterol to the poor souls being served in the Hawkinsville Medical Center."

The reverend smiled, giving permission for a small laugh to ripple through the congregation.

"I am also very pleased to announce the Board of Trustees and the Finance Committee, after many prayers, have unanimously approved the addition of a porte cochere to the side entrance of the building. This is a wonderful, God-led improvement to our church that will allow us a much more comfortable entry in all kinds of weather. The structure will handle six vehicles at a time, and the Men's Group is already planning a valet parking ministry for our Uphill visitors at Easter. Think how nice it will be when you can pull up under the covering and walk right into church without worrying about the rain. You know what that means, ladies?" He paused, not really expecting an answer. "No more frizzies—and that's a ministry all on its own." Reverend Dodge smiled again, permitting another small laugh among his congregants.

"This is a fairly big undertaking, and the job has to be perfect. The Board of Trustees put a lot of effort into finding the right person to take on our project. We had fifty or so contractors bid for the work, but no one seemed to be a good match. The whole process was a little discouraging…you know, when you're eager but the good Lord says 'wait.'"

"Amen," a smattering of saints responded to waiting on the good Lord.

"Then," Reverend Dodge continued, "out of the blue, an old buddy who pastors the First Church of Nazareth upstate phoned me. You've heard me talk about my good friend Pastor Ed before. Anyway, in the course of our conversation, Ed mentioned he'd just had an addition done to his church. He said he was skeptical at first because the carpenter was a one-man show, but he had a good feeling and the guy came with great recommendations, so he decided to hire him anyway. From that point, Ed went on and on about the carpenter's unbelievable craftsmanship, his attention to detail, and his incredibly reasonable price. Well, not being one to miss out on an answered prayer, I spoke to the board, and I am pleased to announce we have hired the carpenter from Nazareth to build our porte cochere." Reverend Dodge grimaced at the irony of his introduction. "I am even more pleased to announce he is in our congregation today with both his wife and his son. Joe, would you and your family please stand so we can all give you a warm God's Glory welcome?"

I didn't bother turning around to gawk at the strangers with everyone else, but out of courtesy or conditioning, I clapped with the rest when the applause began.

The reverend raised his hands, letting us know it was time to rise as the piano broke into the old familiar tune that always precedes the offertory. Ushers moved up the center aisle to greet Reverend Dodge at the altar where he ceremoniously presented them with the brass collection plates to be passed among the parishioners. The ushers waited silently to be sent about their duty when the reverend clasped his hands under his chin and decided to make one final announcement.

"Today, brothers and sisters, we have a very special treat for you as we go to God with our gifts, tithes, and offerings. In a few days, we'll be putting on our Christmas Eve service, and after all of these years, one of our most faithful choir members has agreed to do a solo." Reverend Dodge half turned to the choir sitting in the loft behind him. "It's my understanding the choir has been begging this young lady for years to share her gift with us, and I guess you finally wore her down."

Everyone in the choir loft nodded and smiled, indicating Reverend Dodge was correct in his summary.

"But since our soloist is a tad shy," the reverend continued, "and we didn't know how she would do in front of a church full of strangers, we've decided to give her a dress rehearsal this morning. Is that right?"

The choir nodded again as Ms. Davis and Ms. Hall rose to escort a bashful Natalie Wallace to the microphone.

"I didn't realize this was going to be a trio," the reverend said with a smirk.

"Oh, no, no," Ms. Davis replied as she moved to the front, "we're just here for the hand holding."

"And, we'll be in our new robes Christmas Eve, so it won't be total déjà vu when you hear the song over again," Ms. Hall added as she struggled to lower the microphone to Natalie's height.

I'd never heard Natalie sing before, but I felt my stomach turn as I realized we were about to hold up this simple-minded girl, who had a hard time enunciating most of what she said, as a spectacle to prove how generous and kind God's Glory Church of Cunningham truly was. We'll even let a retarded girl with a speech impediment solo on Christmas Eve—provided the audition on the Sunday before isn't horrendous. It was going to be a big show pandering to the heartstrings and purse strings of our Uphill guests, and it made me sick. I leaned up in the pew, resting my forehead in my hand, and stared at my shoes. Mom patted me on the back.

"Well, all right then, we'll look forward to seeing the new robes," said a jovial Reverend Dodge, now fully facing the congregation again. "Ushers, shall we?" He motioned for the men with the collection plates to move into flanking positions, ensuring everyone had an opportunity with the offertory. I cringed, still staring at my shoes, hoping what came next wouldn't be too awful for Natalie or Mr. Wallace.

"'The First Noel,'" Natalie announced, bumping her chin on the microphone.

I couldn't bear to look up.

"Stand back a little, honey," Ms. Hall whispered loud enough for us to hear over the speaker.

Reverend Dodge twisted in his seat as his congregation waited in awkward silence. Ms. Hall finished positioning Natalie and nodded to the pianist to start the intro. The music began, and perfectly on cue, in a voice as pure as a hand bell, "The First Noel" began pouring out of Natalie like cream from a pitcher.

I looked up to see her standing with eyes closed amid a colorful aura cast by sunrays streaming through the stained-glass windows. The piano stayed with her for the first verse, but then out of shame, the music dropped away, allowing Natalie to continue unaccompanied. The pianist folded her hands on her lap to listen with the rest of us.

I could feel Natalie's voice swirling around me, filling the whole sanctuary with every resonant note perfect and clear. The air was heavy and so full of her voice that I thought I might be able to push off the bottom and swim to the very top of the church. Every verse was so rich and every refrain was so personal, I felt myself being singled out and swept away from God's Glory to a place where I promised to be a better person. My eyes pooled as I watched Natalie in a halo of stained glass, lifting those who hadn't stood in years to their feet. It wasn't the appropriate time to stand and it wasn't the appropriate time to sob, but as Natalie's "The First Noel" washed through the sanctuary, no one could resist either urge.

When she finished, Natalie opened her eyes to the congregation clutching tissues and blowing noses. I clapped as hard as I could when the applause began, but I don't know if anyone could tell the difference in how I felt about Natalie's song and the Christmas wreaths hanging in the windows. Somewhere in the back I thought I heard someone stomping their feet, so I did too—until Mom put her hand on my knee to indicate that's not how we behave in church.

We were too exhausted after that to care much about what Reverend Dodge had to say, but he blustered on anyway with a sermon about giving and brotherly love. All I wanted to do was sleep, but Mom kept tapping me on the leg every time I closed my eyes. I guess keeping me attentive helped her to pass the time as well.

When the final verse of the final hymn was finally sung, I slid to the end of the pew and shuffled with everyone else down the aisle and out the side door of the church to wait for my parents to finish the customary socializing that stood between me and a free Sunday afternoon.

The sun was bright but cold. A late December breeze carried enough chill to make me shiver as the crowd thinned around me in a hurry to get to their cars. Ordinarily the people of God's Glory would stand out here patting backs and shaking hands before heading home, but the crisp weather chased them away quickly today. Before I knew it, I was all alone watching a conversation between Mr. Wallace and the carpenter Reverend Dodge had hired. Natalie was standing with them. I thought about walking over to tell her how amazing she sang, but I thrust my hands deeper into my coat pockets instead and waited for my parents to come out and take me home. My feet were getting cold as I watched Mr. Wallace talk things over with the other man.

"Funny how it can be so hollow and so cold on such a bright clear day."

I jerked in my coat, startled by the warm voice at my shoulder. I turned to see a young guy, a little more than my age, standing beside me with his hand to his brow staring up at the sun. "Almost like that big ball of fire forgot its job, you know?"

"Yeah, it's a bit cool," I answered, unable to conceal the surprise of being sneaked up on.

"Oh, I'm sorry. I didn't mean to scare you. I thought you knew I was here," the stranger apologized. "My name is Jesse. I'll be helping my dad build the porte cochere for you guys," he explained.

"I'm PJ," was all I offered as my eyes fell back on the conversation between the carpenter and Mr. Wallace.

Jesse's eyes followed mine. "Wow. Is that the girl who sang in church today?"

I nodded yes.

"Shoot, I need to tell her how great she is, the best I ever heard. I mean really, this church has a true blessing in that young lady…but I'm not telling you anything new, eh, PJ?"

He waited for me to answer, but I didn't. I just kept staring at Natalie from where I stood while she listened to whatever her father and the carpenter were saying.

"Well, it was good to meet you. We'll probably be here 'til Easter, so I'm sure I'll see you around."

"Sure," I mustered and then watched Jesse walk over to Natalie and say something that made her hop up and down like a bunny rabbit. She threw her arms around his waist, almost toppling him to the ground. Mr. Wallace reached over to steady Jesse, laughed, and patted him on the back. The carpenter smiled big and rubbed his son on the head. I stood my distance, never knowing what Jesse said to Natalie, but wishing I had said the same thing first. When my parents finally emerged from the church, I walked them to the car without a word about Jesse or how beautifully Natalie had performed.

7
Winterberries

After Sunday lunch with my folks, I picked Kirby up, and we resigned ourselves to kill the rest of the afternoon driving nowhere in my truck. We rolled slowly through town looking for friends, but when none were seen, we cruised down to Sandy Shores to sit on the tailgate and watch the Chagrin slide by. I was a little uncomfortable hanging out here in the winter when the sand was hard and the water was gray. The river seemed annoyed at the imposition of guests in the off-season, as if we'd rudely arrived at a time we weren't welcome, when the Chagrin should have been given the privacy to do what rivers do when the weather is cold and people aren't around. No, the Chagrin wasn't happy to see us like it would be in the spring, and a chilly December breeze agreed. Kirby and I sat shivering on the tailgate, staring out over the water, and wondering how we ever got bored enough to stop here. Time crept at a painful pace for a teenager in Cunningham.

"So what'd you think?" Kirby finally asked.

"About what?"

Kirby looked at me like I was stupid. "About Natalie's singing, what else? Everybody's talking about it."

"I think," I paused to collect my thoughts. "I think I'd like to sit in the very front pew on Christmas Eve."

I smiled.

"Yeah, me too," Kirby agreed, turning back to the river, "but you know that's never gonna happen. We'll be lucky to get a seat along the wall."

I nodded without looking over because he was right.

The trees swayed, protesting a biting winter gust, but the Chagrin didn't mind the cold at all. It only glowered as it slipped past.

"I heard the carpenter and his family are staying out at Mr. Wallace's while the church addition is being done."

My attention broke from the water. "That's strange. Don't you think that's strange?"

"Nah, I don't think so. Mr. Wallace has all kinds of room out there. Besides, where else are those folks gonna stay? There's nothing around here. They'd have to head clear to Hawkinsville to find a place."

"Yeah, I guess Uphill would be a haul." Still, the idea of a full family at Natalie's house was weird to me. I don't know why.

Another cold wind picked up, sending me deeper in my coat. "Come on, Kirby, let's get outta here. My feet hurt, and my butt's freezing."

I didn't have to say another word; Kirby slid off the tailgate and hustled for the cab. I cranked the truck and pulled out onto River Road, headed for the Wallace farm.

The heater finally started to spit out some warm air as we drove along the back side of town. Beyond the rear of the church, through a couple of traffic lights, past a bunch of buildings facing the other way, a few more houses, and we were out of town with only the railroad tracks still tagging along.

I loved the way the road felt under my tires out here with no stop signs or traffic lights to hinder me. The farmlands spread low and flat on the east side with only an occasional tree or distant house to mark your progress. Looking across the ocean of flat land made you feel like you were standing still, no matter how fast you were driving. Railroad tracks hugged the opposite side of River Road with heavy scrub trees, thick privet, and briars pushing up tight on the shoulder. You could catch only an occasional glimpse of the river through the curtain of brush that flew by in a blur of green and gray so quickly, it felt like you might actually take off. On one side, time seemed to stand still, while on the other, things whipped by as quickly as life itself. I guess everything came full circle out on River Road.

The asphalt was empty and smooth, so I stepped on the gas, sending the blacktop humming beneath my tires. My attention went off through the sleeping fields with the russet husks of last season's crop waiting to be plowed under. Over the dash, I stared out at the occasional farmhouse rising coldly from the flat land with thin wisps of smoke wafting from its chimney into the December sky. The tree line on the horizon marked the bluff and the ascent to Hawkinsville and beyond where the world was a different one. I always felt too big for Cunningham, but out here, where the sky touched the ground, I was tiny, so I pressed down harder on the pedal as we approached the Wallace farm.

"Oh, crap!" Kirby turned around in his seat to look out the back window. "I think that was Carl!"

"What?" I looked into the rearview mirror to see a Cunningham patrol car turning around on the shoulder.

"You blew right past him coming the other way. Crap, crap, crap, I hope it's not Eddy! If it's Eddy, it's gonna be bad!"

I glanced at the speedometer. Somehow I'd pushed it up to seventy-five without realizing it.

"We're in for it now. PJ, you'd better stop."

But it was too late, I was at the Wallace farm, and the infamous bend in River Road was almost on top of us. I touched the brakes, but the truck didn't slow fast enough. I cut the wheel as hard as I dared.

"Oh, craaaaap!" Kirby yelled as we slammed over the Wallaces' mailbox and slid sideways over a bench swing in the front yard. We fishtailed over the slick grass, barely missing another pickup parked beyond the front porch. I whipped the wheel left and right, trying to get control, until we hit a gravel driveway and the tires grabbed enough traction to hurl us forward and out to the road again. The back end fanned side to side on the asphalt, and we swerved over both lanes before I finally slowed down enough to get control and bring the truck to a stop.

Lights were flashing and the siren was screaming as the patrol car caught us and pulled up to my back bumper. Kirby popped the door and leapt from the truck. He turned back, quivering in his winter coat and sputtering to find his words. He pointed a shaky finger at me. "PJ," he finally spit out, "crap!" Then he plopped down on the side of the road and dropped his face in his palms to collect himself. I closed my eyes and put my head on the steering wheel, thinking more about the trouble I was in than what might have happened if someone had been standing in Natalie's yard.

The next moments felt like eternity as nerves flooded my stomach. I didn't lift my head or even open my eyes until I heard tapping on the window. It was Carl, and he wanted me out. I pushed the door open and slid my feet to the pavement. My knees were wobbly, and I had to catch my balance on the side of the truck to keep from falling.

"You okay?" Carl's tone was measured.

Although I wasn't quite steady yet, I managed to nod I was fine.

"How about you, Kirby? How are you doin' over there?" Carl hollered.

"I won't have to poop for a month," Kirby yelled back.

Carl cut his eyes back to me and stepped in closer. His voice went low and hard, as if he was taking my accident personally. "What in the…" his teeth clenched to hold in what he really wanted to say, "…world are you doin', you stupid punk?"

"I didn't mean to," was all I could get out before he cut me off.

"I don't give a rat's behind what you meant to do. Look what you did do, you moron."

He motioned for me to turn around, but I wasn't moving fast enough and his anger was beginning to bubble over. He grabbed me by the coat shoulder and dragged me around the truck to face the damage I'd done. I didn't know what to say. I just stood on the road beside my truck, staring down at my shoes afraid to look up.

Standing like a mute with my head hung to the ground wouldn't do. Carl shoved me forward hard enough for me to stumble to my hands and knees in the Wallaces' yard. The ground was cold on my palms, and I could feel moisture beginning to soak through my pants. I lifted my head.

There were long, muddy skid marks through the grass, and debris from the mailbox lay among dormant rose bushes churned up by the tires of my truck. Stones that had bordered a sleeping flower garden were strewn all over the lawn. Pieces of the swing and an arbor I hadn't noticed before littered the front hedge and lay on the porch steps. Gravel spewed from my rear wheels as we crossed the drive had rocketed through the back window of the other pickup. I was only in the yard for an instant, but the mess I'd left would take weeks to repair.

Mr. Wallace, the carpenter, and his family had come out and were looking down on me from the porch. No one called my name or came to check on me as I knelt in the yard. They watched a moment longer and then filed quietly back into the house, leaving me to Carl. The whole thing was nothing more than a thoughtless accident, which should have absolved my guilt, but as Mr. Wallace and his guests disappeared from sight, I was no less ashamed, even though I didn't mean for any of it to happen.

"This is the third time I've caught you hot-roddin' out here," Carl growled. "What's gonna happen next time when Natalie's at the blackberries?"

I turned to look up at the deputy. "It's the dead of winter; there ain't no blackberries out now."

Carl grimaced, reached down, grabbed me by the collar, and pulled me to my feet. He shoved me into the road. "Why don't we just go have a look, smart guy?" He took a fistful of my coat and dragged me to the other side where the railroad tracks lay buried behind the briars.

"Open your eyes. How long is it gonna be before Natalie finds these?"

I looked down at the thorny bushes growing along the tracks across from the Wallace place. They should have been sleeping like everything else in Cunningham, but the bushes, somehow, were as full as midsummer.

"I didn't know, Carl, I didn't know these things grew in December. I didn't know," I whined. My eyes started to well. "I'm so sorry. I'm so sorry. I'll never do it again. I promise, never again."

The deputy didn't pay me any attention as he stared into the thorns laden with the little black fruit. His thoughts drifted to a different time. His voice faded into a whisper. "My great-granny used to tell us kids something like this was called winterberries, or maybe she said winter fruit—I can't remember. She'd never seen 'em herself. Only happens once in a blue moon, she'd say. It's like the sun's shining special, blessing only a few while the rest of the world's in a deep, cold sleep. She said it's a sign something's coming. Weird—I always thought winterberries were an old woman's fairy tale, but there's no mistake, I'm seeing 'em now."

The deputy shook himself back, and his voice regained a normal tone. "I'm hauling you in. I ain't ignoring this one. Get in the back of the patrol car, and Kirby can follow us in your truck. You're gonna have to see the judge, and we'll be holding on to your vehicle 'til then. You can call your parents from the station."

A couple days later, Dad drove me out to Mr. Wallace's place so I could apologize and offer to fix what I'd done, but by the time I got out there, Jesse had taken care of all the damage. I offered to put some time in working on the farm over the summer instead. Mr. Wallace agreed, and I felt better about having killed some of another aimless Cunningham summer vacation in advance.

8
Christmas Eve

Christmas Eve arrived before week's end, finally burying the last of my parents' tacit disappointment in my brush with the law. For a few days, it was colder in the house than it was outside as Mom and Dad more or less shunned me instead of giving a definitive punishment. That's how they were. But since family discord wouldn't do on Christmas Eve, my sins all seemed to be forgiven, or at least ignored, as I pulled up to the breakfast table under the welcoming smiles of my parents.

"Merry Christmas, sweetie," Mom sang.

"Merry Christmas, son," Dad followed.

I was like any other teenager, too tired to be pleasant, but I couldn't let this toehold out of trouble pass by, so I mustered all I had. "And a very merry Christmas to the both of you as well," I replied almost like I meant it.

"Right after breakfast we've got to get these dishes cleaned up so I can get to cookin'," Mom continued. "Dinner's early, so I'll need your help with the mix and fix." She shot me a smile, and I nodded back over a spoonful of grits.

There were only three of us, but Mom would cook every dish her ancestors ever made. It was a testimony to tradition my mom was charged to keep, no matter how many leftovers or dry turkey sandwiches it would generate. I think most Cunningham women felt the same way. Judging by what was left nearly untouched, I'm not sure my parents even liked all the casseroles

Mom would fix, although she was insistent we have a taste of everything. I would've been happy with a plate of dressing and gravy, a side of cranberry sauce, and a pickled peach, but Mom wouldn't allow it.

With every one of the ladies in town cooking all their special dishes the way Mom did, the women of Cunningham probably prepared enough food to feed every soul in Hawkinsville—yet we never had guests, and we were never invited to a neighbor's home to share the meal. Traditions being what they are, we were all too proud to eat with one another on Christmas Eve.

After breakfast, Dad disappeared into the den while I helped Mom with the dishes and the mixing and fixing of all her annual casseroles. She had me dig through the cabinets for a bunch of old pots and pans as she thumbed through yellowing index cards full of handwritten recipes—every one with its own story.

"Now this, this right here," she chirped as she wagged one of the cards in front of me, "this is your great-great-Aunt Eileen's squash. You see how it doesn't have any measurements written down? It just tells you to use a lot of this, a little of that, and not so much of the other." Mom smiled to soften me for the coming lesson. "That's because they weren't sure how much of anything they were going to have, so they didn't bother to write it down. Those were tougher times. We're spoiled rotten these days, I suppose." She turned to fish her apron from the pantry and continued without turning back. "I just wish somewhere along the line someone had written down how much of everything goes into Aunt Eileen's squash. It's a real pain to fix without the measurements, and it never seems to come out right. Your father won't touch it, and I haven't liked it since I was a girl. I guess your grandmother was wrong when she kept telling me I'd eventually grow into it…'cause I never did." Mom tilted her head to muse for a moment, and I knew she was thinking about Grandma.

She finished tying the apron around her waist and whirled back around like a giddy child waiting in line at the fair. She gave one little bounce, smiled wide, and clasped her hands to her chin. "Well, my love," she beamed, "I guess we'd better get cookin'. How about getting the squash out of the fridge and chopping it up for me. We might as well start with Aunt Eileen's recipe first."

Mom always said she wanted my help with the holiday preparations, but the truth is, she never kept me in the kitchen long. I chopped squash, crumbled cornbread, and smashed up a bunch of crackers, only to be released to mill about the house or lie on my bed and wait. Even though Christmas was supposedly about family, Dad, Mom, and I always seemed to end up in different rooms with only the smell of roasting turkey to connect us. I love the air of Christmas, but the wonderful aroma filling the house always smelled better than the food ever tasted.

My mother spent all morning cooking and more days before that making cookies and cakes, only to have the three of us rush through her meal, hurrying to clean up the dinner dishes so we wouldn't be late for church. Even as a teenager, I didn't like the way that felt, although Mom didn't seem to mind. I minded. Maybe that's why Maggie and I always took the kids to eat Chinese on Christmas Eve. One of the perks of growing up is you're no longer bound to follow suit.

With the table cleared and the plates stacked, Dad caught a ride to church early, called to duty with the rest of the Men's Group to greet visitors or direct traffic. Mom told me to brush my hair as she headed off to put on her Christmas Eve dress and do whatever else moms do to get ready. We always hurried to church on Christmas Eve, even though we'd end up sitting like we were the last ones there. As Reverend Dodge reminded us, the pews were strictly reserved for Uphill guests. Dad would be stationed in the narthex greeting strangers, and Mom would sit with her friends in their traditional spot outside the ladies room.

Even though the women's restroom was beyond earshot of the service at the end of a tiny, cramped hallway, the humility of the seat made it the most honorable place to be on Christmas Eve. Unfortunately, there was only enough room for a few sacrificial saints in the coveted area, so Mom rushed to church early to secure the worst seat in the house. I remember standing in an empty God's Glory, hours before anyone else arrived, with my mother and her friends crammed together in the little corridor. They were planted for the duration and wouldn't budge even if the building were on fire. They were proud of their humility, but to our restroom-seeking guests who pushed by the tightly packed, rumpled, perspiring women collected in the hallway for no apparent reason, Mom and her friends probably looked crazy.

Christmas was unusually cold that year, but the threat of snow didn't quell the traditional crowd. Conversations of the weather and the beauty of Cunningham followed every visitor who passed by looking for a place to sit. I stood against the narthex wall with Kirby, watching my dad hand out programs and wishing "Merry Christmas" to people we wouldn't see again until Easter. Kirby's mom was packed away with mine, and his dad was directing traffic, so Kirby and I were keeping company for another Christmas Eve.

Visitors flooded in like never before, and soon the ushers were setting up folding chairs along the walls of the sanctuary for the overflow guests. For the first time I could remember, there was no room at all for regular attendees of God's Glory. Even the old folks were sitting in the outside halls still wearing their coats as the greeters let in the cold along with the strangers. Yet, the only lament heard was for missing the choir adorned in their new robes for the very first time. Cunningham would have to wait until next Sunday to see that.

The lights were soft, and the smell of evergreens mixed with crisp outside air stirred through the church, making everything surreal, beautiful, and exciting. The hypnotic hum of indistinct conversations blended in my ears, wrapping around me and keeping me peacefully separate from the people moving by. An unfamiliar nervous expectation fluttered in my chest as the crowd flowed past to fill every seat God's Glory could provide. I was uncomfortable but content with how I was feeling.

"Gah-lee," Kirby leaned in so I could hear through the surrounding buzz, "all of Hawkinsville must have come down this year. Have you ever seen so many folks?"

Every nook and cranny of the church was stuffed with people. "Nope," I shook my head, "this must be a record."

Ordinarily the ushers would close the sanctuary as the service began, but this year the crowd was too tight for the big wooden doors to swing shut, so they were left pinned open against the narthex wall. Kirby motioned me over, and we slid inside. We found a place big enough for both of us to stand near the center aisle behind the very last pew. I wondered how long it would take before someone asked us to move.

I'd never seen God's Glory like this before. The place was packed! There were two rows of people all along the perimeter, the first in folding chairs and the second standing behind them. I noticed a man wrestling comically with a tapestry he'd accidentally knocked off the wall. The whole scene was very entertaining to those of us who noticed, and the woman with him shaking her head in shame only added to our amusement. I smirked to myself as an usher waded over to assist.

Folks were sitting on top of each other or turned sideways in their seats to allow more people to cram in. This had to be miserable for the children whose sole experience with church was on a cold night, laid out and packed in with strangers like a bunch of sardines. I guess there's always the hope they'll grow into it—kind of like Aunt Eileen's squash.

Watching our guests, I was lost in their small dramas playing out in the pews as the murmur of five hundred conversations filled my head. I didn't know a single person in the whole room. One of the ushers stepped up, shouldering me to get my attention. I thought he was going to tell me and Kirby to leave, but he gave a nod of disgust toward the people in the pew directly in front of me instead. From behind I recognized Jesse and his family sitting quietly, waiting for the service to begin. The usher closed his eyes and shook his head in disapproval, letting me know this family should be in the outer corridors with the rest of Cunningham. I'm sure he was looking for agreement, but being caught off guard, I had none to give before he faded back through the crowd to count attendance or dust off the collection plates.

The whir of conversation subsided, and a wave of solemnity rolled over the congregation as the choir processed through the side door of the chancel. Moving with the precision of synchronized swimmers, they must have practiced their entrance for days. I never have been one to notice clothing, but the deep crimson robes swirling under the cross were magnificent in the soft light of Christmas Eve. The new garments cast such somberness over the simple affair of walking to seats that anyone from Cunningham would have gone breathless at the sight. I'm afraid having had no experience with the old robes; our tightly packed visitors couldn't appreciate the full impact of the holy procession. I'm sure it was nice for them, but sitting through a year full of fundraisers and pleas for support creates a special gratitude when God finally provides.

The choir was delighted with their new robes, vowing to wear them only for the first time on Christmas Eve, so the crimson garments were stored, hanging in the original plastic, until just before the singers took their places in the loft. The choir had faith the fit of the robes would be no issue, and their hope was rewarded. They emerged one after the other from the side door as if they were wearing a miracle. Natalie looked like an angel in garnet floating among them.

"Merry Christmas, and thank you all for coming out on such a frosty night," Reverend Dodge boomed over the microphone. I was so captured by the choir that I didn't notice the reverend take the pulpit. He seemed happy and excited and on top of his game. "I know we're in here a little tight tonight, but that's a good thing. We'll all stay cozy and warm. Now if you will pry yourselves out of your seats, we will rise for the opening hymn."

I wondered if Mom and the rest of the ladies sitting by the restroom knew they were supposed to stand up. The piano started as the congregation struggled to their feet, and I mouthed the words to whatever we were supposed to be singing. This was the first time I'd ever been in the sanctuary on Christmas Eve, and I was only here to see Natalie.

As the hymn came to a close, the reverend raised his hands and then dropped them slowly, telling us it was time to sit. The congregation obeyed.

"We at God's Glory are so happy to have you here with us on this joyful night. Don't these ladies and gentlemen look wonderful in their brand-new robes?" Reverend Dodge motioned to the choir as the unfamiliar congregation applauded politely. "Tonight is a night of love, charity, acceptance, and giving," the reverend continued, "and as people richly blessed, we are bound by God to share those blessings with the church. Now let us enjoy the vocals of our beloved Natalie Wallace, a very special young lady, I'm sure you'll see, as we go to God with our gifts, tithes, and offerings."

Reverend Dodge presented the brass plates to the ushers and waved them into position, choreographed so the collection of the offertory would coincide with Natalie's song. The reverend knew what he was doing. With a nod, he signaled Ms. Hall and Ms. Davis to escort Natalie to the microphone and then sat to survey the effect of what would come next on the giving masses. I could see him smile from where I was standing.

The ladies in crimson helped Natalie down and adjusted her mic.

"Don't mind us," Ms. Davis said with a smile. "We're just here for support."

No one stuffed in the pews knew the young lady on stage, but her appearance captured their attention as they fished for their wallets. Butterflies filled my stomach, and I couldn't wait for her to blow the room away.

"I'm nervous. Are you nervous?" Kirby whispered.

I nodded I was.

"This is Natalie," Ms. Hall announced. Natalie smiled and gave a tiny wave to the people in the pews. Some of the strangers waved back. "You're in for a treat. I know you'll love her." Ms. Hall stepped over and brushed Natalie's hair back over her ear and noticing the collar of the new crimson robe was a little crooked, straightened it as well. She signaled the pianist, and the intro to "The First Noel" filled the church. Reverend Dodge nodded again, and the ushers closed in to pass the plates.

Ms. Hall and Ms. Davis stood with Natalie just like on Sunday, but this time Natalie went ghost-white, missing her cue to sing. The music broke for a moment, but the pianist picked back up with the intro and was coming back around as the congregation waited. Reverend Dodge leaned up in his seat. I felt my heart sink, realizing something was wrong.

"Oh, no," Kirby gasped under his breath.

"What's wrong, dear? Are you okay?" Ms. Davis whispered over the speakers.

But Natalie stood frozen in front of the unfamiliar crowd. A low, guttural hum began to eek up through her throat, as if a demon were tying her up inside. She croaked and groaned hideously and started to sway with her gaze anchored somewhere in the back of the church. Something had happened, something had taken hold. Reverend Dodge came to his feet. The collection plates halted in the hands of the congregants who watched poor Natalie in disbelief. They didn't come for this on Christmas Eve.

"Maybe we should sit down," Ms. Hall whispered.

Ms. Davis nodded in agreement, but as the two ladies went to lead Natalie off the stage, she twisted, tearing herself away from their grasp, shrieking horribly, "It hurts! It hurts!"

The ladies reached for her, but Natalie flailed about the altar, forcing them back. She stumbled against the Advent candles, toppling them into the basin of baptismal water, overturning it into the aisle. Natalie swung back around. "Help me! Help me! It hurts, it hurts," she screeched, tripping across a podium and knocking the big church Bible to the floor. She thrashed wildly across the chancel, tangling herself in the Chrismon tree, bringing it down on the altar rail. The congregation gasped in horror, and the choir gaped with their hands over their mouths. Natalie was like a caged animal throwing herself against the bars, flailing recklessly, crying, and foaming at the mouth. "It hurts, it hurts!" she cried over and over again as she crashed over accouterments of the church most of us were afraid to touch. With all of the meticulous planning for Christmas Eve, the pristinely decorated altar of God's Glory looked like it had been ransacked by a pack of wild dogs.

"Get her out of here," Reverend Dodge yelled. "Get her out of here now!"

Ushers moved in to restrain her, but she crashed through the poinsettias and toppled over the altar rail into the front center aisle. She hit the ground like a sack of wet feed, covering herself in potting soil. Natalie squeezed fistfuls of uprooted red flowers as she thrashed and writhed on the floor under the glare of a petrified cross. No matter how she twisted or screamed, she couldn't shake the demon's hold. Strangers in the pews were appalled and turned away from the hideous sight, shielding the eyes of their children and burying their faces into their husbands' chests.

"Take her out of here now!" the reverend yelled.

Two of Reverend Dodge's ushers pinned Natalie, one at her wrists and the other at her ankles, as she continued to wail, but they couldn't move her, needing more men to carry her out.

I don't know where Mr. Wallace was, probably stuffed in an outside corridor somewhere, waiting for the sweet sound of his daughter's voice to soak through the walls. Like most of Cunningham, he had no way of knowing what was happening inside.

Kirby couldn't take anymore and sprinted up the aisle to where Natalie squirmed in the grip of the two men. He wasn't waiting for me again, and not knowing what else to do, I trotted down behind him.

"You boys, get away from her! You don't need to be up here!" Reverend Dodge ordered from the pulpit, but I was committed, so I didn't care.

Kirby slid to the ground beside Natalie. Her face was covered in snot and dirt from the flowers, and her shrieking filled the sanctuary the same way her singing had a few days before. Our visitors in the back pews were already leaving, pushing their way through the outside crowd, unable to contend with the horrible scene playing out at the altar of God's Glory.

Someone had to be looking for Mr. Wallace by now, but he still wasn't here. Kirby stroked Natalie's head, telling her to relax and everything would be all right, but she wouldn't calm and continued to strain against the men holding her down.

"Please, don't leave," the reverend begged over the speakers. "I'm so sorry. We'll have her out of here in a moment. She's retarded. Please stay."

Natalie groaned and struggled against Reverend Dodge's ushers as Kirby attempted to settle her. I was helpless. All I could do was stand there, looking down as the pews emptied behind me. The sanctuary was spinning into a blur when I felt hands on my back moving me over so someone else could step by. Jesse had made his way through the outflow of strangers to help, but what could he do? He was a stranger himself.

Natalie was getting tired but still writhed and moaned pathetically in the grasp of the exhausted men. Jesse dropped his hand to Kirby's shoulder so Kirby would know to make room by Natalie's side. Jessie knelt down, reached around Natalie's neck, and tore out the tag someone else had thoughtlessly failed to remove from her new choir robe. Her demon was cast out. The fit passed immediately, and a slow smile mixed with tears and potting soil crept over her face. Jessie pushed her hair back and leaned down. "All better now," he whispered. He told Dodge's men to let Natalie go, and when they saw she was calm, they did as he said.

Natalie's dirty smile glowed as she grinned up through wet, red eyes. "Merry Christmas, PJ, and you too, Kirby Braddock. Thanks for coming to see me." A hard sniffle shook through her body. "I think I messed up the song? Do you think Reverend will let me try again?"

Jesse helped her up. I braced myself for another fit when Natalie saw her clothes, but somehow her crimson robe had remained clean even though the floor was covered in black soil.

"Those flowers sure had a lot of dirt in them," she noted, wiping her nose.

Mr. Wallace came running through the sanctuary doors to collect his daughter. He hugged her, thanked us, put his arm around Natalie, and took her home. The pews were empty now, but the regular congregation of God's Glory remained gathered in the narthex, not sure what happened and afraid to come in. The reverend was sitting silently under his cross with his face in his hands.

"Hey, man." Kirby touched Jesse on the arm. "Thank God you were here." A tear rolled down Kirby's cheek, and I thought he might hug Jesse, but he didn't.

Jesse smiled. "I guess that concludes the Christmas Eve service, huh?"

"I guess it does." I smiled back. "Thank you."

We turned to leave, headed for the cold and all the traditions our families preserved, but Reverend Dodge came off the chancel and caught us in the aisle.

"Thank you, boys, for the damage control." He put his hand on my shoulder. "You know," he continued, "we can never have that in this church again. She can sit in the congregation as long as she's got someone to stay with her, but she'll never be allowed in the choir loft or at the altar ever again. We can't afford it. I'll tell the choir director, but you're her friends, so you might want to brace her for it first."

In the soft light of Christmas in the calm after the fray, I nodded like I understood, even though I didn't.

As the rest of Cunningham began to filter in, the reverend pulled away from us, careful we were the only ones to hear his plans for Natalie. We left quietly to wait on our parents as the sanctuary filled with parishioners eager to clean up and console Reverend Dodge.

9
Joe's Trees

Cunningham turned out en masse a few days later for the Give Blood to God blood drive. Somehow the town felt the good Lord had been cheated out of a proper Christmas Eve service, and everyone was eager to make up for it with their donation. Even Jesse and his family gave.

After a small ground-breaking ceremony and a prayer from Reverend Dodge, construction on the porte cochere began, adding the distant sound of a hammer to the noise of the town square. Mr. Wallace was supplying all of the building material for the job, and he loaned Jesse a pickup truck to make deliveries to the site. The truck had a big dent in the driver's-side fender where Mr. Wallace hit a deer some years back, so Reverend Dodge asked Jesse to park the vehicle with its passenger side to the street whenever it was on the jobsite. Jesse's dad kept a pristine worksite, often appreciated by the regular passersby coming to check on his progress, but the addition of a dented delivery truck seemed to make the whole picture less ordered and maybe a little less divine. So the reverend told Jesse to park so only the good side showed from the sidewalk in front of the church.

"People should be made comfortable with what's happening," I overheard Reverend Dodge telling Jesse once, "and since the Lord was ordered in his approach, we should do the same. Son, God's work is never messy. Please keep your truck parked so the ugly side doesn't show."

The judge, who was also the town pharmacist, finally got around to hearing my case about speeding on River Road. I told him about making up for the damages by working on the Wallace farm over the summer, but he didn't care and still sentenced me to a hundred hours of community service in the church working for Reverend Dodge. He gave me a claim ticket and told me to collect my pickup from Sheriff Johnson. I was relieved to have my truck back but bent out of shape about having to work for the reverend in addition to the labor I had promised Mr. Wallace. It wasn't fair I had to do both. There is terrible irony in the ability to discern a blessing from a curse only with the passage of time. My parents, of course, were delighted I would have the opportunity to get to know the reverend better.

A hundred hours is an eternity when you're only able to serve on Saturdays, and I counted them to be over three months' worth as I drove in for my first day of indentured servitude. The morning was cold, and most of Cunningham was still asleep. I parked in the side lot, shoved my hands deep in my coat, and headed for the front door of the church. The chilly air stung my ears as dawn was just beginning to break. I'm not sure why Reverend Dodge wanted me there so early, except to add to my penance or to prove he rose as early as any proverb could demand.

"Good morning!" someone said.

I turned, barely able to see Jesse and his dad leaning against a stack of boards in the early-morning light. "Gah-lee, you scared the fool out of me. What are you guys doin' out here?"

"We're just waiting a bit before we start making noise," Jesse's dad answered. "I don't think we've met. My name is Joe." Jesse's dad leaned up off the lumber and offered me his hand.

"I'm PJ," I answered. "It's nice to meet you, Joe." I'd never called an adult by his first name before. I reached to take his hand. It felt like I was shaking a brick.

"How about some coffee?" Jesse held up a thermos for me to see.

I didn't drink coffee then, so I shook my head no, leaving me to search for something else to say. "Wow, you guys sure are using up a lot of trees out here."

"Yeah." Jesse sipped his coffee and put his arm up on the stack of wood. "And by the time it's all scrapped out, we'll be using a whole lot more."

Joe nodded.

"I have a teacher at Hawkinsville High who says we don't have a right to cut down trees like we do to build stuff we don't really need. He thinks it's selfish." As soon as the words left my mouth, I wished I had them back. In my desire to keep the conversation going, I had given my teacher's opinion as if it were my own to two guys who earned a living in lumber. I suddenly felt the need to separate myself from what I said. "But he's the kind who thinks it should be against the law to even climb trees."

Joe sipped from a steaming cup as I backpedaled. I was surprised to see him actually consider my thought instead of reacting to its stupidity. I wasn't used to that.

"Well," Joe took another sip of coffee, "your teacher has a point about respecting trees and all. There was a time, though, when trees didn't mind being climbed on or having their leaves plucked by children at play, and it was an honor to be milled into material for homes or bridges." He shot me a warm smile in the cold morning air. "But just like people, trees have changed, believing they have rights that were never intended."

I didn't know what we were talking about anymore, but I was pretty sure it wasn't lumber or even my teacher at Hawkinsville High.

"It looks about time to start swinging hammers. We'll see you later, PJ."

The sky started to lighten into day, so I waved a short good-bye and headed off to do my time, carrying what Joe said about trees and people with me from then 'til now.

The church door was unlocked, and the floor creaked as I crossed the narthex to the hall leading to Reverend Dodge's office.

I'd never been in the building when it was empty, and the absolute hollowness of the place on an uneventful Saturday morning gave it an apocalyptic air. I half expected to see zombies milling about the sanctuary, so I scooted past the open doors without looking in.

The reverend's door was ajar. I knocked lightly and leaned inside. The room was dimly lit with old books roosting on shelves, staring down at me from every wall. The office seemed more like one of a miserly bookkeeper or an alchemist than that of an eloquent man of God. As I stood waiting to be noticed in the doorway, the back room of the early-morning church whispered contradiction between the larger-than-life pastor of God's Glory and the man who inhabited this place.

The reverend was at his desk scribbling something. "You're late," he announced without looking up. "As the door turneth upon his hinges, so doth the slothful upon his bed."

I didn't know if he was calling me names or quoting the Bible.

"Yes, sir, I'm sorry. I was just talking with the carpenters outside."

The reverend laid his pencil across the paper he was working on and glared at me over the top of his glasses. The books frowned down from the walls in support of their master. "In all labor there is profit: but the talk of the lips tendeth only to penury," the reverend stated as he continued to look me over. "Don't be late again, or I'll talk to the pharmacist about adding to your hours. Am I understood?"

"Yes, sir, I won't be late anymore."

He took off his glasses and frowned. "Okay, young man, follow me."

The reverend stood from behind his desk and led me to a small, musty room stacked high with decades of old pamphlets, books, and other assorted Sunday school material. The smell of mildew and a tiny window curtained in cobwebs told me this place was unvisited with regularity. Looking at the piles on the floor, the books dusty and fat with moisture on the shelves, and a metal cart stacked high with papers, I figured my first job for Reverend Dodge would be hauling this mess to the dump. Based on how much stuff had been crammed into the little room, I guessed it would take about three Saturdays to clean it out.

"This room is full of unused or reusable material," the reverend announced like he was talking to more than one person, "and what I need you to do is organize, inventory, and catalog everything you see into a library for our Sunday school classes to use." He handed me a yellow legal pad and a ballpoint pen. "Don't throw a single thing away without my permission, and even then, I want you to document everything we trash. I need a good record of what this church has wasted. I'll check on you in a couple of hours." Reverend Dodge patted me on the shoulder and smiled for the first time. "Do a good work, young man," he said and then headed back down the hall to his office to scribble some more at his desk.

I was here because I broke the law, so I don't know why I expected anything more than being stuck in a hoarder's closet wasting time on a meaningless task. I guess I was feeling a little like Joe's trees as I picked up a pamphlet from the first pile, trying to decide the best way to go about my punishment.

I pulled the metal cart away from the window, being careful not to put my hands in the spider webs. The glass was dusty, but I could see across the back lawn of the church, out past River Road and the tracks where the trees and thicket covered the banks of the Chagrin. How many times had I driven past this window, neatly placed and hanging over the back hedge of God's Glory, never knowing it concealed the dank and dusty tomes of lessons long abandoned by teachers in the church? Things sometimes look different than expected from inside out. I heard the crack of hammers outside as Jesse and his dad set about their work. I decided to start with the shelf, pulling all the books off and then putting them back up alphabetized by author. I planned to start cataloging only after I had established some sort of order.

My mind was numb and my hands smelled of mildew when Reverend Dodge appeared in the doorway a few hours later. "You know what would be good?" he asked. "An orange cream soda. Go wash your hands. I'll give you some change to run down to the Gas & Grocery to get me one."

I nodded, thankful for even the smallest reprieve from my work in the future home of the God's Glory library-storage room. I washed my hands and met the reverend in his office.

He fished deep in his pants pockets, retrieved some coins, and carefully counted them out in his palm. "Remember," he said, handing me the change, "I want an orange cream soda. If they're out, bring me a root beer instead…but nothing cherry. It all tastes like cough medicine. Understand?"

"Yes, sir, an orange cream soda if they got it, and a root beer if they don't," I confirmed, taking the money. The reverend smiled like he didn't trust me with the errand, but he sent me along anyway.

I caught my breath as I surfaced in the brisk air outside. The crack of hammers echoed off the buildings. It was still too early for most of the shops in town as their keepers busied themselves with last-minute preparations before turning the door signs to "Open." I could see them through windows, standing, sipping coffee, looking out, and waiting on the day. I wasn't used to being on the square this early, and the empty streets with blank people staring out from locked shops roused the apocalyptic feeling I had earlier. I quickened my step and pretended it was because of the cold.

A slight breeze came in off the rooftops, nudging the Bride and Groom enough to make them stir in their sleep. The sound of hardwood limbs rubbing together caught my attention. I paused to turn around.

The two big trees tangled in each other's grasp must have been playing a trick, because they stood as still as statues the moment I looked back. I guess they didn't like being ignored. The trees whispered loud enough to get my attention and then posed silent and dark against the winter sky.

"Look at us, PJ, and never forget *we* are the lords of Cunningham," is what they would have said if I weren't watching—and they would have been right. The Bride and Groom stood older, wiser, and more magnificent than even the big white church building of God's Glory. The trees were patient, but standing there in the cold, waking town, I wondered how much longer they would tolerate being taken for granted. I let go a steamy breath and finished my walk to the store.

The Gas & Grocery was a miniature version of a full-blown supermarket where you could buy anything from cereal to frozen peas and ground beef while it lasted. There was an aisle for hair color and feminine products, one for canned goods, frozen pizza, and ice cream. There were bushel baskets full of fresh fruits and vegetables set up sideways in the produce section and an upright cooler with a vase or two of red roses and white carnations waiting for whoever was having an anniversary in town.

The place was run by Cunningham's mechanic who sometimes closed the store in the middle of the day so he could work on cars or make house calls to repair farm equipment. His wife also worked in the store, but she had some sort of illness that limited what she could do. There were times she simply locked up until her husband returned from whatever else he was working on. People in Cunningham accepted the odd hours of the Gas & Grocery and lived around the inconvenience until there was no inconvenience at all.

A cold wind knifed around my ears, putting urgency in my step as I came off the sidewalk and crossed the parking lot toward the store. I dug one hand out of its pocket, and without noticing the "Sorry, We're Closed" sign hanging on the door, I turned the knob and pushed my way in. Although they were closed, the owners of the Gas & Grocery had forgotten to lock up.

10
The Lady of the Gas & Grocery

The store was dimly lit with long shadows yawning over the aisles. I could see they weren't open, but this was a small town and the door was unlocked, so I didn't worry about it as I crossed the floor.

"We're closed," a woman called from the back.

Accustomed only to accommodating Cunningham merchants, I didn't realize she was telling me to leave. "Yes, ma'am, I know, but the door was open and I have to get something for Reverend Dodge."

I moved deeper into the store to find her.

"I said we're—," but she didn't get the chance to finish before I rounded the corner and found her with a dark figure in the shadows of the baking aisle.

The lady of the Gas & Grocery wore a baseball cap pulled down low with a yellow bandanna draped across her face, covering everything but her eyes. She was clothed head to toe in long, loose sleeves, pants, and gloves so much so she could have been an amateur beekeeper or there to rob the place if she hadn't been the owner. The unexpected sight startled me into a step back. The dark figure retreated as well, knocking a couple boxes of cake mix from the shelves as he scurried out of sight.

"No, no, it's okay," the lady in the ball cap whispered in the dark. "Don't go yet. I have more." She turned to me. "Henry's not here," she hollered.

That's right, now I remember, thank God. The folks who owned the Gas & Grocery were Henry and Mary Miller.

"Is everything okay, Ms. Miller? Who's back there?" My voice quivered, and not knowing who was hiding in the shadows, I was hesitant to approach her. She dropped her chin to her chest as she groped for what to do next, but when she didn't answer, I decided to go. "Okay, ma'am, I'll come back when you're open." Something wasn't right.

"Wait. Come here, away from the front window?"

"Uh, I don't know, Ms. Miller. I think I'd better come back later."

But as I turned to go, she raced up and caught me by the arm. "Please don't," she whispered from underneath her cap. She raised her head just enough to look into my face from under the brim. "I guess I'll have to trust you."

What I could see of her was horribly inflamed and flaked with red skin, but her eyes were kind, so I decided to stay. After all, she said she had to trust me, which, rightly or wrongly, cornered me into trusting her back.

Ms. Miller took my wrist in her gloved hand and led me deeper into the store. When I dragged my feet, she pulled harder. I had no idea what we would find in the dark, and an uneasy feeling began taking hold of my insides as I followed the masked woman into the shadows. I didn't know if I had discovered her in the middle of a robbery or a tryst, but I had the sense I'd walked in on a secret not even her husband knew she kept.

"Come on," she coaxed, pulling me along. "Don't be afraid."

But time for that had passed, and as she dragged me down the gauntlet of cake mixes and pie crusts, I found myself caught between fear and respect of an elder. I was still terribly naïve and didn't know some adults are never to be trusted, so I allowed myself to be led into the darkness when every other instinct told me to run.

Ms. Miller kept me in tow almost to the end of the aisle before she stopped, her grip still tight on my wrist. The friendly smell of flour and sugar tried to comfort me, but the lump in my chest wouldn't allow it. I thought about jerking away and running straight for the sheriff, but Ms. Miller's hold on me was more than I could break.

"It's okay," she whispered. "He won't hurt you."

In the dim light with her back turned to me, I couldn't tell if she was talking to me or someone else.

"Come on now. Let's finish our business before it gets too late. It's okay. We have a bit more to do. Come on…don't be scared."

Ms. Miller dropped my wrist, and I was free but no longer afraid. The smell of flour circled my head as the dark figure moved cautiously from behind the shelves out into the closed store light. It was a girl, about my age and height, tall and thinly dressed—a Tracker. I should have been appalled, but I wasn't. A small one, maybe four or five, clung to the girl's leg and stared up at me from behind a lollipop in her mouth. She wasn't dressed for winter either. I was cold just looking at her.

"PJ," Ms. Miller said, "this is Nya and her little sister Angeline."

I nodded dumbly, not knowing what I could possibly say to a Tracker on a Saturday in the middle of the Gas & Grocery.

"Okay, young lady, let's get you and Angeline packed up and out of here before Henry gets home. I told him I'd be spoiling out a few extra things this week, so I'm thinking some powdered doughnuts might be nice along with the rice and beans."

Ms. Miller turned to me just as a ray from the cold winter sun streamed in through the front window to join us. She looked up from under her ball cap; her soft eyes met mine. "PJ, please go lock the door before somebody else strays in here." I couldn't tell if it was an order or a request, but I did as she asked and then watched as the lady of the Gas & Grocery picked from her shelves to load a bag of supplies for the two timid girls.

"I know your daddy is going to say this isn't a need-to-have," I overheard Ms. Miller tell Nya as she pushed a box of graham crackers into her bag, "but you tell him I said it's a nice-to-have. No charge at all. Tell him it's the cost of doing business with me."

"Yes, ma'am, I'll tell him, ma'am," Nya whispered. She shot a suspicious glance my way, forcing me to drop my eyes in shame. I was an interloper, intruding where no witness was expected or welcomed. Nya turned back to Ms. Miller. "Thank you, ma'am, Daddy says we'll make payment with the warm weather."

The lady of the Gas & Grocery smiled behind her yellow bandana and, pressing another lollipop into Angeline's tiny hand, let the two raggedy girls out the back door for the short walk to their side of the tracks. Ms. Miller watched them from the doorway until they disappeared into the thicket on their way to the riverbank and Tracker Bridge.

I walked up behind Ms. Miller to watch with her.

"They're sweet girls," she mused when she felt I was close enough to hear. "They'll bring a few catfish, some flowers, and a bit of wild honey later to pay me back. Henry never has liked catfish, and the flowers make him sneeze, but he swears the honey is straight from heaven." She took a deep, thoughtful breath. "He'll find something to put that honey on for every meal until whatever we have is all gone. He's always asking me to order a case…thinks we should sell it in the store. Of course, he doesn't know where it comes from. There's a good chance he'd change his mind if he did." She paused as the two distant figures finally moved out of sight. "I'm going to have to ask you to keep this to yourself," she continued. "It's bad enough being here alone…I don't know what I'd do if Nya and Angeline couldn't come by anymore."

Another second or two dragged by before she closed the door. "Now," she spun around, "what was it you came barging into my closed store to get? We won't be open until Henry gets back."

"I'm sorry, ma'am," I apologized. "The door was unlocked, and I didn't realize you weren't open. I didn't mean to—"

"What is it you need?" she cut me off.

"The reverend sent me down here to get him a soda."

"Orange cream." She shook her head in disgust. "He's the only one who drinks those things and insists Henry keep 'em in stock. They taste like wet baby aspirin with a fizz." She brushed past me on her way to the front of the store. "They're over there, taking up space in the cooler," she called back. "Can't sell those nasty things to anybody but Dodge."

I moved along the back wall to the drink cooler. I spotted the reverend's soda through the glass and slid the door open.

"Funny," Ms. Miller called from up front, "the good reverend always seems to send someone else on this errand whenever I'm having a flare-up. I'm not sure if he's afraid he'll catch something or if he's scared of women dressed like stickup men."

I smiled at her comment because, as it turns out, women with low ball caps, yellow bandana masks, baggy clothes, and gloves frightened me a little as well. Listening to her from the cooler, I think she thought I knew more than I did about whatever it was she was talking about. I didn't have a clue.

Everybody considered Ms. Miller to be *off*, rarely in church and never seen around town. Cunningham appreciated her only for the color she added to the community and for the salvation she provided to conversations of women who had run out of other things to talk about. After all, every proper small town needs a recluse and an inspiration for gossip. Ms. Miller was both. Most of us accepted the lady of the Gas & Grocery as another incidental character in the skit of our lives, but seeing her with the Trackers and listening to her talk about the reverend, I began to think it might be the other way around. I'd never considered Ms. Miller as anything other than a fixture in town, but now, reaching into the cooler for the reverend's orange cream soda, I realized she was more of a mystery than anything else…and I liked her. I'm not sure how she even knew my name.

"Come on, hurry up before someone thinks we're open," she hollered. "You don't want to keep our good reverend waiting."

I'd like to blame it on something in her voice or maybe something she said, but in truth I don't know why I reached right over the top of all the orange cream sodas to retrieve a root beer for Reverend Dodge instead. I guess he was right not to trust me with his errand after all.

"He's not going to be happy," Ms. Miller commented as I handed her change for the drink. Either out of mischief or approval, she grinned from behind her mask. The red chafe circling her eyes didn't taint their sparkle.

"He said a root beer would be okay," I shrugged.

She shook her head to contain a smirk and then escorted me to the door, throwing the lock behind me as our only good-bye. I wouldn't see the lady of the Gas & Grocery again for a long time, but we both knew the moment I bought Reverend Dodge a root beer instead of an orange cream soda, her secret was safe with me.

I finished out my day cataloging old books for an irritated Reverend Dodge. Who would have guessed a root beer possessed the ability to sour a grown man's whole afternoon?

I picked up Kirby, and we drove around in my truck for a while before I headed home. I wanted to tell him about Nya, Angeline, and Ms. Miller, but I wasn't sure what I thought about it, so I kept that part of the day to myself. I did tell Kirby about the orange cream soda. He thought it was funnier than it really was. He laughed about it for a good five minutes, wanting a play-by-play of the reverend's reaction when he was denied his special drink.

"I got a feeling that as long as I'm running to the Gas & Grocery for Reverend Dodge, Ms. Miller is gonna be all out of orange cream soda."

"You know what would be great?" Kirby suggested with a snort. "If you ever do bring him one, shake it up first."

It was an outlandish idea, far too brazen and terribly disrespectful, but still, I unconsciously filed Kirby's ridiculous suggestion somewhere in the back of my brain.

When I got home, all Mom wanted to talk about was my day with Reverend Dodge and to make sure I was polite and grateful for the opportunity to work off my debt to society in the church for such a good man. She sat me down at the kitchen table as she made the final preparations for dinner, alternating between interrogating me and chirping about how blessed I was to be doing something as important as establishing a library for God's Glory. Dad sat quietly behind the *Hawkinsville Herald* as Mom went on.

"Okay, we're about ready," Mom announced, pulling meatloaf from the oven, "PJ, go ahead and set the table."

I stood to do as she asked when a question crossed my mind. "Mom, the lady who owns the Gas & Grocery—"

"Mr. Miller owns the Gas & Grocery," she corrected without turning around. "The lady down there is just his wife."

"Okay, Mr. Miller's wife, what's wrong with her?"

Mom continued to busy herself at the stove as I went for the silverware drawer.

"Well, you might not know it, but she's a little *off*. She actually came from someplace Uphill…has an odd ailment that didn't show up until after she and Henry got married. Henry stayed with her, God bless him. I want to say it's acute eczema or something like that."

Mom picked up a boiling pot of potatoes and slid to the sink to dump the water. Steam billowed up into her face, forcing her to turn her head away, but she was back to work as soon as it cleared. She poured a touch of milk in the pot, tossed in some butter, and reached for the masher.

"It's not a contagious thing—comes and goes with the weather, I think—but it sure makes her look like the devil when it's all flared up…just awful. She was scaring the children so bad at church, the reverend finally asked her to sit in the back pew. And of course you know how the people from Hawkinsville are, the ones who only go to church once or twice a year. Well, they would never understand, so Reverend Dodge thought if Ms. Miller stayed home for Christmas and Easter, everybody would be a lot more comfortable. Now she doesn't come at all." Mom hovered at the sink, spooning potatoes into a serving bowl. "Like I said, *off*…Not much of a giver, I suppose. I can't imagine what she must have done to get the eczema like that. Seems like a pretty bad thing." Mom turned from the sink to inspect my table setting. "Good, let's eat."

Dad folded his paper, shaking his head. He hadn't heard a thing Mom said about Ms. Miller. "I don't know about the world anymore," he announced, laying his paper to the side. "You can't believe anything you hear anymore. I just read an article in the *Herald* that says some guy, blind since day one—never seen a thing in his life—was in the bus crash we heard about in Hawkinsville."

Mom nodded as she moved the meatloaf to the table and sat down.

"Get this," Dad continued. "This old guy was the only one in the whole dang accident seriously injured at all. Paper says he was torn up so bad that no one gave him a chance. Almost left him on the gurney without even trying, but they decided to transfuse him in a last-ditch effort. Nice to know the blood we send up there is being used for something. PJ, hand me the potatoes, please."

Dad paused to serve himself.

"Anyway, they're saying not only did the guy live, but when he woke up from the accident, he could see…for the first time ever! What in the world do they take us for?"

Mom shrugged and shook her head, indicating she didn't know.

"It doesn't take a rocket scientist to figure out the whole story is a bunch of hooey, and you know why, son?"

Dad nudged me with his elbow to make sure I was paying attention to the wisdom he was about to serve along with Mom's meatloaf.

"Because real miracles don't get printed on the sixth page in the human interest section behind an advertisement for women's shoes, now do they? If it were truly a miracle, it wouldn't be anywhere but the front page in big giant letters. So we both know," he shot Mom a smile, "the only real miracle we've seen around here in a while is the B you got on your last math test." He grinned and nudged me with his elbow again. "Just 'cause somebody says it like it's true or writes it in the newspaper, don't make it so…at least not anymore. You have to do your own thinking these days, your own deciding." He reached over and squeezed me on the shoulder for emphasis and then asked me to pass the ketchup.

11
The Porte Cochere

It seems like everything dragged by that winter except the porte cochere. I'd never been around real construction before, and I was amazed how quickly Jesse and his dad built the initial structure. A small crowd usually stood on the sidewalk, hovering over the yellow warning tape, observing as the two carpenters called measurements, hoisted lumber, and crawled around the top of the porte cochere-to-be.

Jesse didn't care for being watched; telling me the weight of too many expectant eyes can cause you to second-guess yourself. Even so, I liked seeing the two men work. Unlike the gawking lay carpenters looking on from the sidewalk, whispering suggestions to one another, I couldn't pretend to know much about what was happening, and since I held no expectations, I was continually in awe of the methodical process that raised a structure so much bigger than its builders. And in the end, I found the porte cochere more beautiful in its framing stage—transparent, growing, and hopeful—than it ever was after the Corinthian columns were set with the last coat of white paint lapped on to the final detail.

Every Saturday morning on my way to impressed service for Reverend Dodge, I stopped to chat briefly with Jesse and Joe. I loved being with the two carpenters in the predawn moments with them waiting on work instead of work waiting on them. That was a new experience for me, and I liked the way it felt. I wished I could stay with them to haul lumber or keep the worksite tidy, to be outside and to hear more about Joe's trees, but I was bound to my penance, shuffling mildewed periodicals around a dank room with a dirty window. I wasn't making much progress.

The weather was still too cold for the reverend, so he sent me to the Gas & Grocery every Saturday to fetch his orange cream soda. I was grateful for the reprieve, and the errand took longer and longer every time I was asked to go. I actually started walking the opposite way around the square, waving to Jesse and Joe and stopping by the general store to look through the pocketknife case. When I finally sauntered into the Gas & Grocery, Mr. Miller was the one behind the counter, sipping coffee and waiting on his first customer of the weekend. From the very first Saturday, Mr. Miller knew why I was there, so when I tried to buy the reverend a root beer, the *real* owner of the Gas & Grocery turned me right back around to get an orange cream soda from the cooler instead.

"Wouldn't want to disappoint Reverend Dodge, now would we, young man?" Mr. Miller smiled from the register.

"No, sir, we sure wouldn't. The root beer is actually for me," I lied. I set both the orange cream soda and the root beer on the counter. "I guess I got to thinking about other things. Thanks for reminding me, Mr. Miller." I smiled again as I fished for the money in my pocket.

I counted out the exact change to his palm. He turned to sort the coins into the waiting cash drawer. "Say hello to the reverend for me," he chimed without looking around.

"Okay, I sure will, and you say hello to Ms. Miller for me."

He stopped counting and glanced back over his shoulder like what I'd said was the last thing he expected to hear from a teenager in town. He nodded. "Okay then, I will."

I slid the orange cream soda and the root beer from the counter. "I don't need a bag," I called as I headed for the door. "I'll see you next Saturday." I stepped outside, letting the door to the Gas & Grocery close behind me.

I could hear the crack of hammers a few blocks down, and the sound of morning traffic was finally awake in the square. The outside air made the drink cans colder in my fingers than I anticipated, and I resented not being able to shove at least one of my hands into my coat pocket. I'd been gone longer than usual. My reprieve was over, and it was time to head back to my mildew prison–storage room–church library. I looked down at the orange cream soda as I crossed over to the sidewalk. It lay cold in my fingers, like some overvalued cargo or a spoiled child daring me to swat its behind. I tried not to notice, but the chilly Cunningham breeze around my fingers kept reminding me of my charge. The reverend's soda mocked me, causing my fist to burn in the cold as I walked along.

I would like to say Mr. Miller's smarmy grin or Natalie being banned from the choir or some other great justification crossed my mind next, but the truth is, I don't know what I was thinking. I felt as cold as the outside air as I turned the orange cream soda over in my hand. I was only a few paces away from God's Glory when I popped the top, turned the soda up, and watched as the orange liquid glugged out into the street gutter. I tossed the can into the trash on my way in.

Reverend Dodge's face dropped when he caught sight of the root beer in my hand. The church secretary never had any problem getting an orange cream soda for him during the week, but somehow, miraculously, the Gas & Grocery was always sold out of his favorite drink by Saturday—or at least the Saturdays I ran the errand. Reverend Dodge shook his head. "I don't understand," he sighed.

I shrugged my shoulders, indicating I didn't either.

All my Saturdays doing community service were pretty much the same, with me delivering only a root beer to the reverend, even though Mr. Miller made sure I left the Gas & Grocery with an orange cream soda as well. Kirby kept telling me I needed to shake up a can for Reverend Dodge, but that was only bluster because neither one of us would ever go that far.

The reverend wouldn't let me throw away anything from the library-storage room, so I mostly shuffled books and pamphlets back and forth, writing down titles and counting copies. I wasn't doing much more than moving the same musty piles from place to place around the room. It was torture.

12
Egg Salad Sandwiches

The weather started to warm, and a few jonquils woke early with the promise of spring. Dogwoods and azaleas wouldn't be far behind, heralding the Easter to come. Reverend Dodge had already announced the next blood drive, and the porte cochere was coming to the final stages of completion. It would be ready before Easter and the rainy season just as Reverend Dodge and Joe promised.

The very best part of Saturday was stopping by early to talk to Joe and Jesse and getting a quick tour of all they had completed during the week. I loved Joe's mini lessons in carpentry as he instructed me in the order of things. I remember him telling me how important it is to build the underlying structure without compromise; otherwise you'll spend more time trying to cover up your mistakes with caulk and paint, telling your customers it's "okay" or "that's the way it's done." The trim and all the fancy stuff goes on tight and easy if everything underneath is solid and square.

I was running behind getting to church on what must have been my ninth or tenth Saturday. Jesse and Joe were already up their ladders at work when I walked by. I dreaded being late for Reverend Dodge, who was a fountain of biblical derision anytime I was the least bit tardy, so I rushed by the two busy carpenters with a quick wave. I wasn't even sure they saw me until my foot hit the church steps.

"Hey, hold up there, Speedy!" Jesse called down from the porte cochere. "You're with me today."

I stepped back and craned around to see Jesse on the roof. I wasn't sure I had heard him right. "What?" I hollered back.

"Dad talked to the reverend, so it looks like you're gonna be putting in some time with us—that is, if you want to!"

Hallelujah and thank God in heaven streaked through my mind, but "Sure, that'll work" was all that passed my lips as I accepted Jesse's offer.

I guess I contained my appreciation a little too well. Joe stopped hammering atop his ladder and turned to watch me wander over. I'm not sure if my lackluster response surprised or disappointed him, but under his eyes I felt nothing but shame for how unenthusiastically I had accepted my salvation. As I got closer, he turned and went back to work.

"Are you sure? 'Cause you don't have to if you don't want to," Jesse called.

"No, I'm happy to do it. Thanks." I tried to sound more excited. I put my hand to my brow, shading my eyes as I looked up. "You're sure it's okay with Reverend Dodge?"

Jesse stepped to the edge of the roof, standing above me in just the right spot for the morning sun to spire off the back of his head as he looked down. "Yeah, it's okay. He wants everything finished as much as we do. Dad told him we'd make better time if we had someone to help scrap out the site. So if you're up for it, how about pulling your truck next to mine and loading both of 'em up with that pile of wood, and then police the area for anything else lying around. We'll shoot for lunchtime to haul it off."

I nodded, trotted over to retrieve my truck, pulled around, and started tossing wood scraps into the bed. This would be a good Saturday. Even though the task required no skill at all, I was finally doing something worthwhile. I never thought to ask for gloves because Jesse and Joe didn't wear any.

"Make sure you lay that lumber straight," Joe instructed from his ladder. "Otherwise, you'll never get it all in. No sense in making more trips than you have to."

I shot Joe a thumbs-up and climbed in the bed of my truck to straighten out what I had already loaded.

I loved the smell of lumber, and the weight of heavy work felt good in the early sunshine. The scraps of wood were more plentiful than the musty books in the reverend's church library, but here with Jesse there was a purpose energizing me, and the passersby who stopped to watch inspired me to work harder. I wasn't trying to show off as much as I wanted to seem worthy of the task, even though I knew I wasn't. My time around Joe had been limited to passing by on Saturdays or a quick hello in church, but like the reverend, I guess you don't really see a man until you work with him.

Jesse's dad was as hard as the nails he pounded with the grip of a vise from a lifetime with the hammer. His laugh was full and his heart was kind, so even as powerful as he was, he wasn't a man to fear. Joe was a very good man, I think, even though he didn't have to be.

Jesse listened to his dad and did what he asked. Years of training made Jesse extremely competent at their trade, and the pair worked in such harmony that they rarely discussed the job at hand. Aside from one of the men calling to the other, "Up, up, up, just a little more," or "Take it your way, keep going, keep going, okay, good," they mostly discussed other things. They talked about the big trees in the middle of town, about Natalie, Mr. Wallace, Sheriff Johnson and his deputies. Something was said that made both men laugh hard enough to rattle their ladders. They obviously enjoyed each other's company. I was in and out of earshot as I patrolled the yard for scraps as the two men wondered how big the trout were in the river they could see from the top of the porte cochere and if the water would be warm enough to fish before they left. They talked about dinner and discussed Scripture as if it were an ordinary topic of conversation. That was strange to me.

I didn't realize how much time had passed until Joe called "Lunchtime," and I was left with two overloaded pickups and an immaculate worksite. I noticed the blisters on my sore hands for the first time. I picked at a splinter with my teeth as I waited for Joe and Jesse to lay down their tool belts and inspect my work.

"Nicely done," Joe said glancing around. "You even got the stuff I left by the steps. Good job, thanks."

"This place looks tons better," Jesse agreed. "It's starting to feel close to done."

I was thrilled they were pleased.

"All right then, PJ, why don't you and I walk on down to the store for lunch? Dad, you want tuna or bologna and cheese?"

"Nope, not today," Joe shook his head. "Bring me one—no—better make it two of Ms. Miller's egg salad sandwiches. She makes good egg salad." Joe sat down on a sawhorse. "Don't take too long gettin' back."

"Yes, sir." Jesse nodded and then motioned for me to follow him to the Gas & Grocery.

I hoped we'd eat at the diner, but as it turns out, premade, store-bought sandwiches are the staple of any decent carpenter's diet.

"Good gracious." Jesse shook his head in disgust as we traipsed down the sidewalk. "It's a good thing you and me will be hauling scraps this afternoon."

"What are you talking about?"

"Do you have any idea what egg salad does to that man's system? He'll be moose-callin' and smelling like sulfur all afternoon. It's a wonder somebody doesn't call the sheriff on him. He thinks it's funny to surprise me with a stink bomb. I'll catch a whiff, look up, and he'll just be grinning and giggling to himself. Problem is, I don't have the digestive system of an old man, so there's no way for me to fight back." Jesse laughed. "Doesn't seem fair, does it?"

"No, but it's funny," I said. "Farts are kinda funny."

"Nah," Jesse disagreed, "a universal truth of life is that farts are *always* funny—at least to somebody."

I thought for a moment before I added, "You ever notice how egg salad smells the same whether you're eating it or lettin' it rip?"

"Yeah, it seems like you'd have to be pretty hungry to eat something that smells like a fart, don't you think?"

"That's why I don't eat it," I chuckled.

"Amen to that." Jesse slapped me on the back and held open the door to the Gas & Grocery for me to enter first.

13
Small Prayers

Kirby was standing at the counter, checking out what looked to be a week's worth of groceries. I was surprised to see him in the Gas & Grocery on a Saturday, buying the same kind of stuff my mom does. Usually we're only in here for junk food or soda, but he had all the weekly staples laid out like he was shopping for a full family. He seemed awkward and out of place as Mr. Miller rang up his purchase.

"Hey, buddy, whatcha up to?"

He turned. "Oh hey, PJ. Hey, Jesse. How's Dodge's dungeon? Almost done yet?"

"Gettin' closer. He let me work with Jesse and his dad today." I nodded at Jesse. "We're just down here for lunch. What're you doin'?"

"Mom's had a tough few days...not feeling good. Reverend Dodge even came to see her yesterday. Boy, that guy's a butthole." Mr. Miller looked over his glasses at Kirby's remark but went back to ringing up the groceries without a word. "Dad picked up some overtime, so here I am, pulling my weight."

Jesse rubbed the back of his head. "What's wrong with your mom?"

Kirby shrugged his shoulders. "Just rundown. She hasn't gone to the doctor yet."

"All right, young man," Mr. Miller interrupted as he bagged a carton of eggs. "Looks like you got a week's worth, but no milk. Are you sure you didn't need milk?"

Kirby dug a rumpled piece of paper from his pocket to check his list.

"Shoot, I sure do. Let me go get it."

Jesse and I followed him back to the cooler. Kirby got his milk, and Jesse pulled out a couple of drinks, a ham & cheese, and Joe's egg salad sandwiches.

"Those things smell like a poot," Kirby remarked about the egg salad in Jesse's hand.

"I know," Jesse said shaking his head, "and trust me, they'll smell a lot worse this afternoon."

Jesse grabbed a bag of chips from the shelves across from the cooler and waited for me to decide on bologna and a root beer. I didn't realize how bad the blisters in my hands stung until the cool soda can in my palm provided its relief. I winced to myself.

"You ready?" Jesse asked.

I nodded I was, and we started for the register when the door chimed and the reverend's voice filled the front of the store. We froze. I watched over the top of the chip aisle as Reverend Dodge strode over to shake Mr. Miller's hand.

"Well, good afternoon, Henry. How are you today?"

Although Reverend Dodge was as hearty and resonant as ever, his greeting seemed affected and insincere to me. It didn't belong to the man who inhabited the cramped little office at the back of the church.

"Hello there, stranger. The warm weather bring you out?" Mr. Miller answered.

"Well, I lost my help today, so I thought I'd stroll down to fetch my own drink this afternoon. Got any back there?"

"Sure do. Help yourself."

Ah crap! I knew as soon as Reverend Dodge walked back to find eight or so orange cream sodas waiting for him on a Saturday, he'd know something was up. He'd figure out I'd been messing with him all this time, and a word with Mr. Miller would confirm how far I had taken my charade. The Great Soda Mystery was about to be solved and the mastermind of the caper revealed. I had no idea what the punishment for soda fraud would be, but every defense from tough love to paying for every can I dumped raced through my mind. All my excuses sounded weak. I peered over the bags of potato chips as Reverend Dodge carried on with Mr. Miller. The reverend was only a few paces away from discovering the game before my legal obligation was complete and I was out of his service. I didn't know what he'd do, but I wanted to leave before he put it all together.

"Nothing but prayer, nothing but prayer." Reverend Dodge's voice washed through the store in response to something Mr. Miller had asked.

I took a deep breath, adjusted the root beer in my hand, and started for the register with Jesse.

"Wait a minute, guys, hold up a second," Kirby whispered.

I was too focused on Reverend Dodge to notice Kirby had unloaded every orange cream soda from the cooler and was kneeling on the floor frantically shaking each can.

"Come on, guys, help me put these back."

"What are you doing?" I dropped down and grabbed his wrist to stop him from shaking up another one. Jesse crouched beside me, completing the huddle of hoodlums conspiring on the floor between the drink cooler and chip aisle. I was already worried about being in hot water, and now Kirby was making it worse—much worse. "Stop, Kirby," I hissed.

But it was done, and every orange cream soda in Gas & Grocery was already set to detonate as soon as its victim pulled the tab. I was in a whole lot of trouble.

A slow smile curled across Kirby's face. "Dodge is a butthole," he said. "Come on, help me put these back."

"You know, Henry," the reverend echoed from the front, "nothing ever happens the good Lord doesn't want to happen, so there is always a reason for everything. Sometimes it can be hard to see what it is, but as the Good Book says…"

My heart was pounding, my lips were dry, and I was ready to bolt for the door. Kirby gathered his booby traps to set them back in the cooler where they belonged.

"Wait, Kirby, I've got a better idea," Jesse whispered. "How about this?"

Jesse reached up and grabbed an armful of Fun Doodles to clear about two feet off the chip shelf. I wasn't sure what he was doing, but whatever it was, he needed to hurry before the reverend tired of his conversation with Mr. Miller and discovered us squatting back here on the floor.

"Here we go," Jesse whispered. He scooped up all of the shaken sodas, set them on the emptied shelf and covered them up with the bags of chips he'd pulled off. Perfect, as if the orange cream sodas had never been there at all.

I looked to Kirby. He smiled, and I sighed with relief.

"You boys okay back there?" Mr. Miller called from the register.

"Yes, sir," Kirby answered as we popped up in unison. "They're trying to agree on regular or barbeque."

"Well, come on, son, get that milk up here so we can get you rung out."

We took our purchases to the register. The conversation between the two men up front reached an intermission as they watched us process to where they were standing. The reverend nodded to each of us, and we nodded back.

"Hey there," Reverend Dodge beamed when he recognized Jesse, "how's our project going?"

"Good, sir, it'll be done, no problem. Then we'll hang around on retainer for a few days until you're happy with the punch-out."

"That's fine. It looks great. You guys are doing a nice job," the reverend said with a nod.

"Welllll, Mr. Miller, here's my milk," Kirby interrupted, swinging the jug up high and then setting it carefully down on the counter. His exaggerated gesture and big announcement made it impossible to miss what he was buying.

"Okay, Kirby, there's your milk." Mr. Miller smirked at Reverend Dodge to indicate Kirby was just another smart-aleck kid.

"And," Kirby continued, "heeerrrrre's…" Kirby brought his other arm from behind his back, rolling his shoulder and spinning it like a giant windmill, making it difficult to see what he was holding. He went around three or four times, puzzling an impatient Mr. Miller and a disapproving Reverend Dodge. I didn't know what he was doing, but I was pretty sure I knew what was in his hand. I began to sink again. "And heeeerrrre's," Kirby slowed his windmill and very carefully set what he had on the counter. I could see his mouth curl up the side of his face as he stared for Mr. Miller's reaction. "Here is my…orange cream soda," he announced and then tapped the top of the can once to accent his rightful claim.

The smile dropped away from the reverend's face as he glared through the back of Kirby's head. It's a wonder Kirby's hair didn't catch on fire.

"You know, Mr. Miller," Kirby started again in a big voice, "Mom was saying this morning she prayed there'd be one of these left today…and guess what? There is…one left."

Reverend Dodge twisted and stepped to Kirby's side. "That one or one more back there?" he asked.

"Oh, Mom only prayed for one, Reverend." Kirby reached over and tapped the can again. "So this is it. I guess God answers small prayers after all. I mean, an orange cream soda is a pretty small thing, wouldn't you say?"

I wasn't sure what was going on. Kirby hadn't liked Reverend Dodge since he dumped Natalie from the choir, but his brazenness in continuing the joke went beyond his ordinary demeanor. Something else must have happened to kindle what looked more like a vendetta than fun.

"Do you mind if I buy it?"

"I'd love to, Reverend," Kirby shrugged, "but it's for Mom."

Mr. Miller glanced at Reverend Dodge and then dropped his eyes to ring Kirby out and bag his purchase. Kirby shot me a thumbs-up as he pushed his shopping buggy by on the way out. "Catch you guys later," he said with a wink.

We nodded and stepped up to buy our drinks and sandwiches as Reverend Dodge retreated to sift through the cooler for a stray orange cream soda he would never find… unless he decided to buy eight bags of Fun Doodles instead.

"Thanks for the help back there; I'm not sure what got into Kirby," I said to Jesse on our way back to work. Then as an afterthought I added, "I should never have started that whole orange cream soda thing with the reverend."

"Nah, sometimes a man has to be denied a sure thing to help soften his heart a little." Jesse paused for a few steps. "Then again, it may make him more ornery—could go either way—but at least he has a chance."

I thought about what he said as we moved along the sidewalk, and although I appreciated Jesse's attempt to give my stupid joke a higher purpose, I was pretty sure it was still just a stupid joke.

Joe had set a couple of boards across two sawhorses and was lying on top with his eyes closed, enjoying the Cunningham sunshine. He sat up when he heard us approach.

"Gracious, guys, what'd you do? Wait on the hens to lay eggs for the sandwiches?"

"We ran into Reverend Dodge," Jesse explained as he handed Joe his bag of lunch.

Jesse and I pulled up a couple of buckets to sit on, and Joe offered thanks for what God had provided. I'm not sure if it was the weather, the company, or the hard work, but those were the best bologna sandwiches I ever remember eating. The stars aligned, I guess, making that lunch the pinnacle of my bologna eating experience, and after I inhaled them, the sandwiches sat deep in my stomach trying to talk me into a nap. I didn't feel like getting up.

"Mr. Wallace stopped by, Jess," Joe was saying. "The columns are in, so let's get our stonework done first of next week, get 'em set Thursday or Friday, and finish this thing on out. We'll get it caulked, painted, and done the week before Easter."

Jesse looked over at the porte cochere and nodded in agreement as he chewed a bite of sandwich.

"Mr. Wallace also said he had another project out at his place," Joe continued. "He wants a shed or some kind of outbuilding on the far corner of his property. It seems like an easy build…probably take some time, but the work shouldn't be bad. You know, your mother and me have to head on over to Sardis for a couple of small things after this and then down to Marietta for something bigger, but if you want, you can stay on here for Mr. Wallace's job. You can take the bus and meet us when you're done."

"What about tools?" Jesse asked with a mouthful of chips.

"Mr. Wallace has everything you'll need. You're gonna want some unskilled help, but that shouldn't be hard to find around here. I can leave you the punch-out on this job, and you can collect the retainer for me when you're done. You won't be totally on your own, son. You'll still be staying with Mr. Wallace and Natalie. It's up to you."

My dad would never let me do anything like this, but Jesse was a couple years older and a whole lot more capable than I was, so it wasn't odd for Joe to offer to leave Jesse behind. I got the impression this was the kind of life they led. I'm sure Joe spent the rest of his life blaming himself after that, but fate has its way with all of us, so in the end he was as guiltless as poor Natalie Wallace—whether he believed it or not.

14
Shame of Soft Hands

I hoped he'd stay.

A distant look fell over Jesse's face as he swallowed the last of his lunch. He stood up from his bucket and walked to the edge of the church yard to get a better look at the square of Cunningham and the towering Bride and Groom looming in its midst. It was as if Jesse was seeing the town for the first time, or at least in a different light. He stood a while, looking down the street. Joe and I kept our seats in silence.

"It's okay, son. You don't have to. We can stay, take care of the punch-out together, and then head down to Sardis. We'll pass on Mr. Wallace and be out of here in less than three weeks."

"No, Dad, its fine." Jesse turned around. "I think I'd like to hang back and do the job." He smiled and walked back to where we were sitting. "Besides, I already know I can count on some dirt-cheap labor from Speedy here." He put his hand on my shoulder. "Remember, he's pledged to the farm this summer."

"Oh yeah, I forgot about that." Joe tipped his head toward me in disapproval.

I looked to the ground to keep him from seeing my shame. I could feel Joe staring at the top of my head, but I refused to look up until he started to speak again.

"Well, boys, it's Saturday." Joe slid to his feet. "The place is clean, and we're all caught up, so why don't you guys dump your loads, I'll roll up the tools, and we'll call it a day. Thanks for all your help, PJ."

"Yes, sir, anytime. Thanks for letting me."

I pushed myself up, trudged over, and climbed into my overloaded pickup. I wheeled in behind Jesse and followed him out to River Road. I didn't know where we were going; I figured to the trash container behind Mr. Wallace's store or maybe to the dump, so I was surprised when Jesse turned off into the woods where we parked to hang out at Tracker Bridge. I waited for him to maneuver around, parking face-out so we could unload without having to walk around the truck. I pulled down and did the same.

"You know, we're not supposed to be here." I shook my head. "We can't dump this stuff here."

"Ah, don't worry about it. I doubt anyone will even notice." Jesse slid a couple of boards off the top of the load and disappeared down the path to the bridge.

I was uneasy about this, and for the first time, I was ready to complain about the blisters I'd earned—although I was sure it wouldn't matter to Jesse whose hands had leathered long ago from years of this kind of work. The big sacks of fluid that filled my palms earlier had rubbed off, leaving two wet sores in the middle of both hands. The sharp pain mixed with the dull ache in my muscles made everything more difficult than it should have been. I was beginning to think this was going to be a longer afternoon than I had anticipated.

"You all right?" Jesse returned and caught me staring into my palms.

I nodded I was fine, grabbed a couple boards off my load, and followed him down the path to pile them on the bank. Jesse worked twice as fast as I did, so when he was done with his truck, he helped me with mine until we stood breathing heavy, staring at a tight stack of lumber that looked longer and far more useable than the scraps I remembered loading in the first place.

We sat down to rest, and I noticed the Chagrin's voice in my ears for the first time.

"That's a weird way to trash out a construction site," I remarked.

"Sometimes you have to go a second mile," he answered, and then leaned up with his arms across his knees, and stared at the pile like it might run away if he didn't.

We sat a while until my mind started to drift with the swirling water below. If I weren't so tired, or here with Jesse, I might toss those boards, one at a time, into the river to be swept far out to sea. Any of the teenagers in town would do the same. I thought of John and how Natalie wouldn't set foot on that busted ol' bridge and how all the scraps nailed to it made it look like it had been built by drunk beavers. I smiled to myself as Jesse quietly watched the lumber. I remember thinking the Trackers would probably take the scraps to repair their bridge if the pile wasn't on our side of the river, but since the lumber was safely over here, someone like me would probably come along and get a good chuckle out of throwing it into the water.

A slight wind picked through the trees, and the clouds swimming across the blue above rained intermittent sunshine and shade. A lone jonquil on the bank of Tracker Island waved to me in the breeze. It looked like candy from where I was sitting. *How would Angeline and her sister get to the Gas & Grocery to see Ms. Miller if this stupid thing ever fell down? Wow, weird thought!*

I cleared my throat, breaking the silence and pushing the rush of the Chagrin to the background once more. My eyes fixed with Jesse's on the neat stack of wood resting at the end of the bridge. "Maybe we should move it to the other side," I suggested.

Jesse stood, reached back, and gave me a hand up. "Good idea," he agreed.

As it turns out, the whole time I thought I was waiting on Jesse, he was waiting on me. And even though my muscles ached and my hands stung, Jesse and I made quick work of moving everything we'd brought across the bridge. We stacked it tight and tall, and when we finished, I couldn't imagine how we managed to bring the entire pile down in just two truckloads. The boards looked newly milled without a single short piece and some far too long for any pickup to carry. I remember noticing how the white wood shined against the dingy pre-spring thicket of Tracker Island. It almost sparkled as if it had been freshly conjured by a forest nymph or a covey of fairies. Jesse retrieved a handsaw, a hammer, and a box of nails from his truck and left them on top of the lumber.

"My toolbox is too heavy anyway," he explained as he passed by.

I'd rubbed through the bottom skin of the busted blisters in my hands, and droplets of blood were beginning to seep through the cracks. My palms were wet and sticky and burned like seared meat. I was afraid to look, but I didn't say anything to Jesse as I traipsed behind him back to my truck.

Jesse asked me for one last thing while he had me, to follow him to Mr. Wallace's store and help load some plywood into his pickup. I had to peel my hands off the steering wheel when we arrived, leaving a film of blood and ooze behind. I gritted my teeth, still afraid to look. I wondered what Mom would have to say about me working with carpenters instead of Reverend Dodge. I was sure she'd make a fuss.

"What's this stuff for?" I asked as Jesse and I slid the first piece of plywood into his pickup.

"I have a project I've been thinking about for some time, and now that I'm here through spring, I'm gonna take a crack at it. I've gotta hurry though; we're coming up on the season."

We walked back to the stack of plywood, and Jesse nodded for me to lift my end as he picked up his. We carried the second piece, laying it in his truck on top of the first.

"So what's the project?" I asked as we loaded.

"An apiary. Mr. Wallace has some property out around the bend, and he's already said it's okay. Thing is, warm weather's about to even out, so if I'm gonna have bees for my boxes, I gotta get 'em built pretty quick."

"We got some wild honeybees around here," I offered as we moved another sheet over, "out by the old cemetery. I don't know if there's any honey." I winced when a corner of the plywood cut across my palm as it slid into the truck bed. "We used to throw rocks at it when we were younger."

"Well then, that's one hive I know about," Jesse said as we loaded the last of the wood. Sweat beaded across his forehead. He looked as tired as I felt. "Thanks for the help, especially for moving the lumber across the river. I know that was extra."

"No problem," I answered. Then on an impulse, added, "You know, if you're gonna be around a while longer, it might not be a bad idea to meet a few more people."

Jesse waited for me to complete my thought.

"So do you think…you might wanna come to Sunday school? It's a big group of kids, and they pretty much already know who you are, and I heard you and your dad, and you seem to be religious, and I know Natalie would love it, and I'm sure…."

I don't know why I came so unhinged about inviting him; maybe I was embarrassed Sunday school was the best I could come up with. Jesse stared at the ground as I continued to blurt out all the reasons he should join us until he finally raised his hand to keep me from babbling on.

"I'm not too good at Sunday school, but how could I possibly turn down an offer like that?" He put his hand on my shoulder, and giving an affectionate shake, he added, "How are the blisters?"

I didn't realize he'd noticed, and the question made my fingers curl involuntarily. "They're fine," I lied to hide the shame of soft hands. "Just sore is all."

"You want me to take a look?"

I shook my head. "No, thanks, I'm good."

Jesse nodded like he didn't believe me. "Okay, but next time ask for gloves, all right? Dad doesn't always offer stuff you don't ask for, and I guess I'm the same way. So if you're gonna be doing anymore of this, you need to sing out if there's something you need."

"Okay," I answered without looking at him.

"Being stiff and sore is one thing, but your mom ain't gonna be too happy about doctoring the wounds you got."

"I'm sure she'll pitch a fit loud enough to hear clear out at the Wallaces'," I agreed, "so let me apologize in advance for disturbing your dinner."

"You'll be pitchin' a fit too when she pours antiseptic across those palms." The thought made me cringe. "So here's what you do. When you get home, head to the bathroom sink. Make a couple of loose fists, not tight, just barely curl your fingers around and let warm water run over the outside first." Jesse demonstrated as he talked. "Then, keeping 'em loose, turn your fists thumbs-up and let the water run down through the hole, top to bottom like a pipe. Understand?"

"Got it," I nodded.

"Then," Jesse continued, "open your hands up slowly, turn 'em palms up, and wash off the worst part. No soap. After that, you can show your mom, and maybe she won't be so upset."

Although I didn't see how it would do much good, I told him I'd try his carpenter's trick, and we parted company, Jesse hauling plywood to the Wallaces', and me doing my best to steer the truck with my fingertips.

The smell of Mom's fried chicken filled the house when I arrived from the day.

"Hey, honey, dinner won't be long," she called from the kitchen when she heard me open the door. "Go ahead and get washed up, then set the table for me. Your dad should be home any minute."

"Yes, ma'am," I called as I headed upstairs to the bathroom.

My fingers were stuck to the ooze seeping from my palms, and I could barely peel them away to get a look at what I had done to myself. "Oh, no," I breathed and closed my eyes. From the heels of my hands to the bottoms of my fingers were giant, wet pink wounds veined with threads of blood like rivers on a map. They burned like the devil, and it scared me to look at them. My head started to spin, and I sensed an oncoming swoon. I propped myself on the cabinet and held my head low over the sink to gather myself.

"PJ," Mom called from downstairs, "don't forget about this table."

"Yes, ma'am, I'm coming!" I managed.

Still leaning deep against the sink, I took a heavy breath and reached up over my head to twist on the spigots and wait for the water to warm. I couldn't bear to look at the mess I'd made of my hands again. I let them dangle limply over either side as I hung on the cabinet. I wasn't sorry for working with Jesse, but I sure was sorry for not wearing a pair of stinking gloves.

The faucet gurgled, and when I smelled it beginning to heat, I did as Jesse instructed and let the water wash over my fists. My head cleared enough for me to straighten up. I turned my hands thumbs-up and let the warm water flow down through my curled fingers. The pain eased. I would have stayed like that forever, too afraid to open my palms and finish, until Dad hollered up the stairs, "PJ, your mom's waiting on this table!"

Whenever Mom grew impatient, she turned me over to Dad, and it was never a good idea to keep him waiting.

"Yes, sir, just getting cleaned up. I'm on my way!" I yelled through the bathroom door.

I looked down at my curled fingers, took a deep breath, and began to peel them back, slowly, one after the other, turning both hands palms-up as the drain slurped down all it could take.

What? I closed my eyes, shook my head, and looked again. The terrible sores were floating in my hands like a pair of wet autumn leaves fluttering in my upturned palms. I tilted my hands slightly to the side, and the wounds slid right off, swirled once, and were sucked away by the drain. I heard the faucet cough and spit, and somewhere far away, Mom slid a cookie sheet of biscuits out of the oven. I stared into the sink. It was like the hands at the ends of my wrists weren't mine…no pain…completely healed.

I was terrified and amazed. I wished my parents had seen my blisters before. How else would they believe? I was quivering, and every word seemed to be taken from me as I shuffled down the stairs and into the kitchen.

"Well, there you are," Mom said with a smile. "You must be pretty hungry."

I couldn't answer. I just stood wide-eyed and overwhelmed. I raised my hands for her to see.

"That's nice, dear, all clean. Now please set the table before your father starves to death."

15
Head of a Nail

I ate a couple bites of chicken and pushed the rest of dinner around my plate before excusing myself to lie in bed. I alternated between staring at my hands and the ceiling for the rest of the evening. I don't think I drifted off for a single minute.

When the Sunday morning sun came streaming through my bedroom window, I was anxious to rise, not feeling the least bit fatigued from the day before or the long, sleepless night. Usually I didn't care for Sunday school—it was just another ritual forced on the youth of Cunningham—but today I was eager to see Kirby and talk to him about what had happened. I didn't care if he thought I was crazy, and I knew if he laughed, he'd do it in my face. He was a good friend.

For the first time ever, I was dressed and ready for church before Mom and Dad. I could hear their broken dialogue from the kitchen table where I'd already eaten a bowl of cereal, washed and put away my dishes, and started their morning coffee. Mom couldn't find her earrings, and Dad was grumbling about ironing his own shirt. I felt like I was waiting on a couple of dawdling teenagers while I had someplace important to be. I huffed to myself as they descended into the kitchen with their "good mornings" and remarks on how wonderful the coffee smelled. I smiled, doing my best not to let the frustration show. That would be the quickest way to change my parents' delight with my unusual promptness to a lecture on disrespect.

Dad took his usual long-cut on River Road and the back way into town as I fidgeted in the backseat, biting my tongue and trying not to complain about our leisurely pace. It felt like Dad was crawling along on purpose, perhaps as a lesson for all the times I'd lollygagged us into being late for the start of things at God's Glory. I squeezed the door handle as Dad wheeled the car through the parking lot, finally sliding into a space Mom spotted. I couldn't wait on my parents. I needed to see Kirby, so I popped the door and gave a quick wave as I left them behind. I'm sure my urgency gave Mom the fleeting hope I had somehow found religion, but Dad probably figured it had something to do with a girl instead. They were both wrong.

I didn't speak to any of the adults I passed. I nodded politely and skirted by on my way to class.

The basement of God's Glory was where the youth of the church were trained on God, using weekly pamphlets with cartoon people and a couple of quotes from the Bible. It's hard to tell if the quotes were in context, but it didn't matter as long as the discussion questions on the back page generated enough conversation for our teacher to kill the whole hour. I put my hand on the rail and galloped down the narrow stairwell to find the chairs already pulled around and the lesson begun. I spotted Kirby on the periphery of the group and moved in to sit beside him. I guess I'd have to tell him what happened later.

"Today we're learning about forgiveness," the teacher started from behind a skinny podium. He seemed to be discovering the topic for the first time. "Who would like to read from *The Weekly Word*?" He held up the pamphlet, glancing to our usual readers. A perky chipmunk-faced girl I kissed once on a hayride volunteered. I tried to listen, but the lilt in her voice was too annoying, so I stared around the room instead as everyone else read silently along.

There were generally about thirty youth, too many for a circle, so we sat in a mishmashed cluster of seats that started off in neat rows set up by the teacher, I think…but I don't know. I was always late. The greatest church enthusiasts congregated in the very middle of the group, but as you moved out from the center, participation waned, skepticism grew, and silence was king.

My chipmunk-faced girl was terminally stationed near the epicenter of bodies, and with chairs so tightly packed around, I wondered how she could possibly free herself in the event of a restroom emergency. She would literally have to crawl on top of people to escape. What a terrible predicament for a girl with a full bladder—or anyone she climbed over on her way out. That would probably ruin Sunday school for more than one of the center kids so tightly crammed together in their mutual love huddle. I smirked at the thought of Chipmunk baptizing her friends with pee. I sat on the outer edge with Kirby where issues like that were never a problem. As a matter of fact, it wasn't uncommon for me to slink off to the restroom once or twice every lesson without anybody noticing at all.

"And what does Scripture have to say?" Chipmunk continued reading. "Well, the Bible says…"

I flipped through the pamphlet to find where we were and how much we had left while Kirby skimmed along with his finger. He was better at Sunday school than I was, which was strange considering how much better I was at real school.

I leaned back in my seat, looking over all the heads hung into the paragraph when I saw Jesse sitting by Natalie on the far end of the room. In all my excitement, I'd forgotten about him. I forgot I'd invited Jesse, and now I wasn't sure why I had. As annoying as she was, at least Chipmunk had something to offer a visitor, but I was an outsider even though I had grown up with every kid in the room. I had no business inviting anyone to church.

I nudged Kirby and nodded to Jesse.

"I know," Kirby whispered. "I was here when he came in."

"Thank you so much, that was beautifully read," our teacher announced as Chipmunk finished. She beamed at the compliment like her cheeks were full of acorns as her friends congratulated her for a fine contribution to class.

"Thank you," our teacher repeated as he straightened up behind the podium and turned to the discussion questions. "Now, who gets God's forgiveness?" he asked the group.

There was a long pause as Chipmunk's friends flipped pages to find the correct response. "Everyone," someone eventually offered up.

All eyes went to our teacher to see if the answer would satisfy him.

"Everyone?" The teacher looked up and took off his glasses.

There was a long pause of consideration. "Doesn't the Bible say everyone?" someone else asked.

"How about murderers, rapists, and child molesters? Does God forgive them? How about Hitler or Mussolini? Has God forgiven them, or do they reside in Hell?"

Our teacher was a master of rabbit holes, wrought with conjecture and debate with negligible contributions from those of us sitting on the outside. If the conversation lagged, he would toss in a baited comment under the auspices of getting us to think, but truly designed to kill the hour as a gaggle of goslings honked about the mysteries of God without a shred of credible guidance. The class struggled toward an answer to satisfy our teacher's understanding, although in the end he was as inept and naïve as any of us. But by the time it was over, we would all leave feeling well schooled, thanking a man who wouldn't consider next week's lesson until just before class.

Today was no different as the debate over who God would or would not forgive bounced over the crowd like a shuttlecock. Our teacher smiled and nodded as the argument sustained itself for a solid fifteen minutes before Jesse stood up.

"Did you have something to add?" the teacher asked when he noticed Jesse in the back.

I heard one of Chipmunk's friends whisper something about Jesse being the hired guy working on the church and wondering why he was here.

"Yes, thank you," Jesse nodded, "I'd like to know how many angels can dance on the head of a nail? Uh…a tenpenny nail…to be clear."

"Excuse me?" The teacher frowned and a few in the group smirked at the silliness of the question.

Jesse smiled and reached out, putting his hand on the shoulder of someone sitting in front of him. "I think," he paused, "maybe we should not concern ourselves so much with whom God forgives, but with whom we ourselves forgive instead."

A hush fell through the room, and everyone turned in their seats to hear what he would say next. Even the devoted recognized real teaching.

Jesse took a breath and blew out through his nose as our teacher's eyes locked down on him. "Are we really called to worry about Mussolini or some theoretical murderer, or are we called to be concerned with Uncle Don?"

"Who's Uncle Don?" Kirby whispered, but I didn't know, so I couldn't answer. I remained silent, my eyes glued to our guest along with everyone else.

"Don?" our teacher muttered as if a ghost only he could see had appeared in the room.

"After all," Jesse went on, "Abba's gonna do what Abba's gonna do. We'll never be able to throw a rope around Him or corral Him, even with our Bibles. No, it's best to do as He asks and to forgive one another and to care for our neighbors as we care for ourselves."

"I think you mean *love*," the teacher corrected. "We are to *love* our neighbors as ourselves."

"That would be the angels and nails. What's the difference?" Jesse asked.

Our teacher seemed offended by the question, but the rest of us were eager to hear the answer.

A smile crawled over the teacher's face, and he shook his head as if Jesse's question was beneath a response. "My neighbors are all able to *care* for themselves, so what neighbors would you be talking about?"

Jesse dipped his head and stepped across the room before turning back to face the man at the podium. We shifted in our chairs to follow him. I noticed Chipmunk biting her lip as her friends murmured and whispered to each other. Jesse paused, giving the teacher time to grow uncomfortable with his own question.

Usually the man at the lectern pulled the strings, steering our answers to his own end with very little dissent or revelation. But today, in the name of control, he'd drawn a difference between love and care—a distinction only a Pharisee would make; at least that's what the pamphlets taught us every Easter.

The teacher leaned in on his podium, gripping it hard enough to crack the wood. His tone remained light and friendly, doing his best to spin the illusion of hospitality. Kirby was on the edge of his seat, and we all wondered if our guest would come up with the answer our teacher was looking for. Jesse smiled.

"A girl fell into a river. She was sure to drown, but a man—a man who could not swim—jumped into the water, risking his life to spare hers. The water would have both or none at all. I'm pretty sure, sir, we're talking about her neighbor."

"What does that even mean?" The teacher shook his head. He looked to his students for support, but none was found–not even from his usual readers.

Most of us knew exactly what Jesse was saying, and since he had our attention anyway, he continued for the remainder of class. He talked to us about all he had seen working with his dad at different churches. He talked about love, forgiveness, victory, defeat, carpentry, and building. He sounded like Joe. When hands went up, Jesse answered every question as if he knew God personally. No one wanted to go when the time came to break up, but Jesse insisted we not be late for worship. So we thanked him and asked him to please come back before we filed out of the basement to the sanctuary, carrying our Sunday school lesson along with us for the first time ever.

I didn't see the teacher when we left. I suppose he slipped out to complain to Reverend Dodge. We were told later Jesse wasn't welcome in our class any longer. So much for inviting people to church.

16
Southern Spring

Kirby wasn't himself the whole next week. He sat a million miles away on the school bus, staring out the window as everything whipped by in a dappled blur. The hum of the road captured him somehow, limiting him to nods and one-word answers to any attempt I made at conversation. He went straight home after school, leaving me with no option but to do the same.

Sixteen is too young to notice the pain of others. Everything plays out like the story from a novel where you're always the main character. So as pathetic as it is, adolescent narcissism is my excuse for being more aggravated than worried about Kirby. I didn't know what was going on with him, and I didn't think to ask. Being the center of the universe is a heavy cross to bear for most teenagers, but we all seem to manage it like pros.

Without my usual distraction to keep me company, the week dragged along at a painful pace.

Saturday morning arrived, and even though I hadn't accomplished a single thing of value in the library-storage room, the end of my service to Reverend Dodge was finally in sight. Still, as I crossed the yard toward the church, I hoped Joe or Jesse would rescue me to work with them instead.

The early spring mornings were light and crisp now, full with the sound of robins calling their mates and the smell of trees beginning to open. Jonquils and tulips burst into bloom, and the azaleas wouldn't be far behind. It was chilly enough for a jacket, but the cool air was more of a remembrance than a sting as everything around me was screaming *new life*. It felt like hope. It's how I know God loves the South.

The grass was heavy with dew, and I could feel my socks beginning to dampen through my shoes as I moved toward God's Glory. I could see the worksite was clean, and a crusher run of gravel had been steamrolled into the turf, forming a wide driveway under the porte cochere. It ran from the street front to the back parking lot of the church. All of the temporary supports were gone, and massive Corinthian columns sat on stone pedestals, shouldering the load of the roof. I was astounded by how quickly everything was beginning to finish.

Jesse's truck was parked under the porte cochere, and he and Joe were too busy unloading ladders and paint to notice me until I stood at the tailgate next to them. The ladders rattled and clanked like old men as they were taken from the truck, but it was still too early in the morning to do anything but whisper.

"Wow," I breathed, "this is crazy."

Joe hoisted a paint bucket to the ground and then moved to my side as Jesse continued to unload. "Yeah, it didn't come out too bad. Bigger than we originally agreed, but I guess it's a reverend's prerogative to change his mind."

"It's too big, if you ask me," Jesse added as he hauled the last paint bucket from the truck. "I mean, look at this—four cars wide and two cars deep. It's as big as one from a high-rise hotel. For goodness sake, you could run a marching band underneath this thing." Jesse shook his head. "I think it's too much for the church—doesn't look right stickin' out here like this. Some customers got bigger eyes than sense."

Jesse griped like he built the thing, but I didn't agree with him at all. The porte cochere was beautiful with its broad ceiling and powerful columns wrapped in sturdy detail. The whole structure seemed larger from underneath, and I couldn't resist putting my hand on one of the big columns to assure myself this magnificent work was more than imagination. I wanted to touch it…I wanted to touch all of it. I wanted to pull up a paint bucket and sit right here and watch the rest of the morning warm over a slow cup of coffee. But since I didn't drink coffee, the courtesy ceased being offered a long time ago, and I could see Joe and Jesse were anxious to start work.

"Is there anything I can do to help today?" I asked Joe.

We both knew the answer, but the hope in my voice held him in consideration for a moment before he smiled and shook his head. "Sorry, nothing left but stuff we gotta do ourselves. We'll be done before the week is."

"Just gotta paint this monument now," Jesse muttered over his thermos cup, "and man do I hate painting."

"Yeah, yeah, whine, whine, paint, paint," Joe answered his son. "You can complain all you want as long as you do it where I can't hear." Joe turned to me. "Jesse moans about painting on every job," he explained. "Makes for a longer week than it has to be."

Joe leaned around to continue with Jesse. "Let's get your pickup outta here, throw a tarp over this stone, and stand the ladders up. The church ladies are nipping at my heels about gettin' their flowers and shrubs planted next Saturday, so if we don't have it sewn up by then, we'll have all that mess to work around. Make sure you park this thing so the stupid dent doesn't show. I don't need the reverend's big fat sheriff interrupting what I'm doing to have us turn your truck pretty side out."

Jesse shook his head and puffed in disgust, but nodded he understood all his father wanted him to do.

"Well, PJ, I guess we need to get at it," Jesse said as he opened the truck door. "Have a good one." He slid to the seat, cranked the engine, and wheeled out in a chorus of crunching gravel.

I stood a moment longer in the wake of the exhaust and watched him maneuver the pickup through the yard so Mr. Wallace's dented fender wouldn't taint the façade of God's Glory.

I wanted to stay, but I waved to Joe instead and headed into church to shuffle the mildewed tomes of Reverend Dodge.

17
Standing in the Way of Fate

Reverend Dodge orchestrated the next Saturday so the Give Blood to God blood drive and the workday for landscaping around our new porte cochere would coincide. It was the day before Palm Sunday and one of my last in service to the reverend. Before long he would be able to enjoy his orange cream soda vice on Saturday once again. I'd grown accustomed to walking into church while the town was asleep with only the carpenters up and waiting on the day, but this morning everything was already awake in anticipation of all God's Glory had planned. I felt like I was walking through a carnival that had just rolled out of bed.

Husbands and sons were unloading truckloads of flowers and shrubs, staging them strategically around the porte cochere at the direction of gray-haired visionaries who occasionally bickered among themselves. A pickup stacked high with pine straw sat silently to the side waiting its turn to be emptied at the end of the day. The customary ambulances and fire trucks were parked out front. Banners were being hoisted to announce the blood drive as some Sunday school girls meandered through the early crowd filling foam cups with hot chocolate from a tea pitcher. The whole town would be here soon to give blood and help with the landscaping before the crowds from Hawkinsville descended on God's Glory for Easter service next week.

I didn't see the carpenters anywhere, just the porte cochere looming big and ivory over its servants scurrying about, dressing its feet with flats of begonias and impatiens. Joe had finished, and the final structure was so impressive and so awe inspiring it made the old church building look like an afterthought, added to the porte cochere instead of the other way around. But the growing crowd didn't seem to care as they openly praised the glorious addition. Ecstatic conversations swirled among the people, and I realized Jesse was right. The porte cochere was indeed a monument. I moved faster, hurrying to get inside before God decided to scramble our speech.

Months before, when the board approved the addition, no one anticipated how magnificent it would turn out, but to me, the porte cochere of God's Glory was more inspiring when Jesse was still griping about having to paint it.

I said only the unavoidable "good mornings" to people I recognized as I trudged by to check in with Reverend Dodge. He wasn't in his office. I figured I'd hang around, daydream a little while just to be safe, go give some blood to the Hawkinsville women in white, and then disappear through the fanfare a couple hours early. I was sure Reverend Dodge would be too busy to fuss with keeping track of me.

Boredom was in a hurry though, so I milled about the library-storage room for an indefensibly short amount of time before I meandered down to give my blood to God. I was not disciplined enough to oversee my own punishment, and since the reverend was certain to spend the day occupied with other things, I decided to do so as well. I could always claim I spent the morning shuffling books because, really, how could anybody tell? Progress certainly wouldn't give me away.

By the time I emerged from the fellowship hall with my tiny donor badge and a peanut butter cookie, Jesse and Mr. Wallace were standing on the sidewalk out front watching a mass of landscaping congregants trying to work, but mostly getting in each other's way. They were excited and far more careful about trampling on the flowers than on each other. Now that it was done, I guess everyone wanted to lay some claim of contribution to the church's great work. Jesse spotted me and waved me over, so I sidled up beside the two men as they looked out over the gardening mayhem strewn across the church lawn.

"Hey, PJ." Mr. Wallace smiled and shook my hand. He motioned to the crowd. "All they need now is a dunk tank and a cotton candy machine, and it'll be a full-blown carnival out there. It's a wonder they don't crush every flower they've planted. The whole lot looks like a bunch of chickens with their heads cut off."

"No doubt, it's like trying to plant petunias under a herd of buffalo," Jesse added.

"They might be better off tag-teaming," I suggested. "I mean, how does anyone even have room to push a shovel?"

"I'm afraid that would make too much sense. But then you'd have to decide who gets the honor of going first and who gets the honor of going last." Mr. Wallace shook his head. "They won't even know which they want until someone else voices a preference. Then they'll fight or feel slighted, so I guess it's better for them to step on each other's feet instead of each other's toes."

I laughed and nodded as Mr. Wallace gave his commentary. I always thought he was more approving of church things, but maybe that changed when Natalie was dismissed from the choir.

Jesse watched as the people fumbled over each other in a fruitless attempt to adorn the grand structure he and Joe had built. Then, almost as if he were on the phone with someone else, speaking just loud enough for me and Mr. Wallace to eavesdrop, he shook his head and muttered, "They're excited, and as hard as it is to believe watching this mess now, when it's all said and done, the faithful will pick up the pieces after everyone else has gone and put things as they should be. They believe their money made it possible, so they don't realize the porte cochere isn't meant for them or their valet ministry, but at least they're together doing something not too far off from what they should be. There's hope—for some. We'll see."

It was weird how Jesse said it, like he wasn't talking to us, as if we were overhearing him speaking to himself or someone else nearby. The activity in the church yard was so loud and Jesse was speaking so softly that I wonder now how I heard him at all, but he seemed to whisper straight into my brain, as if he didn't trust my ears already full with distraction. He felt close. A sad smile crept across his face. Jesse obviously saw something in the busy congregants I didn't, and I felt ashamed for agreeing with Mr. Wallace's skepticism so readily. I looked for something innocuous to say.

"It'll look great by Easter—it always does. That's why so many folks come down from Hawkinsville. Reverend Dodge will make sure of it. I guess they're more like busy bees than headless chickens when you think of it like that."

"They are busy bees," Mr. Wallace agreed.

"Yeah, but the work of bees yields honey," Jesse added in a faraway voice. "Speaking of bees," he put his hand on my shoulder and smiled, "all the bee boxes are done. I'll set 'em up this week, and it'll be about time to hunt down some queens. I'm hoping for twelve, but I'm gonna need help tracking down the hives and gettin' 'em to the farm. You up for giving me a hand?"

I'd never fooled with bees before, other than throwing rocks at their nests, but the idea of hunting them with Jesse was an adventure I wasn't ready to pass up. "Sure, sounds like fun."

"Do you think Kirby might want to come too?" Jesse's hand was still on my shoulder, and he gave it a shake when he asked.

"I bet he will," I nodded. "He's been acting off lately, but bee catching sounds right up his alley. Is Joe coming?"

"No, Dad and Mom headed for the job in Sardis last night. Oh, by the way, Dad says 'bye' and hopes he'll run into you down the road sometime."

Disappointment washed across my face, and I dropped my eyes to the ground to better hide the feeling. Even if Joe had said good-bye in person, it wouldn't have amounted to anything more than a handshake and a "see you later," so I don't know why I was hurt by his second-hand "so long," but I was. Maybe I wanted our morning chats to mean as much to him as they did to me, or maybe I knew I wouldn't be running into him down the road, but something disappeared when I heard he was gone, and a faint uncertainty hung in its place. I pushed it back, but not before Jesse noticed.

"He really wanted to see you before he left, but we took longer on this thing here than we planned. When the job in Sardis called last night, he and Mom decided to head on down." Jesse paused to see if his words helped, but even though I understood the legitimacy of all he was saying, disappointment had to run its course. I guess folks don't always know what they mean to other people, especially the ones you only meet in passing.

"Maybe," Jesse continued, "if you want, after I've wrapped everything up for Mr. Wallace, you could ride down to Marietta with me and help us out a couple of days. That's gonna be a bigger job, and I'm sure Dad would love an extra hand—that is, if your folks say it's okay."

I lifted my head to look over the crowd doing their best to plant flowers, all wanting to take their turn at the same time. I knew I would never be going to Marietta with Jesse—my parents wouldn't allow it—but I nodded and smiled anyway to let Jesse know I appreciated the offer.

I never would see Joe again, and I found it terribly odd how he faded out of the story so quickly. I can't tell you what became of him, but I know events would never have unfolded in the same manner if he'd remained. I guess fate removes those who stand in its way.

I stood with Jesse and Mr. Wallace a few moments more, gazing into the tangled people.

"Well," Mr. Wallace piped up, "I guess I'd better go give some blood and then fetch Natalie from Ms. Miller."

"Yeah, I need to go ahead and do my blood too," Jesse said. "Then I'm gonna go meet John and set the bee boxes in the far field."

They made their good-byes, patted me on the back, and strolled off together toward the church. I stood there thinking about Joe and watching for another minute or two, until the crowd finally grew large enough to spill onto the sidewalk where I was standing. It was time to go.

I stopped by the reverend's office and, finding it vacant, decided the coast was clear for me to skip out, pile in my truck, and head to Kirby's. I cranked the engine and wheeled out of the parking lot as my mind unconsciously replayed the last of the conversation between Jesse and Mr. Wallace. When you live your life in a small town, you feel on top of everything, but as I drifted with the hum of my truck, I realized Mr. Wallace and Jesse had mentioned both Ms. Miller and John. It was odd they were all connected, and I began to think maybe more was happening than anyone knew.

18
Palm Sunday

The next day was Palm Sunday, the week before Easter, and the church grounds, with new flowers, shrubs, and fresh pine straw, were as extraordinary as Jesse predicted. The faithful few came through once again. Mom and Dad were astonished at all that had been done when we pulled into the parking lot and wanted to know if I had helped with the landscaping. I shook my head no.

We were handed the customary palm leaves when we entered church as conversations of the magnificent porte cochere circled through the sanctuary full of people greeting their usual friends. The pre-service buzz about the new addition didn't subside until Reverend Dodge took the pulpit and the congregation fell silent.

"I am pleased to tell you," he started in his deep, theatrical Sunday morning voice, "the weather forecast between now and Easter Sunday is for nothing but sunny skies. It appears the good Lord is preparing the perfect day for all we have planned."

There was a murmur of "Amens," and a few waved their palm leaves from the pews.

"If all goes well," Reverend Dodge continued, "the youth will meet here next Saturday night to hide Easter eggs and other goodies on the back lawn. I know this is different from years past, but we have so much to do and we're expecting a lot of folks from Uphill, so we're going to take advantage of the nice weather and get an early start. Immediately following the service, we'll have our traditional Easter lunch for our visitors, and we expect all of you to be there as well. By the way, what are we having this year?" The reverend held his hand to his brow, looking for someone specific in the congregation.

"Fried chicken with all the fixin's, and Mac's going to do the pies for us again," an older lady called up.

"You going to bring peach pie, Mac, wherever you are?" Reverend Dodge smiled wide as he looked down, trying to spot Mac in the pews.

"Just for you, Preacher," Mac hollered from among the people.

"Well then, I guess I'll need to wear my elastic breeches next week." Reverend Dodge patted his belly, giving his flock permission to laugh at the joke. They loved him, but I could no longer get past the man who pouted about orange cream soda.

"Before the Call to Worship, I do want to say one more thing. Yesterday was a glorious day in the life of this church. Everybody was here for the blood drive or to work on the lawn or both." Someone started a light clap in the back. "That's right, go ahead, give yourselves a hand." Reverend Dodge smiled and waited for a soft applause to ripple across the congregation. As the church fell silent once again, the reverend moved back to the microphone. "Now, when we started our latest building project, we were all hopeful God would bless the work ahead, but I have to say, in all honesty, I never expected Him to bless us so richly with the finest carpenters I have ever seen." Applause started, but the reverend held up his hand to silence it quickly. "Let me finish. I have traveled around and seen some of the most beautiful churches in the country, but I'll tell you right now, not a one of them can hold a candle to the porte cochere of God's Glory. It is a glorious testament, leaving no room for doubt about our love for the Lord."

Reverend Dodge was beginning to sound like a politician stoking the crowd, but the emotion in his voice seemed genuine, even to me. We all began to squirm in our pews, ready to bubble over with excitement and gratitude over what he was saying. I was caught up as well.

"Now we all had a hand in helping this come to pass," Reverend Dodge continued, "but I must be truthful. It didn't have to be as magnificent as it is, it didn't have to be the beacon to our Uphill visitors that it will be, it didn't have to be the beginning of something new for God's Glory, and it didn't have to look like it was built by the Lord himself…but it does! And we only have two men to thank for that part of it." The reverend's eyes found Jesse sitting in the crowd. "Now I know your dad isn't with us this morning, but Jesse, please stand up so we can give you the most sincere thank you God's Glory has to offer. Thank you, son."

Reverend Dodge stepped back from the pulpit, smiled down at Jesse, and started to clap. The whole church followed, erupting in such applause that even the reverend seemed startled. He'd outdone himself this time, whipping a near frenzy into his congregation. People flooded out of the pews, waving their palm branches, crushing through one another to pat Jesse on the back or shake his hand. They cheered and hollered, "Thank you!", "Praise God!", and "Hallelujah!" Jesse looked like a bobber on a windy day at the lake, smiling and nodding as people waved their branches high overhead, pushing in around to offer the carpenter their personal gratitude. I've never seen anything like it in church before or since, and I must admit, I was as swept away by him and the reverend's buildup as anyone in Cunningham.

Twenty minutes later, Reverend Dodge finally managed to calm everyone down enough to collect the offertory, remind us not to sit in the pews next week, and offer a lackluster sermon about growing the church. It didn't matter though. Our minds were on Jesse, the Palm Sunday celebrity, who had given us the most beautiful porte cochere Reverend Dodge had ever seen.

On the car ride home, Mom and Dad still hadn't recovered, giddy, chirping about the young carpenter, his wonderful work, and asking me if I knew Jesse or his father.

Time is running shy, and I have a lot to tell, so even if my memory was ironclad, there would be no time to stray or water down my confession with self-indulgent details. I'm nervous about what happens next, fearing what I have to say will be excused as the ramblings of a failing old man. Be assured, although the children slip away from me from time to time, I still hold tight to my beautiful Maggie and my days in Cunningham. The next part of the story is as true as can be remembered. I'll take another pill anyway, if only to make it more credible.

The next Saturday evening, Mom insisted I join the youth to hide Easter eggs at church. The weather was clear and pleasant without the slightest hint of rain in the forecast. It was like God sat on the Holiday Committee and had been delegated the responsibility for a dry, beautiful day. Apparently He had only been given one job, and He was doing it to perfection.

Kirby, Natalie, and I joined the cliquey church kids in hiding a million pounds of marshmallow chicks, chocolate bunnies, and plastic eggs filled with jelly beans. I had a feeling the overnight Easter booty would attract every raccoon and 'possum in the county. No one else shared my concern—probably because they rightfully saw my grumbling as another excuse to put off the drudgery of doing something I didn't want to. A decision was made, however, to hold out some of the Easter candy as a backup in case something unforeseen occurred and the egg hunt had to be moved inside.

I'm not so sure God appreciates a contingency plan when you're doing His work. It's like putting brakes on faith, which, of course, has always been an invitation for rain and marshmallow-eating 'possums. But as the sun drained out behind the trees and the last plastic egg was shoved into the last hedge, there was no hint of anything but a bright morning ahead.

We gathered under the porte cochere for pizza, prayer, and a few songs I didn't sing. Tomorrow was Easter, the second biggest day of the year for God's Glory, and Reverend Dodge would be at the top of his game. Christmas had been a disaster, but now with the grand addition and pristine landscaping, the church never looked better. All of Cunningham felt sure the valet ministry, egg hunt, and chicken dinner would easily satisfy the traditional expectations of our Uphill brothers and sisters. Like well-seasoned stagehands, the working congregants of God's Glory prepared beautifully for our annual performance. I'm sure somewhere in the midst of a final sermon rehearsal, Reverend Dodge could feel the money coming.

19
Easter

Mom was emphatic about getting to church early enough to secure her seat by the ladies room for the Easter service, so she sent me to bed Saturday night long before I was ready to go. I huffed and milled about upstairs, but I had no trouble drifting off once I actually put my head on the pillow. I slept a long time. I'm not sure if thunder woke me or if my body simply had enough rest, but my eyes flicked open to the sound of rain and curtains, filled with an outside breeze, billowing into my room. I tossed back my covers, rolled out of bed, and crossed the floor to close the window. The curtains toyed with me, blowing back into my face as I struggled to push them aside. They would have been happier if I had left the sash open, but the playful damp breeze swirling through my room had already strewn my desk papers across the floor, so I slid the window shut, and the disappointed curtains deflated around me.

I stood for a moment staring through the glass into the streetlight below. I could hear rain falling out of the darkness, but only the drops illumed by the lamppost's halo were visible to me. In the faint circle of light, I could see water collecting in the gutter and streaming by on its way to swell the Chagrin. The sun wouldn't rise for another hour or two, but even so, the day promised to be bleak. For the moment, I was the only one awake in town, but I knew before the morning was too much older, there would be a lot of disappointed folks in Cunningham.

The spring rains were delayed this year, but they were going to come; they always did. Up 'til now, everything indicated God would be smiling down on His brand-new porte cochere with a sunny day, gracing us and our visitors with His approval over what we'd built. I guess when you relegate the Lord to nothing but the weather, you're going to get rainy days that are unexpected to everyone but Him.

Thunderless lightning streaked through the clouds, revealing every detail of the neighbor's front yard as if midday had been momentarily flipped on. I yawned and waited for another flash as I gazed into the street below, but none came, just the sound of falling water. I stepped over the paper on the floor, and had to shake my ankles to keep it from sticking to the bottoms of my feet. I plopped down on my bed and lay across the spread. "The valet ministry will have its work cut out today," I muttered to the shadows as I waited to hear Mom rise and start the rattle of Easter breakfast.

The rain sounded like a bathroom shower on the roof, constant, determined, and hypnotic. I was content in the dark, lying unnoticed and listening to the gutters drain. Besides, there was nothing else to be done but take comfort, roll over, and wish to stay in bed. I drifted.

"Good rainy Easter morning." Dad flipped the light on as he walked into my room. I covered my eyes with a pillow and groaned at the obtrusive pajama-clad man. "Okay, PJ, get those feet on the floor. Your mom's in the kitchen, and it's so nasty outside we're going to get started earlier than planned. Don't make me have to come check on you, you hear me?"

I nodded I heard from underneath the pillow.

Dad was always brusque when he woke me in the morning, irritated at having to prod me into the most basic of responsibilities—getting out of bed. He would be more cheerful at the breakfast table, as long as I wasn't late. I pulled myself up and headed down the hall to the bathroom.

The house lights aggravated the storm, making it seem darker, willing only to reveal my reflection when I peered out the window this time. Somehow we called attention to ourselves, and the blackness outside rushed to envelop us, pressing against the house, seeming more intent on getting in than passing by. The bathroom light was an unintentional slight, but it was enough to turn the storm against me, making it more menacing and less tolerant of my morning rituals. The power flickered as the weather outside threatened to restore our dark harmony, but the storm relented, restraining itself to disapproval rather than dousing the electrical of the house.

I felt small and uneasy as I brushed my teeth, so I snapped off the light, preferring the deluge in the dark. I dressed the same way. The sky began to gray with the backlight of the sunrise, and my eyes grew accustomed to the shadows. I could see plainly all I needed before descending the stairs to breakfast and the artificial light of the kitchen.

Mom was not her usual Sunday morning self. She sighed and kept repeating, "It's such a shame, such a shame." She shook her head. "After all of Reverend Dodge's hard work. Look at it outside." Dad nodded in agreement. I was just happy Mom wasn't too distraught to make her blueberry muffins. Dad had to feel the same way.

"Well," Dad consoled Mom over his coffee, "it's a good day for a porte cochere. Think how messy it would be without it. At least now, only the guys parking cars will get wet. That's good for our guests."

Mom nodded, looked out the window into the rain, and shook her head. I got up to clear the dishes, but she touched me on the wrist before I could move away. "Oh, honey, thank you, but just set them in the sink. I'll get them when we get home." She smiled at me sweetly. "I'm so sorry about your Easter egg hunt."

"It's okay, Mom. We saved enough candy for the little kids to have an egg hunt in the fellowship hall."

"Well, that was smart," she nodded.

"You two ready?" Dad asked, sliding away from the table.

We were, so we pulled some old raincoats out of the front closet—Dad's was a yellow slicker that made him look like he should be stocking fish sticks at the Gas & Grocery—and then we hopscotched puddles to the car.

The wipers slapped away the drizzle as Dad wheeled our sedan around the pools of rain ponding on the streets. When we pulled on to River Road toward church, the weather slowed enough for a clear view of the Trackers huddled together on the railroad tracks. They turned to watch us pass as our car cut through the street water. Dad slowed to maneuver through a large puddle as I stared through my window at the sodden pariahs. I could see them plainly, expressionless and soaked to the bone.

"Gracious," Mom exclaimed, craning to see. "What else can happen today? What a terrible shame. It looks like the sheriff will be working on Easter Sunday…of all days. Where's the dignity? We have guests coming and everything."

I heard her complaining from far away as a deeper puddle rushed underneath the car. But her empty words were brushed away like crumbs to the floorboard when I recognized a small child, shivering and holding her big sister's hand.

Nya and Angeline stood beside John amid their belongings, heavy and melting on the tracks, looking more like a photograph from 1929 than a family living at the edge of town. The guttural sound of water rushing through the under-workings of the car filled my ears as I peered through the beads of rain running along the window. The wipers kept time. I couldn't bear the faces of Nya or John, so I fixed my eyes on Angeline, wondering if she recognized the boy from the Gas & Grocery as he gawked and drove slowly past. She seemed so small in her wet dress, soaked and clinging tightly to her skin. My stomach started to churn, and for the first time, I felt sorry for the people standing in the storm. Perhaps knowing their names changed me somehow, or at least made me wonder how a little girl or the man who saved Natalie could ever deserve this.

Dad reached down to switch on the defroster as he drove by the refugees like he was passing a stand of mailboxes. I leaned back, hoping to exorcise the feeling in my stomach with a heavy exhale. I closed my eyes, trying to push it away, until I heard the crunch of gravel under our wheels as we turned onto the new drive of God's Glory.

"We need to let the sheriff know about those people before anybody from Uphill arrives. After all the hard work to get the church ready, I hate the thought of all those shabby Trackers out where everybody can see them," Mom complained as Dad pulled under the porte cochere to let her out. He didn't answer. Dad told me to get out with her and go inside.

"There's no sense in us both running through the rain if we don't have to." He reached around and slapped me on the knee. "Go on now. Get out with your mother."

I opened the door and did as I was told. I stood under the shelter of God's Glory and watched my dad's car roll over the wet drive to find its place in the parking lot. Mom was saying something about the porte cochere being a blessing on a day like today as she moved safely through the doors of the church, greeting her friends on the other side. I pushed my hand back through my hair and waited a moment longer, but when the sky began to wail again, I followed my mother inside before any more tears splashed the cuffs of my pants.

I guess the thought of calling the sheriff flew out of Mom's head as she wished her other ladies "happy Easter" and lamented the weather. She asked me to move chairs from one of the Sunday school classes to the hall outside the ladies room so she and her friends could plant themselves there, packed in like righteous, hospitable sardines. It was a strange sacrifice, sitting on top of each other in the cramped corridor, unwilling to budge for fear of losing the humble spot. Dad and I wouldn't see Mom again until we sat down for lunch, where she, all rumpled and perspiring, would ask over and over again if all our visitors found a seat.

Dad came in but moved off with the rest of the Men's Group to shake hands and figure out how best to park the visitors. The storm beat down on God's Glory, and standing alone in the narthex, I doubted anyone from Uphill would show. I crossed over to the front window and peered across the square. A curtain of rain kept the shops on the far side hidden, almost like Cunningham was being consumed by the shower one block at a time. The Bride and Groom, dressed in new leaves, lurched back and forth with the wind, making them appear to advance on the church, even though they were holding tight to the ground where they lived. I felt small as I stared out into the stormy world.

"Well, buddy, it doesn't look like we'll be hunting eggs outside today," Kirby commented as he sidled up. He startled me.

"Crap!" I jerked, then covered my mouth with my hands and looked around to see if anyone noticed I said "crap" in church. No one had, so I lowered my voice. "You scared the crap out of me, Kirby."

He smiled. "I guess it was a bad idea to hide the candy last night after all."

I nodded. "Do you think anybody from Uphill is even comin' today? I mean, look at it outside. You can barely see to the street."

Kirby shrugged his shoulders. "I don't know. It's Easter…hard to tell."

"Well, Mom's out by the ladies room for the duration, even if the place is half empty," I said.

"Yeah, my folks are a little beat this morning, so I think my mom's gonna have to park it in a back pew." Kirby looked around. "I guess no Natalie for Easter, huh?"

"I guess not. She told me last night she and her dad thought they might stay home in case the church got too crowded."

Kirby sighed, looked out the window, and shook his head. "The only thing that should be too crowded today is an ark."

Kirby and I couldn't have been more wrong with our prediction of a low Easter turnout. For the gray morning hadn't weathered on much longer before a stream of headlights appeared, creeping along the streets of Cunningham, funneling themselves through the porte cochere of God's Glory where volunteer valets were waiting. The porte cochere was big enough to accommodate eight cars at a time, and the men's parking ministry handled its job with the all the skill any five-star hotel could boast.

Kirby and I stood by the window as the crowd of strangers began wandering through on their way to the sanctuary, extolling our new addition and saying how thankful they were to have benefit of it on a day like today. Some of the children were worried about the egg hunt, while most of the adults couldn't believe the deluge we were having when it was such a clear morning in Hawkinsville.

"Yeah," I heard someone say as the visitors milled by, "it's the strangest thing. The day was clear as a bell right up to the Cunningham line, and then the sky went dark and the bottom dropped out. I thought about turning around, but we were almost here. I sure hope it's not doing this at home."

Their conversations trailed off as they went by.

"Looks like a full house after all," Kirby said, nodding to the sanctuary swollen with Uphillers.

The narthex was also filling fast with familiar faces from our regular congregation, having abdicated their usual pews to the visitors. We wouldn't see or hear much of the service from out here, but that wasn't the point. When I noticed the men of the parking ministry squeeze their way in, I knew Reverend Dodge would soon begin. It was a big day. He needed to make up for Christmas.

"Hey, PJ, let's see if we can get by to check on my mom. I need to make sure she's sitting."

"Sure," I nodded and followed Kirby as he pushed his way through the seams of the crowd.

"Excuse me, excuse me," he apologized.

"Excuse me, excuse me," I echoed, doing my best not to irritate any congregants enough to tell my mom. It wouldn't do for her to know I stepped on someone's foot trying to get into church when I should have kept my place waiting humbly outside with the rest of Cunningham.

"I'm sorry, I'm so sorry." I sucked in my stomach and craned my neck to make myself skinny enough to slide through the last group between me and where I was going. A crowd of glaring eyes followed me as I pushed in to find Kirby standing behind his mother, but I didn't turn back to offer an excuse or even acknowledge my wrongdoing. I moved up beside Kirby and impolitely pretended I didn't know any better.

A colorful array of banners hung around the room, a moat of Easter lilies surrounded the altar, and the big wooden cross was draped in a white linen sash. The Holiday Committee had outdone itself again. On such a dark day, the sanctuary remained light and blissful, ignoring the storm outside. Kirby and I were in the same spot as Christmas when the choir filed into the chancel and Reverend Dodge assumed the pulpit. He waited for the hum of four hundred conversations to taper into silence.

"Good morning," Reverend Dodge greeted in a well-rehearsed voice.

"Good morning," the congregation responded in unison.

"And what a fine morning it is, isn't it?" The reverend motioned to a window streaming with rain and smiled. A light snicker snaked through the crowd.

"You know, on my drive in this morning," Reverend Dodge continued, "I saw a bunch of farm animals lining up two by two, and I was this close—" The reverend held up his thumb and index finger with their tips nearly touching to show how close. "I was this close to turning the car around and following those animals to wherever it was they were headed…just to be sure. There are some boats you don't wanna miss."

Laughter rolled over the congregation, and the reverend stepped back for a moment to enjoy the fruit of his joke.

"But," the reverend raised his hand to reassert himself and quiet the people, "but, we here at God's Glory have a big day planned, so I decided to come on in and be with you instead. Of course, we're going to have our annual egg hunt inside this year—we don't have enough scuba gear to have it on the lawn," the reverend said through a smile. "And you are all invited to join us in the fellowship hall for some Easter fried chicken with all the fixin's and the best pie you ever put in your mouth. There's plenty, and it's our gift to you. So please plan on staying and give the weather a chance to clear before you leave us today."

The crowd murmured and nodded among themselves as the individual families decided to accept the reverend's invitation.

"Before we get started," Reverend Dodge went on, "I want to say, as nasty as it is outside, I don't think you could have come on a day you would have appreciated our brand-new porte cochere or the men's valet ministry more. What do you think?"

The congregation broke into applause loud enough to drown out the beat of the rain as the reverend turned to take his seat. He sat smiling out over the people until the clapping started to wane, and then signaled the organist to play. The choir rose and the service began.

The usual songs and prayers played out with the perfection of a Broadway musical, giving our Uphill visitors every penny's worth they pledged or laid in the offertory. Everything was well timed and beautiful, and the dramatic accent added by the occasional clap of thunder made it seem as if God liked it too. It was easy to be swept away in the warm choreography of God's Glory, making us all feel better and more complete for having been here. A rush of wind howled around the church, stealing my attention and leaving my thoughts with Angeline in the weather outside. I could see her plainly, like a drowned kitten in her soaking dress. I shook my head to break free, but she clung tight until Reverend Dodge began his sermon to rescue me. I stared out the window as his empty words numbed my brain.

The reverend was talking about a lost church trying to trap the Lord with a question of law or logic or something else I didn't quite catch. He raised his hands and, with a voice big enough to hear in the town square, quoted, "And thou shalt love the Lord thy God with all thy heart, and with all thy soul, and with all thy mind, and with all thy strength: This is the first commandment. And the second is like this: Thou shalt love thy neighbor as thyself. There is none other commandment greater than these!" He brought his hands slamming down on the pulpit, startling his congregation frozen in the pews. He came ablaze, and if there had been popcorn, it would have been all over the floor. We hung on the next words he would say as he paused, glaring out over the crowd.

Anticipation crackled and popped like electricity in the air. Reverend Dodge stepped back and wagged his finger, trying to hold onto his next words a little longer, but they seeped out anyway. "And do you know what His very next words were? Do you know what He said to the man who asked the question?" The reverend leaned over his pulpit and lowered his voice into a near snarl. "He said, 'Thou art not far from the Kingdom of God.'" Reverend Dodge paused again to let the words sink down into the people as a slow roll of thunder passed over low enough to rattle the rafters. The timing was perfect. Surely this was the reverend's finest moment—he was more than making up for Christmas.

Reverend Dodge pushed himself away from the pulpit and strolled to center chancel with his hand to his forehead as if he were deep in thought or receiving a message from God. He whirled, throwing his hand up out of his robe, pointing out to the congregation. "Do you know what that means? Do you really know what *that* means?" he shouted as the thunder rumbled over again, leaving us in the wake of a dead silence.

The reverend was magnetic. Every pew was filled with wide eyes and gaping mouths, waiting to be told what it meant. Even I was nervous, lost in what he might say. But before he could answer his own question, someone sitting in the second row rose. We all watched as the figure jostled and bumped past the others packed in the pew, excusing himself to the aisle. The reverend's eyes cut down to the distraction. I couldn't believe anyone would interrupt or get up and leave now, especially from such a conspicuous seat. There was no excuse for such irreverence, and to risk the ire of the reverend was foolhardy. I craned to see who could be so rude.

It was Jesse. Jesse was walking out on the reverend, down the center of the sanctuary as the whole congregation watched in disbelief. I didn't know what to think, but as he brushed by, moving through the sanctuary doors, thoughts of Angeline flooded my brain. I didn't like it.

"I guess he already knows what it means," Kirby whispered playfully as Jesse disappeared through the back of the church.

Reverend Dodge picked right back up, but there was no more thunder in his sermon, only rain, and whatever he was saying wasn't enough to wash Jesse or the Trackers from my thoughts. I spent the rest of the service staring out into the storm as the smell of fried chicken wafted up from the fellowship hall.

20
Mashed Potato Lady

It wasn't the benediction or the closing music that reeled me in, but a nudge from Kirby snapped me back from wherever I'd drifted. The conversations of strangers filled the sanctuary as unfamiliar faces filed involuntarily downstairs like they had been hypnotized by the smell of lunch. Only a few guests decided to brave the weather and turned for the porte cochere to have their cars retrieved and head home. Kirby and I followed them out to watch the volunteer valets and wait for the lunch line to thin.

"Gah-lee, it's still coming down," Kirby said as we pushed through the outside door.

"Sounds like it." I turned back, but Kirby stopped short. I felt the cool, wet air on my neck. The sound of water overwhelming gutters and slapping to the ground filled my ears. Kirby stood drop-jawed in the doorway. His eyes were locked on something behind me, but I was slow to catch on. I raised my voice. "Are you coming or what?" He didn't respond.

A dripping car rolled in from the spray with its windshield wipers going full tilt. I turned around. Valets in rain slickers and galoshes served the last of the early guests with muted "thank yous" and "happy Easters." The porte cochere looked like the inside of a carwash as deafening walls of water rolled off the roof, pounding the drive on either side.

"All right," one of the valets was saying to the other as the last car pulled away, "I don't expect any more 'til after lunch, so

I'm gonna look for the reverend and the sheriff…if he's here." The other man nodded. They shook themselves off and hurried past us on their way into the building.

We were alone outside, and for the first time, I noticed what Kirby had seen right off. It took a moment longer to comprehend.

The beat of the rain droned in my head as I stared across the drive. At the far end of the porte cochere, huddled just inside the shelter, shivered the soaking wet Trackers we had passed on the way to church. There were fewer than I expected: a couple of elderly, a few adults, and a smattering of kids and young children, maybe three families, but no more than four. I'd always thought there were more—there always seemed to be more—but as it turned out, these eighteen or so refugees were all Tracker Island had to cough up.

"Holy crap! What are they doing here?" Kirby gasped.

I was dumfounded. I couldn't answer. I only stared.

"Is that John?" Kirby asked, but I had no response. I only gawked at the timid people pushed to the edge, holding their eyes down to avoid mine. They were afraid, and rightly so.

Curtains of rain continued to roll over the gutters and a rumble of thunder crawled overhead as I surveyed the silent people until my eyes fell on Angeline. She looked up at the very moment I saw her. With the smallest of smiles, she raised her hand and pushed her fingers into a tiny wave of recognition. Without thinking, I pulled my hand up and returned her signal. Her smile broadened slightly before she dropped her eyes again like the rest of her people.

"I think those guys went to get the sheriff," Kirby warned as I began to recover.

My mind raced through everyone I'd seen in church that morning, but I couldn't recall seeing Sheriff Johnson or either of his deputies. I finally found my voice. "I don't think he's here…so maybe just Reverend Dodge."

"Good, you guys made it. We've been waiting on you two." I'd been so captivated by the Trackers I hadn't noticed Jesse. He was soaked to the bone with his clothes drooping deep and hanging heavy off him. He stepped up to greet Kirby and me with a wet pat on the shoulder. "It's storming pretty hard out here, so I thought it might be a good idea to get John and everybody else out of the weather. It took some convincing, but they came around."

"You know John?" Kirby squinted.

"Sure do, he farms with Mr. Wallace - ever since he pulled Natalie from the river. She says he's got a real gift for growing tomatoes and pole beans." Jesse looked over to where John was standing, "Who do you think cleaned up the mess PJ made running his truck through Mr. Wallace's yard? John's a good man, teaching his kids to read, and he helped me build my bee boxes." Jesse took deep breath. "But you know as well as anyone the kind of trouble John working regular on the Wallace place might bring, so let's keep it to ourselves—for now."

I'm not sure why, but Kirby and I agreed to be trusted with the secret.

"Okay then." Jesse grabbed me by the shoulder, his damp sleeve leaking down the front of my shirt. "Looks like God's Glory has a few visitors out under the porte cochere today, so why don't you guys head in and fetch lunch for everybody while I sit here and wait on Reverend Dodge."

I was too stunned to speak, so I nodded and followed Kirby inside, downstairs, where the food was being served.

The fellowship hall was packed with shallow conversation mixed with the smell of chicken and green beans. A long table filled with all the staples of a church dinner ran along the front, but every other nook and cranny of the room was stuffed with Uphillers sitting or standing with plates of food in hand. I wondered how an egg hunt could possibly come off in a place so full of people. The line wasn't long, so Kirby and I grabbed a couple of plates each and moved up. We'd have to make a few trips to have enough to feed everyone outside.

"No, no, boys." A server on the other side of the table wagged her mashed potato spoon at me. I recognized her as a church regular, but I can't remember her name. "You boys know good and well it's one plate to a customer unless you're visiting today."

"Yes, ma'am, I know," Kirby explained, "but we're taking these to guests."

"Really." A suspicious smile crept over the mashed potato lady's face. "Point 'em out to me." She pushed herself to her toes to look out over the crowd before laying narrowed eyes back on us.

"No, ma'am, they're outside," I offered, still holding two plates.

"Really." She smiled again. "That's fine. Have 'em come on in, and they can eat 'til it's gone, but 'til they come through my line, it's only one plate to a customer." She scooped mashed potatoes up from her metal tin and slapped them down on Kirby's plate to emphasize her point. I held my plate up for her to do the same.

Every server down the line was equally accommodating and suspicious of two teenage boys looking for more than their share. As we slid along the table, we weren't given much of any one thing, but there were so many dishes being doled out, by the end of it, we had as much as a medium-sized paper plate could hold. Kirby and I both asked for a chicken breast because it was the biggest piece they had. We picked up a couple of sweet teas and started back upstairs.

"Hey, PJ, and you, too, Kirby Braddock. Happy Easter. You two not staying here to eat?" Natalie spotted us getting lunch and caught up as we were about to leave. She twisted shyly back and forth in a crisp white dress cascading with ruffles and frills. She wore a hat with a fake flower and pink bow, and she had short white gloves to match. She glowed, making her seem like an animated character in a live-action movie.

Kirby knew exactly what she was looking for. "Wow wee, Natalie, that is one fancy dress. You sure are having a pretty day."

She blushed and turned back and forth a little faster at his compliment.

"Hey, I didn't think you were coming," I added, balancing my plate in one hand while holding tea in the other.

"Well, I wanted to show off my Easter dress and I told Daddy I wouldn't pitch no fits, so we been waiting down here the whole time. Daddy didn't think we'd better go to service with the Uphill folks and all, so we came down here 'til time to eat. It sure is hard to wait when everything smells like it wants to be in your tummy. They won't let me have no more chocolate chip cookies, even though they got a whole lot of 'em." She shot a quick glance at a stolid old lady manning the dessert table and stuck out her lower lip.

"Well, you go tell that old biddy I said you can have mine."

"Mine too," Kirby added.

Her eyes gleamed, and her lips pulled into a grin wide enough to cover her face. She whirled about and headed straight for the dessert table to deliver the good news. Kirby and I trudged up the stairs, taking our time, careful not to spill our plates and knowing the pitiful lunch we were bringing back probably wasn't worth the trip. It would never be enough for all those people.

The plate teetered in my palm and the tea sloshed out on my fingers as I backed through the outside door. I pushed it open with my butt and held it ajar for Kirby to pass through. The pound of the rain and the cool, wet air were a welcome relief to the stale heat of too many people waiting for an egg hunt in the basement. I could breathe, but not for long. Although there was no sheriff or deputies, the volunteer valets had retrieved the reverend.

"What I'm telling you, young man," Reverend Dodge was red faced and quivering with anger as he pushed his finger into Jesse's chest, "is that our God's Glory guests do not need to be accosted or panhandled by the likes of those people here at church on Easter Sunday. I'm telling you to get them out of here and off church property right now!"

Anybody I know would have buckled under the reverend's assault, but Jesse stayed calm. "Reverend, these folks aren't doing any of those things. They're just standing here—that's all—and there's still plenty of room to pull the cars through when people want to leave."

"Oh, that's just great. No! They can't be here! Look at them! They look like drowned rats!" But Reverend Dodge didn't look at them; he kept his eyes only on Jesse.

"They're not any wetter than you'd be if you took a few steps left or right—either way, you'd be as soaked as the rest of us."

Reverend Dodge wasn't used to being challenged and became even more incensed with Jesse's observation. He pushed his finger into Jesse's chest again and again, stopping just shy of striking Jesse as he continued his tirade.

The Trackers at the far end kept their eyes to the ground, but Kirby and I watched the whole interchange between Jesse and the reverend in utter disbelief. I hadn't liked the reverend for a while, but to see him spiral into an irrational tantrum at the hands of a carpenter's son was disconcerting. I knew the Trackers shouldn't be here, they had no right, but at the same time I hoped Jesse wouldn't send them away.

"I built this for a reason," Reverend Dodge yelled in Jesse's face. "To keep the rain off my flock, and I don't want them to have to see that." He threw his arm up, pointing to the Trackers without so much as a glance in their direction.

"That's where you're wrong." Jesse shook his head. "Dad built this shelter, not you."

"I paid for it," the reverend snarled back.

"You mean your congregation paid for it."

"That's what I mean," the reverend hissed.

"But not all of it," Jesse said. "You still owe the last installment and a retainer to boot, so as long as that remains outstanding, part of this porte cochere still belongs to Dad. Since I'm in charge of Dad's affairs for now, I think I'll own…the part these folks are standing under."

"We'll see what the sheriff has to say about that, smart guy. You better get these Trackers out of here right now before things start going south for you in a real hurry, boy."

The reverend wheeled around to storm back into the church, but when he realized the plates Kirby and I were holding were for the people outside, he slapped Kirby's out of his hand as he shouldered his way past. Not being enough to satisfy his anger, the reverend reached around for my plate too, but I moved away in time to keep him from sending it to the gravel as well. The reverend wasn't prepared to chase me, so he left me with a heavy glare before pushing his way into the building. Besides us, only the Trackers witnessed the reverend's outburst.

"Can you believe that? That guy is an absolute double A-hole!" Kirby blurted as the doors closed behind Reverend Dodge.

"Don't worry about the sheriff," Jesse announced. "He won't be here today." Jesse stepped toward me. "Let's see what you brought."

"I'm sorry," I apologized. "They'd only give us one plate. We tried to pile 'em high as we could, but now Kirby's is all over the ground. There might be enough here for two people." I handed the food to Jesse.

"It's what we got," Jesse said, "so we'll just have to stretch it. PJ, how about running back inside and getting twelve trash bags. We don't want to leave a mess out here."

Twelve garbage bags was a lot of overkill. It wouldn't take any time at all for the food to be eaten, and I could carry the cups and plates to the trash by hand. I don't know. Maybe I was still in shock over the Trackers and Reverend Dodge, maybe I just wanted to help, or maybe it was the way Jesse asked me that kept me from protesting such a ridiculous request. Instead, I turned around and went back downstairs to fetch the bags from the church kitchen.

21
The Storm

Even from the basement, I could hear thunder rumbling through and the storm pounding against the church harder than before. Every window had gone opaque with a milky fog, making them impossible to see through as billows of rain hurled against the glass. I've always liked thunderstorms, but this one unsettled me somehow, making me feel like God's Glory was listing deep into a great lake where the growing pressure would crush us all.

I grabbed Jesse's bags and headed for the stairs as the youth were setting up for the egg hunt. Of course, the big event would be far less than planned. In a moronic twist of faith, we'd put all our marshmallow eggs in one basket by hiding nearly everything we had outside the night before. Every last piece of candy on the lawn was surely washed into the Chagrin and headed far out to sea by now. I smiled at the thought of Natalie's words as I hustled back upstairs.

A shard of lightning flashed across God's Glory, illuminating every window, followed by a peel of thunder that sounded like giants crashing through trees. The storm pressed in on the church, warning everyone to stay inside. The wind howled at every corner like guard dogs or hungry wolves. The power flickered, and I could hear people in the basement gasp in unison and then applaud when the inside lights found their footing again. Even the porte cochere couldn't provide shelter from gusting rain like this. So with a deep breath and an armload of trash bags, I pushed my way through the door, ready to be assaulted by the weather.

Kirby stepped up and grabbed me by the shoulders. He was right in my face and so excited I couldn't understand what he was saying. "Can you believe it? My God, can you believe it? The grass! The grass!"

"What," I managed to get out as I pushed him away, "are you saying?"

He sputtered to find his words, but he was moving too fast and I was moving too slow, so he hooked me by the collar and started to drag me along.

"Stop, you idiot, you're gonna tear my shirt!" I tried to knock his hand away. But I couldn't free myself and Kirby didn't stop until he pulled me out from under the porte cochere into the sunshine.

Golden rays streaming from a cobalt sky welcomed me as clouds as white as Natalie's dress paraded slowly past. They seemed more like happy stuffed animals, and the afternoon sun smiled as they transformed themselves along the blue canvas. The grass was warm and dry without a puddle to be considered, and laughter was in the air. I never knew Trackers laughed, but their hearty voices carried along the greens and the blues and the whites of an Easter day that could have only been painted by God. They sat comfortably on the lawn, eating and talking together as if they actually belonged.

"What is this?"

"I don't know," Kirby whispered.

"Did you get more food while I was gone?"

"No, he just kept passing the plate you brought. He just kept passing it and passing it, and there was plenty."

A gentle breeze picked up, perfuming the air with dogwood as Kirby and I stared from the shadow of the porte cochere.

"You guys wanna eat?" I didn't notice Jesse move up between us. I couldn't answer, but Jesse took me and Kirby by our arms. "Come on, let's have some lunch," he said, and walked us out to the circle of Trackers.

He introduced us, someone handed me a plate, and I sat down next to Kirby. I didn't have anything to say but a weak hello to Nya and John. I started my lunch in silence and noticed only things I liked were on my plate. Somehow I hadn't been served any of the gross things Mom always made me try, although I saw three-bean salad and pimento cheese being enjoyed by a few of my fellow picnickers.

I had nothing to say to these people as conversations of fishing, gardening, and the weather made their way around the circle. Nya was sitting across from me, but she was too pretty to be caught watching, so I kept my eyes in the grass, not looking up or around until two small brown feet interrupted my stare. I tilted up to see a little girl with a plate full of blueberry pie staring down at me. Everyone was watching.

"Hi," I muttered as friendly as I could, but Angeline didn't flinch. She just stood with blueberries smeared across her tiny face, chewing a mouthful of dessert. The sun was at her back, like a miniature gunfighter, but as uncomfortable as she was making me, I knew I couldn't shoo her away. The whole group fell silent to watch, and it seemed like forever before she finally tired of studying me and turned around. I sighed with relief, but as I leaned over to set my plate aside, she plopped down into my lap to finish her pie. Laughter filled the yard. She tried to feed me a bite, but I politely refused.

Angeline and I drew the attention of everyone on the lawn, so we didn't see Jesse drift back into church until he returned with Natalie and Mr. Wallace. Mr. Wallace was astounded as they approached the picnic, but Natalie skipped along, perfectly at home in the miraculous day.

"Look who I found," Jesse called.

"John," Natalie squealed when she recognized the big man sitting in the grass. She sprinted straight to him and lunged out, forcing him to catch her.

John teetered from the impact. "Now, Miss Natalie, you can't be jumping all over me like that. It ain't right, it ain't right at all. Besides, you gonna go and get grass all over your pretty white dress that won't ever come clean," he half scolded as he set Natalie to her feet.

Angeline started bouncing in my lap at the sight of Natalie. Her plate slid from her sticky blue hands, with the last bite of pie dropping to the ground. She pushed herself off me, *thank God,* and made straight for Natalie.

"No, no, no!" Angeline's mother cried, but it was too late. The little girl caught Natalie in such a tight hug around the waist they both nearly toppled over. Angeline squeezed tight, burying her happy blueberry face deep into Natalie's white dress, grabbing fistfuls in the back. Her mom apologized over and over again to Mr. Wallace, promising to clean the dress, but knowing she couldn't afford to as she tried to pry Angeline from Natalie's waist. The smile sank away from Mr. Wallace.

We knew Natalie couldn't help what would happen next. Kirby and I braced ourselves for the inevitable seizure of hysterics we'd witnessed so often before anytime one of Natalie's Sunday dresses had been soiled. I was uncomfortable sitting with these people, but I didn't want the day to end like this. Natalie was smiling and enjoying the embrace, not realizing the child holding her so tightly was smeared with blueberries that preferred a white dress to a little girl's face. I stood up. Natalie and Mr. Wallace would have to go home.

"I'm so sorry. I'll clean it, I'll clean it," Angeline's mom frantically repeated.

But when she finally pulled her daughter off Natalie, there wasn't so much as a whisper of blueberry left behind. Angeline's mom took one look at the dress and fell to her knees with a damp napkin to clean the blue filling from the cheeks and hands of her little girl. Natalie laughed and treated us to a quick twirl, taking advantage of an Easter breeze toying with her ruffles. She was oblivious, but the rest of us were amazed.

"Now we're all here, and everybody's had enough to eat. Let's clean up and hunt Easter eggs," Jesse announced. "You guys hid a lot of stuff out here last night, right, PJ?"

"Uh, yeah, but the rain." I shrugged, not believing anything we hid could possibly be left after the storm.

Jesse smiled like I was the dumbest guy in Cunningham. "I've got a feeling it's gonna be okay. So how 'bout you and Kirby haul the trash inside and grab a few Easter baskets. I saw a whole stack of 'em somewhere."

God's Glory always gave out Easter baskets to the visiting children for the egg hunt, but I was sure those handing them out would be as stingy as the women serving lunch.

Kirby and I collected four big bags, threw them over our shoulders, and headed to the kitchen trash. We didn't say a word as we hauled the load across the yard. We hated leaving and were in a hurry to get back to Jesse's picnic. But the moment we dragged our bags inside and the doors swung closed behind us, we heard the storm outside beating down on the church like it never stopped. A heavy clap of thunder rumbled over the roof, the inside lights flickered, and the church windows were too thick with rain to see beyond. Kirby and I carried the trash down to find the God's Glory Easter baskets had all been given out to children running around wearing them as hats or using them to beat their sisters. Everyone looked ready to leave, if the weather outside would only let them go.

"Crap," Kirby muttered, eyeing some kids with baskets on their heads. "There aren't any left." For a minute I thought he was going to reach over, grab one away from some child, and make for the stairs like a purse-snatcher, but he didn't.

"It doesn't matter anyway," I sighed. "Listen to that rain. I'm sure Jesse has 'em back under the porte cochere by now, and besides, there's nothing left out there to hunt—not after all of this." I pointed to the ceiling.

Disappointment haunted us both as we climbed the stairwell out of the basement one more time. The storm was louder up here on the deserted first floor of God's Glory, and I wasn't looking forward to going back out in it. Everyone, including Natalie and Mr. Wallace, would be soaked to the bone by now, shivering under the porte cochere, perhaps waiting for another confrontation with the reverend or maybe the sheriff this time. My resolve to return to them softened with every rumble of thunder, and I started to think maybe I'd just stay inside.

"Hey, look at that!"

Kirby darted across the room, stumbling into the church information desk, nearly knocking it over. There were stacks of pamphlets about service times, Sunday school classes, and upcoming events on top, but it was the arrangement of red and yellow tulips that caught Kirby's eye. The flowers were magnificent, of course. The ladies of the Holiday Committee were experts at dressing the church for special occasions, but it wasn't the spray that had Kirby's attention—it was the Easter basket the flowers were sitting in. He righted himself and yanked the tulips out, leaving them strewn over the desk with their soily, wet bulbs soaking through the formerly neat piles of visitor information.

"I got a basket," he exclaimed, holding it over his head. "I don't know what good one basket will be, but we have one! Let's go!"

He was giddy with his find, and although skepticism still had a hold on me, an Easter basket in hand was enough to pull me back.

The wind whistled around the building as I followed Kirby out. I braced myself for the sting of damp spray. I held up my arm to shield my eyes, but instead of a deluge, I stepped into the same sunny day I'd left. I froze in the wonderment and terror of it all. Kirby bolted from where we were standing, galloping across the grass, holding his Easter basket above his head and yelling, "I've got one, I've got one!"

The people on the lawn turned to wait for him, folding around him as he reached them like he'd just crossed home plate. Laughter carried over the air to where I watched, thinking maybe I should go back inside, until Jesse called to me. I couldn't run like Kirby—my legs were too heavy—so I started with small, stiff steps until I was loose enough to stride out at a less awkward pace.

By the time I reached the Trackers, everyone, including the adults, had a basket. They smiled and bounced on their toes, anxious to hunt Easter eggs for the first time in their lives. Nya and Angeline already spotted a multitude of small treasures hidden in the yard and were chomping at the bit to launch out and collect all that was possible, but Jesse insisted they wait for me.

"All right, everybody," Jesse announced. "We have a couple of extra bags here, so when you fill up your baskets, come back and dump 'em in. You'll get a lot more that way, and it sure will make it easier to carry everything home."

From an old man all the way down to little Angeline, not a single one of those Trackers had ever been on an Easter egg hunt before, so even though they twitched with anticipation, they listened carefully to Jesse's instructions for fear of breaking egg-hunting rules. They clung fast to their colorful baskets, hanging on his every word and waiting for permission to go.

"Looks to me like there's a lot to be had out there, so I guess you better get to it," Jesse announced, but nobody moved. He turned to the side and waved them on. "Get going now. Go find something good."

A wave of laughter filled the air as the Trackers moved out into the lawn, bending over to recover treats hidden in the grass. Mr. Wallace, Kirby, and I stood beside Jesse watching the adults skip along as playfully as children, clutching their Easter baskets and filling them with goodies I was sure had washed away. The young ones weren't to be outdone, scurrying to and fro, screaming with glee every time they reached into the grass or under a bush to pull out a prize more delightful than they imagined. I saw John and Nya race across the yard toward something they both spotted, shouldering each other with joyful hoots until Nya reached the quarry first, snatched it up, and sent John tumbling to the ground. It was funny to see, and it made me smile. Natalie was helping Angeline, who plunked herself down in the middle of the fray and was now smeared with chocolate after thoroughly enjoying the first of her candy. I prayed she wouldn't try to hug Natalie again.

I watched the happy commotion, seeing no difference between the young and the old in the jubilation of the new experience. They were honest in their joy, and I was touched. As the cheerful noise hung over the yard, I couldn't understand how I'd ever been conditioned to see an egg hunt for anyone but children as disgraceful.

Kirby, Jesse, Mr. Wallace, and I held the extra trash bags for the Trackers to dump their treasures into when their baskets began to overflow. The old man hobbled over to me, his face wide with a toothless smile. I held up my bag for him to shake in all he'd gathered. I noticed a new hammer and a jar of applesauce among the candy he had collected. That seemed a little weird, and I wondered where he found it.

"Thank you," the old man said with a gummy grin before he skip-limped back to fill his basket once more.

As the Trackers returned trip after trip to deposit their goodies in the extra bags Jesse had me bring, I noticed powdered milk, beef jerky, aspirin, gauze, hand tools, and all manner of durables mixed in with the brightly colored candy. This was an afternoon of continual astonishment that, if left to me, would have remained just another stormy day, for I was so preoccupied with everything the rain washed away, I never imagined all it would leave behind.

When the bags were filled to the top with candy and staples that had never been hidden, and the last treat was pulled from the lawn, the day was done. I lamented its close. We shook hands, Natalie hugged everyone, and the Trackers took their treasures and made their way across River Road. We watched until their conversations faded and they were lost from sight. Jesse, Mr. Wallace, and Natalie said their good-byes and headed for home. Kirby and I went inside to find ourselves the primary suspects in the vandalizing of the information desk flower arrangement. The mashed potato lady led the investigation.

The storm lightened enough for the valet ministry to swing into action and release our Easter guests. The rest of us stayed to help clean up and drive home in the drizzle.

I lay in bed that night staring at the ceiling, considering the day, and listening to the storm trail away. I wrestled with my thoughts until I rationalized all that had happened and all I didn't understand. But even so, somewhere deep, I remained unsettled, knowing everything was changing but hoping I wouldn't have to choose. As it turns out though, the easiest way to deal with a moral dilemma is to avoid having one thrust upon you, although that's rarely possible. These things tend to catch you by surprise.

22
Science and Sorcery

Uh, where was I? I lost my thoughts for a moment…
"Maggie, sweetheart, is that you? Where are you, Mags? Where are you?!"

What is this place? This isn't the home. Is anybody gonna clean up? I'll get sick as a dog in here! Maggie's gonna have a fit when she sees where I am. It's disgusting, and she won't have it—she won't have it at all! Why do they think they can treat me like this? This whole thing makes me madder than hell!

"Maggie! Oh, Maggie, where are you, baby? Where are you? It's dark, it's dark in here!"

They can't make me stay. I'm leaving, and I'm leaving now. Off this chair, over to the door…open, open, damn it! Why won't this damn thing open? There we go, out to the porch…*ah*, a cool pleasant night. The moonlight makes everything look like a black-and-white movie, shaded but crisp and easy to see…much better than inside. Maggie loves the way azaleas sweeten the evening breeze this time of year. I'm sure she'll be along in a minute after she's done fussing with the dinner dishes. I'll sit down on these steps and wait for her. This must be our house.

"Hey, baby doll, would you mind putting some decaf on before you come out?"

I'd love a cup of coffee out here tonight. I don't know why I'm so sore and stiff; maybe more time has passed than I remember. I guess me and Maggie aren't spring chickens anymore, but if that's the case, how is it she's still the same as I remember, right on down to my favorite blue dress. She's right—she's always been right. There has to be a forever because even though I live in this aging, broken body, in my soul I don't feel one moment older.

"Are you coming, honey? The night's getting away from us!"

I've spent most of my life waiting on Mags.

I smell water. Oh yeah, I remember now. There's a lake here. I hear it lapping the bank and whispering to me from beyond the trees. A big fish must've jumped close by.

A lake, a lake…something's wrong.

"Maggie, are you coming? Where are you? Where are you, Maggie?"

A lake, a lake, water…water…my pills! Oh, God, my pills!

Let me dig 'em out of my pocket. One bottle empty—thank goodness I brought two. My eyes are too weak to read the dosage or any warnings taped around the container, so I'll just chew a handful before I lose myself again. There we go…these things work fast…I can feel myself clearing already, but it's unpleasant and it hurts.

"Good-bye, Maggie. I wish I could stay, but I have to finish. I'm scared though, because I know my confession will change me in your eyes. I'm so, so sorry, my dear, but I have to do this."

As a boy, I feared demons, goblins, and ghouls, but as I grew, I came to fear only tangible and temporal things that can't follow you past the grave. How is it I was so much wiser when I was young than I ever was as a man? Maggie used to tell me time heals all wounds, but she was wrong, because in eternity time heals nothing at all.

I have to get back to what I've come for, so let me collect myself while the medication finishes its magic. I have no idea what time it is now, but I can't afford to drift anymore, so I'll sit on these porch steps where the lake and the woods will be sure to prompt me if I lose my place again.

"PJ!" Reverend Dodge appeared in the doorway of the library-storage room to find me staring out the little window at the back. I must have lost myself somewhere in the trees gathering at the Chagrin. I jumped at his voice, startled, knowing I should have been doing something else.

"Well, young man, here's the paperwork for the judge. I've signed off on all your hours." He held up a paper for me to walk over and take. "I have a meeting with the head of the Hawkinsville Medical Center in a few minutes, so I'm letting you go early today. Consider it my gift to you for a job fairly done." He smiled without looking around.

"No orange cream soda today?" I asked.

"Not today." He shook his head and smiled. "Go on and take the rest of the day. I'll see you on Sunday…enjoyed having you here." He turned without waiting on a response and headed for his office.

I have to say I was disappointed, because today, being my last of service to the reverend, I was actually going to bring him an orange cream soda, if only to show I could have retrieved one at any time. But with being let go early and Reverend Dodge saying he enjoyed having me around, guilt tugged for the first time. The reverend was scribbling at his desk, so I waved a silent good-bye to the top of his head as I passed his door.

The outside felt like time served, and a free Saturday morning threw its arms around me like a long-lost friend. The weight fell away like winter clothes as I trotted to the Gas & Grocery to make small amends for my chronic rebellious prank. By the time I returned, voices from the reverend's office indicated his meeting with the guy from the medical center had already begun. With a cool orange cream soda in hand, I moved silently down the hall, debating whether or not to interrupt. I wanted to. I thought the reverend might appreciate the gesture. I leaned against the wall, shy of the office door, to consider it further. I could hear clearly all that was being said inside.

"So what are you saying, Doctor?" I overheard the reverend say. "The blind man we read about in the paper wasn't a hoax?"

"When that guy rolled in from getting hit by that bus, Reverend," answered an unfamiliar voice, "I was sure he was a goner. He wasn't responding to anything, but when that second bag of blood hit him, it was like somebody turned the lights back on. He started mumbling about being able to see and moving around on the table so much we had to sedate him several times to calm him down. It was like nothing I've ever seen. When he came to, he claimed he'd been blind from birth, kept thanking everybody, saying how pretty the nurses were, and begging to go outside. The next day, he was gone—never checked out. He just left. I have no idea how he managed it. He shouldn't have been able to walk for weeks. I chalked him up as another nut job, and when I saw he talked to the papers, well, that pretty much confirmed it for me."

"Okay, so what's that have to do with God's Glory?"

"Well, we don't have any way to trace our blood back to individual donors, but we do know when it was donated, and since we're a pretty small operation, the date on the tag lets us know where it was collected. Do you see what I'm saying? Anyway, the blood in that second bag came from Cunningham."

Reverend Dodge cleared his throat. "I'm still not following you, Doctor. Who cares where the blood came from?"

I decided not to interrupt. I wanted to lean over and peek through the cracked door, but I was afraid to give myself away, so I didn't move, satisfied to only eavesdrop.

"Okay, here's the thing," the stranger explained. "A few days ago, it happened again."

"What?" Reverend Dodge gasped.

"Only this time it happened to a girl, one of *my* patients with cystic fibrosis. I've been seeing her since she was an infant.

Reverend, CF is genetic, cannot be cured, and always ends badly. This girl had an accident; she needed some blood…and…well," the man sighed. "By the time she woke up from the operation…her CF was gone. I tested her and I tested her and I tested her again…but it was simply gone, cleared away, not even the slightest scar on her lungs, like she'd never had it." There was a pause. One of the men cleared his throat. "I can tell by the look on your face you don't fully understand, so let me be clear. To shed something like that, whether it is congenital blindness or cystic fibrosis, is totally and absolutely impossible."

The room fell quiet while the stranger waited on Reverend Dodge to digest the story. Then he whispered barely loud enough for me to overhear. "The blood I gave her was from our last drive in Cunningham." More silence. "So that's why I drove all the way down here to bother you on a Saturday. We need another blood drive as soon as possible to locate the donor. When can we do it?"

"We had a blood drive scheduled for the summer." I heard the reverend push his chair back from his desk to stand up. "But in light of what you've told me, I guess we'd better postpone it."

I was stunned.

"What!" The stranger's chair fell over as he came to his feet. "Why would you postpone it? Maybe you don't understand!"

"Do not raise your voice to me, Doctor!" the reverend threw back with the full force of his pulpit voice. "It sounds to me like you're toying with something dangerous—something *you* don't understand. So don't tell me what *I* need to do. What *I* need to do is keep my flock clear of your witch hunt!"

Reverend Dodge's outburst caught the stranger off guard, and I could hear the surprise in his voice when he answered the reverend's charge. "Witch hunt? I'm talking about medicine!"

"You're not talking about medicine, Doctor. You're talking about miracles, and there are no miracles outside of the church—only science and sorcery! I refuse to let you encourage or accuse us of the latter here! No, the blood drive is off!" Reverend Dodge's words were heavy and powerful enough to rattle the walls. I can't imagine how his guest wasn't knocked to the floor.

"I'm sorry you feel that way, but I don't need your permission to have a blood drive here in town."

The reverend seethed. "Oh, Doctor, you have no idea what you need down here. Set foot in my town again, come down here jeopardizing my flock with your ungodly talk of miraculous healings, and you'll spend a very long night or two with our Sheriff Johnson. You do not want to test this shepherd's devotion. Trust me on that."

The meeting was ending, and I certainly didn't want to be discovered outside the door. I started to retreat, but on an idiotic whim, I shook the reverend's orange cream soda as hard as I could and set it on the floor next to his office door before I left. I tip-toe ran down the corridor and around the corner before anyone knew I was there. I don't remember Reverend Dodge making any announcements canceling the Give Blood to God blood drive, but we never had one again and no one questioned why.

23
Prophecy at Sandy Shores

I stepped out as the stranger's angry steps came down the hall. He burst from the church behind me, banging through the door hard enough for it to come around and slap the outside wall. I could feel heat coming off the man as he bolted down the front steps. He jumped into a black sedan and took the street corner with squealing tires. He leaned on his horn as he maneuvered through the square and out to the road for Hawkinsville. I stood and watched as the Give Blood to God blood drive circled Cunningham like a drain before finally running out and disappearing on the only highway out of town. I wonder now if it was the decision of a single man that fated an entire community or if what was coming was already destined and as purposed as the Chagrin.

"Hey, PJ, you big dummy, you gonna stand there like a statue all day or what?" Kirby yelled from the passenger side of Jesse's truck.

I shook off everything I'd heard in Reverend Dodge's office and galloped down the steps to hang my head through the window. Natalie was sitting between Kirby and Jesse. It was good to see them.

"Hey, man." I smiled at Jesse. "Don't you know the sheriff don't allow this dented piece of crap on the square?"

"PJ," Natalie protested, "this here truck is my daddy's piece of crap, and you should be a more respectful young man than to say the word 'crap' around a lady." Then she threw her hand up to cover her mouth. "Please don't tell Daddy I said 'crap.'"

If she'd meant to, she couldn't have been funnier, and the three of us laughed just long enough not to hurt her feelings. The tops of her ears reddened, and she buried her face in her hands until we assured her we wouldn't tell her dad what she'd said.

"So what are you guys doing?"

Jesse leaned into the steering wheel so he could see me past Natalie and Kirby. "We're gonna grab some sandwiches at the Gas & Grocery, and then Kirby's gonna show me Sandy Shores. Natalie wanted to come along, so that's where we're headed."

"I'm the lady," Natalie announced, which was more untimely than random since I knew she was clarifying who I should be more respectful of. I nodded I understood as Jesse smiled and patted her knee. She bobbed her head and grinned. She was almost pretty sitting in the truck between my two friends.

"You know the water is still way too cold to get in. It'll be another few weeks before it's warm enough to even wade to the rocks."

"I know," Kirby agreed, "but Jesse ain't been down there yet, so we're just going to go. When are you done today?"

"I'm done for good right now."

"You want to jump in and ride down with us?" Jesse offered.

It was a ridiculous question; he'd barely finished asking before I'd swung myself into the truck bed and sat down on the wheel well. I banged on the side with an open palm to let Jesse know I was ready. We made a short stop at the Gas & Grocery, pulled out on to River Road, and finally maneuvered down the narrow gravel turnoff through the woods to Sandy Shores. My butt took every bump the old road had to offer as Jesse's truck crawled along under the tree branches.

I reached out and banged on the side to complain. "Are you trying to hit every single hole there is? You about broke my tailbone!"

"Yeah, that's one boo-boo even your mama wouldn't kiss," Kirby hollered out the window as the truck bounced again.

I slid down to sit with my back against the cab and stare out over the tailgate at the trail of dust following behind. I was uncomfortable, but it was better than being popped over the side.

When we finally made the clearing where everybody parks, there were already several pickups pulled in tight. Others were here ahead of us. I didn't recognize any of my friends' vehicles and it was too early for anybody from Uphill, so I figured the trucks belonged to church volunteers who'd come to tidy up before the weather warmed enough to attract seasonal guests. God's Glory was the self-proclaimed caretaker of this place, believing that pulling a few weeds and tightening up the picnic tables gave them a right nobody else shared. I hoped they wouldn't mistake me for a volunteer. Although my parents would love it, the last thing I wanted was to find myself yard working on my first free Saturday in months.

Jesse parked, and I hopped down as Kirby helped Natalie from the cab.

"Crap," I said, looking at the other trucks.

Natalie shot me a disapproving glance, and Kirby rolled his eyes with an exaggerated huff at my lack of discretion. I apologized for saying "crap" again in front of a lady.

Sandy Shores was the only place on the whole Chagrin safe enough to wade into the water without having to worry about dangerous eddies or undertows. Picnic tables and trash receptacles in need of annual repair loitered under shade trees, but the river didn't mind, at least not here. The Chagrin was calm and predictable around Sandy Shores, almost affectionate, offering this one spot along its banks and on its rocks for people to touch the water without the threat of being sucked to the bottom. Here, the river was patient, but its benevolence didn't last long. Just downstream the water was as capricious as ever, full of water devils and secret currents even the most accomplished swimmer could never manage.

We couldn't see the river from where we stood; it was still a few paces away over a small rise tapering down to the beach.

"Well, this stinks. When nobody's here, we usually drive right down to the water," Kirby explained to Jesse as we gathered in front of the truck.

"Looks like they're starting the cleanup already. Maybe we should head to the bridge or to the old cemetery instead," I suggested.

I wanted to leave before we were noticed and forced into yard service for God's Glory, but I should never have mentioned the old cemetery. It was just another place we weren't allowed to go, hidden back in the woods surrounded by a crumbling iron fence and irresistible to beer-drinking teenagers or younger boys on a dare. It's where Cunningham buried vagrants and undesirables.

"I ain't goin' to that creepy graveyard." Natalie threw her hands to her hips and stomped one foot. "You know as well as me that place is haunted full of scary spookies, and we ain't goin' out to that old bridge neither. You 'member what happened last time, and so do you, Kirby Braddock." She wagged a stern finger at Kirby in case he'd forgotten. "Jesse told Daddy we was comin' here, and so I can't be runnin' off somewhere's else when we told him I'd be right here! Besides, I got my picnic sandwich from Ms. Miller's gas store, and where else am I supposed to eat it?" She crossed her arms and scowled at me like she was my third-grade teacher. I didn't know what to say.

"No, it's okay, we're good right here," Jesse muttered without giving much attention to anything being said. He took a few steps and turned back to us. "Do you hear that?" He froze, and we all fell silent to listen.

There was faint shouting muffled by the noise of the river. A moment of concern stirred among us before Jesse broke for the rise. Kirby was at his heels. I took Natalie by the hand and pulled her stumbling along up the hill to where Jesse and Kirby had stopped.

Looking down, we saw seven or eight men armed with yard tools shouting out into the water. They were terribly agitated as they stomped along the cold Chagrin waving their shovels and rakes, but we were too far away to understand what was being said or why they were so upset. As I watched with Natalie's hand in mine, I wondered if this was some sort of bizarre ritual the cleanup volunteers of God's Glory observed before starting their chore. For a moment, they seemed so riled I thought they might sacrifice one of their own to the frigid river in order to appease the god of raking and weed pulling. I held my hand up to shade my eyes for a better look, and as a passing cloud pulled the glint from the Chagrin, I was able to see what had them so agitated.

Low in the chilly river, sheltered behind the boulders of Sandy Shores, bobbed the heads of a handful of Trackers who'd come to swim in the safe waters while they were still too cold for the rest of the world. The church party arrived at a terrible time and was now stalemated, wanting the Trackers gone without allowing them to leave. The shouting men sounded angrier, more dangerous, and far less comical after I saw children in the water.

Jesse and Kirby trotted down to the beach, and I did the same with Natalie in tow. She stumbled without complaint as I pulled her along. I think she enjoyed holding my hand.

I recognized most of the men as God's Glory ushers or from the Men's Group. I'm sure I never liked any of them.

"How in the hell do you expect us to get this place put back together with the likes of you down here!" a man holding a shovel shouted into the river.

"Don't you know you're trespassing? We're gonna go get the law if you stinkin' Trackers don't come outta that water right now! You hear me?" a man brandishing a sickle hollered in support of his shovel-wielding friend.

I'd never seen men so angry and out of control. I could feel Natalie's hand tighten in mine, or maybe mine tightened in hers, as we stood watching in disbelief while the Chagrin slipped past. Kirby stared wide-eyed, and Jesse stood like a statue carved without expression as we watched the self-proclaimed keepers of Sandy Shores lather into a deeper frenzy.

With all their fury aimed at the Trackers taking shelter in the water behind the cold rocks, the men didn't see us move in from behind. They fumed and huffed and kicked at the sand, but not one of them was crazy enough yet to wade into the freezing Chagrin for the trespassers. I was pretty sure we were safe with these men I'd grown up around, but pretty sure left a whisper of doubt seeping through my bones. I was terribly uneasy. I wanted to leave before we were noticed.

"Hello." Natalie, still holding my hand, stepped up and tugged on the sickle man's shirt. He wheeled around like he might strike her but, realizing who she was, dropped his arm and smiled instead.

"Fellas, fellas!" he called to the rest of the men, having to slap a couple on the shoulders to get their attention. "The kids are down here."

All the ushers of God's Glory except one turned around to look us over. They smiled the way they did when seating guests in the pews Sunday morning. It was weird and out of context. "What are you doin' here?" the sickle man asked.

"We got some sandwiches from Ms. Miller's gas store and come down for a nice picnic on this fine Saturday afternoon," Natalie told the men. "What are you doin' down here?" she asked back.

"We came to tidy up and make this a pretty place for everybody when it gets warm enough to swim," the shovel man answered like he was talking to a two-year-old.

"That so?" Natalie stared up into his face. "'Cause it don't look like you're doin' much more than pitchin' a fit and scarin' the birds away. Is something gettin' you in your clothes? We might can help you cut it out if you need."

The shovel man didn't know how to respond. He shot a glance to his friend with the sickle and shook his head.

"'Sides," Natalie continued, "we picked a terrible day for picnickin', and you all picked a worser one for yard workin' too." She paused to peer up into the cloudless blue sky. "'Cause we gonna get soppin' wet." The ushers of God's Glory looked upward for a moment as well and then chuckled among themselves at what a funny girl Natalie truly was.

"Here they come, here they come!" the man who didn't turn around hollered, and all of Natalie's audience wheeled around to see. The reprieve in the shouting fooled the Trackers into thinking it might be a good time to leave, but when the men saw John standing waist deep in the cold water with his hands on his head, their anger kindled again.

"You come on up outta there right now! You hear me, Tracker?" yelled the man who didn't turn around.

But John didn't trust the men on the beach, so he kept his distance as the Chagrin swirled around him like any other boulder.

"I got kids back behind these rocks, sir. We ain't doin' a thing but learning 'em how to swim. We didn't s'pect nobody to be here on such a cold river day, and I sure didn't know this was your property." John dropped his hands to the water. "It's so, so cold, I'm startin' to get a worry about the little ones. They been in too long, and I'm afraid they might be gettin' a chill in the bones. But, sir, I got to be real sure there ain't gonna be no trouble when I bring 'em on out."

"John! John!" Natalie screamed, but I held fast to her hand to keep her from plunging into the river.

"Hey, Miss Natalie," John called without taking his eyes off the man who didn't turn around, "you just stay on up there with your friends now, you hear me?"

She nodded to herself, and I adjusted for a tighter grip on her hand.

"You listen to me, Tracker. You get your hide up outta that river so you can fix all these picnic tables your people broke," the man who didn't turn around demanded.

"You know, sir," John answered, "we may live down on the river like the lilies of the field, dependin' on what comes for provision, but we're faithful and we're God-fearin' folks what respects the belongings of other men."

"I'm not gonna tell you again. Come on over to me, and I mean right now," the man who didn't turn around snarled as he raised a brush ax to his shoulder.

I remember thinking, *That's an odd way to hold a brush ax*, but a moment later my brain caught up with my eyes, and I realized the man who didn't turn around had drawn down on John with a 20-gauge shotgun.

"Things gonna change, by God, I know it…things gonna change for us all," John muttered as he raised his hands, and it sounded more like a prophecy than a prayer.

24
The Churchmen

I'd never seen a man aim a gun at another, violating everything I'd ever been taught about firearms. Numbness took my body from the hair follicles down, and even though I tried to hold on, I felt Natalie's hand fall away from mine. I seemed like a bit player in a movie with every twitch of my eyes being a slight break in the film. All vision in the periphery faded to black, so all I could see as the callous river flowed past was the man holding a gun on John.

"Buster, what are you doin'?" the shovel man yelled to his friend with the shotgun. But Buster didn't flinch as he stared over the barrel at John, aiming to put an end to the stalemate one way or another.

"You heard what I said, Tracker. Now you come up here like I told you and jail might be all that happens today," Buster demanded.

But John didn't move. He stayed where he was, not giving any further advantage to the man with the gun. Buster pulled the stock of the 20-gauge tight to his cheek, adjusted his grip, and caressed the trigger. The ushers protested and pleaded, but Buster was beyond anything they could say as a bead of sweat ran from his hairline to the crook of his broken smile. I swallowed hard. I couldn't believe what was about to happen.

"Hey, what are you doing? Stay put!"

I heard some of the churchmen squabble, but their voices dropped in and out of my ears, failing to yank me from the haze. I turned blankly to see them wrestling to restrain someone, but it wasn't until I saw Jesse pass right through their grasp and into the water that my senses returned, making every detail of what happened next as crisp as Maggie's wedding dress.

The yelling and protests of the ushers faded to babble, as if they had suddenly been cut to slow motion while the gurgle of the happy river filled my brain. It was like the Chagrin rolled over to have its belly scratched as Jesse descended into the water.

"Get outta there!" Buster yelled over his barrel as Jesse moved along the line of sight on his way to John. The only shot Buster had now was straight into Jesse's back, but that didn't seem to matter. The 20-gauge remained raised to the gunman's cheek.

"Put it down, Buster!" the sickle man yelled, but Buster didn't lower the weapon. He wasn't ready to give up just because an Uphiller strayed out where he didn't belong.

"Please, sir," John begged, "point that scatter gun somewhere else and not at this boy. Ain't none of us here fit to tie his shoes, much less see any harm come to him. Please, mister, I'll come out."

Jesse never turned back to face Buster or to ask for mercy; he simply waded out in a way that any shot fired at John would strike him first.

Perspiration made the shotgun slippery in Buster's hands, and when he twitched to shake off a sweat bee, we thought he'd fire. John grabbed Jesse, and with the power of his size, forced him under the water. Buster had a clean shot now, and he may have taken it if a squadron of mourning doves hadn't exploded from the woods the instant Jesse was immersed. They swooped low over the river like a cooing cloud of miniature gray angels obscuring the gunman's target. They circled twice and evaporated into the trees like avian ghosts.

I nearly jumped out of my skin, being caught so off guard by the mass of birds, and it's a wonder Buster didn't accidentally let off a round, as twitchy as he was. Instead, he dropped the gun to his waist and watched as the doves vanished as quickly as they had appeared.

"Wow," Natalie breathed, "and now for a soakin'."

Jesse came up out of the water, and the sky opened up with a deluge fierce enough to drive the churchmen off the beach and back to their trucks. When the last of them pulled off, the spring sun swept away the clouds and painted a perfect rainbow across the river. The sharp band of colors looked like something from a cereal box or a cartoon, tangible enough to think fairies had fashioned it as a bridge or a leprechaun was counting his gold somewhere in the distant cattails. Kirby fetched the sandwiches, and we swam and we ate more than we brought. There was enough for everyone.

The water was warm, and even though we were in long pants, Kirby and I gave swimming lessons to the little ones as Jesse, John, and Natalie talked on the beach. The sun favored those three together and seemed to save its brightest rays just for them. We laughed, and I even talked with Nya, which would have been easier if she wasn't so pretty.

As the Cunningham sun headed for the reeds, Natalie kicked off her shoes and eulogized our day with "Let's Go Down." Her voice floated like silk above the river. If we lived in an animated world, cute woodland creatures would have appeared shyly from the forest to sit and nuzzle one another at her feet, but as there were only real animals about, they remained invisible, contenting themselves to listen from the tree line.

Ordinarily it's odd for someone to break spontaneously into song, but not Natalie. All conversations dropped away as we stood listening in the water, captured by the only gift God gave the former angel of the church choir. When she finished, not letting go of her last pure note until it nearly pulled me over, she dropped her chin to her chest, and the world fell silent except for the purr of the Chagrin. I was exhausted, but I felt good, like I had just gotten out of a hot shower. I wiped away an unconscious tear with the back of my hand. The fading sunshine skipped over the river and shimmered across her dress. I stood in the quiet water watching Natalie with her head bowed. She was easily the most beautiful person I'd ever seen. It didn't seem right to say anything until she did, so we waited as she slowly raised her head and smiled. I anticipated something remarkable.

"That, that, that, that's all folks," she giggled as she danced up into the sand.

Kirby slapped himself in the forehead, rolled his eyes, and fell backward into the water. Natalie snorted up a big belly laugh. I wanted to splash her, but I didn't know how that would go over, so I copied Kirby instead, throwing Natalie's laughter into the next gear for a moment longer. When she slowed, Jesse took her in a full embrace, brushed her hair back, and whispered something in her ear. She nodded. John patted her head, but before he could move away, she threw a tight hug around his waist. Nya, Angeline, and the others moved out of the river to see Natalie as well. They thanked her. Natalie told them they were welcome.

The day concluded the way Easter had, with us all going separate ways. But as we walked back to Jesse's truck, this time he asked us not to tell anyone about the day's events. We agreed, and Natalie did too.

25
The Secret Meadow

The next day at church, the shovel man, the sickle man, and Buster were handing out bulletins in the narthex. They smiled like they didn't know who I was, but I knew them…*cowards and bullies.*

My parents demanded I respect adults, but because of these men, I never made the same requirement of my own children. By parental decree, my kids had to be polite to grownups, but something as valuable and fragile as respect had to be earned, even by their elders. I never saw being honorable or being a turd as contingent on age, so good manners was as much as I was willing to demand. I figured my kids would choose to respect more-deserving people than I could force on them by a blanket rule they would never embrace anyway. I don't think Maggie ever appreciated my perspective on the matter, and maybe I was wrong, but what's done is done.

Kirby was sentenced to several weeks of cleaning off pews and stacking chairs in the basement after church for his crimes against flower arrangements on Easter Sunday. Although I was a suspected accomplice, Kirby admitted to the caper solo, keeping another black mark off my already tainted slate. His punishment was easy and straightforward, amounting only to a half-hour on Sundays, and because I felt a little guilty for Kirby taking the full blame, I didn't mind helping him out.

By the time we emerged from church, nearly everyone had gone home or to the diner, so the parking lot was all but empty. There were a few stray cars sprinkled about, waiting on the remaining saints who were likely tied up in a meeting about a meeting about something. I'm sure someone was taking notes.

Kirby and I were headed to Mr. Wallace's farm to help Jesse with his apiary. He told us he'd already picked up a few swarms, but Jesse was afraid if we didn't jump on the rest pretty quick, he'd have some empty bee boxes, and it would be a shame if the full twelve hives didn't make. Of all things, beekeeping seemed to be at the farthest edge of what I would expect from a carpenter. I can't imagine why that struck me as so odd above everything else.

"Okay, lead foot," Kirby cautioned, pulling himself into my truck, "keep it at the speed limit so we don't go sliding through Natalie's yard again."

I rolled my eyes and cranked the engine. "I'll do my best, buddy, but it all comes down to the spirit of the road." I gave him a slow smile and stomped the accelerator, throwing the truck into a fishtail as we tore out onto the street. "Yeehaw!" I yelled and slapped Kirby on the leg with a big laugh.

"Damn it, asshole," Kirby snapped, adjusting himself in the seat. "You haven't learned shit, have you?" He glared at me, and I tried not to look back. "What are you gonna do when you kill somebody? What then, huh?"

"I'm just kidding, Kirby. Don't be such an old woman. Gah-lee! If I didn't know better, I'd think I was riding with my grandmother. You want me to drop you at the knitting circle?" I slammed my open palm down on the steering wheel and shot him a cool glance before turning my attention back to the road.

But Kirby already said what he had to say and was now staring out the window, not listening to any of my stupidity. I stepped on the gas to provoke him once more, but he kept silent as we sped out past the "Natalie" signs along River Road.

I let my speed drift upward and out of bounds, but this time I took the curve in front of the Wallace place with confidence and control, emerging blindly on the other side with nothing but clear pavement ahead. It never crossed my mind there could be a slow-moving tractor or animal in the road as I gunned around the bend—maybe because there never was. Dumb luck looked after me back then.

The blackberries along the tracks looked as big as plums as I slowed to find a turnoff onto the property. I didn't realize Mr. Wallace owned so much land. Except for the piece he'd grown on last year, he'd let his farm rest fallow a long while. I was amazed to see it now plowed in and planted. Even with John's help, I couldn't imagine how he'd done it and still kept up with his business in town, or how he would ever find time to harvest everything that was growing now.

I spotted Jesse's tiny truck parked under a stand of trees deep on the Wallace place. I touched the brakes and eased off River Road. The field between us was wide, and the grass was bumper deep. I pulled to a stop and leaned into the windshield to figure the best way across.

"Over there." Kirby pointed to a path farther down.

I nodded, wheeled the truck around, and we bounced and squeaked across the grassy expanse toward the trees on the far side. The pasture was much larger than I thought, and by the time we rolled up, the trees that looked like they belonged to a model train set from the road turned out to be a sturdy grove of seventy or eighty ancient pecans. I pulled up beside Jesse's vehicle and parked. Kirby popped his door and stepped out. I followed.

"Wow," Kirby gasped, "it looks like we drove into a fairy tale."

A breeze brushed by and scurried under the orchard's skirt, kicking up a few fallen leaves before vanishing altogether. I couldn't tell if it was friendly or not.

The grove was old and had been left to herself a long time, but unlike her haphazard cousins growing in the forest, she was disciplined. Her canopy may have been tangled, but her tree trunks held formation, like a silent phalanx ready to turn and slap your hand for picking her fruit.

Bathed in shade and matted in clover, the orchard seemed surreal, like it had been transplanted from a dream or somebody's imagination to catch Kirby and me in a spell—and it did. We stepped in. The temperature, the fragrance, the hue, and every other change under the trees was a comfortable one, meant to go unnoticed and seduce us further. I'm not sure if it was novelty or magic that drew us along, but before either of us realized it, we'd wandered to the middle of the grove without calling for Jesse once.

"Hey, guys, we're over here!" Jesse waved to us from the back edge.

"How come we didn't know about this place?" Kirby whispered as we made our way out of the trees.

I didn't know, and I didn't have a chance to say before we emerged to find Mr. Wallace, Jesse, and John standing together in the adjacent meadow. A cloud's shadow slid along the wild grass, clearing the sun just as we stepped out from the grove. It was as if someone flipped on a light when we entered the room.

The field was far away from the rest of the world, sprinkled in wildflowers and clover, gated at the front by the ancient pecans and guarded at the rear by thick briars and twisted underbrush. Jesse's bee boxes were standing white and fresh at one corner, and a neatly built deck had been constructed in the middle. Up on posts about two-and-a-half feet high, the rectangular wooden structure looked like a stage sticking up from the matted grass. I realized immediately it was the foundation of whatever Jesse was building for Mr. Wallace. There was a pickup parked alongside loaded with lumber.

The day was breezy and pleasant, and Natalie was playing chase with Angeline and a few other Tracker children. They climbed up on the short end of the foundation and ran across the deck, leaping off the other side into the grass. The children laughed hard, and they didn't stop when Kirby and I showed up.

The woman with them watched us intently as we approached the commotion. I didn't see Nya anywhere.

"Watch me, watch me!" a boy called when he caught sight of us and then bolted across the deck, launching himself into the air as high and far as he could go. His momentum sent him rolling through the straw and black-eyed susans before he stood up giggling to make sure we witnessed his flight.

Kirby clapped, and I shot the boy a thumbs-up, catalyzing a whole chorus of "Watch me, watch me!" as the other children sought to impress us by outdoing the first. We continued to be an approving audience as we crossed the meadow to where Jesse and the two men applauded the children as well.

"Good gracious, Mr. Wallace, your place looks great!" Kirby exclaimed as we got closer.

Mr. Wallace turned to greet us. "Well, thank you. I'm afraid I haven't had it in very good use for a long time, but it really seems to be coming along, thanks to this man here." Mr. Wallace smiled and put his hand on John's shoulder. "He's done a remarkable job."

John dropped his eyes to the ground with the praise, but I could still see the smile on the big man's face. "Thank you, sir. You been real good for letting me and mine have a chance to work your property," he answered without looking up.

"Please don't thank me. Please don't ever thank me," Mr. Wallace murmured.

John glanced up enough to give a short nod before his eyes fell back to the ground. I had a sense they'd talked about this before, and I think John wasn't used to being on the right side of a grateful man.

"Look at me, look at me!" Natalie shouted as she ran across the deck. We all looked up just in time to see her leap directly at John. "Catch me!" she screamed with delight as she sailed through the air. The big, unsuspecting man barely had enough time to react, but even so, he easily plucked Natalie from the sky before she tumbled to the ground.

"Good catch, John," Natalie giggled.

John secured her in his arms. "You scared the fool out of me, Miss Natalie. You have to give me some sort of warning next time, you hear?"

"Natalie, don't you do that again!" Mr. Wallace scolded. "What in the world were you thinking? That's a great way for someone to get hurt."

Natalie glanced at me and Kirby. Shame rippled through her eyes. She stuck out her bottom lip and turned to her father. "It was still a good catch, Daddy," she muttered as John set her to the ground.

Seeing Natalie in John's arms stirred a haunting memory deep in my stomach. The day on the bridge seemed a million miles away, and maybe it was to everybody but me. A switch threw in my brain, and I finally realized why John was here and why Mr. Wallace was letting him work his property and why John wasn't supposed to say thank you. The association of Mr. Wallace and John was understandable, but it wasn't common knowledge in Cunningham, and I knew why. I grew up here, and I knew all about the laws of tradition and what happens to those who break them.

"I didn't know you had pecans," Kirby piped up. "Your grove is beautiful."

"I'm glad you think so," Mr. Wallace said with a nod, "but those old trees were long past producing when I bought this place years ago. I'd had a mind to cut 'em down, but Natalie's mom, well, she liked 'em. She'd come out here and sit under 'em, even after she got sick. She said they weren't hurting anything way out here, so I just let 'em go."

Kirby looked back over his shoulder to the stand of trees. "So you're saying you don't get anything at all out of that big orchard?"

"Not one single nut, young man, not one single nut."

"Too bad," Kirby sighed.

"So whatcha got going here?" I asked as I reached over and slapped the top of the deck.

"That's the beginning of the new bunkhouse." Jesse pushed himself up to sit on the edge of the structure as the children raced around on top. "Yeah, we got a well predrilled over there." Jesse pointed to some spot in the field. "We're thinking about putting in a windmill to pump it. We'll bring in a gas tank for cooking and a stove for heating the place when it gets cold."

"Sounds like a pretty big job."

"It's a little bigger than I thought." Jesse shrugged, "Sometimes these things have a tendency to grow on you. Ain't that right, Mr. Wallace?"

Mr. Wallace smiled and nodded to confirm the job was bigger than he thought too.

"Anyway," Jesse continued, "it should house twenty easy, and if the weather is good to us and we don't waste too much time, the whole thing should be done before summer's out." He slid to his feet. "But you guys aren't here for the bunkhouse today. We need to finish up these hives."

I glanced over his shoulder at the dozen bee boxes standing at the back end of the field. I could see activity in almost every one of them. "Looks like you got a lot of bees already."

"Yeah, I couldn't wait on you guys to get free, so Nya and I filled all but three of 'em."

"Nya?"

"You know, John's daughter." Jesse gazed over the apiary. "She's an honest-to-goodness bee charmer…been trading honey at the Gas & Grocery for years. I wouldn't have a single swarm without her. But we're going it alone today. You guys ready?"

I wasn't sure if I was ready to mess with a bunch of bees or not, but Jesse didn't wait for me to say so. He started toward the grove, turned around, and taking a couple steps backwards, hollered, "See you later! Wish me luck!"

A chorus of "See you later, Jesse! Good luck, Jesse!" threaded with giggles followed in response.

Mr. Wallace, John, and the woman waved us out as Jesse turned back. Kirby and I followed him into the trees. We trotted a few steps to catch up.

I didn't like bees, but I didn't want to sound like a pansy, so I was glad when Kirby spoke up as we headed for the trucks.

"Hey, Jesse, do the honey bees we're catching bite?"

"Nope"

I felt better.

"Really, they don't bite?" Kirby seemed surprised.

Jesse shook his head. "No, Kirby, they really don't bite."

Kirby and I exchanged a silent glance of relief.

"They don't bite at all," Jesse continued. "They sting."

"They sting!"

"When they get mad."

"Are we gonna wear bee suits or something?"

I was thinking the same thing, but I was happy to let Kirby do the asking.

"Nope."

"How do we keep from getting stung?"

"Don't get 'em mad."

"Oh...okay."

I don't know if the "don't get 'em mad" strategy made Kirby feel any better, but it certainly didn't do much for me.

We piled into Jesse's truck and bounced across the field to River Road. He wheeled his truck toward town.

"I only parked my truck out front of the grove so you could see it. Next time you guys can pull on through to the site, okay?" Jesse kept his eyes on the road as he talked.

He didn't seem to be in a hurry as we rolled along, and the growing anticipation of messing with bees made me good with our leisurely pace. There's something to be said for delaying the inevitable.

26
The Court of the Dinosaur Tree

I cleared my throat, breaking the silence as the farmland gave way to the buildings of Cunningham. "So, no bee suits?"

"Nope," Jesse shook his head without looking over, "not even gonna smoke 'em." I wasn't sure what that meant, but it drew a nervous sigh from Kirby.

We pulled through the back of town, behind the church, and finally turned off where we go for Tracker Bridge. Jesse parked, and we got out.

"Grab one," Jesse instructed as he reached into the bed of his truck and hoisted out a wooden box. The top was framed window screen with a hinge and a hasp so it could pivot back but be locked down securely when it was closed. Kirby and I reached in and pulled out the other two. "Ready?" Jesse asked. "Let's go." Then he turned and headed down the path toward the bridge.

The woods were cool, and the sound of the river grew in my ears as we trailed Jesse with our boxes. I'd been down here a million times, but it never occurred to me where we were going today until Jesse crossed over the old bridge and through the brush on the far side without missing a step. He was gone, and left to ourselves, standing in the middle over the swirling water below, Kirby and I stopped to consider the boundary. Kirby's eyes were on the far bank where Jesse disappeared, but mine drifted downstream where John had saved Natalie a year ago. "Coward," the river whispered, but Kirby didn't hear because the Chagrin was talking to me.

Jesse reappeared from the brush. "What are you guys waiting on? Let's go get these babies boxed." He gave us a "come on" head-wave and pushed back through the bushes.

We weren't supposed to be on the bridge, and the most I'd ever been on Tracker Island was the day Jesse and I stacked the lumber. I was scared to go farther—I guess the river was right—but when Kirby started to move, I shifted the box in my arms and followed along. I noticed new lumber on the bridge, nailed there to postpone its collapse. The white wood looked like a band aid on a broken arm. I guess someone else also believed the inevitable was worth delay.

Butterflies woke in my stomach. This island was filled with generations of lore and absolutely forbidden to everyone but the sheriff and his deputies, who crossed on occasion to roust the people living here. "Have to keep 'em in place, let 'em know who's boss," I'd heard Sheriff Johnson laugh with his deputies over coffee at Katie's Diner. So even though I was supposed to be in my rebellious years, I was finding it difficult to overcome all I had been taught as a child. Kirby wasn't worried about anything but the bees, and Jesse marched on across like he'd been here a thousand times before. Maybe he had. I shuffled up behind Kirby, and we pushed our way through the thicket to find Jesse waiting.

"Come on, granny-one and granny-two. Let's get movin'. I can hear 'em up there buzzing like crazy, and I don't want 'em taking off on us." Jesse smiled impatiently and turned to press his way through another curtain of brush. We filed in behind him like a couple of box bearers on safari. I did my best to be quiet as we cracked through the bushes…I'm not sure why.

We emerged on a narrow, deeply furrowed path sloping upward and disappearing around a bend in the thicket.

"I didn't see any poison ivy. Did you see any poison ivy?" Kirby huffed.

I shook my head no.

The going was better on the path, although the dirt was crunchy and the sides collapsed easily into the ankle-deep ruts. I stumbled several times in a mini avalanche when the path gave way and threatened to keep my shoe. I don't know how Kirby managed to stay up, but he did.

Tracker Island wasn't very big, so it didn't take long to get where Jesse was going. We wound around a couple times, dense underbrush on either side, moving uphill, stumbling but not falling, filling our shoes with sand, until we reached the pinnacle of the island—the high ground, never touched by flood—and on it sat the ruins of the greatest tree I'd ever seen.

The ancient trunk was about ten feet tall with nothing above but open sky, testifying to its former reach. All else had been toppled and long since carried away by time and the river. Where the tree had been broken away, gnarled spires of twisted wood reached upward like a jagged crown in remembrance of previous glory. The old trunk was as wide as it was tall, and its exposed roots looked like the claws of a dragon, perched and holding fast to the meat of the earth. The deep wooden wrinkles of the prehistoric tree held ages of stories, perhaps even some the river didn't know, and if I hadn't been so awestruck by its terrible beauty, I might have expected to catch a whiff of cookies baked by elves inside. If that were possible, this is where it would happen.

Humble briars and underbrush didn't dare to grow too close, staying beyond the reach of the crawling roots as if to keep court out of fear or tradition. The dinosaur tree lived and died ages before Cunningham ever graced the banks of the Chagrin, and standing in its shadow now, I had a sense its dark, ligneous bones would remain long after the town was dust.

"Here we are," Jesse announced. "It's a pretty big tree, huh?" He set his box down among the monstrous roots. "There's probably five, six, maybe seven hives right here in this one stump."

I noticed bees vectoring in from every direction, dropping down, hovering, and lighting to pass through some dark, hidden entrance in the tree. They paid no attention to us as they buzzed in and out of their fortress to and from the adventures of honeybees. The old king tree protected them, and they protected it, for anyone taking an ax to this trunk would be sprayed with ten million bees. And looking up at the swirl of comings and goings, both high and low, around the middle, and on all sides, I knew Jesse was right; the massive stump was an apiary all on its own, maybe as many as seven hives strong.

Kirby couldn't take his eyes off the tree. "Uhhhhh, Jesse, what are we gonna do without bee suits?"

"Don't worry," Jesse said with a grin. "There's so many bees in this thing, even a suit of armor wouldn't protect you very long."

Okay, that's a terrible reason not to worry, I thought, but I kept my mouth shut and let Kirby express our mutual fear.

"Besides, what we need to do is pretty much done. Take a look." Jesse pointed to something hanging dark and heavy in the thick privet just beyond the tree's roots. It was smaller than a cinderblock, appearing to be a tuft of dry leaves thatched by a bird or maybe a squirrel.

"Get your box and come on," Jesse whispered to Kirby. They moved toward the bushes, and I followed with my box. Kirby gasped to a halt. Jesse put his hand on the back of Kirby's neck and gave him a gentle shake. "Just relax, buddy. This is gonna be easy. No problem."

As I came up from behind, I saw what I supposed to be a clump of leaves was really a teaming column of bees, humming and swaying on the end of a small branch. I gulped. The scene was right out of a horror movie where instead of running away, a couple of idiots do something stupid and wind up with bees flying up their noses and stinging them in the brain. It never ends well. I was glad Kirby was going first, even if all it meant was I would be the last to die.

Kirby and Jesse moved closer, but after seeing what was ahead, I decided to hold back.

"Okay," Jesse instructed, "open your box and hold it underneath."

Kirby was shaking but did as he was told. Jesse fished a knife from his pocket, reached up above the swarm, and cut the branch. The bees fell to the bottom of the box like eight pounds of ground beef. I could tell Kirby was scared, but he held on, and not a single bee flew out. Kirby exhaled and set the box to the ground so he could swing the screen lid shut, but Jesse kneeled down to stop him.

"Be careful," Jesse cautioned, leaning over to sweep a couple of stray bees into the box with his bare hand. "You don't want to squash a single one. If you do, it'll give off the scent of danger, and buddy," Jesse's eyes locked into Kirby's, "that's the best way of all to get 'em mad."

"Don't get 'em mad, that's the plan," Kirby stammered. "It's a good plan."

He watched Jesse tend the quarry, but as his uneasiness began to wane, Kirby reached over to help brush the last few bees into the box. Then he closed the lid as cautiously as if he were diffusing a bomb.

We found two more swarms rallying in the bushes, and Kirby, confident with success, volunteered to help Jesse with both. I was happy to let him. We shoved twigs in the hasps to secure the tops, lifted our boxes of bees, and left the court of the old tree, following Jesse a different way back to the bridge.

Kirby was giddy as we wound down the back side of the island on a cleaner, better traveled path. He kept asking his bees if they might have honey to spare in the best little bear voice he could manage. As irritating as he was, his imitation was dead on. Jesse walked in silence, and I had nothing to say, so only Kirby's one-sided conversation with the honeybees broke the hush of Tracker Island.

"Oh, honeybees, my honeybees, I would be most grateful if you might have a small taste of honey for a hungry bear," he repeated over and over like he was rehearsing for a part in a play.

As we neared the river, the brush began to thin enough to see through to the banks on the other side. Kirby finally shut up as Jesse traipsed ahead without giving notice to anything to the left or right of the trail. But, having only been here in rumors and nightmares, Kirby and I slowed to a shuffle and stared through the blind of twisted trees and underbrush. What we saw captured us.

The river went to a murky crawl as a bog of weeds and cattails choked the life from the Chagrin. The river wouldn't split around the island for many more years before this side was dammed in silt and muck, good for little more than mosquitoes and pollywogs. Without so much as a second thought, the Chagrin would put all its effort into the Cunningham side, gurgle past, losing this part of itself like a tree loses a rotten branch. Dust lay on the decrepit river like gray hair, and the smell of slow-moving water filled my nose. It smelled…old.

Along the bank, we could see a shallow lean-to made of a rusty piece of corrugated steel and burlap bags. A low fire was burning at its entrance, and a string of worn-out clothes hung drying from a line in the trees just beyond—everything from men's overalls to a tiny dress. A big piece of canvas was draped into a makeshift tent, half in the trees and half on poles, with dirty, worn-out bath towels and sheet plastic thatched together for its sides. An eclectic pile of broken pots and dishes was neatly stacked outside, as if someone still found value in the hopeless mess. There was an old, warped dresser leaning against a tree and a one-eyed baby doll with a cracked face leaning against it. Patient milk jugs floating in the lethargic river marked a trout line, and a string of black catfish hung from a pole by the lean-to. The whole place looked like the Chagrin had detoured through the Cunningham dump and discarded all it was tired of carrying right here. If not for the fish and the fire, I would never have guessed anyone lived here at all.

We stood gaping from behind the thicket, remaining hidden but at the same time taking in the whole scene as clearly as if it were being played out on stage.

Kirby nudged me and raised a slow finger to point out something I hadn't noticed until just then. Directly opposite the tent and the fish and the fire and all the broken dishes, about five feet high, up on stilts, stood a freshly pink-painted, powder-blue-shuttered, shingle-roofed playhouse. It would have been the pride of the most well-to-do child in Cunningham.

The house was a contradiction, standing surreal in this place as if it belonged somewhere else, like when they mix cartoons into movies. I stared and tried to comprehend. Somehow, the pink playhouse frightened me more than the old tree full of bees. Maybe it was a Hansel and Gretel thing, or maybe because it declared something unafraid of Cunningham tradition, or maybe it was the water moccasins hanging like Christmas stockings from a clothesline woven through the supports underneath.

"What is that?" Kirby whispered. "It's like voodoo."

"I don't know," I whispered back, "but it's scary as crap. Why would they do that?"

"Protect it. Ward off evil spirits. Summon the dead. Curse their enemies. Witchcraft…maybe." Kirby's voice was shaky, and I knew he wasn't trying to be funny. He and I were raised on the same stories about Trackers and the hidden things they do.

I adjusted my grip on the box of bees. I'd never seen so many dead snakes before.

River chickens.

My heart leapt into my mouth, and Kirby jumped back, stumbling over his own feet but catching his balance and holding onto his bees. I heard it in my brain as much as I heard it in my ears. I whirled around to find Jesse standing behind us.

"They're river chickens." Jesse nodded to the vipers hanging from the playhouse. "At least that's what Nya calls 'em."

"River chickens?" I breathed.

"Look out there. The water moves like molasses, and the swamp, well, it's right on top of the camp. This place was custom-made for leeches and snakes—it's like snake Valhalla down here. I think every snake in the state comes right here to vacation—and then decides to stay and raise a family. I'm saying it like it's funny, but it's not. This place is overrun with river chickens, and they're aggressive. Did I tell you guys to watch your feet?"

I shook my head. *Snakes.* "What are they gonna do with them?"

"They call them river *chickens*, PJ. What do you think they do with them?" Jesse's voice cracked for the first time since I met him. "They do…what they have to do."

"Where'd the house come from?" Kirby asked.

"Scraps from the church…just scraps from the church." Jesse shook his head and looked to the ground. "Now come on. Nya's about to come out of that tent to finish her chores and start dinner, and it's not your place to see her do it. Besides, we've got bees to tend to, so let's get moving."

I almost asked Jesse why we'd walked around the island instead of going straight back to the bridge, but I didn't want to appear any dumber than I already did, so I kept my mouth closed. Only the bees hummed their farewells to Tracker Island.

We set our wooden boxes carefully in the truck and rode to the Wallace farm the same way we left the island—without a word. Jesse pulled across the field, through the pecan grove, and into the secret meadow to find it empty except for the tireless honeybees of the apiary working like they understood forever.

I helped lug the new swarms down to the rows of bee boxes, but sat up on the deck and watched from a distance as Jesse and Kirby transferred the honeybees to their new homes. Jesse talked as he worked, and Kirby nodded, eager to learn and amazed at all he had accomplished that day. Although I couldn't hear anything passing between them, it was easy to tell they were content, and from my spot across the meadow, I was too. This was a good place, and even though I had no idea what it would come to, I was ready for school to be out so I could help Jesse build it.

27
Kirby's Mom

Season to season seems to drag by when you're young and rich with time, but in reality, things move as quickly as if they never happened at all, with only ghosts of memories testifying otherwise. Some are kind and some are wicked, but one thing I know—*all* ghosts lie. I'm sure the weeks from that spring to that summer were painfully slow, wrought with all the ordinary tribulations high school boys of my time faced. But those memories are incidental, unworthy, and buried too deep for even my memory pills to resurrect. I can only hope if I need to remember, I will, but for now the next thing I recall is Saturday morning—the first day of summer vacation.

"Good morning, early bird," Mom sang from the stove as I came into the kitchen. "I was going to let you sleep in this morning now that you're going to be a senior and all." She smiled. "Have a seat. I'll make you some oatmeal."

I pulled a chair from the kitchen table and did as she asked. I wasn't crazy about her oatmeal. It had a funny taste no amount of cinnamon, brown sugar, or milk could cover, and she always served it in a bowl big enough for Papa Bear. I shoveled in spoonful after spoonful until I was full to the gills, yet the trough of Mom's viscous goo never showed any signs of my progress. It just ran back down, reclaiming whatever void I'd left with my spoon, mocking me and refusing to recede in the slightest. Mom's oatmeal was magic, but not in a good way. Whenever I slowed, she'd encourage me to continue eating by saying it was good for me and it would stick to my ribs, and she was right, if what she really meant was it would bloat me and stick to my colon. I loved Mom, so I did my best to keep the complaints to a minimum, finding now the discomfort I suffered at the hands of that sinister gruel a small price to pay for the sweet memory of her oatmeal.

"Thanks, Mom, that'll be great," I answered.

She busied herself with my breakfast a few moments longer and then joined me at the table to wait with her coffee. She took a sip and smiled.

"So what are your plans today?"

"Remember, I have to do some work for Mr. Wallace on account of the accident."

"That's right," she nodded, "I'd forgotten all about that. It seems like such a long time ago. Do you think you have to go out there on a Saturday, your first day off?"

"Probably," I shrugged. "Farmers don't seem to care what day it is."

The water started to boil on the stove.

"They sure don't," Mom agreed as she put her cup down and stood to mix my oats into the pot. "Toast?" she asked over her shoulder.

"Yes, ma'am, thank you." I paused as she continued to fuss. The comfortable smell of percolated coffee filled the morning kitchen, and I thought maybe I'd start drinking it over the summer. "I'll run by Kirby's house on the way out to see if he wants to go with me," I added.

Mom's back was toward me as she stirred my oatmeal and waited on the toast to pop. "How's Kirby doing?" she asked without looking around.

"Okay, I guess."

Mom turned slightly, half to me, half to the stove, still stirring. "Do you really think he'll want to spend the day on a dirty old farm after the news this week? I'd imagine he might want to stay close to home."

"What are you talking about, Mom?"

She reached to the cupboard for a bowl, the big one, set it on the counter, and turned back to the oatmeal.

"You know, Ms. Braddock hasn't been feeling well for a while now. Reverend Dodge has been visiting a lot." Mom paused to ladle my breakfast from the pot to the bowl. "And well…she went up to the medical center a few weeks ago for some tests."

Mom paused again to retrieve a spoon from the silverware drawer and grab the cinnamon and brown sugar from the pantry. She set them in front of me and took her cup to pour some more coffee. She leaned back against the kitchen cabinet for a sip, watching me stare at her over the box of brown sugar. "Are you sure Kirby didn't tell you this?"

"Tell me what?"

She took a slow sip with both hands around her cup, as if she was about to do something she'd rather not. "We've already set up prayer circles, and the Women's Group at church will be ready to start making dinners as soon as it gets worse. I'm so sorry. I know you and Kirby are good friends."

"Mom, what is it?"

"Leukemia," she whispered into her coffee as she took another halfhearted sip, but I heard it anyway.

The toast popped. Mom buttered it and brought me a glass of orange juice. Then she sat with me and watched me watch my breakfast until it was too cold to eat.

28
The Windmill

Even though it was early for teenagers, the heat of the day had already chased away all remnants of a cool morning. I couldn't believe how hot it was, and I hoped this wouldn't be the prelude to a blistering summer working at the farm. I rumbled up to Kirby's house and threw the truck into Park. Ordinarily I'd just honk for him, but after what Mom said, I figured I'd better knock this time. I didn't know what I was feeling, but I knew it should hurt, so I wanted to seem like it did. I opened my door to get out, but before my feet hit the pavement, Kirby came bounding out of the house like he was running down an ice-cream truck. He loped over the lawn, slung open the passenger door, and sprung into the seat. He was excited and smiling wide. I watched from my perch half in and half out of the truck.

"What's wrong?" he asked.

I pulled myself into my seat and closed the door. This was not what I expected. Maybe Mom heard it wrong.

"We're headed to the Wallaces', right?"

I nodded we were, still stunned by his demeanor. He bounced in the seat, drumming happily on the dashboard a few moments before noticing my stare. *Curiosity, disappointment, or horror. Which one was pasted across my face?*

"What's wrong? Come on, let's get out of here. It's been a long time, and I can't wait to see how the bees are doing. Gah-lee, it's hot already. It's gonna be a hot summer, don't you think?" He drummed on the dash again looking at me, bright eyed and grinning. "What are you waiting for? Let's go."

I pushed the shift into Drive, and we rolled through town and out to River Road without conversation. Kirby tapped on the dash and bobbed his head singing some stupid song under his breath. I didn't understand, and he didn't notice when I took the curve in front of the Wallace place too fast and nearly clipped a stray dog on the other side.

I was supposed to be working for Mr. Wallace, but it never crossed my mind to stop at the main house to check in with him. Instead, I pulled over on the shoulder to look for a way across the field to the secret meadow beyond. I spotted a path matted through the tall grass, so I pressed the gas and turned in. I stepped on the brake as my windshield filled with the Wallace farm. I swallowed hard. I could feel Kirby's astonishment rub up against my own.

The heavy sea of dark and light green crops growing over the Wallace place looked to be two or three weeks ahead of every other farm we'd passed on our way out. There would be very few Saturdays left before the first of the harvest would be ready. I've never been big on plants or growing things, but the order, the richness, the neatly turned soil painted out before us pulled another breath from me. It felt like I was seeing outside for the first time.

"Beautiful," Kirby gasped.

I noticed a few Trackers moving in the distance among the pole beans, tenderly lifting the leaves to examine the plants and pull the occasional weed. They were as much a part of the scene as the okra and tomatoes, adding both depth and beauty to the story of the farm.

"Is this what happens when you plant on fallow ground?" I breathed out loud.

Kirby shook his head. "This is what happens when you plant on blessed ground."

I could have stayed all day, watching the cucumbers and squash grow as the dusky caretakers moved gracefully among the plants. But since a moment lasts only a moment, I recovered enough to touch the accelerator and bounce across the field, through the pecan grove to the meadow and Jesse's apiary.

We pulled up to find Mr. Wallace's truck parked beside the bunkhouse-to-be. The exterior walls had been framed, righted, and braced off, giving better definition to the vision. The construction was impressive, but in reality, the stick walls were only a few hours of a carpenter's work. Natalie leaned from the window of Mr. Wallace's truck to wave when she heard us roll up. We waved back and got out.

"Hey, PJ, hey, Kirby Braddock," she sang. "How you boys doin' on such a hot summertime morning?"

"I'm just fine," Kirby called back.

"I'm hot," I muttered to myself as Kirby and I traipsed over to get a better look at the framing.

"Daddy says I have to stay in the truck 'cause if I don't, I'm liable to pull the bunkhouse walls down all over myself," she explained and then sank into the seat, crossed her arms, and huffed. "So I gotta sit right here…it ain't right, and it's not fair too."

"Where's Jesse at?" I asked as we approached, but either Natalie didn't respond or I didn't hear what she said before Kirby slapped me on the arm, drawing my attention to something new in the field.

"Look at that...cool," Kirby gasped as he pointed out a windmill looming like a silent giant in the late-morning sun.

Kirby was right. It was cool. The windmill stood thirty or forty feet tall, and with its clean white undergirding and rust-red propeller, the tower looked like the offspring of a roller coaster. The base was wide, and a giant tub sat underneath. I wanted to touch it, and so did Kirby. We moved past Natalie in the truck, hypnotized by the structure towering among the wildflowers.

Mr. Wallace paced toward the windmill from behind the bunkhouse, careful to keep his steps even, counting silently to himself the whole way. We didn't say a word, careful not to disturb his tally, until the three of us met at the foot of the tower and Mr. Wallace pulled a rumpled piece of paper from his pocket to record his findings. He smiled and leaned in on the big tub.

"So what do you boys think?"

"I think it's great," Kirby answered.

"It is *so* cool," I added, staring up through the white undergirding laced with blue sky.

"I have to say," Mr. Wallace held his hand to his brow, looking straight up, "even I was impressed." He paused as a slight breeze came over the trees and the pinwheel on top turned to greet its friend. It reminded me of a dog wagging its tail in a delighted overreaction to a slight touch from his master. The wind was halfhearted, but the spinning wheel responded with vigor.

"Wow, that thing is sensitive," Kirby commented.

"We balanced it the best we could. John and Jesse do pretty good work, and even an old builder like me isn't totally worthless. Besides, that's not even the best part. Look here, boys."

Mr. Wallace moved around to where some metal workings and a spigot overhung the tub. He reached down, struggled a moment, and then pulled a lever to engage the pump. Another breeze brushed over the meadow, and the vane turned to take all it offered. We waited. The metal workings gurgled. They sputtered. They spat hard to clear the spigot's throat, and when the pump and the pipes were fully rousted, clear water flowed from the spout and drummed to the bottom of the tub. It lasted as long as the wind.

The windmill was a blue-collar structure, plain but magnificent, and even more beautiful because of its purpose. People weren't lining up to landscape its feet and pitchers of hot chocolate weren't being passed around to celebrate its completion, but there was a blue sky above, wildflowers nearby, and a pouty girl sitting in the truck who believed her daddy had built the best thing she'd ever seen. That was so much more than enough. If they could pick themselves up and move about, I wondered if the porte cochere and the windmill would be friends. They seemed so different and yet so much the same. I thought they might enjoy each other's company—if the people of Cunningham would allow it. Then again, I don't know how much influence any of us would have over those wooden souls, brothers and sons of the carpenter who fashioned them. But that's silly; after all, they were just lumber and nails, fated to become whatever we make them by however we use them.

Mr. Wallace bent down and pushed the lever to disengage the pump.

"So what do we have going out here today?" Kirby asked when Mr. Wallace finished.

"Not much, boys. I was just out here pacing off for some pipe to the bunkhouse. I wasn't gonna put water in, but this morning over coffee I thought, *why not*, so I came out to see if I could make it work. Looks like there's plenty of fall, and if I reduce the pipe a time or two, I think I can get enough pressure to push it right up to a kitchen sink."

Kirby and I nodded like we understood what he was saying.

"Of course, if I do that," Mr. Wallace paused, put his hand to the back of his head, and cast a pensive gaze over the future bunkhouse, "I'll have to figure how to drain it, but we can work that out." Mr. Wallace turned back to me and smiled. "Anyway, running water doesn't get you out of digging an outhouse, and it'll need to be double deep."

"Yes, sir," I nodded.

"Yeah, that's a good job for you." Kirby smirked and shouldered me hard enough to make me take a step. I didn't have the energy or inclination to push back, so we just leaned silently on the big basin underneath the windmill a few moments longer while Mr. Wallace contemplated his pipes.

I felt like I had to say something. "Where is everybody today?"

"Jesse wanted to work, but I wouldn't let him. I told John to take the day off too, but he's already been in with his folks jarring honey, and now they're out in fields somewhere working. I can't get 'em to stop. I guess they don't have much else to do."

"Your farm looks prettier than a postcard," Kirby chimed. "Who'd have thought a bunch of Trackers could do all this?"

Mr. Wallace snorted in through his nose, cleared his throat, and spat on the ground. He took a deep breath and glared across the big basin at Kirby. "You mean John, Elizabeth, Nya, Angeline, Zeke, Tommy, Esther, Josiah, Pearl, David, Sam, Lilly, Kaden, James, Henry, Emmeline, Addie, Livvy, Anna Claire, and Tuttle? Is that who you mean when you say *Trackers*, boy?"

His tone stunned me, and Kirby was so taken aback he looked like he might cry. He was trying to compliment the farm, never anticipating his words would cause offense or draw such a steely reaction from Mr. Wallace. For a moment I thought we were going to be told to leave.

"No, sir," Kirby stammered. "Yes, sir, I meant all those people you said. I don't know their names. I'm sorry. I wasn't trying to be a jerk. I just—"

Mr. Wallace held up his hand to silence Kirby's pitiful babbling. "I'm sorry too, son. Let's not use that God-awful word out here anymore, okay? It upsets me."

We could see it did, so we nodded and agreed to never use the term "Tracker" on the Wallace farm ever again.

Mr. Wallace held a hard expression a moment longer until he was confident his point was made, and then he softened, letting a slight smile slip across his lips. "I sent Jesse to Sandy Shores for the day. It's hot, and it's the first day of summer vacation, so I figured there'd be plenty of pretty girls down there to talk to. We won't have any decent produce to sell in the square for another couple of weeks, so I imagine everyone coming to town will be on the river. If he did what I told him, Sandy Shores is where he'll be."

"Yes, sir, okay then, that's where we're headed." I pushed away from the big tub and stepped out from under the windmill.

"Do you want us to take Natalie?" Kirby asked.

I wasn't interested in bringing Natalie along, but Kirby put his foot in it, so all I could do was stop and wait for Mr. Wallace to respond. I stood in the grass, too far away for anyone to notice my disgusted sigh.

"Thank you. You boys are so good to Natalie, but I don't think you need a tagalong today with your Uphill girls. I'm afraid she'd probably cramp your style beyond all hope. There'll be plenty more summer; maybe some other time. Thanks though."

"Well, okay," Kirby said as he stepped out from under the windmill, "but I wouldn't worry about PJ. He doesn't have a style to cramp."

Mr. Wallace laughed. "No work tomorrow, but I'll expect to see you first thing Monday morning. Right, PJ?"

"Yes, sir, see you Monday."

We said our good-byes to Natalie, climbed in my truck, maneuvered through the pecan grove, over the field, and out to River Road on our way to Sandy Shores. I didn't say anything to Kirby about inviting Natalie to the river with us. That stupid idea had resolved itself. But the folly of a windmill and a bunkhouse standing hidden in a remote corner of a newly replanted farm was an even dumber idea, with its only resolution a dangerous one. I finally realized what was going on. Jesse and Mr. Wallace were out to change everything—or they were about to try—and there was no escaping my part in it. That die was cast the day I kept Kirby on the bridge and John saved Natalie from the Chagrin.

29
Woman at the River

An unusually hot first day of summer vacation falling on a Saturday proved perfect for drawing everybody and his brother to our pleasant little bend in the river. Vehicles lined both shoulders of River Road for over a mile, and when Kirby and I pulled up, we found Eddy leaning against his squad car blocking the entrance of Sandy Shores. I slowed to a stop, and Kirby rolled his window down. Eddy pushed himself up to stroll over and give us parking instructions.

I never liked Eddy. He was long and lean with the personality of a switchblade. He was the sheriff's unpredictable dog, fully obedient with the master present, but unencumbered and capricious when left to himself. For Eddy, the star pinned to his shirt made everything legal, justifying every greasy thought passing through his head and every slimy remark crossing his lips. He peacocked around Cunningham in his neatly pressed uniform, but in the end, he was nothing more than a punk whose badge saved him more than once from prison or being stomped to death in a bar fight. He was handy for Sheriff Johnson to have around.

Eddy moved up, stopping short so he could see into the truck without having to lean in the window. He acted strange and overly cautious, like he didn't trust us. I guess he was playing some sort of game involving deadly fugitives to help pass the time on traffic duty. He thumbed his holster and turned his head to look back down the road. It was all very dramatic.

"Sorry, boys," he drew out, "no more chubby or dorky locals allowed in."

"What?" Kirby huffed.

"You heard me, you little turd," the deputy snapped. Then he smiled and pushed his hat back on his head. "Apparently all the pretty Uphill girls complained about all the porkies and dorkies, so I've declared martial law, and I ain't lettin' no more road apples like you two down there today."

I heard what Eddy was saying, but somehow it wasn't registering. "That's fine. We'll park down the road with everybody else and walk up," I agreed.

"Did you hear a word I said?" Eddy snarled. "You ain't going to Sandy Shores today, no matter where you park."

Kirby turned his hands palms-up in his lap, looking to me in disbelief. We started to protest, but Eddy started first.

"Now you get this piece of crap off my road right now, or I'm gonna have to ask you boys to get outta your truck, and that ain't gonna lead nowhere good…at least not for you."

I was furious, but I bit my tongue long enough to turn around and head back the way we came. In my rearview mirror, I watched Eddy saunter over to lean against his patrol car and pull his hat low over his eyes for a standing nap. As soon as he was out of sight, I pulled to the shoulder, parked in the long line of cars, and Kirby and I picked our way through the woods to the river.

It was a miserable walk, but the anger and defiance in us made it tolerable. Before long, the trees and brush thinned, and we emerged at the edge of the beach from a way we had never come before. We said our "excuse me's" and "I'm sorry's," when we stumbled around a family of picnickers with a checkered cloth and deviled eggs as we stepped into full view of Sandy Shores.

After seeing all the cars parked on the road, I don't know why I was surprised at the number of people lounging along the riverbank and cooling off in the friendly waters. Maybe it was the overwhelming patchwork painted over the sand by yards of brightly colored beach towels, T-shirts, and neon swimsuits that struck me more than the crowd itself. I guess the trappings of people are often quicker to catch the eye.

Blue-and-white cabanas stood behind lifeless red banners as a smattering of weak-willed kites tried to find a suitable breeze. It seemed like Kirby and I had walked up on a human anthill with enough bodies to crush Sandy Shores right into the Chagrin. Footballs and Frisbees flew rudely overhead as people tried to pick their way around each other. Now I understood why Eddy closed the place off. I couldn't decide if I liked the commotion or not, but it made the place seem alive, bearing no resemblance to the spot where Buster almost shot Jesse in the back. I wasn't sure I wanted to stay.

Kirby and I stood by the deviled egg family, awed by the sea of bodies sunning themselves and all listening to different radio stations.

"I guess we're the only people on the planet Eddy didn't let in," Kirby snorted.

"I guess. Have you ever seen it like this…ever?"

"Nope." Kirby shook his head. "There're more folks here than I've seen in Cunningham on two Easters and two Christmases."

"Yeah, too bad Dodge isn't here to pass the plate," I smirked.

Kirby slapped me on the arm and grinned wide. "You know, that's right. That guy's nothing but a giant butthole."

Kirby had a problem with Reverend Dodge he never wanted to talk about, and now wasn't the time to ask. I sighed and gazed over the swollen tide of sunbathers as the hypnotic drum of their conversations filled my head. A slight breeze picked up, dousing us in the cloying aroma of tanning lotion and coconut oil.

"We should leave. We'll never find Jesse down here today, and I don't feel like hanging out at the beach in my work boots and farm clothes."

I just realized we were still dressed to work at Mr. Wallace's. I don't know what we were thinking, coming up out of the woods dressed like a couple of hayseed bumpkins from the back side of Tracker Island. No wonder the deviled egg family told us we could take whatever we wanted if we just kept moving. We were horribly conspicuous, and it wouldn't take long for the kids from Hawkinsville High to recognize the two idiots wearing overalls at the biggest swim party of the century.

"Hang on; let's see if we can spot him from here before we take off. I'd hate to miss him. Besides, he may be able to give us a ride out instead of walking back through the woods."

"Come on, you'll never find Jesse in all these people. Let's go."

"Wait a second," Kirby insisted again, curling his fists into makeshift binoculars and holding them to his face in order to scan the crowd. He looked like an idiotic Peeping Tom standing at the tree line in his farmer's clothes, zeroing in on some sunbathing girl. I started to move back.

"Wait a second." Without looking around, he dropped one hand and grabbed me by the arm, instantly transforming his binoculars into a telescope. I pulled away, but before I could take another step, Kirby found what he was looking for.

"There," he said, "center middle, twelve o'clock." He sounded like a sniper.

I held up my hand to take the sun from my eyes, and sure enough, on top of a picnic table with his feet on the bench, Jesse sat all alone. He seemed to be in the eye of a storm or maybe Fort Apache—I couldn't tell from where we were standing—but he had the table to himself as a tide of people in colorful swim clothes swirled around.

"Let's go, he's waiting on us." Without giving me a moment to protest, Kirby waded out into the bodies and headed for Jesse.

I wanted to leave, but not alone, so I plowed in behind Kirby, doing my best to follow his lead over and around those sprawled in the sand. I figured it was better to double annoy folks than annoy double the folks, so I stayed close behind Kirby, echoing his apologies to the same people he stepped on or pinched with his big feet. It's hard to be graceful in work boots. We trampled beach towels, stumbled over radios, and kicked sand on everyone in our roundabout way. I lost my balance once or twice but didn't fall, and although Kirby and I were elephants in the room, no one seemed to recognize us from school. Traversing the minefield of sunbathers took longer than our walk through the woods, but we finally made it to the table as the wake of agitated people settled behind us. Jesse slid over to make room for us to climb up.

"Nice threads," Jesse noted. "Not exactly dressed for a day on the beach, are you?"

"We came from the windmill," Kirby answered, settling to his seat.

"Plus, we had to pick our way through the stupid woods to get down here because Eddy wouldn't let us use the road," I added.

"So what'd you guys think of the windmill?"

"Unbelievably cool," Kirby answered with a grin.

The sea of visitors buzzed around us in their private goings-on, so even though we were among thousands, we were truly alone in the commotion as we watched the Chagrin slide around boulders decorated with summer people.

"And what'd you think, PJ?" Jesse asked, staring over the water.

I wanted to say it was awesome and it was great, but I got caught in the folly of it all and decided to be helpful instead. I was a lifelong resident of Cunningham, and I knew things Jesse didn't. "Fact is, Jesse, Mr. Wallace is headed for real trouble if he lets those Trackers—" I paused to correct myself, "I mean, John and his group have run of his farm. The town will never let him do it, even if they live invisible back behind the pecan grove."

Kirby twisted at what I said, as if he finally understood where this business with the bunkhouse was headed.

"I know he feels like he owes John for saving Natalie and all," I continued, "but that's the hard facts of the matter."

The whir of the sunbathers offered a deafening silence as I let the realities of Cunningham soak through Jesse's skin. I thought about Buster and the mashed potato lady as we looked over the peopled river. I was more assured than ever things here would never change.

"You see those big rocks out there?" Jesse interrupted my thoughts. He was whispering, but it was like he was right in my ear instead of the other side of the table. I could hear him plainly through the surrounding noise, like I was listening to him on the phone. "Those boulders are as hard and cold as any fact could ever be. People stand on 'em all the time, but in the long of it, those rocks ain't going nowhere. All they do is sit and wear out. They're big and awfully sure of themselves, but they don't change one drop of where that river's headed. It just flows right on by on its way to the sea. Facts are just like those boulders—to be negotiated on the way to the truth."

It sounded exactly like something Joe might say, and I had only a vague idea what it meant. Kirby nodded in agreement, but I'm not sure if he understood or just accepted what Jesse said. I guess the truth is easier to recognize than understand. I sat for a moment, trying to pick it apart.

Whoa, whoa, whoa! I was surprised as a woman from the crowd suddenly landed deep in my lap. I couldn't tell if she fell or jumped, but my initial instinct was to push her away and get some distance between us. I squirmed, and so did she, mostly undoing each other's effort to get untangled before Jesse and Kirby slid off the table to help the lady right herself.

"Wow," she laughed. "Thank you, thank you, and thank you for the use of your lap, young man. If you hadn't been there, I would have cracked my face wide open. I'm a bit teetery these days."

Her smile was worn but still let life out, and even though she seemed unusually frail, the beauty of her younger self flickered through. I don't take to people well, but I liked her immediately. It was hard not to.

She balanced herself on the table's edge with Kirby and Jesse at her side, ready to give support should she collapse again. She looked like she could go at any second; if she had, I'm afraid she would have broken apart in their arms. Jesse and Kirby inched along with her like they were following an old woman carrying a newborn as she worked her way over to sit down. When she did, we all felt better.

"Whew." She wiped her brow with the back of her hand and settled into her seat. "Thank you so much, guys. I'm okay for now. You don't have to hover. Sitting I'm good at, but walking through sand on a crowded beach…not so much." Then, as if she just remembered something else she wanted to say, she reached over and tapped me on the knee and drew her crooked hand back to cover what thirty years ago would have been a flirtatious giggle. There was something gray about her, and her eyes shone like the embers of a dying fire. "I'm so sorry I fell on my face in your lap like some wanton young hussy," she laughed from behind her hand. "It probably gave you quite a turn when you saw it was me, huh?"

The truth is, I had been so surprised by her sudden and intimate appearance I was just glad she wasn't trying to bite me, but I didn't say that. "That's okay, ma'am. I don't have a girlfriend," was the best I could manage.

I wasn't trying to be funny, but she held her bent hand up to hide what remained of her laugh. She swayed, provoking a simultaneous start from Jesse and Kirby before realizing she wasn't going over. Her eyes flickered up.

"That's hard to believe of a good-looking fellow such as yourself, but even if you did, I'm certainly nothing to be jealous of."

Sitting at the table among the bright summertime whir with this fading stranger should have been awkward, but somehow it wasn't.

"I'm so sorry," she continued. "I don't always think the way I used to, so sometimes I can be a tad impolite. I don't want to intrude on your day, guys, but is it okay if I sit here and rest a few minutes? The sand is giving me trouble with my poles."

We all nodded hospitably, as if we owned the place we were sitting, agreeing she could rest here as long as she wanted.

She reached over and touched me on the knee again. "Hey, handsome, would you mind looking to see what happened to my sticks?"

I peered around to see a pair of metal crutches, the kind that go up around your forearms, one stuck leaning in the sand and the other lying at the foot of its mate. I slid down to retrieve the pair and leaned them against our table.

"Thank you," she said. "By the way, my name is Margie, and even though I'm old enough to be your mother, please call me Margie. It sounds better nowadays than ma'am."

We introduced ourselves, taking her outstretched hand in turn as cautiously as a crumbling butterfly wing at the end of a brittle twig.

"So, Margie," I piped up, "why the crutches? Was it hang gliding or rock climbing that put you in those things?" I knew it wasn't either, but something was bad wrong with this ashen whisper of a woman, and I had no other way to ask. I half expected her to laugh at my ridiculous question, but she didn't.

"Actually, I've been on crutches for both of those things before, but not today, not today…" Her voice trailed off, and her eyes clouded with a momentary trip to the past. "I'm armed and accessorized with these metal things because of my MS."

"MS?" Kirby asked.

"Multiple sclerosis," Jesse explained. "It's pretty bad."

"Yeah, it's bad," Margie agreed with a weak smile, "and the worst part is, it has my mind so frazzled and my tongue so tied

I can't even pronounce multiple scl…sis, multiple sc…sis anymore. It's terrible not to be able to say the name of what's going to kill you."

Jesse slid down next to her.

"My husband, Paul, and I used to bike in from Hawkinsville almost every weekend, and after the boys were born, we just outfitted our cycles with car seats and kept coming. Cunningham is a beautiful place to ride. Eventually our sons got too big to haul down here on the back of our bikes, but they were still too young to make the ride pedaling themselves. Paul wanted to put sidecars on our ten-speeds." She shook her head with a sad smile. "I told him it was ridiculous, and we could drive the car down until the boys were old enough to make the trip on their own bikes. We didn't come much after that…I guess it was more about the ride than the destination. Anyway, I got my diagnosis before the boys were ready." She paused to swallow a fading smile. "I should have let Paul put the sidecars on."

I didn't know what to say, but Kirby slid down next to Margie, flanking her between him and Jesse. We must have been quite a sight on the beach that day, if anyone bothered to notice, three big, hearty boys, hanging on the last words of a small, frail ghost-to-be.

Kirby leaned over and buried his face deep in his palms. I thought he might be crying, but when he let his hands fall to his lap, he appeared more indignant than sorrowful.

"I'm so sorry, ma'am, it's not right. It's not right at all," he choked.

"Kirby," she patted him on the knee, "just because it's not fair doesn't mean it's not right...and please, don't call me ma'am."

Kirby nodded. "Yes ma'am, I mean Margie. But doesn't it make you angry or sad or something?"

"At first I was shocked." She held her crooked hand to her brow to shade her eyes from the glint off the river. She was searching for something in the water and speaking to us now only as background people. There was no hurt in her voice. "But it doesn't make me sad anymore, although I do mourn sometimes—not so much about what I can't do, but what I won't do. There! There they are!" A triumphant smile leapt to her face as she raised a thin arm to point out her family. "You see that man by the big rock, the one in the red trunks and no hair? That's my husband. You see the two goofballs he's splashing around with? Those are my boys, Ryan and Scotty; not too much younger than you guys." She beamed around at us as hard as she could, like she was watching her favorite movie or had just written something she really loved and wanted us to enjoy it too. "They're beautiful, aren't they?"

"You have a good-lookin' family," Jesse agreed.

"Yeah." Margie's grin fell away. "My grandchildren will only have stories of me. I doubt I'll even see my sons get married." Her eyes went out to her husband and boys playing in the river again, drinking in the view. "I guess that's the blessing of being sick. Everything is so much more valuable…the economics of supply and demand." She smirked, but her words were too honest to be funny. "I'd love to get rid of my MS," she sighed, "but I wouldn't trade it to somebody else for all the tea in China. It's too awful to wish away with 'why me's.'"

We sat like we were waiting on a dinnertime prayer as a small world of trivial conversation spun around us. No one knew what to say, and Margie looked like she'd settled at our table for the day until Jesse spoke up.

"So, Margie, where were you headed when you dove all over PJ?" he asked more flatly than I liked.

She looked to him. "Actually I was on my way down to put my toes in the water, but it's longer than I thought and I can see my family fine from right here, so if you guys don't mind…I mean, if I'm not scaring off the pretty girls," she turned to make sure Kirby and I could hear her, "I'd like to sit here until Paul and the boys get done and walk me back to our cabana."

Kirby and I both agreed immediately she could stay, but Jesse reached down, took her hand off her lap, and shook his head no. "I think you'd be better off going to the river," he said, clasping her hand in both of his.

She huffed out loud at his unexpected refusal, and I thought she would protest, but the years of carpentry in his touch somehow put her at ease, and the startle in her face faded.

"Will you walk me?" she whispered to Jesse.

Again, he shook his head a silent no. "I think everything will work out better if I carry you instead."

"You're funny!" she snorted and rocked back without pulling her hand from his. "But I can't let you do that."

"Why not?" Jesse's lips curled in delight. "I thought you were a hang-gliding, rock-climbing, bike-riding, sidecar-wishing kind of gal, so I'm pretty sure you can be a cowgirl for another forty feet to the water. We'll do it piggyback, and you'll see what going in style really means."

"We'll be a sight," she laughed.

"We will be a sight," he agreed.

"I'm heavier than I look," she laughed again.

"I'm stronger than I look," Jesse volleyed.

The silly thought of riding a strange young man over a crowded beach ignited tiny blue flames in Margie's eyes, and after a moment's consideration, she gave a quick nod, indicating she would accept Jesse's offer. He knelt to the sand, and she draped her arms over his shoulders and around his neck. When he stood, Margie gave a faint chortle swirled with illness and fear.

"Giddy-up," she said. "Giddy-up before I change my mind. Yeah, yeah, you better hurry and giddy-up." She hooted and called back for me to look after her crutches.

30
Why People Get Sick

Sitting on the tabletop, dressed for farm work, Kirby and I watched Jesse pick his way over the minefield of self-absorbed sunbathers not having enough courtesy to get out of his way until he and Margie already passed them by. The laughter and static of a million conversations drowned away all other sound as the carpenter's son and the ashen ghost piggybacked their way to the river. If anyone even noticed, their attention wasn't held for long, and then only to complain about being stepped on or over.

Jesse and Margie descended into the water, and when they were deep enough for the Chagrin to hold her weight, Jesse rolled her off his back so they stood face-to-face as the river swirled around them. Words passed between them, and whatever was said made Margie shake her head no twice before she gave in with a nod, indicating a reluctant yes. She fell against Jesse with as deep an embrace as her body would allow. He pulled his hand from the river and stroked the back of her head once before they separated and Jesse left her with her husband and boys. I remember thinking she looked like the cutout of a paper doll in the presence of her colorful young sons. I was sad for her.

By the time Jesse picked his way back to us, the summer sun had licked away all but the last bit of dampness from his body. He smelled fresh, like the river, as he climbed up to sit between

Kirby and me. We sat a while, watching the gray lady enjoy her family, until the weight of Margie was too much for Kirby to bear.

"Why do you think people get sick?" he pondered in a faraway voice.

Jesse sighed deep without looking over. "Some to be healed, some to be cared for, and some to remind us we're human," he answered with the same expertise he would have if Kirby had asked about framing a house.

"So you think there's a reason for it all?" Kirby followed.

Jesse shook his head. "Not usually, but we can find a good purpose in whatever chance happens to bring, and I guess sometimes that purpose can be mistaken for a reason."

"That's not what Reverend Dodge thinks. He says it's God's will when people get sick—to teach them a lesson or put them in a position to do something for Him."

"Is that what he told you about your mother?"

"That's what he told my whole family," Kirby sniffed, "right in front of Mom and everything. My mom is a good lady…puts up with all of us, goes to church on Sunday, and does everything she's supposed to do." A long, silent tear ran down Kirby's cheek and dropped off his chin. He sniffled and paused to collect himself. "If God wanted something more from her, why wouldn't He just ask instead of giving her leukemia without saying why?"

His question hung over the picnic table as summertime falderal buzzed around us. Jesse waited, and I waited too.

"Hurting somebody," Jesse started, "or making 'em sick so they'll do something for you is like buying yourself a present and forcing someone else to give it to you. What's the point? What does it really mean? That's not to say we're not singled out to do certain things, but mostly doo-doo occurs and we build our gifts to God from there. It's all terribly complicated and so simple at the same time, but Kirby, the Lord didn't make your mom sick to get something out of her. It doesn't mean she won't do something beautiful for Him on account of it though. Most times it's about *our* end of things and what *we* do when bad things happen, and not about God extorting good works from us. Does that make sense?"

Kirby shrugged his shoulders, and I felt the same.

"Reverend Dodge hates that he can't reconcile all that happens with Father's Will," Jesse continued as he watched Margie with her family, "so he mixes it around to suit his own recipe instead of opening up to the possibilities. He fights to preserve what he thinks he can prove, and nobody around here questions him, even when he's disgusting enough to tell a family God made their mother sick on purpose."

Kirby sucked the summer air in deep through his nose and blew it back out like he was filling an imaginary balloon. He held his emotions back, although anger and sadness were strong allies, desperate to get out. He dropped his face into his hands to reinforce his position against them and cover his eyes in case they leaked. I could sense tears coming, but since I didn't know what to do or say, I remained silent as my best friend wrestled the mean-spirited feelings.

What Jesse was saying sounded right, but it didn't make any difference to me. Kirby's mom was still dying, and Margie would never know a grandchild. I couldn't see how it mattered if God, the Devil, or bad luck did this to them. All the explanations, excuses, and theology in the world were no more than placebos without any real power at all. But I appreciated Jesse trying to make Kirby feel better. It was more than I could do.

"No, Kirby, don't hide your eyes," Jesse was saying. Then in his same strange whisper like he was right in my ear, he said, "You need to watch Margie now."

We turned our attention to the river and found the gray lady in the water with her family. She clung loosely to her husband, splashing weakly at her sons as they laughed and splashed gently back. At one time she may have been able to cycle for miles, but today her greedy illness had already taken its toll and weariness consumed her hollow smile. Her trip home, back to bed, was overdue. It was a sad and tired scene that still plays in my head.

"Remember what I said," Jesse whispered. "Some are to be healed."

The day was coming to an end for the lady who spilled into my lap as she and her family began to move off the rocks toward shore. I reached for the metal crutches to go meet them, but Jesse put his arm up to stop me. "Hold on," he said without looking around.

The sun glinted off the river like it had all day as a hot breeze at our backs toyed with sleeping banners, inspiring a few young boys to stand and try their kites. The people here weren't like the single-minded honeybees or even the landscapers of the porte cochere; they lived in tiny worlds with borders ending at the hems of their beach towels spread neatly on the ground. So even though the banks teamed with witnesses, the three of us were the only ones watching as Margie and her family made their way in from the water.

The sun cracked off the river, filling my eyes with yellow and blue spots that moved around in my brain like the goo of a lava lamp. The wind that blew an occasional cloud overhead dipped briefly to caress the treetops. The sound of the swaying branches washed through my head as I cleared my eyes to find the Margie again. I reached for her crutches so I could be the first to meet her.

The river was chest high on the gray lady, with her husband and boys in close escort. I could see she was searching for our picnic table among the others where she left me in charge of her metal poles. But as the water began to shallow, something made her stop. Margie lifted her arm from the river to examine her palm. She shook her head, spread her fingers wide, and turned her hand over and over to get a better look before showing it to her husband. He stared in disbelief, and then realizing he was no longer holding his wife, stepped to catch her before she collapsed—but as he reached out, she moved away. She waded up from the river, emerging no longer ashen, no longer hollow, and looking twenty years younger than when she sat at our table. It was as if the Chagrin washed the MS right out of her.

The sun sparkled off the water again, but the summer breeze lay still as we watched Margie searching for us in the crowd. When her husband and boys joined her on the beach, she showed them her arms and legs. They grabbed her, examining her as if they were buying a horse, bouncing and screaming when they realized she was well. Margie did a happy twirl before falling into embrace them all. In the midst of the laughter and tears, one of the boys toppled over a stray cooler and fell into the corner of someone else's world. I could see the sunbather lift her head, but after an apology or two, she lay back down to sleep or listen to music or whatever most people do at the foot of a miracle.

Margie waved her arms, explaining something emphatically to her husband as her two sons listened. She turned back to scan the crowd once again to find the table where she rested and the young man who piggybacked her to the river. Jesse sat silent. Kirby's eyes streamed either for his mother or Margie, I'm not sure which, but I didn't want to look at him, so I stood up on the picnic table and waved my arms to get Margie's attention.

We were only forty feet away; somehow though, amid the colors and the flags and the cabanas and the kites, she didn't notice me standing or hear me shouting her name. I was astonished and sat down, not understanding how she could have missed me. I continued to watch her search as her husband and boys did all they could to help.

"How is it she didn't see me?"

"It's okay," Jesse remarked.

I waited for him to explain, but he wasn't talking to me. My eyes went back to Margie. She'd given up looking for us and had fallen to her knees in the sand. She was staring straight up into the summer expanse with both hands clasped under her chin. Her family moved down beside her.

"I know," Jesse continued softly, "but we'll see each other soon enough." He paused. "Yes, but not yet..........You're welcome..........Enjoy your family, dear, and keep doing the best you can........I know.......I love you too."

Margie dropped her hands, and she, her husband, and her boys collapsed on the riverside into a pile of laughter and tears. I'm sure everyone around them thought they were crazy.

We walked back to Jesse's truck and crouched down in the cab so Eddy wouldn't see that Kirby and I sneaked in. The deputy stopped us long enough to hassle Jesse about the truck's unsightly fender but waved him by anyway. Jesse let us out at my pickup, and I dropped Kirby off before driving home. I can't remember anything else about the first day of that summer except how unremarkable it had been for nearly everyone at Sandy Shores.

31
Lunch and Labor

The moon has retreated to the middle of the sky, watching and keeping its distance like it's afraid I may jump off this porch to snatch it. If I had something the pale light wanted, I might be able to coax it to my hand, but nothing seems tame enough tonight, and if the moon drew too close, it would surely sense my fear. No, it's better for us both if it remains tall and out of reach.

It's chilly on these hard steps, but I'm afraid to seek a more comfortable spot inside. The cold in my bones and the ache in my body seem to be the pinch I need to keep my mind and stave off the sleep that keeps threatening to take me. At least here with an audience of dark trees, I can remember to take these pills, but when I'm done with what I have to say, I'll let myself slip into remembering only Maggie…if You will allow it, dear God. Please let me have at least that.

I don't know a time I didn't love Maggie, and although I can't clearly recall the day we met, it seems to me there was straw in her ponytail. It hurts not to be able to connect it all, but I'm sure I loved her right off. It took longer for her to love me back, but when she did, it was without reservation. She never was one to hold back. We had laughter at our dinner table and intimate coffee talks in the morning before the children got up. I can't remember ever being angry with Maggie, and I can't ever remember Maggie *staying* angry with me. She was my best friend, and I loved her to the bone. We had a family. I hate to say those names and faces fade in and out for me now, but I know we had children I loved dearly.

This cabin was the only secret I ever kept from her. I traveled for work, so a spring business trip to Hawkinsville was never a *total* lie…if there is anything but. How God ever let me have so many beautiful years with Mags without forgiving me first, I'll never know. I almost thought He'd forgotten. Then, just like Kirby's mom, Maggie came down with cancer, and it wasn't long after she died…and, well…I started to die too. I always counted on going first. I guess I fooled myself into thinking there wouldn't be a price for what I did in Cunningham.

I find now I'm chained to a drowned past like an unforgiven ghost too feeble to go haunting. I guess I was never really whole after all, for even with everything I had, this place still beckoned me, summoning me every spring. Why spring, when my crime was committed at summer's end, I don't know…or maybe I forgot. But I'm not ready for that yet. A couple more of these damn pills while I'm thinking about it, and I can begin to finish the story.

We didn't go back to Sandy Shores for a while. Work at the Wallace place took precedence even on Saturdays, and on Sundays, I was too tired to do much more than go to church and watch TV.

I was digging the pipe ditch from the windmill, and Jesse had Kirby building more bee boxes for the apiary. Jesse, John, and another Tracker named Sam worked together to finish framing the bunkhouse.

The work was terribly slow compared to a seasoned carpenter's pace. I remember standing up from my shovel to wipe my brow as Jesse was moving back and forth from his sawhorses to the bunkhouse to take another measurement or make another cut with his pupils, John and Sam, in tow. He explained all he was doing, and they seemed eager to learn, but Jesse was still doing the skilled work himself. I wondered how long it would take for Jesse to trust the two men enough to remain at his sawhorses as they shouted for the cuts and measurements they needed, or for them to be able to set walls without Jesse having to climb up and help. I thought how quickly the porte cochere had gone up with only two men working, but those two men spent Jesse's lifetime building their skills and their trust in each other. I watched Jesse instructing his students as they nodded in understanding. Even though I wished he was teaching me, I knew it was better for them to learn, because I already knew firsthand what one carpenter's faith in another could accomplish.

I worked harder than I ever have that summer, and digging the pipe ditch was just the start of it. There was an outhouse to dig, lumber to haul, grass to mow, and a million other jobs ending with a dirty sweat and sore muscles. All my time was spent working in the meadow, even though a vast farm rich with chores lay just beyond the trees. It didn't matter. Work was work, and my hands grew tough and calloused as I dug, hauled, and drank from the basin under the windmill. It was the sweetest water I ever had.

The days were long and the sun was hot, but I never goldbricked, not once, because no one else did. I began to take pride in how much I was able to accomplish before needing a break. Even so, when the Trackers appeared through the pecan grove bearing lunch every day, I was ready to rest. Whoever brought food usually joined us in the shade of the trees, and I loved sitting and listening to them talk as we ate.

I was fascinated hearing how John came to be a Tracker and the day Nya was born. Sam had a different life at one time, somewhere else with a house and a family, but an accident took both before he wound up on Tracker Island. I never shared anything about myself at lunch. What could I possibly say to compare with Jesse's stories of traveling with his parents or John talking about the war and how God gave him Angeline?

John's wife, Elizabeth, told how she walloped Nya the first time she ever dug honey out of the old dinosaur tree. "I'll never forget it," she laughed. "That child wasn't much bigger than Angeline is now when she showed up at the house as sticky and nasty as you please with a jar full o' that ol' dead tree honey. When I asked her where she got it, she was too scared to tell me, so I spanked that girl 'til she did. Then I spanked her some more 'cause I thought she was fibbin' me. She cried and cried, but she wouldn't give up her story, so I knew she was saying the truth, so I said I was sorry. Then I walloped her one more time for messin' with them bees. A good way to wind up in an early grave is swiping honey from a bazillion bees, and the Lord knows ain't no doctor gonna help if she got bit and turned up allergic." Elizabeth smiled and shook her head. "Poor girl swole up more from my beatin' that day than anything them bees ever did. I know now I was wrong, 'cause as many times as Nya's put her arm down in that ol' trunk, she ain't never been bit…not once. Always scares me when she goes—always does—even though those little critters never seem to mind sharing with her." She paused to stare across the meadow. "Thanks to Mr. Wallace, we're all gonna have a chance to do better for a while…work this farm…and I'm so grateful to the good Lord I won't have to worry about my girl being bitten to her death for a handful of honey."

I remember thinking, *bees don't bite; they sting,* but I didn't say a thing and took another mouthful of sandwich instead.

For a few short weeks filled with long days, Kirby and I worked and ate lunch with the Trackers. It's funny how hard labor, dirty clothes, and a good meal can wash away many of the things we tell ourselves about one another. Mr. Wallace had a store in town to run, but I wished he could have been with us more than just Saturdays. In the honesty of lunch and labor, I'm sure I would have learned more about him than I had the courage to ask.

Everyone shared some story as we ate or worked together, and in those summer weeks, I let myself enjoy the company of the outcasts of Cunningham. I didn't have anything to tell, but Kirby talked about his mom and everyone said they'd pray. The water pipe was run, the outhouse was built, the bee boxes were assembled, the bunkhouse was ready to be roofed and sided, but the tiny fruit forming overhead in the pecan trees went as unnoticed as their green flowers two months before.

I was hardening and softening at the same time, and through the heat, labor, and lunch, I couldn't imagine ever passing these people in the rain again. I knew their names, I knew their stories, and my parents knew nothing of what was happening to me.

32
A Better Place

It must have been Saturday. Mr. Wallace was standing with Natalie beside his pickup filled with windows when Kirby and I rolled through the pecan grove. Jesse and Sam had already tacked up felt paper and were moving bundles of shingles to the bunkhouse roof when we stepped out of my truck. Natalie bounced on her toes and waved to us smiling big. We hadn't seen her in a while.

"Good morning, boys," Mr. Wallace nodded.

"Good morning, sir," we answered together.

"Well, well, just in time," Jesse said with a grin as he came down off the last rung of the ladder. "You're just in time, Kirby, to tote these shingles up to Sam. The ridge is done, and the first couple runs are on. Sam knows what to do, so get these bundles up the ladder and put 'em where he says until he tells you to stop. Then load up the back side after that. When you're done, jump up there and give Sam a hand. It's gonna be hot, so work fast enough to get off that roof before too much of the morning gets away."

"Sure, no problem." Kirby beamed as he hoisted a stout paper bundle to his shoulder and started up the ladder.

"And Kirby," Kirby stopped to look back for further instructions, "don't fall."

Kirby nodded.

"And Kirby…don't drop any shingles on me or PJ either."

"Gotcha." Kirby smiled and turned to move up the ladder with his first load.

"Now you, me, and John are gonna unload these doors and windows, and I'll show you how to set 'em. We'll take care of the soffits first, but that'll go pretty fast as long as Sam and Kirby don't kill us."

"Sounds good." I clasped my hands and glanced at the load in Mr. Wallace's truck. It looked heavy, but I didn't mind. I was excited about learning some carpentry, and I was happy to be working with Jesse and John.

"All right, let's get this stuff off the truck so Natalie and Mr. Wallace can get into town. It's a vegetable stand day, and if they don't get there quick, all the best spots on the square will be taken."

"I know!" Natalie exclaimed. "And we got so much more than boring ol' tomatoes this year. We got peas, we got beans, we got squash, we got cucumbers, okra, and a whole bunch of other stuff. We don't got any blackberries though," she stuck out her lip and eyed her father, "'cause I get walloped every time I pick 'em…but we do got about a million jars of honey! So, PJ, you need to jump up, hop to it, and get all this stuff outta Daddy's truck so we can hitch up the trailer and get to town. I think everybody's gonna be real happy when they see how gooda farmers our friends is—and we have honey!" She glowed as she talked, but I was pretty sure Mr. Wallace wouldn't allow Natalie to talk about how good of farmers his friends were in the Cunningham town square.

"Yes, ma'am, will do, ma'am." I gave her a salute and started moving windows to the bunkhouse with Jesse. John was doing something inside but came out to help as soon as he realized we were unloading. What took Jesse and me together to lift, John could do by himself, so we had the truck empty in no time, and Mr. Wallace and Natalie were back through the pecan grove and off to the square to sell vegetables and honey.

The work went fast. Sam and John had gotten good with their hammers, and I did my best to learn all I could about soffits and setting windows without slowing things down. By the time Mary, Elizabeth, and Nya appeared through the orchard with lunch, we only had an hour or two left of the workday. We made the meal a quick one, said our thank yous, and finished our work in short order. Jesse said the siding would be in Monday, and we would set the stove and sink after we hung that next week.

The bunkhouse was wide instead of deep, like a horizontal shotgun set on a wooden foundation with steps and a porch that hadn't been built yet. The windows and shingles gave it a face and hair, but sheathed only in plywood, the structure still seemed naked and vulnerable, like a new fawn finding its legs in the meadow. Without shutters for dimples or a porch to give it a smile, it was hard to tell if the bunkhouse was happy, but the windmill approved of its company.

Even though we'd worked 'til after lunch, the day was still young for a Cunningham summer, so we rolled up our tools said our good-byes, and Jesse, Kirby, and I climbed in my truck to head for town. We left John and Sam to do whatever they did without us, probably collect honey or help the others with farm chores before heading back home to Tracker Island.

I thought of that place with its snakes, broken dishes, and cracked-face doll as I drove off. The meadow beyond the pecans with its apiary and windmill was a far better place for Angeline, and I was satisfied with my part in building it.

33
Mr. Adleman

Even on a summer Saturday with vegetable vendors in full swing and half of Hawkinsville in town, the drive in on River Road was always a smooth, straight shot, and parking behind the church was never a problem. So we were stunned to see cars lined up on the roadside two or three miles out as groups of excited people walked among slow-moving vehicles headed for the square. I'd never seen a traffic jam in Cunningham—*ever*—but I touched my brakes, coming to a complete stop as other trucks and cars circled around the church looking for a nonexistent parking spot.

"What's going on?" Kirby asked. "All these people can't be here to shop, can they?"

"No way." I shook my head and let the truck roll forward as someone up ahead took their turn in traffic. "Something else must be happening. You see the plates on the car ahead of us? That ain't a Hawkinsville tag. Some of these folks are coming all the way in from Monticello, maybe even Waynesboro."

"What's going on?" Kirby repeated as a group of Uphillers walked by.

"Let's go past the church up here," Jesse directed. "Turn in behind Mr. Wallace's store. I have a key to the loading gate. We'll park there."

On and off the brakes, being as patient as I could, I followed Jesse's directions until we finally squeezed into a spot between a stack of lumber and a pile of cinderblocks behind Wallace's Hardware & Lumber Supply. We climbed out to try the back door but found it locked, so we followed a group of chatty Uphillers around the building into the square.

The Bride and Groom were in their full summer glory, casting a deep green shadow across the farmers, their produce, and the people squeezing and sniffing what they had to sell. Indistinct chatter and laughter buzzed through the crowd as strangers milled across the lawn, moving in slow herds over the streets and sidewalks, in and out of overwhelmed shops. Excitement sizzled and popped like static electricity. I couldn't tell what was happening, but above the multitude, past the open shops, and beyond the big smiles and farmer hats, I noticed the largest concentration of Uphillers gathered at the church steps.

"Come on," Jesse touched me on the arm. "Let's find Natalie."

He stepped into the street and in an instant disappeared in a wake of strangers. The crowd was tight, but I followed the best I could, with only glimpses of Jesse's shirt to keep me from being lost among the people. I pushed, jostled, and bumped—trusting Jesse knew where he was going because I had no idea where Natalie might be or if she was even still here. But I followed just the same. I hoped Kirby was keeping up, but I couldn't turn to check and risk losing sight of Jesse. Nobody seemed interested in excuses, so I didn't bother with apologies as I pushed rudely past. I just kept chasing Jesse's shirt until I found myself at the midway where the farmers were selling their produce. When I spotted Jesse with Mr. Wallace and Natalie, I was confident enough to turn back to check on Kirby. He'd stayed with me the whole way.

Mr. Wallace was telling Jesse he'd never opened the hardware store. So many people were buying produce; he had to come help Natalie right away. He said he felt terrible because, like last year, the other farmers insisted he charge more for his vegetables, so he tripled the price, but it didn't matter. Customers were delighted to pay the premium.

"We haven't had a chance to sit down once," Mr. Wallace was saying as Natalie bagged what was left of the pole beans for a woman in a big white hat. "And now it looks like we're out of everything."

The air was heavy with the smell of sweat and fresh okra, but the scent of resentment wasn't difficult to detect. Other stands had steady lines of customers too, but their bins were still full, not having had the same success as Mr. Wallace. Farmers cut their eyes and made excuses about everybody wanting to buy from a retarded girl. They never considered the testimony they made to the superiority of the Wallace produce by forcing up the price on everything Natalie sold. Competitors sought an advantage, but they only validated the best of Cunningham, doing more for Mr. Wallace's financial success than he would have been brazen enough to do for himself. The other vendors soured on their stools.

Jesse was oblivious, but I'd lived here all my life, and I'm sure Kirby felt it too. Loose tongues and suspicion fueled by jealousy wouldn't be so hushed once Natalie and her father were packed up and gone for the day. Butterflies sprung to life in my stomach as I watched the other farmers pretend not to watch Jesse and Mr. Wallace talk. I was worried. I knew what Mr. Wallace was doing behind the pecan grove, and I knew who was tending his farm. I'm not sure it was a full secret, but I know it should have been—and people with secrets should know better than to call attention to themselves in the Cunningham town square.

Maybe Mr. Wallace overestimated his influence, or maybe he was just excited by the success of the day, but he didn't seem to notice the sharp eyes and pursed faces stabbing him from every direction. It reminded me of boiling a complacent frog by gradually turning up the heat. He was a smart man, so I don't know what he was thinking.

"I felt like I was charging an arm and a leg for the honey, Jesse, but it sold out straight away, and I had to restock everything else six or seven times. I was sure we were hauling too much down here, but it's all gone now, and…" Mr. Wallace leaned in closer so only we could hear what he was saying, "they made me sell it all at triple price."

"Wow, that's pretty good," Kirby commented.

"Yeah, it's good," Mr. Wallace agreed, "because, boys, we raked in enough today to pay for the windmill and the bunkhouse with some to boot." Mr. Wallace snorted through his nose and smiled as he thought about what he'd just said. "I was planning to pay the construction debt down over the next several years, but here it is, all taken care of in less than a day." Mr. Wallace shook his head. "Unbelievable isn't it?"

"I guess we'd better believe it." Jesse put his arm around Mr. Wallace's and gave him a shake. "As long as you counted right."

"Oh, believe me," Mr. Wallace said with a grin, "if there is one thing I can do, it's count right."

People milled past, looking over the empty bushel baskets as Natalie apologized and explained everything was gone for the day. When asked if she'd be back tomorrow, she shook her head and told them, "Not on Sunday."

Mr. Wallace motioned us in to say something else he didn't want overheard. "That's not the best part. Do you know who Mr. Adleman is?"

"I think I know the name," I lied.

"You know Red Apple grocery stores?" Mr. Wallace whispered.

Kirby and I nodded, because that was the big grocery chain in Hawkinsville.

"Mr. Adleman owns those. He's got a dozen or so in Hawkinsville, Monticello, and some other places. Anyway, he asked me if I'd be willing to sell to him farm-direct. Said we grow the most beautiful vegetables he's ever seen, and he wants 'em special in his stores. Said he'd take all we had at a regular price, and he'd send a truck on Wednesdays for pickup. He wants the honey too, as long as we give it a name and a label. Can you believe it? That old place is gonna be a real farm. I might even be able to sell the store…if things keep goin' like this."

"Wow," Kirby sighed. "Has anyone ever done that much business with Uphill before?"

Mr. Wallace shook his head. "Not for a real long time."

The conversation broke momentarily as Mr. Wallace, Kirby, and I considered how Cunningham might respond to one of its own monopolizing the business of an Uphill buyer. I thought the other farmers might be happy as long as it kept Natalie and Mr. Wallace off the square.

"Well, looks like you guys are done for the day. How about a hand packing up?" Jesse offered.

"Nah." Mr. Wallace waved us off, looking around at his empty stand. "Natalie and I can manage. You boys have the rest of the day off, so go enjoy yourselves. Maybe you can find out what all these people are doin' here. We've been so busy, I never thought to ask. I'll see you tonight, Jesse, and I'll see you two on Monday. And, boys…thanks."

Mr. Wallace turned to Natalie, gave her a hug, and began packing their things. We headed out through the multitude to find out what was happening on the steps of God's Glory. The day was hot, and the crowd grew heavier and less patient with us moving by as we approached the church. A balding man with an elderly woman growled at us to get back in line. I'm sure he would have chased us down to enforce his demand had it not been for his infirm companion, but Jesse kept going and so did me and Kirby.

34
The Ghost in his Arms

The hum of the crowd droned in my head, isolating me down to the soul. Even though Jesse and Kirby were nearby, it felt more like we were underwater than truly together.

I pushed past a sad man holding a hollow girl whose eyes were tired as bedtime. Through all the whir, I heard him tell her everything would be okay. I don't know why that caught me or why I stopped for them, but I turned for a better look.

Against a curtain of nondescript Uphillers, the sad man swayed gently with a six- or seven-year-old girl draped against his chest. Her arms were limp around his neck as he stroked her hair and sang softly into her ear. Sweat beaded his brow and bled through his shirt as he held the little girl in his arms, waiting patiently with a child who couldn't wait much longer. I could feel the sorrow, and it made me shudder.

"What's wrong?" Kirby found me watching the sad man.

I shook my head. "What are they doing here?"

But before Kirby could respond, Jesse moved up and answered instead, "Why don't we ask them?"

The man who seemed so distant in the crowd was no more than a half-dozen steps away. We slid around until we stood by him and the weary child in his arms. He held her like a dried flower someone pressed into a family Bible long ago.

"Hey," Jesse said to the sad man, "looks like you have a sleepy girl here."

"I do." The man half smiled. "I wish I could get her to doze off for more than a few minutes."

Jesse nodded and patted the girl gently on the back. "She's not feeling too well. What brings you down on such a miserably hot day?"

The man adjusted the little girl in his arms. He was exhausted with his load. "We came in from Patterson this morning for the river, but when we got there, the deputy turned us away, saying we needed to buy a pass at the church if we wanted to go in." The man raised himself to his toes and craned over the crowd toward God's Glory. "Doesn't look like we'll make it today, not with all these folks ahead of us wanting the same thing."

"What? Since when do you need to buy a ticket for Sandy Shores?" blurted Kirby.

"That's weird," I shrugged, and then I leaned closer so the man could hear me better through the noise. "Why does everybody want to go to the beach all of a sudden? It's like a flippin' gold rush around here."

The man adjusted his daughter again and sighed. "Kind of it is," he nodded. "They say a woman from Hawkinsville with cancer or MS or something went into the river down here a few weeks ago, and the water healed her fresh and healthy. She's been declining interviews left and right, but her doctors aren't, and they say it's nothing short of a miracle. So here we are, me and this bunny rabbit." The man dipped his head so we wouldn't see the slow tear run off his nose. "I don't know if it's true or not," he sniffed, "but it's all we have left."

Jesse drew a deep breath and pushed his hand back through his hair. "So, you have to buy a pass at the church on account of that, huh?" It wasn't really a question, so nobody answered. "Well," Jesse continued, "it's awfully hot out here, and this sweet girl ain't feeling her best, so I don't think you should worry about going to Sandy Shores today, especially when there's nothing there that can help."

The man looked at Jesse with welling eyes. "Really, it was all a hoax?"

"No," Jesse whispered, and I could hear him again like he was in my ear. He reached over and touched the little girl on her back. "It's time to get up, Caroline. Your daddy's tired, and your mommy's making tater tot casserole at home. Come on, sweetie, rise and shine."

Caroline's father's eyes swelled, and tears flooded his face. For a moment, I thought he would pull away and tell Jesse to cut it out, but before he could, the ghost in his arms pushed her head up off his shoulder and turned to Jesse. "I love tater tot casserole." Her eyes were weak, but she mustered a dim smile.

A tear crawled off Jesse's cheek. "I know you do, sweetheart."

He touched her shoulder, and Caroline leaned from her father's arms to hug Jesse around his neck. He welcomed her embrace and kissed her on the ear. She squeezed Jesse as hard as her illness would allow, and when they let go, the sad man's daughter pulled away as a healthy child.

"I feel better, Daddy," she chimed. "I'm hungry."

She squirmed to get down, but before she could, her daddy threw his arms around Jesse sandwiching her in between. Caroline's dad held tight, convulsing into sobs and broken thank yous before letting go and wiping his nose on his shirt sleeve.

"Thank you," he choked as he set his daughter to her feet. Somehow, Kirby and I were the only witnesses, but even so, I still wasn't sure what had happened.

Caroline took her daddy's hand and waved before they faded away through the crowd of tragic strangers waiting to buy a ticket for Sandy Shores. Funny, I remember her name.

"C'mon," Jesse slapped me on the chest with the back of his hand, "let's go see."

35
Mary Miller

Kirby and I followed Jesse through tightly woven strangers. Most of them complained bitterly as we squeezed by. Jesse seemed to pass through without issue, while Kirby and I stumbled behind, tripping over feet and crutches with every step. I almost fell, but caught myself on the arm of a wheelchair. I apologized profusely to its pilot.

We pushed up to find the church steps roped off and funneled down to a single-file line where people ascended to buy passes from church volunteers changing money from a metal cashbox. The mashed potato lady, the sickle man, and several others sat like magistrates behind a folding table as Uphillers approached to trade bills for paper stubs that would allow access to Sandy Shores. A big banner hung across the doors of God's Glory, indicating the price for adults and children. Carl, in his neatly pressed uniform, stood adjacent so everyone would know the church had the law. He seemed disgusted with his post.

Jesse dipped under the rope and started up the stairs, but when Kirby and I tried to follow, the deputy protested.

"You two hold it right there." Carl stepped toward us. "Ain't no locals allowed at Sandy Shores today—not as long as all of this is going on. So you boys get yourself somewhere else, you hear?"

"What's going on, Carl?" Kirby motioned to the ticket table.

"You don't worry about it. You two just need to get and get now," he snarled, taking another step down and tapping his nightstick.

Carl was a nice guy, firm but not hostile or aggressive like Eddy, but the contradiction between the decent cop and the storm trooper fingering his baton made Carl nearly as intimidating as Sheriff Johnson. I remembered the day he slung me across River Road, and I stepped back as Jesse moved by unchallenged. Carl didn't notice him at all until Jesse was standing at the ticket table.

"What are you doing here?" the mashed potato lady snapped. "Tickets are for out-a-towners only. No locals allowed at Sandy Shores."

"Why not?" Jesse asked.

"Too many visitors," the sickle man answered. "Now move out of the way and let these people get past."

Carl moved up to Jesse's flank, and while his back was turned, Kirby and I eased up a couple of steps as well. We were careful not to get within easy reach of the deputy in case a hasty retreat became necessary. I was sure Carl would take Jesse's arm and escort him away from the table, but he didn't. Instead he offered Jesse a more plausible excuse than the sickle man had.

"We have too many people in town, so the sheriff figured we needed to regulate 'em—you know, keep 'em safe. We got a gate down at the turnoff, and Eddy's there checking tickets so the river don't get overcrowded." Carl had been harsh with me and Kirby, but he was speaking with Jesse like he was apologizing to a friend. "Sheriff Johnson thought we should issue passes, but it was Reverend Dodge's idea to collect donations with the tickets."

"Listen, boy, you need to get out of the way," one of the magistrates barked from his seat. "Deputy, clear him outta here! We got people waiting."

But instead of reaching for Jesse, Carl dropped his head to cover his face with the brim of his hat. When we arrived, I could tell Carl wasn't happy with his job, and he saw something in Jesse that made him terribly uncomfortable with his part in all this. The deputy's shame spilled over the church steps like a cup of soup, warm with compromise and smelling of regret. I felt sorry for Carl.

Jesse turned to the table of volunteers. "And what are they waiting for? To buy hope from a bunch of crooks and charlatans selling their indulgences like thieving pardoners at the foot of my Father's house! You're selling tickets to nothing!"

The mashed potato lady and the other cashbox magistrates, stunned by Jesse's words, sat wide-eyed and open mouthed, as if they never anticipated their provocations would bear fruit. I'm sure they hadn't been openly insulted since grade school, so it took a moment for the first of them to shake off Jesse's assault and respond.

"First of all, young man," one of the volunteers snarled, "this is not your father's house. He only built the porte cochere, and you've been paid for that. This place belongs to Reverend Dodge and the people of God's Glory, not to you or your dad. Second of all, who do you think you are to stand up here and call us names? I've got a good mind to…"

But Jesse quit listening and turned back to Carl. "Deputy, do you know where Reverend Dodge is? I need to go talk to him."

"I think he's at the Gas & Grocery with the sheriff," Carl muttered from under his hat.

Jesse nodded and reached out to put his hand on Carl's shoulder as the cashbox magistrates continued to squawk in the background. "You're doing a good job keeping these people safe." Jesse glanced over the tide of people rolling up on the church steps. "Keep doing what you're doing and don't worry about it for now."

Carl lifted up just enough to see out from under the brim of his hat and give Jesse an understanding nod.

"Deputy!" the shrill voice of the mashed potato lady broke in. "Are you going to let that hoodlum come up here and talk to us this way?"

Her words made no difference. Carl stepped back to his post and ignored her complaint. Jesse turned to descend the steps of God's Glory, but that wasn't good enough for the sickle man, who jumped to his feet to hurl a last insult at Jesse's back. But before he managed to get out what he wanted to say, the sickle man bumped the ticket table just enough for the front legs to slide over the edge of the steps and send it toppling into the crowd. The cash box and paper tickets spilled out among the people. By the time I got home that evening, my parents already heard how the young carpenter, in a fit of rage, tossed over the money tables at church.

We dipped under the rope and pushed our way out. People were happy to let us leave as the cashbox magistrates collected themselves enough to resume business behind us. The Bride and Groom watched as we dodged our way through the thinning fringe of people and headed to the Gas & Grocery. We hustled to keep up with Jesse's angry gait. When we arrived, Jesse pulled the door wide, leaving Kirby and me to catch it for ourselves as we walked in behind him.

The flood of strangers filling the other shops on the square hadn't bothered with the little grocery store. Only a smattering of locals were milling through the aisles when we stepped in. Mr. Miller stood at the register with his palms on the counter, leaning over directly across from Reverend Dodge. He didn't bother to break off his conversation with the reverend when the door chime announced our entrance. The sheriff was leaning against the endcap of the cereal aisle, sipping a cola, half listening to Reverend Dodge and Mr. Miller as customers began lining up with their purchases. Chipmunk was there with a couple of her friends, waiting to buy a cold drink and a bag of bubble gum. Mrs. Miller, with her ball cap pulled low and her yellow bandanna covering her face, stood barely visible in the mouth of the baking aisle. She looked like she might disappear at any moment.

"What are you saying, Reverend?" Mr. Miller spat. "I've lived here forever, and I can't take my wife to Sandy Shores to see if something might happen with her condition?"

"Come on, Henry," the reverend bellowed back, "you know as well as I do if there was anything there that could possibly help Mary, I'd have the sheriff drive you down right now. But God doesn't work like that. There are no quick fixes. There's a purpose for Mary's illness, a reason the doctors can't heal her, a plan, something He needs her to do. God's will is a mystery and all we can do is pray it is carried out."

"Reverend," Mr. Miller started to protest, but Reverend Dodge held up his hand to silence him.

"Now, Henry, there's no use in discussing it any further. We already have too many people down there as it is, and Eddy's not letting any locals in." Reverend Dodge turned to confirm what he said with the sheriff. The big man gave a silent nod and took a sip of his drink. "So you can't get in anyway, but don't worry, we'll keep Mary on the prayer list. I'll even include her in my personal prayers, and if it's God's will, she'll get better."

Mr. Miller, still leaning over the counter, dropped his head between his shoulders, exhausted from begging for his wife.

"Why do you say, 'If it's God's will'? Why not just ask the Lord to heal Ms. Miller and expect it to be done?" Jesse stepped up.

Mr. Miller lifted up to see who had interceded, and the growing line of customers shifted uncomfortably as Jesse's question hung in the air. My toes curled in my shoes. It was one thing to challenge the mashed potato lady or the sickle man publicly, but this was Reverend Dodge with Sheriff Johnson standing close at hand. Kirby twisted at my side. I noticed a faint smile flicker in the sheriff's eyes, but I couldn't tell if it was from the enjoyment of Reverend Dodge being challenged or from the anticipation of crushing Jesse.

"Young man," Reverend Dodge flipped on a patronizing smile, "I love *all* of my flock, and I wouldn't want to hurt *any* of them by giving false hope. I'm sure you understand that."

It was a reasonable response, and the room breathed a collective sigh of relief Reverend Dodge had provided such a profound answer, but Jesse wasn't ready to let go.

"You don't want to give them false hope in God or false hope in yourself, Reverend?"

Sheriff Johnson leaned up off the endcap, taking a long, slow sip from his can to cover a smile his eyes couldn't contain. Ms. Miller peeked out from the corner of the baking aisle, and I thought Mr. Miller might reach for the broom to sweep the reverend's face off the floor.

We remained silent as Reverend Dodge cleared his throat. "What?" was all he managed.

"When you abide in the Spirit honestly and fully, will not the Spirit also abide in you honestly and fully?" Jesse fired.

"I suppose," Reverend Dodge mumbled, too stunned to search for a rote biblical verse in defense.

Jesse was angry. "You suppose, Preacher! What does your almighty Scripture tell you?"

Reverend Dodge looked like a champion who'd been clipped on the jaw for the first time. His eyes were wide, and he took a single step back in retreat, offering no response to Jesse's question.

"And if you are submitted to the Spirit, is not His Will yours and yours His?" Jesse fired again, moving forward.

"I suppose," Reverend Dodge muttered, not ready to retaliate.

"You suppose again! How else would Peter, a mere man, be able to heal the lame or Paul raise the dead if their will and the Will of the Spirit were not one? It doesn't matter, Preacher, that you are like most, lacking in holiness, but you shouldn't pretend to be something you aren't, passing judgment on your flock like you are closer to God than they. Leaving them with 'if it is God's will' is nothing but a colossal cop-out, offered out of guilt instead of faith. And make no mistake, it is out of *your* guilt, not theirs, you offer such a lame, halfhearted prayer. You don't always know, so why pretend to at the expense of your parish?"

Jesse paralyzed the store with his last question. All eyes slid to the reverend, who was beginning to find his legs again. He cleared his throat, righted himself, and drew a breath deep enough to flutter the shades in the windows. He mustered the full force of his pulpit voice, ready to lay Jesse low with bone-crushing resonance.

"How dare you speak to me this way, you arrogant twerp!" Reverend Dodge thundered, rattling all the glass in Miller's Gas & Grocery. "How would you know better than I the mind of God?"

The fearsome reverend fumed like the wrath of God itself, forcing the rest of us, including the sheriff, to draw back in dread. I wasn't sure if the Gas & Grocery could contain the reverend or if the building would burst from its foundation and collapse around us. Dust spilled from some unknown place in the ceiling, and if the fury in the reverend's glare could set one afire, Jesse would have been cinders. A dusty pause wafted over our heads as Jesse waited for the rattling walls and tinkling glass to settle. He stood like David before the Philistine.

"I speak with Him every day," Jesse answered.

"You mean you *pray* to Him," corrected Reverend Dodge.

"I mean I *speak* to Him."

"That's blasphemy, boy," the reverend erupted. "Who do you think you are to tell me you talk to God?"

"I know who I am, and I know who you are as well. So I'll ask you, is it easier for me to say I talk with God or to ask Ms. Miller to remove her hat and bandanna and be free of the ailment you wouldn't let her wash away in the river? Well, Reverend?"

"What are you saying? Are you really that crazy?" Reverend Dodge looked around for support from Mr. Miller's customers, but we were too frightened to weigh in on either side.

"You like to blame all that happens on God's Will, as if we are powerless to change any of it, yet you ask God for stuff all the time. It's no problem for Abba…but for you, it waters down your petitions, so in the end you request healing with all the faith and sincerity of asking for a new car or a better golf game. You ask for so much, you're not devoted to what is holy, and you fail to recognize the difference between God's work and your own. It turns you into a pompous blowhard making all of your excuses *God's Will*, and you lord it over your flock as if they are as impotent as you."

I was at least five full paces away, but Jesse's words filled my thoughts like I was listening to them over the phone. Reverend Dodge twitched and Sheriff Johnson fingered his ear, so I knew they had heard it in the same way. In fact, every customer at the Gas & Grocery seemed to shake their heads or rub the side of their faces like they were being tickled by a secret whisper no one else could hear.

"Let me be clear," Reverend Dodge roared back. "Of all the things I will discuss, debate, or entertain, blasphemy will never be one of them!" Reverend Dodge wheeled around to Mr. Miller. "Henry! *No locals at Sandy Shores!*" Then he stormed out, shoving the door open hard enough for it to slap against the outside wall. Sheriff Johnson stepped up to follow, but paused to lean into Jesse's face before he went by.

"If I was you, boy, I'd pack up and get the hell out of Cunningham," the sheriff growled. "Otherwise…you're dead." He rose up, lumbered to the door, and turned back, eclipsing the exit. "Have a pleasant day, folks." He tipped his hat and disappeared into the parking lot.

Groceries littered the floor at the feet of a broken line of frozen people who had been waiting to ring out when the confrontation began. Eggs, having slipped from the hands of a would-be customer, lay cracked and oozing from their carton. A puddle of milk seeped around a loaf of bread, making its way toward a box of cookies, and Chipmunk's bubblegum spread across the ground like a game of jacks. Everything anyone carried to the front slid unconsciously from their fingers during the altercation and now lay wet or broken on the floor of the Gas & Grocery. I felt like someone had forgotten to turn off the gas at the dentist. We could've stayed blinking at each other the rest of the day if Jesse hadn't spoken up.

"Mary," he called to Ms. Miller. "Mary, let me see you."

Ms. Miller stood at the corner of the baking aisle where she had dropped a bag of flour. The white dust piled on her shoes like a crumbling iceberg from a tiny frozen world. Jesse raised his hand to her, but Ms. Miller only gaped from behind her bandana as if the flour on her feet was too heavy to move. I couldn't see her eyes from under her ball cap, but I saw her head twitch ever so slightly, like Jesse was in her ear. Still, she remained.

"Mary," he called again as the store watched in silence, "let me see you Mary," but she was paralyzed.

Our eyes went from Jesse to Ms. Miller and back, wondering how this would end. No one moved—that is, except for Henry Miller. Without a word, Mr. Miller slid from behind his counter and crossed the minefield of broken groceries to be with his wife. He took her by the arm. "C'mon, sweetheart, let's go see this man," he whispered.

Ms. Miller gave a hesitant nod. She took her husband's arm and tore away from the tiny mountain covering her feet, grinding it to a pair of dusty white footprints leading to Jesse.

"Here she is," Mr. Miller said.

Jesse kept his eyes on Ms. Miller. "Mary, let me see you."

Mary Miller looked to her husband, dropped his arm, and reached up to slide the baseball cap from her head. She let it fall to the floor among the other broken things. Her dark hair cascaded over her shoulders like pent-up satin falling to the middle of her back. The sun glinted in, dressing her head in golden white sparkles. Ms. Miller took a deep breath, summoning her courage as she reached around to untie her bandanna for a witness other than the mirror. She took another breath as it dropped away.

Time slowed to a crawl as the mask drifted to her feet. Ms. Miller looked to her husband and, seeing his eyes, tore off her gloves and threw her hands to her face to feel the absence of sores. Her eyes filled with tears, and she laughed as she danced out of her baggy clothes until she stood in her underwear. There was no evidence of affliction.

"Will it last?" Ms. Miller choked.

"Forever," Jesse whispered back.

I couldn't take my eyes off the nearly naked town recluse who kept herself hidden and wrapped in the secret world where I first met her, buying a root beer instead of an orange cream soda. It had been a world of shadows, shared only with Nya, Angeline, and me for a moment one day. I felt separate but a part, like a dream where I'm not myself but at the same time I am, as the Millers embraced each other and kissed Jesse as if no one else was there. They laughed through their tears as they examined Ms. Miller's clear skin.

The rest of us stared like there was nothing left outside the Gas & Grocery until Jesse said it was time to leave. He held the door for us to file out before him. Everyone, including Chipmunk and her friends, went out of their way to brush against Jesse or touch him as they left. He was gracious about it all. Kirby and I were the last ones through the door, and as we stepped out to the parking lot, I heard Jesse tell Mary Miller to go show Reverend Dodge.

I felt like an intruder watching Jesse pass final words with the Millers, so I turned away, stumbling over Chipmunk standing right behind me. She was staring at the same scene. Our small collision forced our attention to one another. She was in a blue dress. She had a pretty, round face.

"Who is he?" she asked.

"Just a carpenter who works for Mr. Wallace," I answered.

"Nah," she shook her head, "I don't think so." She glanced around me at Jesse and the Millers. "You saw what he did, right? You know what just happened, don't you?"

I wasn't sure what she wanted me to say as her eyes searched mine and found less than expected. "If Sheriff Johnson hadn't closed down Sandy Shores," she continued, "and Mimi hadn't wanted gum, I wouldn't have been here at all. Do you know that? I would have missed the whole thing with Reverend Dodge, and I wouldn't have seen Ms. Miller…well…get better. It's…" her voice trailed off, "like this was meant for me to see. Do you know what I mean?"

I didn't.

"I know what you mean," Kirby answered. "I know exactly what you mean."

A crowd of chattering strangers swelled around us, moving across the parking lot, bumping past to buy provisions at the grocery store. They flowed by like the Chagrin around its boulders, and while Kirby and Chipmunk contemplated what they'd seen inside, I wondered if Ms. Miller would have time to get dressed before the Uphillers came through the door. We stood in the bright afternoon waiting for Jesse, but when the customers finally drained out of the Gas & Grocery, he was gone. We figured we just missed him.

We parted without good-byes because even in a small town, we didn't belong with Chipmunk's friends any more than they belonged with us. I was sure I wouldn't speak to any of them until necessitated by some future event at school or church.

Kirby and I walked back to my pickup. I don't know that we were done with the day, but the day was done with us. We waited a while for Jesse, but when he didn't show, we hopped in the truck and I took Kirby home. I fought the stop-and-go traffic in silence as Kirby stared out the passenger window. Even though we hadn't spoken since we left the Gas & Grocery, I knew what he was thinking. He had a bad deal going and I didn't want to see him bruised anymore, so when we rolled to a stop in front of his house, I said what was on my mind.

"Hey, Kirb, if you're thinking what I think you're thinking, well…" I searched for the words, "we're not even sure that woman, Margie, was even sick, and whatever Ms. Miller had, it couldn't have been all that serious…not like leukemia. I guess what I'm trying to say, buddy, is don't get your hopes up. I know Jesse's our friend and some weird things have been happening lately and he's really cool, but he's just a carpenter. If he was anything more, do you think he'd be building a crappy shack in the middle of nowhere for almost no money at all? That's like miracles being printed on the back the page of a newspaper…it don't happen."

Kirby didn't turn around. He kept staring out the passenger window as the truck idled and my words bounced off the back of his head.

"I guess what I'm trying to say is," I continued, "maybe we shouldn't get any false hope…you know, like Reverend Dodge said."

I don't know why I thought Reverend Dodge's name would add credibility, but as soon as I mentioned him, Kirby popped the door and slid out. I could tell he was mad, but it wasn't until he looked back I could see how angry he really was.

"If you think about it, if you really think about it, asshole," he growled, "that's nothing but a stinkin' Dodge lie…'cause how can there ever be *false* hope? There ain't no such thing."

I thought he would slam my door, but he didn't. He closed it like ordinary and crossed the yard into his house, leaving me to wrestle with the notion of *false* hope for the rest of my life.

36
Chipmunk

Kirby's parents couldn't make it to church the next day, so we swung by his house to pick him up and drove through town to God's Glory from there. The square looked like the circus had pulled up stakes in the middle of the night and left without cleaning up. Trash spilled over the tops of every receptacle, and paper cups, wrappers, bottles, and cans lay strewn under the Bride and Groom like a dew of sleeping refuse.

"Oh, my goodness," Mom breathed at the scene as Dad maneuvered around double-parked cars piled in the street. I could see people sleeping in them.

A line was backed out the door at Katie's Diner, and a group was already gathered at the steps of God's Glory to buy tickets for Sandy Shores. Yesterday seemed exciting with all of the strangers in town, wading in and out of shops, buying vegetables, and standing in line, but in the aftermath, on this breezeless Sunday morning with its overnight cars and litter in the streets, Cunningham reeked only of desperation. Even with the windows rolled up tight, it was impossible to keep it from seeping in. "Oh, my goodness," Mom sighed again. This didn't seem like home, and I didn't know if I should feel sorry for the families camping in their cars or be afraid of them.

Dad found a parking spot somewhere, and we kept close, not looking around, as we moved across the yard, under the porte cochere, and through the side door of the church. A smattering of strangers leaning on canes or crutches and daddies holding sick, sleeping children hung in the narthex, waiting for the early service. Dad nodded hello to a man mussed from a restless night and lack of a morning shower, standing at the handlebars of a quiet boy's wheelchair. He and Mom slid by the hodgepodge of unfamiliar faces to their Sunday school class to drink coffee and talk about the rabble in the church.

Somehow I knew we wouldn't be asked to give up our seats for our visitors today. I stood with Kirby a moment longer, wondering what these people were doing here or thought they might find in Cunningham, but I didn't ask. I touched Kirby on the elbow. "Let's go." And we descended the basement stairs to see what our weekly pamphlet had to say about the love of God.

The old stairs creaked and popped with their customary complaints as Kirby and I made our way down to find Chipmunk holding court with a small contingent of the regular youth. They huddled around her in chairs, shaking their heads as she gabbed on about whatever she was saying. Her friends from the Gas & Grocery weren't with her and she was so involved in her single-sided conversation, a full minute passed before she noticed us. There was no teacher in the room to prevent what happened next.

"PJ, Kirby, great!" she chirped and waved us to join the group.

We had no choice, so we pulled up a couple of chairs. Cursory chatter about the state police being called in to clear out Sandy Shores last night circled the group, but that's not what Chipmunk wanted to talk about.

"PJ, I was telling everybody what happened yesterday at the Gas & Grocery," she finally said.

Whatever she told them, her influence wasn't enough to pull these kids over the edge of belief. They looked to me for a toehold either way. Why they cared what I had to say, I'll never know—maybe it was the unlikelihood of collusion between Chipmunk and me that made it matter.

"Jesse got mad at Reverend Dodge. Is that what you're talking about?"

Kirby hissed, dropping his head in disgust with my answer.

"Did he really throw the ticket tables down the front steps?" someone asked.

"Nah," I shook my head, "that was an accident."

"I tried to tell everybody what happened at the store, but they all think I'm crazy," Chipmunk added.

A murmur of agreement rustled among the tightly packed chairs.

"Not crazy, just mistaken," somebody else clarified.

Chipmunk had always been one of the Sunday school favorites, a regular reader with all the right answers. She was a goody-goody with a cartoon faith she used to define herself and bolster her popularity with both her friends and the adults of Cunningham. She behaved like she had something I didn't, but I never considered it to be anything but an act. Whatever she'd told this group, she'd gone too far and needed me now as an unlikely ally to save her popularity. I could feel Chipmunk's credibility hanging by a thread, and I wasn't sure I wanted to help. I hesitated, considering my options, when I caught a hard, unfriendly elbow from Kirby. He charley-horsed me in the meat of the upper arm and it hurt!

"Just say what you know," he growled.

"I don't know anything," I complained, rubbing my bicep.

"Fine, then," Kirby snarled back, "tell 'em what you saw…no commentary, no opinions…just what you saw."

Even though there weren't any more than a dozen of us sitting around, the weight of their eyes was heavy. I dropped my head and reluctantly began to tell what I saw.

"Well, we went to the store because Jesse was mad about the church charging people to go to the river. He might have felt responsible or something because of what happened with the sick lady down there a few weeks ago."

"That was real?" someone gasped, but I didn't answer because I wasn't sure I believed it anyway, and Kirby told me no opinions, just what I saw. "We went in, and Reverend Dodge was saying the Millers couldn't go to Sandy Shores and that made Jesse even madder, so he started to argue with the reverend. Reverend Dodge called Jesse a blasphemer and walked out with the sheriff."

"The sheriff was there?" another in the group asked.

I looked up and nodded. "Then Jesse called to Ms. Miller."

"My mom says that woman's crazy and is all eat up with some kind of skin disease from marrying Mr. Miller for the wrong reasons," someone added.

"My mom says the same thing," I nodded, "but I don't think she's right."

"What you saw," Kirby whispered.

"Well, Jesse told Ms. Miller to take off her mask and stuff, and when she did, she wasn't sick at all. Her skin was as clear and smooth as any you'd see. Then they laughed and cried a lot, and I was glad when Jesse said it was time to go."

"See, I told you!" exclaimed Chipmunk.

"That doesn't prove anything," somebody challenged. "She could've been faking all this time. What's that carpenter doing here anyways?"

"Working for Mr. Wallace," I answered.

"Doing what?" came a snide retort followed by a chorus of hushed conjecture.

I didn't look around to see who owned the question, already knowing my answer wouldn't matter. I held no weight with this group and whatever Chipmunk was trying to do; my testimony hadn't helped at all. I could feel her stare, waiting for my answer, as she began to drown in the murmurs of her friends. She had not convinced them, and being unconvinced myself, I had nothing more to say. Chipmunk threw her lifeline to the wrong boy. If there was so much as a spark of belief among any of us sitting together in the basement of God's Glory, a swirling riptide of cynicism was already threatening to snuff it out.

"Making things better," Kirby answered in a voice too soft to break the conversations about how phony Chipmunk was. Kirby slid from his chair and rose slowly to his feet. I dropped my face into my hands, but I didn't try to stop him. It seemed like he stood forever, alone among the youth hissing their not-so-secret secrets, but it was probably no more than a couple of moments before he was noticed and someone shushed the crowd.

Kirby cleared his throat. "You asked a question I'm not sure you want answered. You asked what he's doing, and I'm telling you—he's making things better."

A moment of low whispers bubbled up through the youth before they finally quieted again and Kirby continued. "I don't know if you know, but my mom has cancer, so I'm not like the rest of you, especially you, PJ." He dropped his hand to my shoulder, but I didn't look up. "So when I see a woman walk out of the river healed, knowing it wasn't the water that made her well; or a little girl dying in her daddy's arms get down healthy and skip home to tater tot casserole; or a woman, every one of us knows is ill, made clean before my eyes; or there's enough to eat when there shouldn't be; or the sun shines in a storm; or I find myself putting a roof on a new home for people I've been raised to ignore and despise…well, maybe it's because of Mom, but I can't afford to be blind to even the smallest part of it."

Kirby took a deep breath as the rest of us sat silent. He glanced over at Chipmunk and continued, "I'm not trying to convince you of anything because what you think doesn't matter a lick to me. I'm just saying what I'm saying. But if anything we've ever learned here in the basement of God's Glory is even close to true…well…it seems to fit." He took his hand off my shoulder. "If Mr. and Ms. Miller are here today, go greet 'em when the time comes and decide for yourself." Then Kirby sat down and no one said a word.

"Hi-ho, gang!" The spell cast by Kirby's words evaporated as soon as our belated Sunday school teacher entered the room. He talked as he crossed the floor, like all we'd been doing was waiting on him to arrive. It took a second to catch up to what he was saying.

"Wow, I had a heck of a time finding a place to park. I've never seen such a motley group of people in all my life hanging around town." He grabbed a chair on his way over to join us. "Looks like the sheriff has his work cut out for him today…might even have to call in the state police again." He plunked his chair down at the periphery of the group and plopped in it like he was already exhausted from the day. "I can't figure how rumors like these get started or how ignorant people have to be to buy into 'em."

The class swallowed hard as our Sunday school teacher grinned through his teeth, and we all fought the urge to look at Kirby. As it turns out, all the rehearsed lectures in the world reveal less about a man than a moment of casual conversation. Our teacher wasn't much more than a wax figure that lit up every Sunday morning to monologue over miracles he secretly regarded as myth. He smiled and nodded to prompt our agreement about ignorant people, but expressionless faces were all that returned. His crass disbelief so seasoned Kirby's words, even I wanted to believe something special might really be happening in Cunningham…if only in defense of my friend.

"Well then," our teacher coughed, "I'm sorry for being late, but it's about time to head up for service, so let's bow our heads and have a prayer."

We did and then filed up the stairs through the narthex filled with pitiful strangers. I thought we'd sit with my parents in our usual spot, but Kirby turned and slid into the very back pew beside Natalie and Mr. Wallace. They hadn't been in church for a while, and I almost passed by until Natalie waved me over. I guess it didn't matter if I sat with my folks or not. Natalie scooted over, making me a spot between her and a couple of strangers who'd settled in the last pew as well.

"I'm glad you and Kirby came to sit with me," she whisper-blurted. "Reverend don't let me sit with the choir no more in case I have a fit, but he says I can sit back here all I want…it's special just for me. Wish I could see the singers and the hand-bellers better though. PJ…you forgot to tell me my dress was pretty today."

Her dress was pale blue and frilly like ones they make for expensive dolls to wear, so that's what I told her. Natalie blushed and took it as a compliment. "And my bow matches too," she added.

It did.

Mr. Wallace reached over to shake my hand and wish me good morning. I wished him the same.

God's Glory was packed tight up front where members considered the holiest pews to be. There was a dusting of overnight Uphillers in the middle of the sanctuary and a full five rows of empty seats between where we were sitting and the next closest person. Instead of an even wheat field of congregants, I'm sure we looked more like patches of dandelions and crabgrass growing in a bad lawn from the pulpit. Plenty of strangers were seated in the church, but judging by the concentration of Cunningham squeezed to the minimum fanny-space in the front third of the sanctuary, our visitors were the opposite of the kind you give up your seat for. No one looked around, so we sat unnoticed in the far back where Natalie wouldn't get into trouble.

"I'm glad you sat with us today." The stranger I was sitting by touched my knee, and I realized it was Ms. Miller. She looked like Christmas, beautiful and smiling in a dress not too different from Natalie's…but grown up. I'd only been this close to her once before, but this time there was no yellow bandana or red chafe around her eyes. She seemed younger, maybe prettier than she should have been, and as she held her husband's hand on her lap, it was easy to see their love. *Inside out…this must be what a good person looks like inside out,* I remember thinking, and as I sat next to her, I realized why the ladies of Cunningham hadn't shed a moment's dismay when Mary Miller fell ill. Even if they'd known, I'm not sure they'd understand the difference between sitting outside the ladies room at Easter and secreting powdered doughnuts to a couple of hungry little girls.

"Me too," I blushed.

The music started and Reverend Dodge took the pulpit. He paused when he noticed the Millers and the Wallaces in the back, but collected himself quickly and proceeded with his announcements. Something about ticket sales, not going to Sandy Shores if you're a local, and some other stuff I didn't care about. When he asked us to greet each other in love, I shook the Millers' hands, Mr. Wallace's again, slapped Kirby on the back, and gave Natalie a half hug. The rest of the church mixed together up front as our visitors spoke to one another in the middle. It seemed all the greeting that would be done had been done, and the congregation was settling back into their seats when the Sunday school youth, with Chipmunk in the lead, scooched to the center and headed down the aisle to tell us good morning.

Natalie was elated and waved frantically at the approaching teenagers. Most of them waved back as they filed into the pew ahead of ours for greetings and handshakes.

"Good morning, Ms. Miller," Chipmunk stuttered. "I, I, I just wanted to say…well, I wanted to say…I was there." I watched as an instant of awkwardness flickered by, and without knowing what else to do, Chipmunk leaned over the pew and threw her arms around Ms. Miller. Mary Miller hugged her back.

"I know you were," Ms. Miller whispered. "I know everyone who was there."

"Ahem," Reverend Dodge broke in, "let us all be seated to praise God on this glorious day which He hath given."

We all sat to listen to the reverend's opening prayer. No one returned to their original seats. Instead, we filled the two back rows of God's Glory—the place where Ms. Miller and Natalie had been asked to sit so they wouldn't horrify visitors. With all the empty pews separating us from the rest of the congregation, we probably looked like a tree line of dark parishioners sitting too far back for the reverend to read our expressions. An usher stopped by to quietly ask us to move up, but Mr. Wallace shook his head and we kept the seats on the outer edge where big sermons only ripple and the reverend didn't seem quite so large.

Reverend Dodge fumbled over the non-scripted portions of the service; perhaps the previous day's events, the motley visitors, or the sight of Mary Miller stunted his clever ad-libbed lines. His sermon, however, was eloquent and without flaw. Something about blasphemy and false prophets—I'm sure it would have been good if I didn't know who he was talking about.

When the final hymn was sung, we hugged our good-byes in the back with promises to see each other soon—an easy promise to keep in a small town—but somehow it meant more today. Kirby and I slid out without shaking the reverend's hand and met my parents at the car. Dad wheeled through the crowds, picking his way around pedestrians and overnight people forming long lines to buy tickets on the steps of God's Glory. If things didn't change, we wouldn't be spending much of the summer at Sandy Shores, leaving only work at the Wallace place to distract us. But for now, that was fine by me.

37
Ms. Braddock

I tossed and turned as hazy thoughts of Jesse, Trackers, Chipmunk, and the overnight people taunted me through a restless night. That tip-of-the-tongue, end-of-the-brain feeling made slumber evasive, but when sleep finally took me, it held me 'til late the next morning. My room was brighter than it should've been, and the instant I opened my eyes, I knew my alarm had failed me. *Crap!* I was hours late for work. I threw on my clothes, galloped downstairs, grabbed some cookies from the jar, and bolted to my truck. I can't remember seeing Mom, but I yelled good-bye just the same.

I drove by Kirby's long enough to realize nobody was home and then pushed on the gas, hightailing it to River Road. I couldn't believe how late it was, nearly lunchtime. I wondered why Mom didn't wake me or Kirby hadn't called to find out where I was. They let me down. My frustration burned into anger, and I beat on the steering wheel. I stepped harder on the accelerator, sending the summer landscape whipping by in a blue-green blur.

We'd be siding the cabin today and adding the front porch later in the week, but after that I wasn't sure what came next. Thinking about building soothed me, so with every passing farmhouse, my frustration began to settle out as the hum of the wheels on the blacktop lulled me into contemplating the order of things. Thoughts of the Trackers moving up from the river drifted into memories of Natalie and the bridge. Out of shame, I tried to push them away but couldn't help connecting that day to all the good happening now. Was my cowardice justified, or was I excusing failure for reasons like Jesse talked about that day at Sandy Shores? I didn't want to think about it.

Where's Kirby? He'd probably be whining his pants off about slowing down if he was with me right now. I am moving at a pretty good clip.

I surfaced. I was coming up on the bend in River Road far too fast to make it around. I had enough time…*I wasn't sure*…I'd make it…*I didn't know.* I touched the brakes, hoping not to flip as I squealed deep into the turn. I felt the back end fishtailing, so I cut the wheel, somehow managing to hold it in the road as I flew blindly around the curve. *There it was again!* That same stupid dog I almost clipped that day with Kirby! He was standing in the street, frozen, staring as I barreled down on him. He was mesmerized by the screaming wheels, showing no concern over what a ton of flying steel would do to him. There wouldn't be enough left of the mutt to hose off my bumper.

"Move!" I screamed.

I couldn't adjust. I cut the wheel to the left and then back to the right, trying to regain control. He didn't move…*why didn't he move?* Adrenaline slowed everything to a crawl as the dog flashed by my side window, melting into the blur of the thicket. Dumb luck was all that kept me from splattering the stupid thing all over the blacktop. I went hand over hand on the wheel as I brought the truck around the curve and slowed to a manageable speed. My heart was pounding and my breath was short. In the rearview mirror, I caught a glimpse of the mutt crossing the blacktop into the blackberries behind me. That had to be the dumbest animal I'd ever seen.

I made the turnoff across the Wallace farm, and I could see unfamiliar vehicles parked at the pecan grove. Something was wrong. Ordinarily I drove right through the orchard to the meadow, but as I rolled up, I found my usual path blocked by a dozen cars nosed into the trees. I pulled up directly behind another pickup, cut my engine, and got out.

The vehicles may have been recognizable if they'd been in the church parking lot or at Katie's Diner, but out here on the border of a secret, nothing seemed familiar. I should've sensed trouble, but I guess I was like the dog in the road—too bewildered by what was barreling down to realize how deadly it might be. I started into the trees.

"PJ! PJ!" someone called.

I turned to see Mr. Braddock waving me over. It was like seeing a clown at a funeral. He was so out of place I had a hard time recognizing Kirby's dad, even though I'd known him all my life. I hadn't seen him much in the last few months, and for him to show up here among the strange cars, where I least expected, made me wonder if I was actually awake.

"PJ, come here," he yelled.

"Hey, Mr. Braddock, how are you?" I called as I made my way over. "What are you doin' out here?"

"Kirby needed a ride to work—pitched a helluva fit about it at the house. I came this close," he held up his index finger almost touching his thumb to show how close, "to taking his butt in the yard and knocking his teeth out." He glanced back at his car. "He knows his mom can't be left alone."

I leaned around enough to see beyond Mr. Braddock into his sedan. There was nothing there but a couple of rumpled blankets tossed over the passenger seat.

"I didn't know I'd raised such a selfish punk," Mr. Braddock seethed. "We were fighting and woke his mom." He dropped his head into his hand and rubbed his eyes the same way Kirby does when he gets frustrated. "I've never been able to say no to that woman, even when I should. She heard us and insisted we take him." He turned for a long look at the blankets in his car. "She's not as strong as she used to be, but she still knows how to push my buttons. We just pulled in before you got here." He dropped his head again and rubbed his temples with his fingertips. "Kirby asked me to wait and then took off through those trees. I need you to go tell him he's got five minutes and we're leaving. This is too much on his mom, no matter what she says."

His eyes were wet, and his face was red. How wide the pendulum sweeps between anger and sorrow in the face of tragedy. It's a wonder we don't all break.

I nodded I understood and turned to go, but Mr. Braddock caught me by the arm. "Wait, Kirby's mom wants to see you first." He took a deep breath. "Between the cancer and the chemo, she won't look how you remember. Please, don't let her see it in your face…she knows."

I felt like I was dreaming as I followed Kirby's dad to the passenger side of his car. He pulled the door open and motioned for me to step up. I wasn't sure what seeing Ms. Braddock had to do with a pile of blankets.

I didn't pay much attention the last time I saw Kirby's mom. It must have been in church; I remember Kirby wanting to check on her. I'd always seen her as the mother of my best friend—prettier than most moms, I think, or maybe it was her sense of humor that made her more appealing. She had a nice smile. Kirby was a lot like her. Her cookies were as good as Mom's, and when we were little, she would stay up with us 'til midnight, watching scary movies on TV when I stayed over. No other mom could do that and make it fun. Ms. Braddock was something special, and when Kirby and I first became friends, I think I went to his house as much for his mother as I did for him. She actually liked me, and if you knew her at all, it was easy to tell Kirby was her son.

Mr. Braddock leaned over the blankets in the car. "Maggie," I heard him say—no, no that's not right, not Maggie, not Maggie. It was…it was…Peggy. "Peggy," I heard him say to a quilt in the car. "PJ's here."

I looked over Mr. Braddock's shoulder, and for the first time, I saw the rumpled blankets flutter like a tiny kitten was trying to free itself from underneath. The movement was so faint, so very slight; I never would have noticed it from two steps back.

"Please help me, dear," a raspy request crawled from under the covers.

Mr. Braddock obliged, carefully pushing a corner of the blanket away and backing out of the car. He nodded for me to approach the open door. I paused, looking for a hint of what to expect in Mr. Braddock's face, but none was given, so I stepped up. The covers were as flat on the seat as they would have been on my bed at home, so when they moved again, I wondered if Mr. Braddock had Kirby's hamster with him.

"PJ, oh PJ…hi, dear." The voice was weak, almost imperceptible as it crackled my name like static. I noticed a sunken face that could have been mistaken for a shadow in the fold of the blanket. "Hi, PJ, don't I look a mess…so much worse since Easter."

"Ms. Braddock?" I exhaled, sounding more stunned than I meant to. I shuddered, and my knees buckled, forcing me to kneel. I would never have known it was her…so small and thin, not much more than a rumple in the smocked bedspread…only not quite as stout. She was careful not to let me see too much of her.

"Please, don't look too close," she wheezed. "I'm afraid I look like a mummy without the wrappings. That used to scare you pretty good on Friday night TV." It felt like the memory made her smile, but I couldn't tell. "Do you remember watching scary movies at my house with Kirby?"

"Yes, ma'am, I do."

There was a pause as she collected enough of a shallow breath to continue. "Good, that's good." She gave herself another moment while I waited on my knees beside her. I couldn't see her clearly, but when I heard her labor to collect air again, I knew she was ready to speak.

"Can you believe I came all the way out here?"

"No, ma'am, I can't," I whispered, feeling the pressure behind my eyes. I fought with it, not wanting her to see me cry.

"Help me. Help me get my hand out, please."

She tapped on the underside of the bedspread so I would know where her hand was, and I reached down to fold the cover back as gently as I could. Her fingers were dead gray, looking more like the claw of a subterranean creature or part of a skeleton ready for the final layer of skin to fall away. I never knew she was this bad, and suddenly I was infuriated with Kirby. I didn't let it show.

"Take my hand."

I slid my hand across the blanket and took hers in my mine. Her fingers were cold. I'm sure if I had squeezed even a little bit, they would have crumbled like a dry leaf.

"Ah, you're warm. Thank you for coming to see me…I had something I wanted to say." She broke off for a moment, and all I could hear was the faint whistle of Kirby's mom breathing through wet lungs. I thought she'd fallen asleep. "Oh, yes…I know what it was now. I'm sorry. My thoughts drift, and sometimes I think I'm dreaming when I'm still awake."

I felt her cold hand tighten ever so slightly in mine.

"I'm too tired to make long speeches, but I did want to thank you…for being Kirby's friend. It's nice to have friends, especially ones from childhood. You boys are growing up so fast." She paused like every word hurt. "Stay friends, PJ, stay friends."

My temples felt like they were being drilled out as I tried to keep the pain in check. The wake of an involuntary sniffle rushed up in my body. I did my best to stay collected. "Yes, ma'…am." I tripped over the words.

Mr. Braddock touched me on my shoulder, and my conversation with Kirby's mom was over. I was sure she would be over soon too. I pushed to my feet and wiped away the rogue tears that somehow found their way out. My head was pounding. I should have let myself weep. I don't think Kirby's parents would have minded at all.

"Tell Kirby four minutes," Mr. Braddock huffed and then leaned into the car to tend to his wife.

I started to walk back down the row of cars and into the grove, but I couldn't stand it and broke into a run instead. I was alone, so I let the tears come as I dodged around the old trees on my way to fetch Kirby. He was walking when I came up and caught him by the arm. I jerked him around to face me. I was furious! My eyes were swollen, and my face was red and smudged from running and crying.

"So," he said flatly, "you saw Mom." Then he turned and continued on his way.

I grabbed him and whirled him around again. "What the hell are you doing? Going to work on that stinkin' bunkhouse or with those damn bees? I would've picked you up. You didn't have to drag your mom all the way out here just so you wouldn't miss nailing a bunch of stupid boards together! Your dad said they're leaving, and you need to get back double-ass quick and go home with 'em!"

"I don't have time for your crap!" Kirby jerked away and started back toward the meadow. His gait quickened, and his pace was determined. I followed alongside.

"What's wrong with you? Have you lost your flippin' mind?"

"How was I supposed to know all those stupid cars would be blocking the way? How did I know we wouldn't be able to drive through like normal? Have you ever seen that before? Where'd they come from anyway? I just wanted Mom to see Jesse, that's all! That's all I wanted! Now I have to listen to your shit and Dad's too!"

"Why do you want her to see Jesse?"

"Did those words actually come out of your mouth?" Kirby huffed and began to trot. "You really don't get anything, do you?"

I kept trying to talk him into going back, but he quit responding to my protests and name calling altogether, and before I could start to beg, we stepped out of the trees into the meadow.

It was lunchtime, and a group of teenagers was sitting at the foot of the windmill eating with the Trackers. I heard Chipmunk's laugh carry over the field, and I knew right away she was the reason for the cars parked outside the grove. She'd really been taken by what happened with Ms. Miller, but I'm sure the rest of her company wouldn't have been there at all if Sheriff Johnson hadn't closed down Sandy Shores. Ironic how even our misdeeds push the story along.

I saw Elizabeth, John, Sam, Nya, and Angeline sitting among a host of regulars from the youth of God's Glory. Jesse was standing, making wide arm gestures the same way Joe did when he was telling a story or imparting wisdom about trees. I wondered if I looked as much like my dad.

"Look at you two, sleeping the whole workday away!" Jesse hollered across the field when he noticed us. "You boys better get on over here!" He gave a big roundabout wave, and Kirby sprinted across the field. I was embarrassed to run after him, but I did anyway so I wouldn't be stuck strolling up like an aloof idiot all on my own.

"Jesse, Jesse!" Kirby yelled as he ran. "I need you!"

As ill-fated as it was, I knew why Kirby was in a hurry for Jesse. His father was two minutes away from pulling out of the Wallace farm and taking Kirby's misbegotten hopes with him before they could even be proved wrong. Jesse smiled and waved back as he continued talking with the group at his feet.

Kirby waded through the crowd, toppling over people without excusing himself. I followed, but stopped at the edge to watch my desperate friend flailing about in the false hope Jesse would do something impossible.

"Jesse," Kirby puffed, "I need you to come with me."

"Hey, Kirby, how are you?" Jesse smiled. "I'm taking lunch and telling a story right now, so have a seat, and we'll talk in a minute."

"No, no, I need you now, Jesse, I need you right now!"

"Kirby," Jesse was stern, "I'm taking lunch and telling a story, so I need you to sit down and listen."

Kirby didn't say another word. He dropped his head and did as he was told. His face washed pale as hope ran out through his feet, soaking into the ground beneath. It was eerie how fast he changed color. I wanted to take him home, but I wasn't sure he was ready to go.

"Well," Jesse looked away, "ah yes, you were asking me about teachers. Just because they say it doesn't mean they believe it, but just because they don't believe it doesn't mean it's not true. So at times, it's better to look at what's being taught more than the person teaching it. After all, nothing's taught that isn't learned, and in the end, we're responsible for our own understanding and our own actions…nobody else."

He smiled and sighed through his nose. "Now I'm going to sound like my dad. Some people are like dry leaves when they hear Scripture. They walk out of the church and are whisked away by the first breeze or dust devil that blows by. Others are like the leaves of the maple; wide and well anchored throughout spring and summer, but when the weather turns cool and the winds pick up, they drop and are carried off by the gusts of the world as well. Then there are pine needles; never failing to be green in all seasons, cold or warm, and when it comes time to fall, they simply feather straight down into the bed of those who came before, never being cast to the wind. There will be hypocrites in your pulpit, but that's no reason to abandon the church. Learn and discern what you hear for yourself. In the meadow around you, bordered by briars and pecans, the words you've heard at God's Glory are not empty."

I had no idea what Jesse was saying, or even what the question was, but I thought it was weird to be talking about church at work on a Monday. He wasn't even telling a real story. I liked Joe's better.

"I want to say," Jesse continued, "thank you all for coming out, and you are more than welcome to visit and have lunch with me, John, and everybody else anytime. Everyone has enjoyed your company. It's good gettin' to know each other. Also, some of you asked, but there won't be much to help with out here for another week or so, but we'd love for you come after that and help us paint…if you have the time."

The youth at Jesse's feet nodded and murmured in agreement to all he said, but none got up to leave.

"PJ," Jesse called over the heads his audience, "why don't we call it a day and get a super-early start tomorrow."

I shot him a halfhearted thumbs-up.

Kirby's mom hung like rusty chains in my guts, and the sight of Kirby hunched on the ground with his face in his hands made my temples burn. I needed to take him home, and after today, I doubted if he would ever come back. I moved closer, excusing myself over the covey of visitors.

"Kirby, is an early start okay with you?" Jesse asked.

Kirby raised his head without an answer, but when Jesse offered him a hand up, he took it. We stood together in the crowd. Kirby's face was striped with drying tears. I'm not sure if he kept his silence out of grief or anger, but I kept mine because I was too embarrassed to cry.

"Kirby." Jesse slid his hands around the backs of our necks and pulled us in tight so our foreheads touched. We were so close Kirby's tears ran down my face and everything else in the world squeezed away. It was like Jesse was going to tell Kirby and me the biggest secret of all that neither of us wanted to hear. "Kirby, remember what I said that day at Sandy Shores?" Jesse whispered. "Some are meant to be healed, some are meant to be cared for, and some are meant to remind us we're human. Do you remember?"

Kirby whimpered and nodded into our heads.

I couldn't take it anymore; my eyes puddled, and my nose started to flow. I squeezed my eyes shut, and I could feel Kirby's tears as he seized in gentle sobs. I didn't care about the crowd watching anymore. I just wanted to pull back before Jesse finished saying Ms. Braddock was here to remind us we're human. She'd already done that for me at the car. I tried to move away, but Jesse held fast.

"Kirby," Jesse whispered into our wet faces, "Kirby, some are meant for all three." Then he kissed Kirby, let us go, and pointed across the field of wildflowers.

I wiped my eyes the best I could, smearing away tears and snot with my forearm. When I was clear enough to see, there were Kirby's parents, standing at the orchard waiting for their son. No blankets, no shadows, and no mummy; just Kirby's mom and dad as they should have been.

"Jesse," Kirby choked as he stared across the meadow, "I'll see you tomorrow. PJ," he continued as he wiped his wet face with his shirttail, "pick me up early." Then Kirby took off, cutting over field faster than I've ever seen him run. He nearly tackled his parents before falling into a roundabout embrace with his mom and dad. The Braddocks' laughter and tears rose over the daisies as they stumbled in each other's arms under the shade of Mr. Wallace's trees.

I watched. We all watched, but I wondered if anyone else knew what really happened. I wasn't even sure.

The Braddocks wept and laughed a moment longer, waved to me, and turned to fade back through the grove. I would definitely pick Kirby up early tomorrow.

38
King Tree Honey

Ms. Braddock greeted me from the porch when I pulled up in front of Kirby's house. It was strange to see her, and honestly, I was a little unnerved by the change in her appearance. The feeling would pass in time. I rolled my window down so she could see me waving back.

"PJ," she called from the stoop, "can I interest you in some blueberry pancakes? There's no better way to start off a hard day of work than blueberry pancakes."

"No, thank you," I hollered back. "I've already eaten."

I was relieved when Kirby emerged from the house ready to go so his mother wouldn't pursue the invitation further. He hugged her, and she kissed him on the head before he stepped off the stoop, crossed the lawn, and hopped in the truck. Kirby's mom watched him the whole way. She waved. We waved, but she didn't go back inside until we pulled out of sight.

"These are for you," Kirby tossed a paper sack in my lap. I didn't even have to open it. I could smell right through the bag—oatmeal raisin cookies, still warm.

"She's been cooking and cleaning ever since we got home yesterday." Kirby smiled. "Says she wants to get rid of the sick smell in the house. She sent Dad to Wallace's store this morning to get some paint for the kitchen—said she didn't care what color he got as long as it was cheery. I'm not sure Dad knows what cheery paint looks like."

"Natalie will help him, but I don't think Mr. Wallace is open yet," I remarked, wheeling on to River Road.

"Me either," Kirby agreed. "I guess Dad will have to wait it out at Katie's Diner until he is."

"If he can find a seat with all of the Uphillers in town."

"How long you think they'll be here?"

"I have no idea. There's as many as ever. I'd just like 'em to open up Sandy Shores."

Kirby nodded and turned to watch the passing farms roll by. The morning was somber, full of wonder and unanswered questions. I kept my speed reasonable out of respect. I glided the truck around Natalie's curve without incident, finding no stray dog waiting for me in the road. I didn't tell Kirby I almost ran it down. I slowed to make the turnoff.

"PJ," Kirby piped up, "I know this is silly, but Mom was wondering if you might like to stay over Friday night. She says there's a mummy movie on and it won't be the same without you and me…like when we were kids…says she wants to do it one more time before we're too old and busy."

I thought about the woman who lay like ashes underneath the blankets in the car and the woman who made blueberry pancakes this morning. Was she really the same person? The truck bounced over the field.

"Sure," I accepted, but I can't remember if I went or not.

There were no cars blocking our path today, so I drove through the grove and parked beside Jesse's truck. He was still in the cab when we pulled up but stepped out as soon as my pickup was in Park. He was alone.

"Good morning," Jesse greeted us over a thermos cup of coffee. "Looks like it's just us today."

"Why, what's up?"

Jesse sipped his coffee, "Adleman is sending his first truck for Mr. Wallace's produce tomorrow, and everybody'll be picking, packaging, and doing whatever else needs to be done before it gets here. John, Sam, and the whole crew will be working the farm today and most of tomorrow."

I glanced at the stack of siding and the pile of lumber for the porch. "Looks like a load to do for three people."

Jesse shook his head and held up two fingers like a peace sign to indicate my count was off. "It'll only be you and me on the bunkhouse. Kirby, I need you to get building some more bee boxes. Everything you need is in the back of my truck."

"Really, more bee boxes already?" Kirby was surprised. "I've been reading up on honeybees in the encyclopedia, and from what I can tell, we shouldn't expect to split the hives 'til at least next season. We have time. Shouldn't I help with the house?"

Jesse reached over and put his hand on Kirby's shoulder. "I know what the encyclopedia says, but what I need you to do is build enough boxes to fill in that whole corner of the meadow. After that, I want you to help Nya jar up as much honey as you can. She's filled nearly a thousand by herself and it's getting to be too much. Maybe you can help her think up a name so when the label machine gets in, we can get the jars stickered and sold to Mr. Adleman. That stuff fetches a pretty penny. Those bees and their honey are a lot more valuable than you think."

Kirby seemed hurt being pulled off the bunkhouse to work on something he thought was less important, but I knew he enjoyed the apiary more than building anyway. I was the opposite, preferring construction…although I never bothered to research it in the encyclopedia. Kirby was a strange guy.

Kirby unloaded his materials, and Jesse and I set about siding the bunkhouse. I listened carefully to his instructions, and we found our rhythm quickly. Building felt good. The whine of the saw, the feel of the hammer, and the smell of lumber held lessons on the kinship of carpenters I wanted to learn. I could have worked on the Trackers' home forever, but very little of the morning had passed when Jesse and I held the final board against the back wall and nailed it into place.

"Not bad, not bad at all," Jesse said as he stepped back to survey our work. "It's all good and straight. Dad would be impressed."

I was giddy with his praise. I tried not to let my excitement show, but I'm sure it bubbled over just the same. He smiled, and I was happy.

"Okay now, buddy, there are a handful of kids you know—they were here yesterday—walking through the trees right now. They'll be here in a minute." Jesse said it like he could see them coming, even though the bunkhouse fully obstructed our view of the orchard. "When they get here, they'll ask what they can do to help. I'm gonna send a couple to work with Kirby, keep one with me, and give one to you. We'll split up and take opposite ends of the house."

"What do you mean? I want to work with you. Who are they?"

"No," Jesse shook his head, "we'll get a lot more done if we take the time to train a couple guys. You can run the job. Show 'em what to do, talk 'em through everything, but don't let 'em measure or do anything skilled yet. If all else fails, just have 'em hold the boards for you. If you run into trouble, walk around and get me."

I started to protest, but Jesse smiled, and I knew my objection wouldn't matter. I needed more practice and I wasn't happy about newcomers working on the bunkhouse, but I knew that wouldn't matter either, so I kept it to myself.

When the extra help arrived, Jesse divided them among the jobs, and I did as I was told. My helper was slow but eager, and I was shocked at how well the job went. I guess Jesse's faith in me kindled my knack for carpentry, and we finished our end of the bunkhouse not far behind him. Jesse walked over to have a look at my work, smiled, and walked off without a word. I knew I'd done well. We all moved around front to complete the final side together.

The summer sun beat down and the tools were slippery in our hands, but the refrain of saws and the chorus of cracking hammers never rested until the job was complete. It didn't take long with four of us working across the front, and when we were done, I was satisfied with what we'd accomplished. I could hear Kirby across the meadow instructing his crew on the construction of bee boxes. He seemed frustrated. As it turns out, Kirby was a tougher taskmaster than I ever thought about being.

When Mr. Wallace and Natalie drove in through the trees with lunch, all work ceased and we sat to eat. The sandwiches tasted as good as the day at the porte cochere when Jesse decided to stay in Cunningham. Jesse talked about his family, the places he'd been, and the things he'd built. We laughed at his jokes, even the ones I'd heard before. Lunch was as leisurely as an hour would allow, so even though the newcomers were probably thinking about naps, I knew it wasn't in the cards…and that special knowledge made me feel important. I smiled to myself.

I looked around at the others chewing and reclining, trying to get comfortable in the shade of the pecan trees. I'd known these boys all my life. We all grew up in Cunningham; played ball in the square, rode the same bus to the same school, attended the same church, and got in the same trouble with the same sheriff. And even though I can't remember any of their faces or names, I'm sure at the time I considered them friends.

As far as Cunningham was concerned, I was just another adolescent among them, but on this day, in this moment, by the simple virtue of being here longer, I felt special and trusted above the others. I'd known Jesse since the Sunday Natalie sang her solo at church. I'd worked with Joe. I helped collect honeybees—Kirby and me—and now Jesse was letting me work on my own and I wasn't screwing it up—just the opposite. Funny, I felt a tinge of jealousy when Jesse told me new people were coming to help, but sitting around now, waiting to go back to work, the addition of volunteers made me feel important, necessary, and I was determined not to let that feeling go.

When Jesse was ready, we rose to our feet, and Kirby took his crew back to the apiary. The front porch was next, and even though the task looked daunting, after Jesse took the time to explain, it didn't seem so bad.

"The important thing is to lay out our frame square and get good angles on the rafters. When we do that, it's only a matter of cutting straight and filling in, but if we're not careful about keeping the framework right, we'll have nothing more than a big mess that'll have to be torn down when it's all said and done." He shook his head, looking up at the bunkhouse. "There's not much worse than rework—I hate tearing stuff down. So," he turned around, "today we'll get the porch roof boxed in and braced. I'll make sure it's square, but PJ, you're gonna have to make sure it stays that way. I'll show you how. You can check it as often as you need, but I'm the saw man, so I can't be running up and down the ladder if we're ever gonna get this thing done. Understand?" Jesse smiled at the newcomers. "We have all the muscle we need to do a good job as long as we keep it the way I lay it out."

I was nervous, but Jesse seemed confident in my ability, and as it turns out, I had a small talent for building. With every measurement I called and every nail I drove, I got better at what I was doing, and so did the rest of our novice crew. Other summer distractions could have stolen our volunteers, but we stayed together all week. With every passing hour, we became more skilled, drawn into brotherhood by the work. More newcomers drifted in over the next few days, but Jesse sent them with Kirby or had them sit at the tree line out of the way in order to preserve the rhythm of our crew. When John and Sam returned from the farm, Jesse gave them something to do on the interior.

It was then I discovered the poetry of construction, how much greater the whole is than its parts and how beautiful even the most pragmatic creation can be to the one who fashions it. The smell of sawdust and the glow of bright lumber have always put my mind at ease. Ever since that day, I've found nothing so contenting as building something useful.

As a carpenter, I was to become nothing more than a talented hack, able to impress family and friends with a new porch, a deck, or a remodeled room. Still, carpentry was my secret panacea…my last defense against the melancholy constantly nipping at my heels, threatening to drag me down. Maggie always had a project for me just as I was starting to blue. Funny, it didn't matter whether I was building a shelf or a tool shed for her; I was always swept back to this moment with Jesse as the saw man and me calling down measurements, trying to keep things square. I wish I'd considered what that meant before now.

Tended by youth and inexperience, the porch started slowly, but like anything else of consequence, what began as a crawl finished in a sprint. By Saturday, Jesse was teaching me to cut steps as the rest of the crew installed the handrail. As the last nails were being driven, I looked to see Kirby's bee boxes in the lower corner of the meadow. They shone white against the tall summer grass like the village huts of remote rice farmers I'd seen in my history book at school. It was a pretty picture.

Jesse fitted the stair stringers, I hammered on the treads, and we stepped away to survey our work. The bunkhouse beamed with its new wooden smile. After all this time, the Trackers' home was finally born.

The pecan trees approved, and the windmill turned slowly in the breezeless meadow to thank us for what we'd done. Onlookers waiting in the shade to volunteer on paint day broke into light applause as we laid our hammers down and they realized we were finished. The four of us turned for a quick bow as Kirby and his crew traipsed up after setting the last bee box. Jesse waved everyone over and climbed the steps of the new porch to better address the crowd. John and Sam came out to join him.

"I'd like to thank you all for coming out this week. I know we didn't have much for you to do. I enjoyed having lunch with you guys, and even though they're not here right now, let's put our hands together for Mr. Wallace, Natalie, Mary, Elizabeth, and Nya for fixing our meal every day." Jesse stepped back and started to clap, and we all followed suit. "The best thing about this week is you got to spend time with John, Sam, and everybody else from across the bridge. I have to believe you came out more for that than to watch us nail boards on a house. Carpentry is not a spectator sport, and it's easy to lose interest if you don't have your fingers wrapped around a hammer, so I appreciate you staying for the company. I think we've all learned a lot."

Jesse smiled, and a murmur of agreement ran through the youthful gathering. "That's it for today. We're gonna finish up inside the first part of next week and be ready to paint by Wednesday. So if you're up for it, wear something you don't mind getting splattered."

A ripple of excited chatter bubbled from the opportunity to help. Jesse raised his hand to hush everybody for his final announcement. "Just remember, that won't be until next Wednesday, and tomorrow is Sunday, so there is no work. Get yourself to church, and be sure to thank the good Lord in Heaven for all He's doing out here."

"Are you coming to church?" someone asked from the crowd.

Jesse paused. The question was a natural one, but somehow, it struck me as strange and terribly naïve. With all that had passed between Reverend Dodge and Jesse—from pulling the Trackers out of the storm to sticking up for the Millers—I knew Jesse wasn't welcome in the reverend's house. It was one thing for Jesse and Reverend Dodge to rub up against each other occasionally in town, but Jesse taking a pew in God's Glory would be picking a fight he could never win. It wouldn't take much to find out Jesse had the children of Cunningham consorting with Trackers—setting what *is* and what *should be* on a collision course that would swallow us all like a snake swallows its babies. The slightest provocation would put a quick and tragic end to Mr. Wallace's folly. Of course Jesse wouldn't go—that would be crazy. He hadn't been since Easter—and even then he walked out early.

The question hung on the porch. "We'll see," Jesse answered.

I was satisfied he would stay away, leaving the rest of us to go through the motions, not having to own up to the truth or invite the wrath of the reverend and our parents. We would finish, Jesse would leave, and hopefully things wouldn't change back all the way.

"All right, everybody," Jesse called from the porch. "You guys get home and we'll see you next week…thank you."

"Thank you," John echoed.

"Thank you all so, so much," Sam added as the youth of Cunningham began to meander back through the trees to spend the rest of their Saturday somewhere other than Sandy Shores.

As the group began to thin, Chipmunk and a couple of her friends pushed their way up to Jesse. Whatever they wanted would prolong our workday, but I didn't mind. Fanfare was in my blood and my heart swam in delight of the bunkhouse, so I welcomed any delay that would keep me here even a moment longer. I moved up to hear what Chipmunk had to say.

"Jesse, we have an idea, but we wanted to ask you first." Chipmunk fidgeted and looked at the ground like she didn't know how to proceed. Three friends stood with her. "We were wondering…well, we kinda got to know Nya this week….and Angeline, Tuttle, and the other kids are so cute. Well, it seems like there's a lot of stuff they might need after their house is done. We have fundraisers at church all the time, usually to pay for a retreat or to send the choir to sing at some church on the beach…but we were thinking, you know, there are clothes and books and regular everyday stuff they might need out here…so we were thinking," Chipmunk motioned to the three God's Glory girls standing with her, "we were thinking…we might do a fundraiser to help out…you know…if you'd let us."

Chipmunk fumbled awkwardly over her words. It seemed overdone until I noticed John and Sam leaning against the porch post with heads hung low. I couldn't tell if it was out of shame or gratitude they refused to look up.

Chipmunk's offer was honest, causing her as much embarrassment to make as it did the two men on the porch to hear. I think it was not so much Chipmunk's proposal, but her fear of making it that made her so beautiful to me. On the outset it seemed like a great idea, but it's a wonder how much good never gets past the gates of fear and pride.

Jesse took her hand. "That's very nice," he said, "but it's not my decision. You'll have to ask the men behind me."

John and Sam shifted uncomfortably on the porch. Their eyes were anchored to their feet as they grappled with how to accept or reject Chipmunk's offer. They hadn't been able to provide for their own families safely, and now some stranger from town was asking to do it for them. The Trackers accepted all Mr. Wallace had done, but that was partly for working the farm. A fundraiser was out-and-out charity with no fair exchange for those on the receiving end. Without a word between them, John and Sam twisted on the porch, trying to decide. I thought Chipmunk might have to ask again, even though they heard her clearly.

"I think, young lady," Sam broke the silence without looking up, "I been wrestling with my pride a long, long time now…maybe like Jacob and the angel."

"Yeah," John picked up, "it's one thing to work this farm and tend them bees to get something better, but how can I…" He stopped. "I been taught a man should stand on his own two feet," he paused, "but sometimes…well, maybe the Devil might use that against him."

Sam nodded. The two men looked tired.

"Pride's what kept me on the river all this time, miss, and my own pride's what kept my family down there with me. It's all I've had for some time now, but maybe pride ain't something I can afford no more…not if it calls me to refuse my children the love of a fellow human being."

John reached over and put his arm around Sam. Sam nodded and looked to Chipmunk with a tearful smile. I couldn't tell if he was grateful or just at the end of his rope.

John cleared his throat to continue from the porch. "You know, miss, it's not always about who you'll help, but who you'll take help from." He paused to consider his final decision. "I won't keep my family from your friendship because of some demon what lives inside of me. Thank you, young lady, and I pray one day I'll be able to pass your blessing on to someone else. I promise me or mine will do that for you."

The moment should have ended in a handshake, an embrace, or a slap on the back, but Chipmunk wasn't Natalie, and although she may have welcomed it, a Tracker could never touch a town girl. Sam held up his hand, John nodded good-bye, and the two men disappeared into the bunkhouse to finish their work for the day.

"There you go," Jesse said with a grin.

"There we go," Chipmunk repeated with a smile. "Kirby, PJ, I'll see you guys in church tomorrow. We've got a lot to plan."

I thought she would leave, but a simple "so long" wasn't enough for her to go on, so Chipmunk bounced over and threw her arms around Jesse's neck. She hugged Kirby and me in turn. Her friends hugged us too. I suppose some moments demand that kind of thing. She spouted her good-byes once more, waved, then half danced back through the grove, talking and giggling with her friends the way excited girls always do.

Kirby and I stood beside Jesse, watching the girls fade into the trees. For some reason, I couldn't take my eyes off them as they moved away with their conversations trailing behind.

"Kirby," Jesse said without looking around, "did you and Nya come up with a name for the honey?"

Kirby sniffed and wiped the sweat from his brow as he watched the distant girls. "We had two names, but I think we'll call it *King Tree Honey* because…well…because we both like it."

"That's a good name. Don't worry about painting. You'll have your hands full splittin' the hives again next week—but it'll just be you and Nya. The bees know you two, and I don't want anyone gettin' stung."

"Okay," Kirby nodded.

"Okay," Jesse repeated, "thank you."

When Chipmunk and her friends finally disappeared from sight, we picked up our tools, piled in my truck, and left Jesse, John, and Sam to finish up inside.

39
Duty to Cain

The next day Sunday school was a fiasco. Our teacher arrived late and was never able to wrangle control of the class away from Chipmunk. He wanted to talk about the mark of Cain, but she had everyone so whipped up over what was going on at the Wallace place and what we could do to help, our teacher never managed to assert himself. He rolled his eyes and scowled as teenage ideas ricocheted around the basement. The disruptive behavior of his usual pets and their ill-conceived plan of putting all he taught them into practice ruined a perfectly good lesson. A date was set for a fundraising carwash after church in two weeks. Our teacher left before the hour was up, probably to tattle on us to Reverend Dodge the way he'd done when Jesse taught the class. Without an adult to keep us prompt, we sauntered into the service later than usual.

The Wallaces, the Millers, and Kirby's folks were seated in the back. Our tardy group seeped around them like mortar and bricks to find our places as well. A void of at least four rows separated us from the next inhabited pew. I'm sure our parents thought we were rebellious and ill-behaved for separating ourselves from them, but in truth, we wanted to be as close to the Millers and Braddocks as possible. Sitting by a miracle doesn't happen every day, especially in church.

The fine citizens of Cunningham were crammed to the front of God's Glory with a looser contingent of shabby Uphillers sitting like weeds the in middle pews. Crutches, white canes, and wheelchairs were folded among them. The strangers were pale and drawn as a variety of maladies sucked the life from their faces. They coughed and cleared their throats, filling the rafters with the repugnant sound of illness as they picked and pulled at their rumpled clothing. Sickness and misery—the sanctuary stank of them both as visitors waited patiently for the church to sell them a ticket to Sandy Shores. The Cunningham congregation up front murmured to one another in disgust without turning around.

Ms. Braddock reached over to pat me on the knee. I leaned forward to wave down the row at Ms. Miller and then to Natalie. An usher stopped by to ask us to slide closer to the front, but Mr. Wallace and the Millers shook off the request.

"Suit yourself," the usher whispered and moved away to kick the stops from the sanctuary doors.

I caught a glimpse of Eddy in his uniform standing in the narthex as the doors fell closed. *A strong police presence to keep the riffraff in check*, I thought, and even though it was Eddy, I was glad he was there.

I thumbed through a bulletin and looked over the crowd. The pianist started, we all stood, and Reverend Dodge took his pulpit.

"Welcome, everybody, welcome to God's Glory. We're delighted you're here." His warm voice blanketed the sanctuary like we were being tucked into bed. "We have a couple of announcements before we begin. As you all know, our Sandy Shores has become quite a popular tourist attraction, hosting many more people than our town is equipped to handle. Sheriff Johnson asked the church's help with regulating the number of visitors to keep everyone safe and sound as they come to enjoy Cunningham." Reverend Dodge leaned out in a mock whisper. "Keeping people safe is godly work, wouldn't you say?"

The people in the front pews shifted and nodded their heads.

"Yes, I would too," the reverend agreed. "And since God blesses godly work, He has blessed us richly for our efforts in His service. I am happy to announce, because of what we've done to manage the safety of our pilgrims, we will not only be able to retire a couple of long-term debts, but we'll most likely be able give our staff some long overdue increases in salary—provided the tourism continues to flourish in Cunningham."

The front rows erupted into applause, and Reverend Dodge stood back from his microphone and clapped as well. He gave a moment and then stepped up, raised his hand, and the room fell silent. "Now, I know this boon has caused some inconvenience, especially for our teenagers. Not being able to enjoy the river as you have in past summers has left extra time to fill, and with idle hands and all, we want to ensure *you* young people are filling your time with the right kinds of things." The reverend gave an exaggerated wink, and light laughter rippled through the front rows. "Anyway, to show our appreciation for your sacrifice in these strange and wonderful times, we're going to throw the youth a full-fledged, dyed-in-the-wool, big and fancy, with all the trimmings, last-all-day and stay-up-all-night dance here at the church. How will that do you?"

Everyone in the front of the church came to their feet in applause and for the first time turned, looking back over the shabby people to us. They clapped to show their approval and appreciation for all we had endured. It was surprising and exciting, and we were delighted to have something to look forward to, something just for us.

"Okay, okay, please be seated," the reverend interrupted. "Parents, you have a great group of kids back there, and they deserve to have a wonderful, fun-filled day. This celebration of our youth will be an all-day, all-night event, starting with breakfast. So whatever else you do, make double sure the kids' calendars are absolutely clear two weeks from today."

Reverend Dodge beamed, and our parents agreed nothing would take precedence over the Youth Celebration on the day

Chipmunk had planned the carwash. I guess our Sunday school teacher was a tattletale after all. I was torn.

The usual theater of church proceeded with a prayer, a collection, and some songs I stood for but didn't sing. My mind drifted around the pathetic people buying tickets, hoping for the miraculous Chagrin to wash away their sickness. I thought about Reverend Dodge paying off the debt, raises for the staff, and daddies with sick little girls buying us a church dance. I wondered how much longer the ruse of a magical river would line the pockets of the master of God's Glory. Rumors fueled crowds as big as ever, and if the reverend was already spending the money, he had to believe the gold mine ran deep.

I gritted my teeth as Reverend Dodge cast his spell over the front pews. I saw him clearly, but I didn't speak up. I'd like to say I kept silent to protect our work at the Wallace farm, but that's a lie I'm beyond telling. Besides, I think the reverend already knew what was happening.

Reverend Dodge cleared his throat for the sermon as God's Glory council members spent the church's windfall in their daydreams. Intentions may have been noble, but the reverend would have the final say.

Reverend Dodge latched on to the pulpit, pursed his lips, and tilted his head, adding drama to the moment. Like a roller coaster clicking up the first hill, he knew how to pull Cunningham to the edge of its seat before he said anything at all. I wonder how many of us could have held both arms up for the entire sermon.

"Cain!" he boomed. His voice bounced off the walls like he was shouting into a canyon. He waited for the building to settle. He must have had a good week because we could tell one of his better efforts was coming. "Cain was a man cursed by God for an unspeakable crime against his very own brother. God put a mark on Cain so all would know of His disfavor, and Cain was cast into the world alone. Was this an actual mark God placed on Cain, or was it poverty or poor fortune or some sort of terrible illness so others would know Cain was under God's curse?

Possibly…probably." Reverend Dodge paused to let reason saturate his congregation. "And how many people who crossed paths with Cain after that knew the cause for his suffering?" He paused again. "I'll tell you—none did. But what they did know was Cain's punishment, his despair, was the will of a just God. Nothing happens outside His will, and if His will was for Cain to suffer, who among us would dare second-guess or oppose His judgment? We can't know everything, but we must open our eyes and discern what we see! There are Cains in this world, but who is willing to interfere with God's plans for them?"

Passion was overtaking Reverend Dodge, and his words began going off like fireworks around the room, seducing feelings rather than contemplation. "Who would prolong Cain's suffering by attempting to ease God's curse before its measure comes full circle?!" He slammed his fist down on the pulpit. "Who dares change God's plans?! Who dares to intercede?! Who dares put himself as God's equal? Who?!"

Ordinarily I didn't listen to the sermon, but the authority of the reverend draped in his robes, pounding on the mahogany, grabbed me from the back pew. And although I didn't want them, I could feel him sowing seeds of his theology in my soul. He must have been irresistible for those sitting up front.

"Who?!" the red-faced reverend thundered again…and waited…glaring down into his flock. No one made a sound as the reverend stood like silent stone waiting for the unanswerable question to fully settle in the hearts of his congregation. Suspense drifted through the room like the morning mist of the Chagrin. Even Natalie kept silent as the question "Who?" hung in the sanctuary of God's Glory.

We waited in the uncomfortable air until something caught the reverend's attention. He sniffed, thumbed his nose, and took a sip of water. The reverend seemed angry, but he held his tongue, not wanting to break the spell he'd cast. He sighed and held up his hand to summon the door usher with a brief flourish of his fingers. As his minion neared, Reverend Dodge nodded at someone in front, and the usher moved quietly down the row to invite that someone to leave.

Jesse rose. He slid to the middle aisle with his escort. I couldn't believe Reverend Dodge interrupted a sermon to have Jesse thrown out of the service. What's more, I wondered how in the world Reverend Dodge missed him in the front pew all this time, right up to the big question of his finest message ever. But the reverend would not suffer a blasphemer in his church, so before he proceeded with his inflamed rhetorical question the parish believed couldn't be answered, Reverend Dodge had Jesse rise to leave—perhaps in a testimony lost to all but Kirby's mom and Ms. Miller.

Maybe it was the effect of the reverend's sermon, the shock of seeing Jesse being led out, or both that made me feel like I was watching from an outside window. There was a tickle in my ear, and my legs were suddenly too heavy to move. I watched as Jesse followed the usher past the front rows where the saints of Cunningham congregated so tightly. They turned to stare. Reverend Dodge glowered from his chancel perch, but I couldn't tell if he was irritated at the interruption or delighted by his demonstration of power.

Jesse didn't look back. But as he followed the usher beyond the rows of Cunningham, he reached out to both sides of the aisle and let his hands brush against the ends of the pews where the ragged people sat. As he touched their seats, our visitors stirred, shook their heads, and finding their legs, rose to follow him out. Some were laughing, and some were crying as they left a litter of crutches and canes behind. Jesse pulled his hand away before he touched our pew and trailed the usher through the doors with the healed following along.

"It's blasphemy anyone should stand when asked who is equal to God," the reverend growled to the congregation now devoid of visitors.

Without Uphillers filling the pews between us, the back row seemed more distant than ever. The front of the church turned to hear Reverend Dodge finish what he had to say about Cain and then Ishmael and what happens when we interfere with God's providence. He reminded our parents about the Youth Celebration and not to schedule the slightest chore for the day. He told us to leave through the porte cochere because the Sandy Shores tickets were being issued on the front steps and too many folks going in different directions would cause a mess. He called us to the final hymn, and suddenly I could stand. I left before the song, exiting the front of God's Glory against the reverend's instructions.

The cashbox magistrates were setting up, but the steps and the lanes roped off for their customers were empty. The double-parked cars and the overnight people who flocked in from five counties to buy hope had disappeared. Driving in this morning, Dad had to weave his way through the pathetic mass as Mom did her best to wish them all away. Now there was nothing but scraps of paper, overflowing trash cans, and empty lines at the foot of God's Glory to testify the Uphillers had been here at all. Abandoned wheelchairs, crutches, and other artifacts of the lame, sick, and blind dropped by their former owners were the only witnesses to what happened outside while we listened to Reverend Dodge tell us about God's will.

The cashbox magistrates went about setting up their tables, to sit and look out over an empty town. They wouldn't make much money today. I wondered if Reverend Dodge would still be able to afford the Youth Celebration, given the terrible turn of events in the Cunningham tourism business.

"What do you think Dodge will do now?" I didn't realize Kirby had come out beside me.

"I don't know. But I'm sure it will be something. Did you see how happy he was about the money from these ticket sales?"

"Dodge will blame Jesse for this," Kirby added.

"How can he?" I shrugged.

"How can he not?"

We stood for another moment and then walked around the building to say our good-byes under the porte cochere and head to our car. I'd ridden in with my parents, but everyone else from the back pew—the Braddocks, the Millers, Chipmunk, and the others who'd driven themselves to church—found their back right taillight smashed out and conveniently ticketed for the offense by our zealous deputy, Eddy.

On the way home, Mom chattered about the dance and commented how good Kirby's mom looked. Dad knew better than to make the same observation of Ms. Miller. He did say Reverend Dodge had a fine sermon and how much he liked messages with practical value. Mom agreed. And although the fruit wasn't quite ready to drop, I knew it wouldn't be long before my folks associated Cain with the people I was working with on Mr. Wallace's farm.

40
Ghosts in the Trees

It seems like…it seems like…oh, I feel myself drifting away from what I know. It's like drowning with a safety line at your fingertips, being sucked into oblivion where everything familiar is out of reach.

It's colder than it was before, and the moon is playing hide-and-seek with the clouds, throwing an intermittent blanket of darkness over the trees. My parents have been watching me from the woods for some time now. I haven't mentioned them because they keep to the shadows, but I recognize them just the same…they frighten me. I think the mashed potato lady is with them.

My back hurts and my bones ache. I can't…seem to remember why I'm here. Damn it! Why am I here? The pills…that's right, the pills will help. I'm not sure how many bottles of these things I had, and I'm not sure how many I'm not supposed to take, but remembering is everything, so I'll chew the rest. Funny, memories can be as bitter as these damn things and just as hard to swallow. I'll go down to the dock. The water will be better company than the ghosts in the trees, and after all, it knows the story as honestly as I do.

With all the help, the bunkhouse at Mr. Wallace's finished quickly. Kirby split the hives as Jesse said, and it became a full-time job for several Trackers to collect all the honey they produced. Mr. Adleman's trucks kept rolling, and before long, he had to send three more to retrieve everything he bought from the farm. Mr. Wallace joked about retiring from his store in town, but it wasn't until he noticed the ancient pecan grove laden with fruit, he began taking his own jest seriously. He and Natalie never peddled Tracker tomatoes on the square again—didn't have to—and in one season's time, his place became more profitable than all the other Cunningham farms combined. Natalie had been kicked out of the choir only last Christmas, and Reverend Dodge was already regretting that decision.

But I'm getting ahead of myself, I think, going out of order. I'm feeling a little nauseated…the unsteady dock or maybe the pills…I can't puke 'em up…just wait…just wait...deep breath. Hold on…deep breath. Okay…I'll lie down and keep going…but not to sleep, I can't sleep yet.

"PJ, you better get out of that bed! Didn't you hear me calling you? This is not the morning to be acting lazy bones!" Mom stomped across the floor and tore the curtains back. Sunshine filled my cluttered room. Flecks of dust hung in the dry rays.

"Mom?" I moaned.

"You need to rise and shine, young man," she continued as she marched toward the door. "Today is the Youth Celebration with Reverend Dodge, and I have to deliver a breakfast casserole. So hustle up. It won't do to be late today." She was in and out of my bedroom, still talking even after she left and started down the hall. It took me a moment to catch up.

I rolled out of bed. My body was tired. There was so much more to do finishing up at Mr. Wallace's place than I imagined. The Trackers were used to much less, but we didn't use that excuse to wrap things up with anything but our best effort.

The farm was in full swing with multiple Adleman trucks coming regularly for all it produced. John's people had been doing everything they could to keep up, leaving only Jesse and a group of youth volunteers to put the final touches on the Trackers' new home. For so long, the adolescents of Cunningham lived together like the threads on a frayed pair of pants, but with Jesse, we found a common purpose our parents never had—and it felt good.

The bunkhouse was one big room with built-in beds at both ends. We hung heavy curtains to be pulled across the sleeping areas for privacy, dividing the living space into thirds when closed. I hooked up the pipe I'd buried from the water basin at the windmill and set the sink. Mr. Wallace was right, the pressure was fine. The original design called for a propane cooktop, but John and Sam thought it would be better not to rely on a gas delivery truck from town just yet. Instead, we installed a wood-burning stove, which delighted the ladies like it was the latest modern kitchen convenience.

I hate painting, so I found other ways to busy myself as coats of antique white were brushed on. I'm not sure if it was sadness or satisfaction that leaked from my eyes when the last volunteer stepped away with an empty paint bucket in hand. The bunkhouse looked like a pearl. I stood back. It was done.

We cheered, and when the Trackers broke from their farm chores to come see, we all cheered again.

Elizabeth, Mary, and the other women sobbed in their husbands' arms, and even though I'd pegged Nya as a tough one, she came to the meadow with wet eyes as well. Natalie laughed, and Mr. Wallace applauded and slapped me on the back. Emotions ran like horses through the wildflowers as a covey of giggling children played chase and danced circles around their new home. A tearful chorus of appreciation swirled through the field, and although it should never be done, in all the hysteria we shook hands and hugged our Tracker brothers and sisters.

Chipmunk kissed me on the cheek.

I looked around at all we had done. A thriving apiary, a proud windmill, and a sturdy little bunkhouse was more than I would ever accomplish again. Summer was nearly over and so was our work with the families of the river. They'd be moving up soon, school would start, and Jesse would leave. At least we had the carwash to prolong this season of our lives, if only for a moment more.

"PJ, get your feet on that floor," Dad bellowed from the bottom of the steps. "I do not want you to be late."

"There's loads of fun today," Mom added. "Reverend Dodge says he's going teach you kids the chicken dance, so get your fanny moving. You'll need to drive yourself."

I slid up and sat on the end of my bed. I dropped my face into my palms to clear the remaining sleep. I was too proud to wear gloves, and my hands had grown hard with the summer. My parents hadn't the faintest notion what they'd done for me when they insisted I work off the damages I caused to Mr. Wallace's place…*funny*.

I'd go to breakfast at the church, listen to Reverend Dodge from the back pew, and then I was cutting out for the Gas & Grocery to wash cars with everybody else. Even though the overnight people disappeared from our streets, Uphillers still dropped in on Sundays to buy vegetables and picnic at the Chagrin, so we could make enough to buy some blankets or clothes or books or something.

There was no point in explaining to Mom and Dad or asking their permission. Too much had happened, and anything I said would be secondhand reasoning that would never stand up against the generous façade of Reverend Dodge—at least not in my parents' eyes. If I asked to be excused from the Youth Celebration, I'd be dismissed as an ungrateful teenager and escorted to the basement of God's Glory where I would remain under guard for the duration of the party. No, it was better to do like everybody else and say nothing at all.

Mom's high heels clicked across the floor. I thought she was coming upstairs, so I stood up and started to dress.

I was angry with Reverend Dodge, but he was no different than he'd always been. Jesse hadn't done anything but hold a candle to it, even though most were too far gone to see. Trouble was coming, but I didn't know how much until it was too late.

If I'd just gone to the chicken dance, maybe things would have worked out better, but I didn't, so here I am sprawled out on this dock, listening to the water lap beneath, praying to be done before the shadows drag me away.

The pancakes were stiff, the bacon was cold, and the syrup was thin, but the adults of God's Glory served breakfast like it was a four-star meal. Paper cloths sprinkled with glitter covered the tables, and jubilant signs announcing how great we were and how much everybody loved us were taped to the walls. Colorful streamers dangled like jungle vines from helium balloons insistent on hugging the ceiling. By the time I arrived, Kirby had cleared away a swath of them above the table where he and Natalie sat. She eyed the streamers hanging like razors from their floats. They were at the mercy of the slightest breeze, and she didn't trust them at all.

I moved over and sat down. "Hey, Natalie, you sure look pretty today."

She wasn't ready for the usual compliments until Kirby shooed a few more balloons away, but when she felt safer, she turned to answer. "Why thank you, this is a Sunday dance dress Daddy got me in Hawkinsville. He ain't here today on account of he's using his truck to help John. I'm not supposed to say nothing 'bout it out loud—Daddy told me that."

"I think we're Natalie's dates for a while," Kirby said with a grin, "at least until Mr. Wallace comes to take Cinderella home."

"He's coming to get me right after church." She pooched out her lower lip to show her disappointment and then reached over to pat my hand. "But Daddy says there'll be other dances soon enough, so don't fret too much, PJ."

"Okay," I nodded.

Kirby stood to corral a couple more suspicious balloons and drag them away. I noticed the rest of the room for the first time. There were speakers set up for music, a big bingo ball cage, and freshly rented casino games staged in the corners waiting to be dragged out later in the day. Activity schedules printed on bright green paper littered every table. The fun started immediately after the service with a fried chicken lunch and dance lessons from Reverend Dodge. Later, we would play capture the flag on the lawn, then inside for Bible trivia, and finally a casino night, dance, and dinner with door prizes and everything. We were supposed to bring extra clothes for each event, and Mom made sure I did.

The church adults had been electric all week with the buzz of this celebration. The work and cooperation needed to fulfill the generosity of Reverend Dodge created an unprecedented tide of unity and single-mindedness throughout God's Glory. Members who weren't known to be friendly were, and every difference was put aside for a time to build the best Youth Celebration possible. It was remarkable. This was more than just balloons and banners; our congregants shouldered a common purpose, making them feel close, trusting, and worthwhile. This was the testimony of God's Glory's commitment to its children, and nothing imaginable was more important. Reverend Dodge knew exactly what he was doing as a tide of anticipation filled the church, rising high, threatening to burst out the doors. Adults scurried about, eager to play their parts. Watching their wide smiles left me uneasy. How quickly their grins would turn to growls when we abandoned them.

Any other time, we would have loved all that was being done, but our carwash became as much against Reverend Dodge as the Youth Celebration was against us, and the virtues of a dance always pale next to a fundraiser for the poor…we believed.

No matter what our parents thought, we couldn't see the celebration for anything other than an assault on our teenage freedom. It impassioned us. Sometimes it's best to run with feelings and sometimes not, but when the lines between right and righteous are blurred, we often do things we regret. We could have rescheduled the carwash, outmaneuvered Reverend Dodge, and spared our parents heartache and embarrassment, but we didn't. Instead, we pushed our petrified breakfast around our plates and whispered under the noses of our elders as they set the stage for lunch and dance lessons with the reverend.

When it was time for the service, Kirby and I wandered upstairs with the rest of the youth to sit in the back pew with the Braddocks and the Millers. Natalie sat between us, insisting on holding both our hands in her lap. Of course, we let her.

The reverend offered a sharp sermon on misguided teenagers, false prophets, the danger of cults, and how blessed the youth of God's Glory were to have so many caring adults to protect us from all three. "Amens" popped like corn over the congregation, and when Reverend Dodge concluded, everyone came to their feet in applause.

The benediction was said, and the pews emptied as the whole church filed back to shake our hands, offer their blessings, and tell us how fortunate we were. We stood a while, milling about and thanking people. The smell of fried chicken and green beans seeped from the basement, and I heard the muffled chicken dance being played through the floor.

Kirby and I needed to walk Natalie out, so we slid by the crowd and through the front doors. Mr. Wallace was waiting at the curb. Natalie whined about having to leave but climbed in his truck anyway. I wanted to go too.

I was cornered in a decision of betrayal. I was going to disappoint someone either way. *Would I go in and chicken dance, or would I wash cars?* I thought I knew what to do all week, but now, with the outpouring of effort from the church, leaving, even for a few hours, seemed ungrateful. I wanted to delay all I could.

I stepped to the truck. "Hey, Mr. Wallace, Natalie says it's moving day."

Mr. Wallace put his window down to answer. "Sure is, and I'm mighty happy for it. Those folks deserve better than they have, and thanks to you boys, they're gettin' it."

"You need any help?" Even though skipping out with him wouldn't have been much better than heading to the Gas &

Grocery, somehow it seemed more defensible. Mr. Wallace was a better alibi, and I'd still be helping. I prayed he'd say yes.

He lifted his arm to rest it on the open window. "No, we're okay. John's folks don't have much, and most of what they do have, I think they'll leave. It's not like they can take Jesse's playhouse with 'em, and we'll replace most anything else." He shook his head. "No, they're just bringing up a few sentimental things, so I'm really just shuttling everybody back and forth so they can make their good-byes."

He reached over to pat Natalie on the leg and cranked his truck. "Thanks though. You go on in and have fun. Seems like the whole church is set up for you kids, and the people inside don't even know how much you all deserve it, but that's okay. The Lord works in mysterious ways, don't He?" He looked to Natalie again, and she raised a thumbs-up in agreement. "Have a good time…you, too, Kirby. I'll see you boys tomorrow."

"See you soon!" Natalie echoed.

"We're almost done with the summer, huh, PJ?"

"Yes, sir, we are."

"Maybe they'll open up Sandy Shores, and you can take the last few days off to enjoy yourself. You've paid me back plenty for running through my yard. As a matter of fact, I'm sure I owe you by now."

I didn't know how to respond. It didn't seem like I'd worked for Mr. Wallace at all…only Jesse, and even that seemed more like a privilege. The summer had flown.

I stepped back. Mr. Wallace gave a short wave to Kirby and pulled away. He didn't know what we were planning, but I'm sure he wouldn't have approved.

Kirby touched me on the shoulder. "Let's go. We're already gonna be the last ones there."

I sniffed as I watched Mr. Wallace's truck wheel out of the square, and then turned to follow Kirby, letting my feet decide what was right for me to do. I wondered how long it would take before a posse of angry parents would find us and drag us back to

Reverend Dodge. With all of the carwash signs spontaneously popping up around town, it wouldn't be hard to figure out where we were.

41
Charity Carwash

Kirby was right; we were the last ones to arrive, strolling up on a soapy-sudsy scene of bikini tops and cutoff jeans. A couple of girls were waving poster board signs that read *Free Charity Carwash – Generous Donations Appreciated.* A green garden hose ran across the parking lot where buckets of wash water overflowed with foam. Laughter filled the air as the boys scooted the girls and pretended it was just an accident. One boy caught a soapy sponge to the side of his head after *accidentally* spraying Chipmunk. The joyful sound of play circled the parking lot as the boys chased the girls with the hose and the girls retaliated with buckets of suds. I'm not sure if the hard work at the farm or the deprivation of Sandy Shores seasoned the moment, but soapy water on hot summer pavement has always smelled like happiness to me.

Kirby brought extra clothes and headed straight into the Gas & Grocery to change. I accidently left my stuff in the truck, so I was stuck in church pants and penny loafers unless I was willing to walk all the way back.

"Hey, PJ, why you still dressed for Sunday school?" one of the guys yelled from the cheerful fray.

"Yeah, PJ," Chipmunk chimed in. She was soaking wet from head to toe, armed with a soapy sponge she tossed lightly in her hand. A mischievous grin covered her face. "You better go ahead and change before someone hits you with a sponge." Her eyes sparkled above a wide smile, and I couldn't help but smile back. She was pretty, and for one long moment, as she stood there against a backdrop of spray and foam, I wondered if she remembered kissing me on that hayride so long ago.

"Car!" someone yelled as the first customer of the day rolled into the parking lot. The horseplay subsided, and Chipmunk turned to join the others in their work. Kirby emerged to help, and before the first car was even finished, a half-dozen more were lined up for their free charity carwash.

If Chipmunk had asked me one more time, I would have walked back to fetch a change of clothes, but she didn't know to—not that it would matter anyway. I sat down on the steps of the Gas & Grocery, not for attention or pity, but to watch the commotion and feel sorry for myself. I've always been an honest pouter.

I wondered how much longer the carwash would be allowed to continue. Kirby and I had been here forty minutes, and I was sure Reverend Dodge was seething by now. He was not one to be ignored, and I couldn't think of anything more humiliating for the reverend than waiting to give dance lessons in an empty basement as grease from lunch congealed in silver metal pans. Sitting on the steps watching, I couldn't say whether the reverend deserved the snub, but I was sure he wouldn't tolerate it. Since there were few in town who could resist him, I was sure Cunningham wouldn't tolerate it either.

"What's up?" Mr. Miller stepped out of his store behind me. "Why aren't you over there gettin' wet?"

Without standing, I turned to look up at him. "Wrong clothes," I shrugged.

"Yeah, I see." He paused to watch the youth rinse off a station wagon.

I felt awkward with him standing behind me, so I looked up again and said the first thing that came to mind. "Thanks for letting us use your parking lot."

"No problem. It's the least I can do for a good cause. Just make sure you get back to church before too much longer. No sense in getting yourselves in more trouble than need be."

Yes, we were certainly going to be in trouble, but our transgression would eventually be excused for youth and stupidity. The Millers, on the other hand, would be a different story. They would be in trouble too, but I'm sure they knew that before they gave permission for the charity carwash to be held at their store.

"Yes, sir," I agreed.

"And, PJ, when you guys slow down a little, I have a tow truck that needs a good rinsing. That should be worth a pretty sizeable donation."

"Yes, sir, thank you."

He looked down with a faint smile and then disappeared inside.

Across the parking lot, laughter erupted in the mist of the green hose as another car pulled up to be washed clean.

Everyone was so devoted, but Cunningham would only understand this as a rude teenage prank, a slight to God's Glory, and an insult to everyone who prepared the Youth Celebration. Ordinarily when caught, we would justify ourselves to parents who wouldn't listen, ending with standard punishments and forced apologies to all we offended with our adolescent self-centeredness. But with his latest Sunday sermons on Cain, God's will, false prophets, and the dangers of cults, Reverend Dodge planted a minefield more explosive than we imagined, and the whole town was dancing across it.

I saw Kirby's folks come through with their car, but I didn't go speak. They waved as they passed by in their dripping sedan headed for home.

Maybe the Youth Celebration was never about canceling the charity carwash but to invite it instead. Maybe it was set to expose the misguided children of Cunningham, incite the church, and rid the town of a lingering, insolent blasphemer. If that was the case, the plan had been perfectly laid. Maybe the reverend wasn't seething after all, and maybe that's why no one had come to get us yet. Maybe Reverend Dodge was giving us time to be fully involved in our crime, letting our selfishness ripen while he spun some sympathetic tale mustering the full support of God's Glory. Jesse was never part of the carwash, but that wouldn't matter when his association with Trackers was exposed—especially when *our* association with Trackers was discovered by our parents. Hell was coming, and it would have to be paid.

But maybe in this last hour, sprawled out by the lake struggling to recall, I credit Reverend Dodge with more than he deserves. Maybe his theoretical scheme occurs to me only now in some effort to share blame for what happened that day. But Dodge is dust, and whatever part he played has surely been judged by now…which leaves only me…only me…without whom neither tragedy would have unfolded.

42
The Doctor

Even over the commotion, I could hear the engine of a speeding truck all the way down the street. It came tearing past the line of cars and skidded into the parking lot. The happy ruckus of the carwash went silent, and I came to my feet as the truck kicked a puddle of soapy water over the gas pump. It roared straight to the door where I stood, forcing me to take a couple of quick steps back before it squealed to a stop. Until the pickup sat rumbling a few feet away, I didn't realize it was Mr. Wallace. I was too startled to cuss out loud.

Mr. Wallace leapt from the vehicle. He was alone. "PJ, PJ, my God, have you seen the doctor?" He didn't wait for me to answer. He turned sweating and out of breath, yelling to the frozen car-washers staring from across the lot. Buckets and brushes hung silently in their hands as water from the garden hose slapped the pavement. "Has anybody seen the doctor?! I can't find the doctor!"

The door to the Gas & Grocery banged open as Mr. and Ms. Miller sprang to Mr. Wallace's side. The gaggle of youth abandoned their customers and trotted over to see what was happening. Mr. Wallace drained pale and quivered as if he'd been touched by a ghost. I'd never seen a heart attack or a seizure, but this looked like both. Ms. Miller put her arm around Mr. Wallace to get him to sit on the steps, but he wouldn't.

"Okay, it's okay. We'll send someone to get the doctor for you," she said.

"Wait, what?" Mr. Wallace took a shaky breath. "No, not for me…it's Angeline, little Angeline…she's been struck…getting her doll at the river…she's been struck by a river chicken…a moccasin…John said its head was big as a saucer. He carried her back…all the way to the bunkhouse…everybody's there. Her arm's black up to her neck, and she was barely breathing when I left. Now I can't find the damn doctor anywhere!"

"Where's Jesse? We need Jesse," Ms. Miller demanded, but Mr. Wallace shook his head he didn't know.

"Okay, where's the girl?" Mr. Miller took charge. I don't know if he knew who Angeline was, but his wife certainly did.

"At the bunkhouse," Mr. Wallace panted.

"Who knows where that is?" Mr. Miller turned to the group, and everyone raised their hands. "Mary, get the first-aid kit and a snake bite kit too. I'm pretty sure we still have some of those." He turned to Mr. Wallace. "We're going to follow you. Everybody else, go find the doctor and get him to that bunkhouse now!"

We broke from the Gas & Grocery, running back to church where our cars were parked. No one stopped to turn off the hose or rinse the last soapy vehicle as we sprinted past the line of Uphillers waiting their turn for a carwash. We'd barely made it to the Bride and Groom when Mr. Wallace drove by with the Millers following in their tow truck. We raced up the sidewalk past God's Glory and around the corner to the church lot. Teenagers filled their cars, and those who didn't have one piled in with someone else. I was breathing hard when I popped the doors and Kirby and I slid into my pickup. I was never so glad in all my life to have driven separately from my parents. I was determined to be the first to find the doctor.

Word was passed to lean heavy on the horn when the doctor was found to signal everyone else to break off and head for the Wallace farm. Cunningham was small and anyplace the doctor could be was close by, so a long horn blast through town was a good plan. We rolled out of the parking lot like honeybees from a dead tree as Youth Celebration volunteers and Reverend Dodge watched from the windows of God's Glory. If they'd known, they may have understood. We never even considered the doctor may have been among them.

Some drove straight for the doctor's office in case there were some Sunday odds and ends he was tying up, while others trolled the square looking for his car. Chipmunk waited behind the wheel as her passengers hopped out to check Katie's Diner on the chance the doctor decided to have lunch there. Kirby and I headed for his house. I knew where he lived.

With every passing side street, an uneasy feeling began to sink around me as I recalled what happened the day Carl went to get the doctor for John. I wondered if we should be looking for the veterinarian instead. Surely this was different; Angeline was a little girl…but she was also a Tracker. I didn't know if the doctor would be willing to help or not. Surely he would—but I didn't know.

I turned the corner toward the house as Kirby held up two sets of crossed fingers. "Kirby," I said, "let's not tell the doctor who Angeline is. I think we need to get him out there first."

Kirby nodded his head without looking around from the window. "I agree. We'll say what we have to. After he sees her, he'll help."

I slowed the truck as we rolled up.

"Good, good, good!" Kirby bounced in the seat. "Look there. There's the old man's car in the driveway. Hurry up, hurry up, pull over!"

I did, but before I could come to a full stop, Kirby sprung from the truck, sprinted over the yard, and was pounding on the door. The doctor emerged, and I watched an excited one-way conversation play out on the front stoop. I had no idea what Kirby was saying or how much of the truth he was telling, but the doctor nodded…nodded again and then disappeared into the house without closing the door. Kirby shifted uncomfortably on the front porch until the doctor re-emerged carrying a medical bag. *He was coming, he was coming…thank you God!*

Kirby jumped off the steps and trotted back to where I was waiting as the old man locked up. He stuck his head through the open window. "I'm riding with the doctor…I'm taking him to the farm…you have to find Jesse."

"What? No, you guys are following me out there."

"Damn it, there's no time for this crap," Kirby snapped. "Jesse needs to know what's happening. He needs to get to the bunkhouse. I have the doctor, you find Jesse, and we'll see you there. Just do it, PJ!"

Kirby didn't wait for me to protest again. He met the doctor at his car, got in, and I watched as they backed down the drive and turned the corner at the end of the street. The horn sounded, signaling everyone but me to meet at the Wallace farm.

I slammed my palms against the steering wheel, closed my eyes and took a deep angry breath. I ran my hand back through my hair and then wheeled the pickup around to head through the square, back by the abandoned Gas & Grocery, and out to the locked gate of Sandy Shores. I didn't look too hard and I didn't see Jesse's truck anywhere, but I'd done what Kirby wanted, so he would have to be okay with it. I loved Jesse and I knew he'd want to be there for John, but Kirby managed to get the doctor, and that's what was needed.

I dipped into the Sandy Shores turnoff just enough to make a U-turn and head out River Road to the Wallace farm. Dark summer storm clouds were gathering on the horizon.

43
The Dog

The library-storage room window stared at me over the hedge as I passed along the back of the church. I was worried about Angeline, but I must admit some small part of me cared only about being present for what was happening. My mind went elsewhere as God's Glory slid by. I was sure we'd done right with the carwash, so I didn't give a single thought about the anger a youthless Youth Celebration might cause Cunningham or who would take the blame.

I touched the accelerator as the buildings of town disappeared from my rearview and the pastels of summer farms and the overgrown banks of the Chagrin smeared by in a rich amalgamation of seasonal colors. Earlier storm clouds mustered into black ramparts in the distant sky ahead, blocking out the light, making ready to claim their boundaries with a wall of silver rain. I pressed the gas again, hoping to beat them to the Wallace farm.

It didn't take long for the harmony of the wheels and the road to send my mind sideways with their hypnotic lullaby. I had a special weakness for it, almost like a space traveler who climbs into a sleeping pod for the long journey home. *I wonder what they dream about.*

Angeline's arm was black up to the shoulder. The snake's head was big as a saucer…the cracked-face doll…bees don't bite…I still can't believe Natalie saw me and Kirby in our underpants…orange cream sodas really aren't that bad…I wonder if they're still behind the chips…why would anybody eat something that smelled like a poot?

I smirked as the last thought tiptoed across my mind.

The blackberries are big as apples this year.

Warning drops pinged against my windshield, sounding more like pea gravel than water. I'm not sure if it was the weight of the raindrops or the speed of the truck that made them sound like they might break right through. But the click of pebbles and glass was enough to reel my mind back from wherever it strayed.

I was on the curve…*again*! Going way too fast…*again*! I pulled my foot from the accelerator and touched the brakes…*again*…trying to manage the line between cutting speed and flipping the truck. As I flew around the blind, I felt my back end start to go, and I worried the blacktop may be wet even though the storm hadn't let loose. Dark clouds marched across the sky, forcing an early twilight. Everything went gray. I felt the truck slide and begin to tip. I cut the wheel as I barreled around my nemesis. *I've got it, I've got it!* My tires grabbed, and I shot forward. *Dog!* It was too late. I hardly felt the bump as I crushed the animal beneath my wheels. A pitiful yelp pierced the screaming engine and squealing rubber. It turned in my stomach like sour milk. Hitting a dog is different than hitting a 'possum.

I regained control and stopped to take a breath. I surveyed my victim through the rearview mirror. It looked like a pile of splayed waste from a butcher shop, or maybe a shredded roll of pink-and-red carpet padding that had fallen off a truck. I dropped my head to the wheel. I made it around…*again*. My truck idled patiently. *Me and that dog…it was bound to happen.* I hoped the stupid thing didn't belong to Nya or Angeline.

I looked up in the mirror at the twisted heap. I was going to get out and check, but the storm clouds chose that moment to release their deluge, dropping a curtain of heavy rain between me and the animal I'd crushed on the curve. I couldn't see a thing. I reached down to flip on the wipers.

"It was just a mangy stray mutt," I told myself.

Thunder dragged along the sky, and fat drops washed the blood from my bumper as I idled a moment longer. The storm would be strong enough to wash the body into the briars, so I pushed my foot down on the pedal and rumbled on out to the bunkhouse.

44
The Littlest Tracker

The sky was black and the air hung gray, but there was no rain on the other side of the pecan grove. You could smell it though…all around. Deep thunder rolled like boulders across the sky, and lightning flickered high among the clouds. It wasn't ready to strike the earth. Dull wildflowers bobbed in the meadow, agitated by an imperceptible breeze as the windmill watched like a tall, silent ghost from beyond the bunkhouse. Everyone was there, standing quietly in the afternoon twilight outside the Trackers' home. No one spoke, they only stood. I pulled my truck alongside the other vehicles, killed the engine, and got out. I felt like a fated character watching myself in an old black-and-white movie. I had to adjust. I spotted Kirby standing among the others. I moved up beside him.

"What's going on?" I whispered.

He turned, looking directly into my face, not recognizing me for a moment.

"Hey, the doctor's been inside with Angeline a while now."

"No problems?"

Kirby shook his head. "No problems at all. He didn't say a word, and he didn't ask about this place. He went in, told everyone but John and Elizabeth to leave, and started to work."

I nodded and looked around. Nya was sobbing gently into her hands as Chipmunk and one of her friends stood with their arms around her. Sam and the other Tracker men sat like headstones in the grass with Mr. Wallace and some boys who'd worked on the bunkhouse. Everyone else held hands or tried to calm little ones who were growing bored with the whole affair. Muted tears and hushed voices in the light of the dark clouds made everything feel like a broken, grainy film with the sound turned too far down to hear. Faint weeping rippled in the gray. We waited—and despair waited with us.

"I couldn't find Jesse." My voice cracked louder than I intended.

"I know," Kirby whispered. "He's down at the apiary right now."

"By himself?"

Kirby nodded.

"What's he doing? I mean, why is he there?" I glanced beyond Kirby to see a lone silhouette standing among the bee boxes.

Kirby shook his head. "I don't know. Mr. and Ms. Miller walked down to ask him, but he wouldn't come up. He's just there…maybe praying…I don't know…standing…but I wish he was here. I didn't like the way the doctor looked when he saw Angeline." He paused. "She looks bad."

I didn't know what to say. I thought about going to get Jesse but waited with everyone else instead.

I remembered seeing Angeline for the first time with her big lollipop at the Gas & Grocery and later at Easter when she plopped in my lap with the blueberry pie. I smiled. A stray drop of water ran from my eye to the crook of my mouth. I wiped it away with the back of my hand.

It's hard to tell the passage of time when it's neither night nor day and you're caught somewhere between prayers and hopelessness. I may have been a few minutes or a few hours standing with the others. I couldn't imagine why the storm spared us this long or why the doctor hadn't emerged to tell us Angeline was okay. I didn't know why Jesse was so interested in those stupid bees or why he wasn't here with the rest of us. He stood down there in his stinking apiary like he was waiting on a bus! Thoughts and feelings whipped up inside me until I was ready to bust. But I kept my place, lingering quietly on the brink like everyone else.

We stood and we waited. Then I heard it—a low guttural moan from inside the bunkhouse, spreading out through the twilight, growing into an unnatural howl like grief itself screaming in anguish. Elizabeth's cries for her lost child were joined by an upheaval of wailing from the chorus of mourners who'd waited outside for different news. Misery spilled in from all around, overflowing the meadow in a flood of heartache. I felt myself drowning in it. I gasped for breath, fell to my knees, and without permission, everything living inside me tore free and my tortured voice joined the others'.

We knew, even before the doctor appeared on the front porch, Angeline was gone.

"He didn't come," Kirby sobbed. "Jesse didn't come."

Thunder rumbled, and a few moments later the doctor stepped out. His shirtsleeves were rolled to his elbows, and he held his medical bag in one hand. He moved across the porch to lean on the railing. The doctor looked like he'd been punched in the stomach. He wiped his face with his palm, leaned up, and shook his head. "I'm sorry" was all he choked before the sobs of the crowd drowned out anything else he might have said.

A minute or two went by before John and Elizabeth appeared from inside. John was holding his wife in both arms as she wept into her hands. Her legs were unsure with the weight of sorrow, and she would have dropped if John had let her go. They stumbled to the bottom of the steps where Nya rushed to meet them, throwing her arms around her parents. Mr. Wallace was next; then the rest of us collapsed around them, joining Angeline's mother and father in a great embrace of tears and loss.

I pressed in with the others, seeking comfort from people whose faces I couldn't discern in the darkness. I tried to hold back, but couldn't, so I cried with the rest, grieving for the littlest Tracker.

45
Angeline

I thought we would stay forever. I couldn't think of one good reason to let go. All of this seemed so wrong. What was it for? How would these families ever recover? I don't know how long we stood together until the group began to sway and people in the center struggled to breathe. We stepped back from the outside, and the massive embrace slowly split into individuals or pairs still weeping and holding on to one another.

John and Elizabeth pulled away and started up the steps to be with their daughter one last time before the final good-bye. Nya moved between them, and the three held tight as they climbed to the porch together. My head swam as they moved up in slow motion. The gray, the dog, the Youth Celebration—nothing seemed real, and I hoped to wake soon, roll over, and shake it off as a terrible dream. I felt Kirby beside me as what was left of the family paused to steady themselves on the top step. But before they could proceed, someone reached out and took Elizabeth by the arm.

"Elizabeth, what's going on?" The sorrow in Jesse's voice ran back down the front steps and puddled at our feet. I was too distant to hear him clearly, but his voice was in my ear again, like he was whispering only to me. By the twitch in the crowd, I could tell others heard him the same way.

Elizabeth put her arms around Jesse and wept on his shoulder. I don't know where she found the tears. She pushed back, wiped her face with one hand and then her nose with the other.

"It's my girl…she…she…" Elizabeth paused to collect herself enough to say it. "She done gone away, Jesse…she done gone away."

She turned to John, and he took her in his arms. Tears welled in Jesse's eyes, and somehow seeing him cry made me feel worse. Jesse put his arms around the family.

"He's too late," Kirby muttered.

Jesse pulled himself away, wiped his face, and looked at Elizabeth. "Are you sure?" he whispered.

The doctor reached over and touched Jesse on the elbow. He wanted to answer so Elizabeth wouldn't have to.

"Yes, son, we're sure. There was too much poison for the child…went straight to her heart…she never woke up. I'm so sorry. I tried everything I know."

The doctor kept his voice low and hushed, but I could hear him the same way I could hear Jesse, like eavesdropping on a conversation we were meant to hear. Jesse's eyes pooled, overflowing in slow tears down his face.

"No," Jesse said shaking his head, as he dragged his wrist across his nose and wiped his eyes. "No, she's just sleeping…she's only asleep."

"Please, son, don't," the doctor interrupted, but Jesse paid no more attention to him.

"Elizabeth…Elizabeth, look at me." Jesse touched her on the side of the face. "Call Angeline…she's only sleeping," he said, but Elizabeth sank deeper into her husband's arms without looking up.

"Stop, Jesse, just stop," Kirby mumbled to himself as we watched from the yard. His voice cracked, and I could tell without looking he was crying again.

"Call your daughter, Elizabeth. She's not gone, she's asleep." Jesse's words were like daggers twisting in the grieving mother's heart. She couldn't bring herself to lift her head from her husband's chest. She started to moan and pulled one feeble hand free to wave Jesse away.

"Jesse, please," John choked, "please stop."

"Jesse," Mr. Wallace pleaded from the bottom of the steps, "what are you doing? Son, it's over."

But Jesse didn't stop. "Angeline," he called, "wake up, sweetheart. Your mommy needs you."

Elizabeth began to wail, Nya buried her face in her father's side, and the crowd moaned. Screwdrivers jammed into my temples, and tears puddled my sight. This was terrible, and Jesse was making it worse. I wanted him to stop…but he didn't…he wouldn't.

"Angeline," he called to the dead girl, "it's time to get up now. Your mommy and daddy are looking for you. It's time to come back now…you've been gone long enough."

Anguish rippled over us all, thunder scraped over the clouds, and a heavy mist fell through the gray. I dropped my head. I couldn't take any more.

"Angeline," I heard Jesse's voice deep in my ear, "Angeline…well…hey there, sleepyhead."

What? I looked up to see a small silhouette hugging Jesse around the legs. He reached down and stroked the back of her head as she tilted up to see into his face. Elizabeth, Nya, and John, quaking, unable to speak, collapsed to their knees and took the child in their arms. I stood among the others, not understanding the commotion on the porch until John whisked Angeline up for us all to see. The pendulum was swinging too wide for me to comprehend.

"Good Lord," Kirby gasped.

Angeline gazed over the crowd, rubbed the sleep from her eyes, and gave a tiny finger wave from her father's arms. We watched, dumb with disbelief. I swallowed hard. This was surely a dream. Angeline turned to John and took his face in both of her hands. "I'm hungry, Daddy," she announced.

Sometimes events overwhelm words, so there were none to be found. The mourners in the yard erupted in howls of laughter and tears of joy. The doctor had been wrong…but that was impossible. We moved toward the porch, falling together again in a giant embrace, bouncing and laughing this time, stumbling and trying not to fall.

The miraculous coursed in my veins. No other event of my life—not my wedding day with Maggie or the birth of my children—would compare to the contentment and satisfaction of the moment I spent in the arms of the Trackers. Angeline was alive and I nearly understood, so I howled and laughed and danced and gave thanks with the rest.

The mist grew to a light rain, and the windmill turned slowly with the heavier drops. My clothes began to soak through but a terrible weight was lifted, and I didn't mind the damp at all. I rose up enough to see the doctor pull Jesse into his arms, and although I couldn't hear what he was saying anymore, I'm sure it was "thank you."

The ebb of the crowd eventually pulled everyone around to kiss Angeline on the head and shake Jesse's hand. Even though it was dark and heavy, cold clouds dipped to the ground, the day was a good one, and the charity carwash and the Youth Celebration seemed as distant as if they'd happened to people other than us.

46
Unfriendly Lights

So here I am now, lying broken, old, and lost…sprawled out on this dock without the strength to wipe my own tears. I can feel the shadows of Cunningham watching from the banks, hoping for me to join them before I say too much. I'll be with them soon.

The dock rolls and groans as Able Lake swells from something it swallowed in the distance. The faint smell of wisteria sweetens a breeze, making the water in my eyes colder than it was before. Everything feels darker now; somehow the night feels darker. It's hard to believe that's the same moon that watched over my boyhood.

My arms and legs are heavy with pins and needles, and my thoughts are mushy and crisp all at the same time. Has to be the pills…I don't know how many I've had since I've been here…it doesn't matter…I'm at the edge…it doesn't matter…it was always going to be like this. My wife is gone, and I have no children I can remember. Every reason to lie has been taken from me, so all that's left for me is to confess before the abyss, and then maybe, just maybe, I can forget everything but Maggie. Please don't take Maggie again. This is why I've come.

Chipmunk hugged Kirby, and I hugged Nya as Tuttle, Kaden, and the other children giggled and played chase through the flowers. I looked around in the mist, finding it hard to tell the

Trackers from the youth of God's Glory as they blurred together, mingling, shaking hands, and slapping each other on the back. Just last season, we didn't give a second thought to passing these people in the rain, but the seasons changed, starting with the carpenter hired to build a porte cochere.

Mr. Wallace's laughter broke above the happy noise, and John's followed along. Someone touched me on the shoulder, and I turned to find the Millers making their rounds. Ms. Miller was as pretty with wet hair as she was dressed for church. She thanked me for keeping her secret all those months ago when I walked in on Nya and Angeline, and I thanked her for keeping mine about the reverend's orange cream soda.

Mr. Miller shot his wife a sly smile. "You told me about the kids, Mary, but the sodas—" He looked at me, shook his head, and smirked. "Well, that explains a lot!"

"Yes, sir, I'm sorry," I apologized. "I…well…there may be some cans behind the Fun Doodles."

"Yeah, I know," he laughed. "I found them right after I placed a whole new order. We didn't have a clue how they got there. You sure know how to push the reverend's buttons, don't you?"

"It's not hard," I said with a smile.

Mr. Miller chuckled, and Ms. Miller covered her mouth to contain a laugh.

"I know," Mr. Miller agreed. Then he congratulated me for not getting caught in my joke but told me never to hide any of his stock again. He had more orange cream sodas than Reverend Dodge would drink in six months. Ms. Miller hugged me, Mr. Miller shook my hand, and they turned to look for Chipmunk among the happy crowd. I watched them disappear.

"Hey," Kirby touched me on the arm, "let's go talk to Jesse."

It was a good idea. I could see him still on the porch.

As we started to pick our way over, cheerful carnival lights appeared swirling over the meadow and across the bunkhouse. If

I didn't know better, I'd say fairies were dancing just for Angeline. They stabbed magically through the gray, illuminating every tiny raindrop in whites, blues, and reds. They were so beautiful, catching me in the moment, until the familiar blast of a police siren turned my stomach, and I realized the lights weren't friendly at all.

We looked around to see two Cunningham patrol cars followed by the reverend's black sedan crawling through the foggy pecan grove. Silence hung across the meadow like a spider's web as the encroaching vehicles moved in. I noticed the rain and my wet clothes for the first time. I wanted to run, but all I could do was wait for the trouble in bright lights coming through the trees. It didn't take long.

The two police cruisers forced us aside as they pushed up to the porch. The reverend rolled to a stop a few feet behind them. Why had they come all the way out here? We weren't breaking any laws. We'd skipped out on a stupid church party…for a really good reason—Angeline was sick—but that wouldn't matter, and I was scared. Sheriff Johnson, Eddy, and Reverend Dodge stepped out of their cars.

"Well, well." A greasy smile slid over Eddy's lips as he looked over our damp gathering.

"Shut up!" Sheriff Johnson barked at his deputy. "Go check those vehicles."

Eddy lingered a moment, gave a two finger salute, pulled his flashlight, and started over to where we all parked.

Reverend Dodge popped his umbrella and sidled up to the sheriff.

"This is my property." Mr. Wallace stepped off the porch. "You've got no issue with us." He was furious with the intrusion. "What the hell are you doing here?"

"Back off, Wallace," Sheriff Johnson snarled. "That ain't the question. No, that ain't the question at all. The real question is, what are *you* doing here?" The sheriff's eyes shot to the Trackers standing in front of our summer's work. "What do you got, some kind of cult going on, mixing our kids with river trash so you can snatch a higher dollar from Uphill? Is that what you're pulling, Wallace? Is that it?"

"Hang on, Sheriff." Mr. Miller stepped in, but Sheriff Johnson drew his baton faster than a fat man should be able to, pointing it at Mr. Miller as a warning to stay back.

"Sheriff, take it easy," Reverend Dodge interceded. "These are our friends," he nodded toward Mr. Miller and Mr. Wallace, "and these are our neighbors." He motioned to John and Elizabeth standing on the porch. "They haven't done anything wrong. They're victims being manipulated by a shrewd Uphiller who knows how to twist the truth. False prophets…" Reverend Dodge stopped when he saw the doctor. "Doc? I'm surprised to see you here. I didn't know the malignancy had gone this far."

"Reverend," the doctor spoke up, "I've seen the most amazing thing. It's beyond explanation, defying what I know about medicine. This little girl—"

"Enough, Doctor!" Reverend Dodge's pulpit voice cracked like a shotgun blast. "*What* I know, is children are standing in the rain instead of standing in church! *What* I know, is a group of kids who used to sit at the front of God's Glory has separated itself to the very back! *What* I know, is mothers and fathers are dishonored by the secrets being kept in this place! *What* I know, is in our hour of greatest need, you were here instead of serving your fellow saints...that's what I know!" His voice dropped into guilty, theatric remorse. "It hurts me I've let it come this far, but that's not why I'm here."

The reverend took a deep breath to calm himself under his umbrella. He turned to Mr. Wallace. "Bill, where is your daughter?"

Of all the questions Reverend Dodge could have asked, I expected that one least. My mind flew through the day, and I realized I hadn't seen Natalie since Mr. Wallace picked her up after church. I searched for her face among those standing in the mist but found it nowhere. She was probably in the bunkhouse or maybe at home, or she could be out on the road picking those stupid blackberries she likes so much. She had to be somewhere, so why did Reverend Dodge come all the way out here to ask Mr. Wallace about Natalie?

The rain came harder.

Mr. Wallace glared at the preacher.

The reverend's question began soaking through.

Mr. Wallace's face drained to the color of ghosts.

"Natalie! Natalie!" he called. He looked to John who stepped into the bunkhouse, shaking his head as he reemerged. Kirby ran to check Mr. Wallace's truck, but Natalie wasn't there.

"Natalie!" Mr. Wallace's strangled voice echoed through the meadow as he cried out for his daughter. "Natalie, where are you, sweetie? You need to answer your daddy right now!"

All but the sheriff and Reverend Dodge joined in, looking through the apiary and underneath the bunkhouse in case she was playing a game, but even with all of us calling for her, Natalie didn't answer.

"It's okay, it's okay," Mr. Wallace muttered to himself as he bit his lip, searching the day's events to find where he'd last seen his daughter. He approached the reverend. "Dodge, you need to get off my property, and I need to go…I have to go home. Natalie's probably at the house."

"No, Bill," Reverend Dodge shook his head, "she's not. Please get in my car. Let's get out of the wet."

"But I have to go home to find my daughter," Mr. Wallace whimpered.

"Natalie won't be there. Please, Bill, get in the car. I'll take you where she is."

Every worry was written across Mr. Wallace's blank face. "Mary? Henry?" was all he could manage to get out.

"It's okay, Bill. We'll come. We'll be right behind you," Ms. Miller assured.

Reverend Dodge opened his door and then, almost as an afterthought, called out, "Come on, Doc. You're goin' too."

We watched in silence as Mr. Wallace, Reverend Dodge, and the doctor got into the black sedan, pulled around, and maneuvered back through the trees to the main road. The Millers followed in their tow truck, leaving the rest of us alone with Sheriff Johnson. Lightning flickered dimly above the clouds, and a dark roll of thunder promised the storm wouldn't wait much longer. The sheriff watched for the reverend's distant headlights to disappear before turning back to us.

"Well, that leaves just us now, don't it?" he snarled. He tapped his nightstick against his leg and began to pace like a temperamental hound biding its time with a cornered cat.

"We haven't done nothin' wrong," a weak, anonymous voice spoke out. It was easy to tell it wasn't a Tracker—they knew better.

"You ain't done nothin' wrong?" the sheriff barked. "You ain't done nothin' wrong?" He laughed even though it wasn't funny. "You embarrassed the town by vandalizing a bunch of Uphill cars today. You disrespected your parents by choosing to come out and play with trash in the rain instead of goin' to a stupid dance. They waited on you…all of 'em…they waited with Reverend Dodge—who you humiliated and burdened with terrible worry about the path you're choosin'." He stopped to face us full on and smiled. "Yeah, the reverend laid it on heavy, boys and girls, sermonizing to a full house about you turds and how your folks have fallen short in their God-given responsibility. He had 'em stirred up pretty good too. I hated to interrupt him." Sheriff Johnson snorted like something amusing crossed his mind. "I expect most of you are in for a serious ass-whippin' when you get home." He grinned.

The rain picked up, and thunder toppled through the heavens like a bag of bricks. I could feel my church clothes, soaked and clinging to my body. My shoes were full of lakes.

"Hurry the hell up, Eddy!" Sheriff Johnson hollered to the deputy inspecting our cars. "It's about to throw down out here, so move your ass!"

"Almost there, boss," Eddy yelled back.

The sheriff grumbled to himself and then started on us again. "Yeah, you kids are in for a pretty good ass-kickin', but don't worry too much. Even though what you did to Reverend Dodge was a terrible, terrible thing, he is a good man, and he doesn't want any of you to be unnecessarily hurt…although it would probably do you some good. The reverend was very clear with your folks; it's been the conniving Uphiller keeping you astray—filling your heads with ungodly ideas, associating with Trackers, and embarrassing the town. Reverend Dodge took all the responsibility on himself for bringing that troublemaker and his family to Cunningham in the first place. Oh yeah, you should've seen your folks spittin' fire, looking for anyone to blame but themselves for your shit. You may be in for a thumpin', but Lord help us if Cunningham gets half an excuse to do anything but run that stupid-ass Jesse kid out of town."

All I could do was stare at the big man in the rain poncho with the plastic cover over his hat. He was saying a lot of things and I knew we were in trouble, but my mind hung on Natalie, so the sheriff's words faded to the background of my thoughts. My mind raced to find her as Sheriff Johnson went on, but Natalie was nowhere else in the day. Not my day anyway. I started to worry…like I'd walked through a cobweb with every faint strand on my skin the possibility of something awful.

"Sheriff," Kirby sounded meek beside me, "where did Reverend Dodge take Mr. Wallace?"

"Well, that brings us down to it, now don't it, Kirby Braddock?" Sheriff Johnson pointed his baton at Kirby and then straightened himself up so we could all hear his answer. "The reverend is taking Wallace down to Mort's Funeral Home to see his daughter."

What? What did he say? No, that's not right. Natalie's back at the house or maybe at the store.

"Or what's left of her," the sheriff continued.

Everything stopped—not one breath, not one heartbeat—as we waited for what Sheriff Johnson would say next.

47
The Dented Truck

"Yeah, we found her right up here on River Road, across from her own damn yard in them blackberries. She looked more like hamburger than anything else." He tapped his baton against his leg. "By the time we got out there, couldn't do nothing but call the coroner to come scrape poor Natalie up off the pavement…and fetch the reverend so he could break the news to Wallace." He shook his head. "Whoever done it splattered that child doing near seventy…then drove off like she was a dog in the road."

I hadn't thought about that stupid dog since I arrived, but as soon as the sheriff mentioned it, my stomach drained through my knees. The bunkhouse, the windmill, and the rest of the meadow retreated to the background, like I was standing in front of an oil painting or beginning to wake from a bad dream I wasn't sure was real. Everything faded on the periphery and Sheriff Johnson was all I could see.

My breath shallowed, and my throat felt like it was full of paper towels. I choked and heard myself asking, "What about the dog?"

"Do you think you're funny?" the sheriff snarled. "There ain't no dog…just a stain on the road where Natalie Wallace used to be."

"But there was a dog."

"Shut the hell up!" The sheriff aimed his club at me. "There—ain't—no—dog! The only *dog* I know about is the scum that ran down that poor retarded girl, and if," he raised his voice so Eddy could hear, "my deputy would hurry up inspecting those vehicles, we'll know who the scum is soon enough!"

What did he mean there was no dog? There was a dog! I saw it on the curve with a fist full of blackberries! I hit it! I heard the yelp! I felt the bump! Why was the sheriff saying there wasn't a dog?!

"Got it, boss, right here!" Eddy stood up and slapped his baton across the hood of Jesse's truck. I jumped at the hollow, metal sound. "Big dent in the driver's side fender. No doubt, this is the vehicle!"

Sheriff Johnson lumbered over, trying not to slip in the wet grass. He pulled his flashlight to inspect what Eddy found. We watched as brief, muted words passed between them. Sheriff Johnson and Eddy were in agreement about something. They returned together.

"That truck, right there, who does it belong to?" Sheriff Johnson was calm—scary calm—but nobody answered—nobody wanted to. Besides, the sheriff already knew whose truck it was. He tapped his baton against his leg, waiting, but no response came.

"I said, who does that truck belong to?" the sheriff roared.

"That's Mr. Wallace's truck," John answered from the porch.

"Shut up, Tracker, before I run your ass in for lying to the law," growled Sheriff Johnson. "I want to know from one of you." He waved his club, indicating he wanted to hear from the youth of God's Glory. I saw Chipmunk standing wet, shivering with her friends, and I wondered if she'd ever been in this much trouble before. Thunder slid above the clouds, and light rain began to fall again; still, no one said a word.

"Well now, looks like we got a bunch of mutes here, impeding justice and obstructing a lawful investigation, don't it, Eddy?"

"No doubt about it, Sheriff," the deputy said with a grin.

"So here's what's gonna happen if one of you don't tell me what I want to hear. We're gonna take this man," Sheriff Johnson raised his baton and pointed to Sam, "to the back side of this shack and interrogate him with great and extreme thoroughness. It will be highly unpleasant—might even crack a rib or two, *if one of you pipsqueak punk-ass pukes don't tell me who drives that truck!*"

I was afraid to speak, and I was afraid not to. What did it matter? Sheriff Johnson already knew it was Jesse's truck, and they would beat Sam if someone didn't step up and say what the sheriff wanted. *Would it be me?* Surely this whole mess would be sorted out easily at the sheriff's office. The whole town knew the truck had been banged for up years. For goodness sake, Reverend Dodge told Jesse a hundred times to park the truck so the dent wouldn't show from the street. This would be resolved in less than a minute, and everything would be okay if we could get past right now. I could save Sam—if I'd say the truck was Jesse's.

"Um." I dropped my head so I wouldn't have to see anyone else. "Um." The sheriff's attention turned to me. I thought it out and I knew what to do, but somehow, deep somewhere—maybe from our walk to the Gas & Grocery to get Joe's egg salad or the day Jesse touched the child who loved tater tot casserole—something didn't feel right. "Um," I stammered. I wanted to protect Sam, but I wasn't sure, so I kept my words as long as I could. The sheriff moved in. "Um," I hesitated. I was going to tell, I think, but I held on just long enough to keep betrayal from my sins.

"I drive that truck," Jesse announced from the porch.

Sheriff Johnson turned away from me.

"Well, looky, looky who's here. I didn't notice you up there. Figured I'd have to get out the bloodhounds for you, boy. Is that your truck?"

"I said it was," Jesse answered flatly.

Sheriff Johnson nodded to his deputy, and Eddy pushed his way up the steps. The mix of Trackers and youth watched from the yard as the deputy turned Jesse around and cuffed his hands behind his back.

"You're under arrest for the murder of Natalie Wallace," the deputy snarled. He took Jesse by the arm. "Clear a path," Eddy barked to get those standing along the stairs to move off.

A slow smile oozed up from his chin, and Eddy shoved Jesse beyond his balance, throwing him from the porch. Jesse was helpless to break his fall and hit the ground flat at Sheriff Johnson's feet like a bag of cement. The impact drove the wind from his body, and he rolled to his side gasping for air.

"Oops," Eddy laughed.

Kirby moved to help and I started to follow, but Sheriff Johnson raised his nightstick. "Hold your spot," he growled. "All of you…not even a twitch."

Sheriff Johnson reached down with his baton, hooked Jesse's arm, and dragged him to his feet. Eddy came in from behind. The sheriff leaned into Jesse's face. "You should've listened when I told you to get out of Cunningham, boy. Now it's too late. If it had been up to me, I would've run you out a while ago, but that don't matter no more 'cause now it's time to pay the piper."

Eddy raised his club and, stepping deep into his swing, brought it down and around to the back of Jesse's thighs. The thud was sickening, like a baseball bat striking a fresh country ham. Jesse went to his knees with a groan, and everyone in the crowd lurched forward to help.

"Nah uh," Sheriff Johnson warned, tapping his holster. "Don't even think about it, not one muscle. You be statues. Now back up! All of you!"

"My God," Kirby muttered, and suddenly I realized we were all alone—just some teenagers, the Trackers, and Sheriff Johnson. I was trapped in a nightmare where my legs were too heavy to run and my voice was too weak to call for help. The deputy raised his nightstick again, bringing it down across Jesse's shoulder blades, sending a sharp crack echoing through the trees.

Jesse went facedown into Sheriff Johnson's boots. The crowd wailed in protest, begging for the carpenter as Elizabeth held John on the porch.

"And that one is outta here." Eddy laughed and twirled, raising his club over his head like a homerun king. "No applause, no applause," he joked, "just throw money."

"Stop it! Stop it! Please!" Chipmunk screamed through the cries of the hysterical crowd. Tears filled my eyes and I wanted to step in, but the law of Cunningham, with their batons and pistols, held us at bay. Everyone wanted to go to him, but none did. It was like we were watching some horrible movie coming to an inevitable conclusion we were powerless to change. We only sobbed and pleaded for the celebrating Eddy not to strike Jesse again.

It wasn't me…something inside me, stirred by the sight of my friend lying motionless on the wet ground. There was no courage in it, only shock. I never even got close enough to touch him, so it didn't make any difference. The sheriff warned us, but I drifted toward Jesse anyway…up from behind Eddy, who was too busy enjoying his work to notice, until I reached out. I was helpless in a foggy dream, floating by, catching the deputy off guard. I may have taken three steps at most when Eddy caught me in the corner of his eye, whirled around, and brought his baton down across my outstretched arm. The dull crunch sounded far off, and the white bone splitting from my skin looked like it belonged to somebody else. I remember thinking how easily it broke. Pain exploded in my arm, driving me to my knees and a slow roll to my back. I knew I was hurt bad.

48
A Long Time Comin'

"Damn it, Eddy," Sheriff Johnson snapped. "You can't help but take things too far, can you?"

"He was going for my gun," Eddy lied.

The sheriff pushed by his deputy and leaned down to my face. "You okay? Can you hear me, son? I told you to stay put, and now look what happened."

I saw every whisker popping from his chin. He was talking to me, but I couldn't understand what he was saying. I tried to tell him I was hurt, but my words had been knocked away and all I could do was stare at him and gurgle.

"Eddy, you stupid shit," growled Sheriff Johnson, "put PJ in the back of your squad car. I'll take the prisoner. We'll dump 'em with Carl at the station and fetch the doctor. He needs to get out of the weather."

I saw Kirby's face, and I must have passed out, because I don't remember getting in the car or driving out through the grove. The next thing I recall is waking up in the backseat of Eddy's cruiser, headed for town on River Road.

The seat was cold on my face, and I could hear the wipers slapping a comfortable rhythm across the windshield. It seemed like dusk, but I couldn't tell. Dark clouds pressed in lower as the storm waited to make good on its threat…watching, maybe, to see what we would do first. Numbing pain coursed through the right side of my body, and I glanced at my arm but turned away before

I puked. My stomach churned, and my head felt like it was full of helium. I didn't move. I lay there, breathed deep, and tried not to faint.

"Holy crap, Eddy, take a look to your right. Are you seeing what I'm seeing?" The sheriff's voice crackled over the radio.

"Look at that," Eddy snickered to himself and then picked up the transmitter to respond. "If that's what I think it is, boss, it's a long time comin'."

"Dodge has been working this out ever since that kid told him off at Easter, but I never thought he'd get 'em boiling like this." Sheriff Johnson's voice cut out.

"I guess they found out about the girl," Eddy answered.

"No doubt about it. Natalie Wallace gettin' killed is the match on the powder keg," the sheriff came back. "All right, deputy, let's drop these two off with Carl, you find the doctor, and I'll head to the bridge to make sure none of these idiots toast themselves or fall in the river."

"Will do, Sheriff. See you at the ranch," Eddy acknowledged, then clipped the transmitter back on the radio.

I could hear the road speeding by through the seat under my ear. I wanted to stay down so all this could go away. I wanted to wake up in my bed, go to the Youth Celebration, and learn to chicken dance in the basement of God's Glory. I was alone with Eddy, and somehow I felt safer with him thinking I was unconscious. I waited, but even though every instinct told me not to move, I used my good arm and managed to push myself to a sitting position.

The deputy caught me in his rearview mirror. "Well, hello there, Sleeping Ugly. You look like I feel after a night off in Hawkinsville," he said.

I glanced around. It seemed late, but the day had been gray for so long it was hard to tell. "What's goin' on?"

"What's goin' on? What's goin' on?" he chimed. "You mean besides your arm hanging by a thread? Well now, let's see, only the best thing to hit this town…ever!" His eyes glimmered in the mirror. "Take a look over there. We seen that from seven miles out. What do you think that is?"

I was hazy, the whole right side of my body ached, and the wet windows made it difficult to pick out what the deputy was pointing to. I blinked to clear my eyes. I breathed to settle my stomach. If the day had been darker, it would have been easier to see. But through the cage, the rain, and the wipers, over the trees, miles ahead, I saw a faint glow, like the lights of a carnival or a blowout sale at a used car lot in Hawkinsville.

"What is that?" I sighed.

"That's a long time comin' is what that is. Ain't it beautiful?" Eddy paused to stare out the window. "It's a shame a girl had to get herself splattered to make it happen, but if that's what it takes, that's what it takes." He glanced in the mirror to see I still didn't understand. "You dumb shit; they're burning down the bridge! After what happened, I bet all Cunningham came out for it. They're seriously pissed." He hooted and gave the steering wheel a celebratory slap. "They won't be any happier when they see what that punk rabble-rouser made me do to your arm. But don't worry, they won't be mad at you; it's not your fault…mine either. The reverend tried to warn 'em, but most times people don't listen 'til it's too late."

We followed Sheriff Johnson through the mist as the wipers slapped the drizzle from the windshield. The lights of town were haloed by wet air, making everything seem imaginary, like all of this was nothing more than a place in a made-up story. I blinked at all the cars in the parking lot of God's Glory as we drove past. The deputy was right. The whole town must've rallied to finally wipe the bridge from the banks of the Chagrin. I looked for Dad's sedan as we went by. I didn't see it, but I was pretty sure it was there.

The light in the sky grew brighter, and the faint smell of smoke made its way into the deputy's car. I was glad when we turned off and pulled in behind the sheriff's office. Sheriff Johnson dragged Jesse from his squad car like a hooked fish, walked to the back door, and threw him in. I'm sure Eddy would have done the same to me if the sheriff hadn't been close by, but he was careful instead, walking at my side in case I passed out.

Carl met me at the door, catching me under my good arm as I started to stumble. "Good gracious, what happened?"

"A small altercation," Eddy replied as he brushed by.

"PJ, I'm gonna put you on a cot and get some towels." Carl's voice seemed far off and hard to understand. "Eddy, go get the doctor."

"Yeah, yeah, big man," Eddy sneered. "The boss already said that. Sit tight. I'm gonna grab a cup of coffee, then I'm gone."

Carl didn't argue with the other deputy. He ushered me through a big steel door to a small bed in the back. He helped me lay down, and the room began to come into focus. I was in the holding area. There were two full-fledged prison cells with iron bars across from me, but I was enclosed by chain-link that looked more like a dog pen than a place to cool prisoners. The top was caged, but the door was nothing more than a gate with a backyard hasp. You'd need a padlock to keep somebody in. It wasn't closed. There were no windows in the room, and a single massive steel door separated the holding area from the rest of the station. It was cold, quiet, and solid like a concrete tomb.

I heard Sheriff Johnson briefing Carl on the prisoner and the fire and then yell at Eddy about the doctor when he discovered his deputy hadn't left. Orders were given, a door opened and shut, and all conversation fell silent in the front office. My head was clearing, so I slid my legs off the cot and sat up. Jesse was crumpled on the cell floor across from me. His head lay in a shallow pool of red. I guess the sheriff took his turn in private before Carl brought me in. I picked up my arm and tried to stand.

"No, no," Carl waved me down as he came into the cage, "you need to sit."

"But, Jesse," I managed to get out.

"He'll be fine. Eddy's gone for the doc. He'll be locked away for a long time for what he did, but he won't die tonight." Carl draped a towel over my shoulders.

"He didn't do anything," I gurgled up.

"Sheriff's got proof. He killed the Wallace girl, and then tried to hide out on her daddy's farm."

It was like steak knives behind my eyes as I choked on my tears. I tried to explain to the deputy, but I was drowning in my own throat. All I could do was shake my head no.

"I'm sorry, but that boy ran Natalie down, and that's a cold hard fact. She's gone, and she ain't never comin' back. I was over at Mort's with Mr. Wallace a while…busted that old man to pieces. Too bad." He glanced over at Jesse's cell. "Your friend seemed like a decent guy, but sometimes we do things…make mistakes we can never come back from."

"Are you sure, Carl?" I coughed. "Are you sure it wasn't a dog out there?"

"You mean what we found on River Road? It was Natalie…tore clean out of her shoes. She hung on to them blackberries though, had a fistful still in her hand. No, I saw for myself. It wasn't no dog."

The air billowed from my lungs, and I gasped to reclaim it. My chest and stomach began to heave and convulse. I'm sure Carl thought I was going into shock, but the truth is I was being crushed by the weight of what I'd done. *There was a dog! There was a dog! Oh, dear God…there was no dog!*

The reel flashed through my mind…the truck, the rain, the curve, the blackberries, Natalie and the yelp! I could hear myself in the holding area echoing off the concrete walls like a wounded animal too dumb to speak. I couldn't catch my breath. Carl put his hands on my shoulders, pushed me down on the cot, and dragged a thin blanket across my chest.

"Take it easy. I know your arm hurts like hell, but stay with me now. The doctor will be here soon."

I looked up into his face. He didn't understand! He didn't know! *There was never any dog!*

"Jes, Jes, Jes," I panted, not finding air enough to say it. "No, no, no," I shook my head, choking on my tears. I tried to move, but Carl leaned on my shoulders, pinning me to the cot.

"Relax. Hold still before you hurt yourself. You're going into shock."

I wanted up! I wanted up! I kicked and twisted to stand, but I couldn't break free. I tried to scream, but only low, wet burbles escaped my throat. The doctor appeared over me with a syringe. He thumped the barrel with his finger, squeezed liquid into the air, and put the needle in my arm. I felt better, like moving from a nightmare to a dream. Carl let me go and I lay still.

I wasn't asleep. I heard the doctor and Carl like they were speaking in a can.

"His arm looks bad," the doctor was saying. "See this…and this here?" He was pointing something out to Carl. "It should never have broken like that."

"What do we need to do?" Carl asked.

"We need to get him to the Hawkinsville Medical Center straight away. I don't have what I need to deal with a break like this. We can't wait on an ambulance."

"Okay, let me call the sheriff, and I'll get Eddy to run you both up there."

Carl disappeared from the cage, headed for the office to radio Sheriff Johnson, but he wasn't gone long enough to make the call. He barely stepped out when he turned around and shouldered the steel door closed behind him. I heard shouting and screaming in the front room. He threw the big lock and backed in with a gasp.

"What's out there?" the doctor asked in my dream.

"The whole town, Doc. The whole town is out there."

"What do they want?"

I lifted my head up from the cot and saw the deputy motion back over his shoulder. “Him,” he answered, and I knew he was talking about Jesse.

49
The Steel Door

"We have to get PJ to Hawkinsville."

"I know, Doc, but we ain't leaving through there…not right now. We're gonna have to wait for the sheriff to get back and clear everybody out. This Natalie Wallace thing's got the town all torn up, and I'm afraid if they get their hands on the prisoner, they'll do something stupid."

"They're my friends. Maybe I can talk some sense into 'em," the doctor offered.

"No way, not a chance. You should've seen 'em, like a bunch of animals beyond being talked outta anything. They're mobbed up, so the best thing we can do is sit tight. Sheriff Johnson will be here soon. He'll cool 'em down and send everybody home. We'll get PJ outta here then."

The conversation in the holding area played out over a chorus of breaking glass and toppling furniture in the front office. Muted voices were screaming for justice, for vengeance as angry sounds of destruction whipped around outside. Heavy vibrations of steel on steel flooded the room like a dull gong as someone started to pound on the door with a metal chair. The clamor pulled me from the cobwebs, and I sat up. The doctor and the deputy were too distracted to notice me.

"Don't worry," Carl tried to sound calm. "Ain't nothing short of a tank bustin' in here without a key, and we only got two. One's right here in my pocket," he patted his leg, "and Sheriff

Johnson has the other on his ring. So they can beat on that door 'til the cows come home, but they ain't never gettin' through."

Someone struck the door with another metal chair. Carl patted the doctor on the back and turned to unlock Jesse's cell. "Tell you what, Doc. Why don't you have a look at our prisoner while you're here?"

Carl slid the iron bars open, and the two men hoisted Jesse to the cot. The steel door rang out again, but this time with heavier, more determined blows. Someone found a sledgehammer.

Carl stepped out of Jesse's cell and saw me sitting up as the methodical ring of metal pounding metal echoed through the room. "Don't worry. That's reinforced steel with armored hinges, and these walls are two foot of concrete. They couldn't get in here with all the dynamite in town."

My arm didn't hurt much anymore and I believed the deputy about the door, but I didn't understand the frenzy outside. It frightened me. Everything was muffled through the thick walls, but I could hear enough to know the sheriff's office had been ransacked. The brazenness of that alone told me the people on the other side had thrown themselves far beyond right and wrong. I imagined them spitting and nipping at one another like a pack of dogs at the foot of a treed coon. I wondered why they weren't offering comfort to Mr. Wallace at Mort's instead of beating on the door. These couldn't be the people I grew up with. Mourning twisted itself into hate, but none of it made sense…unless something else was fueling their anger…encouraging it from somewhere offstage. As the sledgehammer rang hard against the door again, I wondered if it would make any difference if they knew I was the one who killed Natalie Wallace. Maybe I would've seen things differently from the other side…but that steel door would separate me from Cunningham from that day to this dock.

Static buzzed in my ears, and I heard Reverend Dodge's voice crackle through the room. "Carl, are you in there? Can you hear me, Carl?"

The deputy stepped to a small tan panel on the wall, and I noticed the intercom for the first time. Carl pushed the button. "Thank God, Reverend. What in the world's going on out there?"

There was a pause before the reverend's voice came back deep and resonant through the tiny speaker. The mob hushed, but I heard them pressing in and breathing behind the reverend as he spoke. "Don't worry about any of that, just open the door. You, PJ, and Doc have nothing but friends out here."

Carl turned to scan the holding area. I had my head lolled back against the cage, and Jesse was finally sitting up as the doctor whispered instructions and flashed a tiny light in his eyes. The deputy pushed the button. "Sorry, Reverend, I think I need to wait on Sheriff Johnson."

A muffled roar of indignation erupted in the outer office, more breaking glass, and the sharp ping of something else being thrown against the door…maybe a snow globe or a nameplate from an upturned desk. We could hear Reverend Dodge calming the crowd before he pressed the intercom button again.

"Carl, as a man of God and the shepherd of this community, I hate to lose even one of my sheep, but if you think it's best to put your faith in the laws of man, so be it. I wash my hands of the whole thing. What will be will be. After all, 'vengeance is mine…sayeth the Lord.' Besides…the sheriff is already here."

I heard every tooth of the key slide into the lock from the outside. The tumblers sounded like thunder in my ears. Carl stepped away from the intercom and watched in horror as the mechanism on the steel barrier with armored hinges flipped open. He threw his shoulder to the door to hold it closed, but the weight of the bodies from the other side was too much and easily overwhelmed the single deputy. A rabid throng poured deep into the holding area.

Carl was swept under and crushed to the floor as the frenzy from outside flooded in. Men filled the room in an instant, groaning and yelling as they were pinned against the walls by the force of their own weight. Red faces crushed against my cage, but I can't say if I recognized any of them. There were too many people to distinguish individuals as the wave of nondescript colors and angry voices rushed in.

I picked up my arm and pushed off the cot. The shot the doctor gave me spun in my head like I'd just gotten off the drunken barrels at the county fair. I leaned against the chain-link to steady myself. A hundred enraged voices drilled in my brain as the tide of men who'd swept into the holding area receded like sea foam from the room. Their jeers became distant as the mob crunched back through the sheriff's office and moved out into the square. I blinked at the open door, listening to the voices fade.

Carl lay unconscious, trampled and busted, in the middle of the floor, and the doctor was sprawled out in Jesse's cell like he'd been dropped from a building.

Jesse was gone.

"Doc? Carl?" I called. Neither answered.

I heard the crowd outside cheering.

"No, wait, it was an accident!" I yelled from my cage. "It was an accident. It was me! It was me! I hit Natalie! It was me, not Jesse!"

I shook the cage with my good arm and screamed my confession with everything I had, but the walls were thick, cold, and deaf, and the doctor and the deputy never stirred. I hoisted my busted arm, stepped over Carl, and stumbled out into the square.

I had to tell. It had to stop. I didn't want Jesse to pay the price for something I'd done…for something so stupid, so careless, and so terrible…belonging only to me.

50
Beneath the Bride and Groom

It was dusk, and heavy clouds licked the streets, making everything hazy and out of focus, colder than it should have been on a summer evening. Streetlamps burned with all their might, attempting to cast their light across the square, but they could do little more than glow in the mist. Lightning flickered in the darkness, and I could smell rain on the way. A great storm held us in its grasp, waiting, as tiny voices jeered from the middle of town. Maybe if it had come sooner, nothing would have happened and everyone would be home, out of the weather, praying their roof didn't leak or their basement didn't flood—but that's not the way God works. He gives us all the rope we need.

I staggered over the sidewalk and up on the curb. Silhouettes flickered across headlights like skittish demons, and howls of delight pierced the river fog as it crawled in. People gathered in the square where farmers would be selling their goods next weekend, and as I shuffled toward the commotion, I noticed a school bus obscured by the mist, parked just beyond the crowd. I sucked in the cool air, and a dull ache settled into my body. My pulse thumped where my arm was broken. I cradled it the best I could and moved across the grass.

A pickup truck fired its engine, and the people roared. They stood with their backs to me, lining the far sidewalk like they were waiting on a parade. The pickup revved its engine again, and shadows I would have known in the daylight pumped their fists and screamed with approval. No one noticed me.

I needed to see, but I didn't want to push through with my busted arm, so I decided to go around. I floated like a ghost while the horde of shadows cheered, remaining fixated on the spectacle in the street. I was invisible, watching a dream in which I had no part…until someone called my name.

"PJ, PJ, oh, my God, PJ!" Chipmunk screamed.

"PJ, you have to stop them!" Kirby yelled from the haze. "Make them stop!"

I could hear them clearly, but my head was swimming, so it took a moment to realize they were calling to me from the school bus. I felt like I was sleepwalking as I moved toward their voices.

The big yellow bus was dull in the twilight, but I could see arms stretching out to nothing from every window. It reminded me of a horrible scene in a Holocaust movie. The bus leaned deep with the weight of all its passengers pushing against one side as the imprisoned youth of God's Glory cried and wailed and called Jesse's name. Dark faces begged and cursed their parents from the prison with Cunningham Elementary stenciled on the side.

"PJ! My God, PJ, what happened?" Kirby cried.

I wanted to explain, but when I saw Eddy standing alongside the bus twirling his baton and the reverend's ushers with ax handles of their own guarding the exits, I turned away before they saw me.

I moved to the corner, a half block down from the heart of the angry mob. Up the street, Mary Miller was kicking and screaming in the arms of two men restraining her under the glow of Katie's Diner. Mr. Miller was pinned facedown in the gutter by several others as they yelled for him to settle down before he got himself hurt. Silent lightning flashed somewhere above the clouds, and a wet fog stirred through the square like an aimless spirit from a hidden graveyard. I stepped into the street for a better look. The pickup roared again and faceless people spilled over with delight.

Swirling wisps surrounded Jesse standing in the road. His hands were cuffed behind him. He was unsteady, swaying, on the verge of collapse. A shadow crouched at his feet for a moment before backing away to join others on the sidewalk.

"One!" they yelled in unison.

The pickup revved as the driver pumped the gas.

"Two!" the crowd howled out.

The truck throttled up once more. Jesse teetered like he might fall. Someone stepped out to steady him.

"Three!"

This time the engine whined, and I could smell rubber and asphalt down the street. The tires screamed to be free. A piercing squeal echoed off the storefronts. The wheels grabbed road, and the truck shot out, disappearing through a veil of fog. Jesse looked like a carpet someone was shaking out when his feet snapped out from under him, slapping him to the pavement. He was gone.

The bus behind me erupted with horror and the crash of broken glass as its prisoners kicked out the windows. It rocked and wailed like a wounded yellow beast. The guards banged on the sides with ax handles, but the captives would not be quieted by their threats.

The truck rumbled around the square once, dragging Jesse behind like a mangled side of beef. I cradled my arm and watched as he went by. I wasn't sure it was him.

"One!" the crowd yelled, and the truck kept going.

I blinked dumbly as the load skidded by for another turn around the misty garden spot of Cunningham.

"Two!" the people yelled…and around again.

Mary Miller kicked and screamed, and Henry Miller struggled but couldn't break free. The bus moaned and swayed like an impotent behemoth begging for mercy. I stood and watched the truck roar by again, praying I would wake up soon.

"Three!" The pickup squealed to a stop, but its limp load continued on, tumbling forward and crashing up under the tailgate with a wet thud. The crowd cheered and yelled for more.

"No," I cried as I stumbled forward, holding my broken arm with the good one. I needed to get to Jesse! I needed to make them stop! My legs were like lead, and my knees kept buckling the way they do in nightmares. I started up the street, but when the crowd realized the truck wouldn't take another turn, they flooded past me and I was lost among them. Someone touched me on the shoulder and told me I should go get on the bus.

Shadows on the curb screamed and laughed as they collapsed around the idling pickup to dig Jesse from its undercarriage. They dragged him out by an ankle and tossed him in the truck bed. The pickup backed over the azalea hedge, across the lawn, and under the Bride and Groom. In the daytime, the two giant oaks were green with summer glory, but in the light of the coming storm, their foliage was dull silver on black arms. The leaves whispered to one another with every breeze, telling tales about the ashen souls gathering underneath.

I noticed two dark figures standing alone on the steps of God's Glory, but unlike the Bride and Groom, no secrets passed between them. They watched in silence, keeping their distance, so in the aftermath they could dispense justice and forgiveness like they had nothing to do with any of this. Thunder rumbled heavy across the heavens, warning Cunningham about the price of vengeance, but no one listened.

My head spun and my steps were unsure as I followed the shadows onto the grass. I had to tell them. I was going to tell them.

Shoving through the crowd was like squeezing through the seams of a stone wall. Someone protecting his spot threw an elbow and caught me in the break of my arm. The curtains closed on the periphery of my vision, and beige filled my eyes as pain threatened to shut me down. I was going out, but if I fell, I would be trampled to death, so I reached out with my good arm and draped myself over the man in front of me. He tried to shake me off, but the crowd was too tight around us. I hung on to him long enough to keep from fainting.

People pushed and shouldered, cramming together under the trees to watch, but when Buster, the sickle man, and one of the cashbox magistrates muscled Jesse to his feet, everyone settled down.

Buster and his friends stood with Jesse in the bed of the truck. They shouted Mr. Wallace was shattered to bits over at Mort's, having to bury his only daughter because of this scumbag Uphiller. They accused Jesse of being a lowlife meddler who exposed good children to a plague of shiftless thieves and panhandlers, giving them wild ideas about skipping church and separating themselves from the rest of the congregation. He colluded with a gang of good-for-nothing Uphillers to steal money from the church and told Reverend Dodge he—could—talk—to—God!

"Bullshit!" a shrill voice in the crowd interjected.

The reverend kicked him out of God's Glory for blasphemy, and he went and killed poor Natalie Wallace like a dog in the street before Sheriff Johnson could run him out of town!

Cunningham exploded. They foamed and lathered and screamed for justice. They pumped their fists, yelling for the criminal to answer Buster's charges.

Jesse's nose was mashed into his cheek, and his jaw looked dislocated. His clothes were shredded and soaked with blood. When he started to sway, the men in the back of the truck reached over to prop him up.

"Well," Buster demanded, "what do you have to say for yourself?"

For the first time since they broke into the sheriff's office, everyone fell silent, waiting for the carpenter to explain. I was ready to hear him say he didn't kill Natalie and the dent in his truck had been there long before he ever came to town. I thought he might tell them if they would take him to Mort's, he would wake

Natalie up and show Cunningham some miracles don't make the front page. I thought he might mention Mary Miller and Ms. Braddock, or tell about Sandy Shores and what happened to all the sick people who'd camped in the square. Surely, he could say enough for them to give him a chance—a chance to save Natalie at least. This would be over soon.

Jesse took a deep breath as the two men at his side kept him standing. He looked out over the gray faces. These people congratulated him and adored all he'd done for God's Glory a few months ago on Palm Sunday. Surely their minds could be changed if he would just say the right thing. Jesse took another breath as the town waited for his defense. But in a dull swirl of mist on a late summer's eve under the shroud of the Bride and Groom, Jesse shook his head, indicating he would say nothing.

The crowd went mad, furious with rage, and screamed for the blasphemer's blood. They shoved in toward the truck. I did my best to protect my arm as the tide of bodies carried me along.

"Hold it! Hold it!" Buster yelled. "Hold on a stinkin' minute!"

The mob simmered to an even boil long enough to hear him out.

"Well now," Buster announced, "we've already taken this SOB for a spin around the square, and he's pretty torn up for the trouble. Don't you think we should hand him over to the sheriff and call it a night?"

"Noooooo!" Cunningham yelled.

"Yes!" I shouted, but I couldn't even hear myself.

"What should we do then?" Buster asked.

The crowd quieted to consider how far they would go. These were good people; surely this was over now. But before reason could settle in, the sickle man popped open the truck's toolbox and produced an orange power cord. He stepped to the end of the tailgate and held it up high above his head.

"Hang him!" a woman somewhere behind me shouted.

"Yeah, hang him!" a man up front agreed.

"Hang him, hang him, hang him, hang him," the rest of Cunningham chanted.

Everything began to list, and I felt like I was going to puke as the rhythm of condemnation droned in my skull. I don't even know if I protested again.

"In that case," Buster answered, "let your will be done!"

I stood frozen, my arm aching, my head numb, as angry voices echoed in my brain. It was hard to believe this was the same day that started this morning. I could feel Reverend Dodge and Sheriff Johnson watching from the steps of God's Glory as one end of the orange power cord was tossed over a lower limb of the Bride. It was like watching a slow dream as the sickle man tied off a slipknot and placed it over Jesse's head. The mob jeered its approval as the cashbox magistrate tightened the line and secured the other end to a concrete park bench. Buster and his friends climbed off the back of the truck. Jesse managed to keep his feet.

The pickup fired to life, and the crowd cheered.

Jesse stood bloody with his hands still cuffed behind him. His head was bowed to his chest, and I could see his lips moving.

"PJ," Jesse's voice was pure and deep in my ear. There was nothing to distract me. "PJ, it's gonna be okay."

The truck revved its engine, coughed, and choked out. Everything I knew of Jesse flooded back to me. Why was I ever worried? Miracles happened for him all the time! Of course Buster's pickup conked out! Everything will be fine! Natalie will be fine! Jesse will make sure!

The people hissed and booed. They started to throw rocks as the pickup whined and sputtered, trying to resurrect itself. The battery started to go, and the sound of a motor on its last legs only clicked with the turn of the key. Buster kept trying. Thunder rumbled across the tops of the clouds, and a gust of wind smelling of rain stirred the Bride and Groom. Disappointment hushed the crowd. Buster pumped the gas, trying to revive the engine. He only needed to move the truck three feet. I knew it would never happen.

Jesse rolled his head back. "Father, forgive them," he breathed into every ear. His words were like a wet winter coat, and in that moment, every obscure soul under the oaks hoped Jesse really could talk to God. Given another minute, they may have cut him down.

The pickup truck coughed again and then found its feet and roared to life.

"It's finished," Jesse whispered, and Buster pulled out from under the Bride and Groom.

The orange power cord snapped taut then sagged under his weight. We watched Jesse choke to death seven inches above the ground.

The world went mute at what we had done. The breeze dropped to nothing, and every rumble of thunder ceased. There was only the horrible creak of the orange power cord straining with Jesse's weight as it gently corkscrewed his limp body around for us all to see. Without words, we watched as he turned slowly about. My ears hummed, and I could feel the pressure building in my head like I'd been underwater too long. All else faded to someplace else, and I was alone with the murder of my friend as I stood shoulder to shoulder with the rest of Cunningham. It was darker now. Everything was cold and silent…but not for long.

Pop! The streetlight in front of Mr. Wallace's store shattered and went dark like someone shot it out with a .22. *Pop!* Another light went out, and for a moment, I thought Eddy had drawn his weapon in celebration, but no loud reports echoed off the buildings to confirm the deputy had fired his pistol. All eyes cut to the exploding streetlights, trying to make sense of what was happening. *Pop!* Another light made me jump. Crack! A car window blew out. The mob peered dumbly through the fog. And when our attention was fully gathered, every storefront, windowpane, and windshield at the far end of the square shattered in a crescendo of broken glass as the angry storm that promised rain sent a barrage of plum-size hail instead.

A thin line of blue lightning spired from the clouds, striking a transformer, sending a burst of white sparks cascading over the buildings and broken shards before plunging the square into darkness. I could only feel the people around me as the shower of cold stones began to shred the town. The sky wailed, and a flash of lightning revealed a curtain of falling ice moving out into the grassy area where we stood. The hail struck hard enough to kick up dirt, and the azalea hedge on the far side had already been chewed up and beaten flat.

Someone screamed, and the crowd turned like herd animals stampeding off to take refuge in Katie's Diner or one of the other shops. Buster and his friends spun his pickup around, and a wave of people flooded over me. My arm exploded with pain as they crashed by, sending me to my back. I felt the weight of every foot fleeing over my body as the dull thud of ice on earth chased them away. Jesse swayed, and I was left knowing I couldn't get up. My arms and legs lay alongside me like dulled pieces of meat as the heavy sound of frozen bullets chewing turf moved in. A blanket of fog folded in around me.

Somewhere in the night, I heard a freight train rumbling along the river. I couldn't remember the last time one had been by, but it rattled the whole world like it was rolling right through the middle of town. I stared up into the Bride and Groom, watching their leaves twist and tear away in a sea of wind. Distant people screamed. The wet grass soaked into my clothes. The orange power cord twisted and creaked. I could see Jesse's shoes dangling, turning back and forth slowly above the ground. In my thoughtless idiocy, I killed Natalie Wallace, and Jesse paid the price for my crime. Now the heavens would pound me to death at his feet for what I had done. I was helpless to stop it…even if I'd wanted to.

"I'm sorry, I'm sorry," was the last thing I remember uttering as the freight train roared in. Agony, terrible agony…Dad's face and all was black.

51
Into the Black

I opened my eyes, alone, staring into a white tile ceiling with tiny black holes. A light blue curtain on rings hung around me, and the faint beeping of a monitor told me I was at the Hawkinsville Medical Center. I dipped into consciousness long enough to hear hushed voices standing beside my bed.

"Your son was in shock when he got here, and honestly, we nearly lost him. A half-hour more would have been too late."

"But he's going to be okay now, isn't he, Doctor?" Mom asked.

"He'll need to stay with us for a few days, but I think he'll be fine."

There was a pause, and I heard papers on a clipboard being turned over.

"Something else folks," I heard the unfamiliar doctor say. "It's very lucky your son broke his arm when he did."

"What do you mean?" Dad sounded raspy.

"Well, it was unusual. Bones don't ordinarily break this way. We had to dig in pretty good to put it back together, and when we did, we found a tumor hiding right there in the bone marrow. We sent it off for a biopsy, but tumors like that are never benign. We'll need to keep an eye on him for a while, but we caught this thing at the best possible time, and we got it out clean. In another six weeks though, I'd be giving you different news."

"Thank God," Mom gasped.

"But he's going to be okay?"

"He'll have limited mobility in that arm for the rest of his life. Your son will be able to use a pencil, but I'm afraid there'll be no baseball or golf, and if he's right-handed, he won't be much with a hammer. Other than that…"

I stared at the dark little holes in the ceiling tile until one pulled me in and I drifted away into the black.

52
Closing

I was laid up in the Hawkinsville Medical Center for four days and in a cast much longer than that. The hail storm destroyed every farm in Cunningham except the Wallace place, and the tornado that ripped through tore up every building but God's Glory and the Millers' Gas & Grocery. The Bride was struck by lightning and split right to the earth. She took a few of her groom's arms with her when she fell. Men from the church pulled Jesse's body from the debris and buried him without a headstone in the old cemetery. Sympathetic stories of how the carpenter was accidentally killed during the storm were already being sown, but questions about the death of Natalie Wallace were never asked.

With the farms destroyed and the square in ruins, no Uphillers came on the weekends for the rest of the season. Without the steady stream of revenue, recovery was slow—too slow for impatient outsiders who eventually found leisurely distractions other than Cunningham. Only Mr. Adleman's trucks rolled in and out for pickups from Mr. Wallace's farm.

The pecans came in with a fury, and King Tree honey was sold in every grocery store in the region. Mr. Wallace boarded up the windows on his lumber supply store, locked the doors, and never went back. He hired a live-in teacher from Uphill to educate the Trackers, but she rarely came to town.

Despicable rumors sprung up all over Cunningham about rich Mr. Wallace, his paid woman, and the Tracker serfs he abused.

That was just loose talk, though, and no one lifted a finger against him.

The Millers sold the Gas & Grocery to an Uphill company and moved back to wherever Ms. Miller was from. Carl and the doctor left too.

When fall came, I drifted through the school year like most others, waiting for my chance to escape. Jesse and Natalie haunted me with every stray thought, so my academic effort was lackluster and my final marks in school topped out at mediocre. With a bad arm, there would be no military, and my grades were too poor for scholarships, so as the schooldays passed, I realized I was doomed to Cunningham where I'd expire before I died. A chain-link cage was closing around me, locking me in with Reverend Dodge, Sheriff Johnson, and the others…until I received the letter from Mr. Wallace.

Mom handed it to me after school, and I took it upstairs to my room. I lay on the bed dreading what Mr. Wallace might have to say. I hadn't seen him since Natalie's funeral. I took a deep breath and tore the envelope open.

He thanked me and told me how important I'd been to Natalie. He wanted me to know how much he, John, and Sam had enjoyed working with me and how much Jesse loved me and Kirby. He said he was blessed to know me and didn't regret me running through his yard one single bit. He was happy I'd been with him for the summer.

His words stung my eyes and twisted my stomach. I tossed the letter on the bed as guilt pushed its way into the room. It glowered at me from the corner as I rolled to my side and stared at the paper. I watched the letter for a moment more before gathering enough courage to pick it up again.

Mr. Wallace wanted to pay for my college, anyplace I could get in. He should be putting me in jail, but he was saving me instead. I knew I couldn't accept his offer, not without confessing about Natalie, but somehow, I never got around to telling him what I'd done. I ended up taking from him what should never have been mine. I left the day I graduated from high school. I loaded my truck, kissed my mom, shook Dad's hand, and never saw Cunningham again. My parents visited me from time to time, but I never went home, not even for the usual holidays. The demons wouldn't let me.

I loved building, but the doctor from the medical center was right. I could tinker a bit, but I lacked the endurance and coordination in my right arm to ever make a living as a carpenter. I studied marketing at a rural college and got a job selling building materials after I graduated. At least I was around the smell of lumber.

I get the sense that Maggie and I had been together for a while by then, and we managed to put together enough money to get married and move to Fair Play. We were happy. We had children, and I was fine with everything I'd left behind in Cunningham. Kirby was the only one I missed.

Mr. Wallace put him through college as well, but Kirby went on to theology school and started a mission establishing apiaries in the poor communities of Appalachia. There was a big magazine spread with a photograph of him painting a bee box with a smiling little girl, and another one of Kirby showing some children how to collect honey. He was grinning, and I could still see the boy in the picture of the man. I was sure he was telling his pupils bees don't bite. I read the article a thousand times, and I knew Jesse would be pleased.

Kirby wrote me once, but I never wrote back. He told me Nya had become a lawyer, Angeline was a veterinarian, and Tuttle had published his first novel. Mr. Wallace paid for it all.

Cunningham never recovered from the day Natalie died, and there wasn't much pride or fight left in anyone when the government announced plans to dam the Chagrin. I'm sure they were glad it was over.

I subscribed to the *Hawkinsville Herald* for the year leading up to the dam, but that's as close as I got to home. I wish I'd realized I needed more, but I was afraid to see Cunningham again for real. There were pictures in the paper of the square with the tall steeple of God's Glory cut from the building and lying in the street. It would be too tall for the new lake. The lonely Groom was limbed to a pathetic height with its arms piled at its feet, while the last patrons of Katie's Diner sipped a final cup of coffee. The human interest stories about the lost town left me cold and bitter and ashamed.

They exhumed the remains from God's Glory Memorial Park and moved all the ancestral bones to another graveyard in Hawkinsville, but when the backhoes dug up the old cemetery, no bodies were found—not a single one.

There was a picture of a man beside a tractor and a big pile of dirt, standing with upturned hands. The headline read "Where Did Everybody Go?" The caption read "Cunningham's Graveyard Hoax." I knew better. There were generations of bones planted under the low trees between the crumbling iron gates. I'd been to Jesse's grave myself. I never understood why the newspaper would lie about an empty cemetery. It was a bunch of BS, so I tossed the paper in the trash and never picked up the Hawkinsville rag again.

The valley filled with water, Mom and Dad moved…somewhere…before they went to the state retirement home, and I started sneaking away from Maggie to come here every spring to be with the lake.

So here I am, flat on my back, staring into infinity, wondering why things had to go so fast. I guess life is kind of like the summer I spent with Jesse—long days make short weeks, and you don't get much of a chance to be a different person. I don't know if it's my age or the medicine keeping me sprawled on this dock. I can't even hear myself breathing above the crickets on the bank anymore. I never meant for this to happen. I needed every pill. I needed this place, and I needed to remember before the final page was turned and all was lost like words in the tomes of Reverend Dodge's office. My memory is worn too thin to know who I'm confessing to, but if my body lets go tonight, I didn't do it on purpose. I couldn't…I'm too afraid.

"Maggie, I'm scared!"

Cunningham is waiting for me. Buster, Eddy, and the mashed potato lady are with the others, watching from the shoreline. They want me back. I hear them whispering in the shadows, and I can feel their feet on the dock, but I can't move.

"Get away! Get away!"

Why should they listen? If abuse of trust is a vile thing, I must be the most despicable creature ever born. I've lied, and I've killed. Jesse hanged for my crimes, and because he did, I was set free. I never got what I deserved, so I've come here every spring, guilty, hoping the Chagrin will tell me why.

"I tried, I tried, but there wasn't enough time, and now…"

Looking up into the starry forever with water lapping underneath and shadows at my ankles, I know every excuse is a lie, and Jesse's sacrifice was wasted on me.

"I wish I'd been more like you. I'm sorry, I'm so sorry. I wasn't worth it. Why didn't you tell them? Forgive me, please."

I can't wipe my own tears, and my nose runs down along my cheek. I have no control, and I'm too heavy to move. A cloud slides in front of the moon. An icy hand takes me by the ankle, drags me a few feet toward shore, and releases me like a hungry jackal testing to see if I'm ready to be eaten. A breeze blows across the bank, and I hear the privet call me by name. The lake rolls underneath. I'm helpless to resist. If the moon hides again, they'll take me in the dark. The ghosts of Cunningham will pull me into the trees.

"Leave me alone!" I try to yell, but it only comes out as a moan.

They whisper again. There are more of them now.

Lights, I see lights, but they are faint and turn away. I hear gravel crunching under the tires of a slow-moving car. The engine cuts, and the sound of doors opening and closing tells me more than one person has arrived.

"Dad, are you out here?" someone calls. "Look around; the trucker said he let him off at the end of the driveway. Here, take a flashlight."

I blink, but that's all I can do. I'm trapped in a corpse who won't stand or obey my commands. If I can get up—if I can just get up or make some noise—the people will find me before the clouds cover the moon…before the shadows come and drag me to the darkness.

I hear people searching the cabin and confirming I haven't been found. They need to come down here, where I am. Someone needs to find me before the sky goes black again. I try to call for them, but nothing comes out. Feet! I feel feet again on the dock, causing it to roll underneath…heavier than ghosts, but not people from the cabin either. I feel the weight of something step up off the lake. The dock lists. I feel it coming. I feel it moving across the dock to where I'm trapped on my back. I can't move! I can't see it! I have to call out! I have to stand up! I have to get up! But I can't!

A figure looms over me, eclipsing the sky. I blink up at the silhouette outlined by thin ribbon moonlight, and somehow…I'm not afraid. He leans over me, and the moon glints off Able Lake to illuminate his face. He extends his arm. "Hey, PJ," Jesse says, "need a hand?"

I reach for him, and he pulls me up away from myself. I turn to see the burden I've carried all this time lying lifeless behind me as my three children rush down the path, calling my name. I know them again, and even though I hear my daughters weep, I will not go back. My son kneels down to check me, but I'm no longer there. He drops his head to his hand the way I do, and my girls sob next to my body. They don't understand the tricks time plays; by tomorrow twenty years will have passed, and this night will be replaced by fonder memories. I watch them lean over my corpse, cradle its head, and hold its hand, but I feel no loss, knowing fleeting moments are all that separate us now.

Jesse touches my shoulder, but I don't wait for him to speak. I throw my arms around his neck and hold on tight as my spirit seizes into tears. He puts his arms around me. "Relax," he whispers. "Didn't I tell you everything would be okay?"

I nod into his shoulder. I don't want to let go, but he stands me away. I wipe my tears with the back of my hand and start to apologize, but he shushes me quiet.

"Can you stop for just a minute, please? I want you to see who came along." He puts his arm around me and motions out over the lake. I can see people walking toward us across the rippling reflection of the moon. There's a gentle breeze, and the smell of dogwoods is stronger than ever. As they draw near, I recognize John with Elizabeth, Kirby's parents, Henry and Mary Miller walking hand in hand, and someone else I can't quite make out. I see Sam and Mr. Wallace on the end with Natalie skipping up beside him. Their gait is lively, and they wave and call my name as they approach. By the time they step up off the water, tears are running off my chin. I'm not sure what to do.

"Natalie," I call out. I want to say I'm sorry, but she doesn't give me a chance. There's something different about her. She runs ahead of the others, twirls once, and falls into my arms. She hugs me tight.

"It's so good to see you," she giggles.

"Natalie," I start again.

"Shhh, PJ, it was an accident, that's all," she whispers in my ear and then pushes back. "Looky here at my new jacket. I always wanted one with fringe up and down the sleeves." She waves her hand back and forth under the loose ties hanging from her coat.

"You sure look pretty, Natalie, the prettiest I ever did see," I choke.

"Now, PJ," she throws her hands to her hips, "it ain't fittin' at all for you to start sweet-talkin' me out here on this moonlit lake. Even if what you say is true, what's Maggie gonna think about you flattering another girl?"

"What?"

Natalie steps to the side, and down near the end of the dock where everyone is gathered, I see a figure push out from behind Mr. Miller and John. *Maggie!*

I stumble to her and take my beautiful Mags in my arms. I sweep her up, and her laughter echoes through the trees. *She's here!* I set her down and look into her pretty round face. "You know?"

Maggie nods. "It's okay."

I hold her, and she's warm, not like the last time I saw her. Still in each other's arms, we turn to watch our children at my body. Jesse moves beside us. "They'll be fine," he says.

"I know. Kirb is a good man," I agree.

"And Nat and Jess are strong women," Maggie adds, giving me a squeeze.

"Maggie! I wasn't going to tell him that."

"You weren't gonna tell me what?" Jesse smiles, but I'm sure he heard what Maggie said.

"Well…uh….my first was a boy, and I named him after Kirby, but after that, I only had daughters. So I kinda…I kinda, well, I kinda…named a girl after you."

"I know!" Jesse laughs and shoves me like I'm sixteen again. I go off the edge of the dock and stumble across the water to keep my feet.

"Hey," I yell, "where's Kirby?"

"There's one more person he needs to meet," Jesse calls back. "He'll be along after that."

His answer lets me know my old friend has done well, and I'm as delighted for Kirby's success as if I had spent my life in the same way.

We gather together and follow Jesse out over the water where Cunningham lies entombed forever by the Chagrin. Our backs are to the world, and all the shadows can do is groan and watch us leave. Maggie takes my hand in hers, and I and take

Natalie's in the other. I'm happy. I'm saved. I can say nothing more about anything. This is the beginning of forever.

Epilogue

Dad never was a churchgoing man. He claimed the religious did little more than serve bad spaghetti and step all over each other's flowers. As for the righteous, he'd say they were either spit on or spit out, so Mom saw to our religious upbringing, and most of it stuck. Dad worked hard, and other than the church thing, I think anyone would be hard-pressed to find a better father or more attentive husband. He loved Mom fiercely, and she loved him right back. We laughed at our dinner table, and although Mom was the storyteller, Dad always had a humorous twist to add. He could be stupid silly, chasing us around as Mr. Tickle or trying to get us to blow out birthday candles with our noses.

He and Mom had big plans after he retired, but Mom was diagnosed with leukemia, and she didn't last long after that. Dad stayed with her every day and then went home after her funeral and never left. My sisters did his shopping, cooking, and cleaning for a while, but when Dad stopped remembering to eat, we decided to sell the house and put him in a nursing home. His memory collapsed until he didn't recognize us anymore. My sisters would beg him to remember Mr. Tickle, but his only clear recollection was of his Maggie in her blue dress. He argued with the nurses and fought with the doctors, asking them if he was here for the blood drive and where were the damn peanut butter cookies. He needed a badge so his folks would know he'd done his civic duty.

Finally, they found a medicine that seemed to help. Dad could mostly dial himself up to the present where he would keep his balance for a while before falling through a hole in the past, plunging him back by Mom's death over and over again. His eyes filled with tears every time he remembered or began to forget.

Even though his pills were doing some good, we still didn't have much time with Dad. We were at my youngest sister's house, going through some old pictures, and I guess it was about that time I realized we knew almost nothing about Mom or Dad's childhood. I knew they'd grown up together, but I couldn't tell you where they were from or anything at all about my grandparents. On a whim, I bought a voice-activated micro recorder, hoping I could convince Dad to record a story or two about being a kid, how he met Mom, or when I was born, but he just got angry and told me to mind my own damn business. He didn't recognize me again, and I watched his eyes water as he slid back to whatever dark place his mind would go. I lost my temper, and out of meanness and because he couldn't stop me, I clipped the recorder in his shirt pocket and stormed out.

The recorder was still in his pocket when we found him on the dock. We heard him break into the pill cabinet, walk across the street to the gas station, and catch a ride with a truck driver. I don't know if he meant for anyone to know the rest. I heard him say he was sorry, yell for something to get away, and tell Mom he was scared. The dying words of my father offer me no comfort for his soul.

I did my best to find some of the people Dad talked about, but without last names, Nya, Angeline, and the rest were impossible to trace. I found a magazine article about Reverend Kirby Braddock, and I went to visit him in West Virginia. He looked older than he should have or maybe just not as hearty as I expected. He was working to establish an apiary in a remote valley in the middle of nowhere. The reverend threw his arms around me and cried when I told him about Dad.

I had a lot of questions, and Reverend Braddock answered all I could think of. He told me about hiding the orange cream sodas, watching scary movies on Friday nights, and how afraid they were the first time they went after honeybees. He told me Dad liked to drive too fast, but was a good carpenter, a better friend, and used to say Mom looked like a squirrel…or a chipmunk…or something. He told me stories, and every name he mentioned I knew from Dad's last night. Reverend Braddock said he and my father stood in the wake of miracles in Cunningham, and that's something that can't be undone between men…even if Dad's annual check to the mission was their only contact as adults. It always came in the spring, without a note, postmarked Hawkinsville. When I asked about Jesse, he smiled wide and answered, "He's the reason I'm here."

I almost told the reverend about Dad's confession, but the day had been long and the old man looked tired, so I decided to leave well enough alone. I shook Reverend Braddock's hand and turned for my car. I'd head home, put the recording in my desk drawer, and let PJ, Kirby, and Natalie collect dust with the Millers, Reverend Dodge, and Sheriff Johnson. In all honesty, that's what was going to happen as I opened my car door.

"Sometimes, Kirby," Reverend Braddock called, "to really tell a story, you have to tell another one instead."

I had no idea what he meant, but his words tugged at me, so when I got home, I pulled out Dad's confession and started transcribing what I could make of the recording as accurately as possible. I learned more about myself than my father with every keystroke. By the time I was ready to send a draft to Reverend Braddock, I learned he'd been taken by the same disease his mother had been healed of so many years ago. I prayed he would find my father where he was going.

So this is the final testament of my father after he ran away from the nursing home on the night he died. I've been as truthful as he was. The story belongs to Dad, and I've always intended on naming it after him, but as I type these final words, I'm not sure he would approve. So I've changed it to *The Gospel of Jesse* for the sake of PJ, and I hope he doesn't mind.

I don't want this to end with my father's final words, so even though I'm not sure what it means, I'll use the last thing his best friend said to me. Sometimes to really tell a story, you have to tell another instead.

Amen.

Made in the USA
San Bernardino, CA
04 May 2015